CRAWLING
HORROR

CRAWLING HORROR

HORROR

Creeping Tales
of the Insect Weird

Edited by
DAISY BUTCHER AND JANETTE LEAF

This collection first published in 2021 by
The British Library
96 Euston Road
London NW1 2DB

Selection, introduction and notes © 2021 Daisy Butcher and Janette Leaf

'An Egyptian Hornet' © 1915 Algernon Blackwood, reprinted by
permission of United Agents on behalf of Susan Reeve-Jones

Dates attributed to each story relate to first publication.

Cataloguing in Publication Data
A catalogue record for this publication is available from the British Library

ISBN 978 0 7123 5349 6
e-ISBN 978 0 7123 6748 6

Frontispiece illustration by Sandra Gómez, with design by Mauricio Villamayor.
Illustrations featured in the book are from woodcuts originally reproduced in
Thomas Moffett's *Insectorum sive Minimorum animalium theatrum*, London, 1634.

Cover design by Mauricio Villamayor with illustration by Sandra Gómez
Text design and typesetting by Tetragon, London
Printed in England by CPI Group (UK) Ltd, Croydon, CR0 4YY

Contents

The bulk of the investigative work on our insect anthology and associated writing was carried out immediately before and during the COVID-19 *pandemic, so in many respects this represents lockdown literature. We have been grateful for each other's socially distanced co-editing and complementary skills brought by Daisy's editorial experience with* Evil Roots, *and Janette's extensive knowledge of cultural entomology. We dedicate* Crawling Horror: Creeping Tales of the Insect Weird *to our partners, family members and friends with whom we have been sharing circumscribed spaces or virtual worlds in challenging times, and whom we hope we have not bugged too much about our book.*

INTRODUCTION

Crawling Horror: Creeping Tales of the Insect Weird proved an irresistible wordplay on creepy-crawly for the name of this short story collection, although our weird insects do not just crawl, they also flutter, fly, burrow, swim and in some cases ride on the backs of other animals. We deliberately excluded spiders on the grounds they have very different associations to their six-legged, arthropod cousins and frequently overshadow them in the popular imagination. We wanted our anthology to provide an environment for insects which is exclusively their own and allows their peculiarities to come to the fore.

These peculiarities reside in numerous characteristics such as their metamorphic life-cycle from egg to larva to chrysalis to adult; their highly organized, alarmingly large eusocial groups; their alien unreadable faces and exoskeletal bodies; their ephemerality or their survivability; their fecundity, and their sheer variety. Distinctive traits like these make insects a rich subject for metaphor in tales of transformation, such as Franz Kafka's "*Die Verwandlung*" ("The Metamorphosis" (1912)), and stories of invasion or parasitism. Weirdness might be said to be inherent in these captivating creatures in the real world, and the writers of fiction within this volume propel it to a further extreme.

Almost invariably the insects portrayed in our collection tap into entomophobic associations of rapid breeding cycles that threaten to overwhelm; of insidious infiltration into man's domestic and personal spaces; of uncontrollability. The entomologist Jeffrey A. Lockwood argues entomophobia is "characterized as a disgust-imbued fear" and is an evolved response to danger.[1] It is an intense emotion arising from a perception—in some cases a misconception—of all insects

7

as vectors of disease, creatures that singly or en masse may invade our bodies. It may also stem from a deep-rooted concern they have the potential to become an invasive force which could overwhelm our communities. The surrealist painter Salvador Dali developed extreme entomophobia as a child because classmates tormented him with grasshoppers. The trauma led him to feature oversized insects in many of his paintings—eating the main subject and functioning in Lockwood's words as "dreadful symbols of waste and destruction [...], mortality and decay."[2] Fear of the insect can also be a manifestation of fear of the unknowable. It is the fear of sentient beings existing in a way so spatially, temporally and imaginatively different to our own, that they stand in opposition to humankind. Eric C. Brown, the editor of *Insect Poetics*, describes insects as "Humanity's Other".[3] It is their expressionless alterity that makes them weird to us.

Our literary insects are natural, unnatural and supernatural. Several appear in brilliant hues and are externally beautiful. Their sizes range from minuscule to gigantic. They may be menacing or innocent and occasionally even comic, but all partake of an unsettling quality. For us, the Insect Weird is the textual territory occupied by these fascinating animals which provoke conflicting senses of awe at their embodiment of the intricacies of Nature, and innate repulsion and suspicion. They are simultaneously wonderful but uncontainable entities which move between real spaces in the world, and imaginative spaces in the human psyche. In the hands of our authors, they take form in print with their own unaltered, unnerving morphology or they are artificially and ter-rifyingly augmented in physical and mental capabilities. The Insect Weird creates an atmosphere in which arthropods are enhanced while humans are diminished.

We have ensured that multiple insect species are included in this anthology, and so beetles, bees, moths, butterflies, ants, a cockroach, a flea, a stick insect and a praying mantis are all here as well as insects in their larval state. We have stories from America, Asia and Europe set in locations ranging from Scotland to South America to South Africa. Our selected tales are arranged chronologically to give a sense of weird insect fiction moving from legendary curse tales through proto Science Fiction, psychological thrillers, the height of the Weird in the 1920s and 1930s, and becoming the stuff of Science Fiction proper all within a timeframe of around a hundred years. Our earlier stories are more Gothic in nature, having been written fifty or sixty years before the Weird as a literary subgenre or mode of writing reached its height; however, we present the mid-nineteenth-century authors as pioneers of the Weird for combining in their writing elements of fantasy, horror and dread.

More often than not women writers are overlooked where ento-mologically inspired texts are concerned; therefore, in putting this collection together we made it our business to seek them out to ensure ours is not an exclusively male preserve. We have included contributions from Jane G. Austin, Olive Schreiner and Clare Winger Harris. Together we scoured the archives to unearth tales long forgotten or by authors meriting far greater attention than they ordinarily achieve such as A. G. Gray, Jun., A. Lincoln Green, Lafcadio Hearn, Christopher Blayre, J. U. Giesy, Arlton Eadie, Garth Bentley, and Carl Stephenson. We blended them with insect writers who may be more familiar such as Edgar Allan Poe, H. G. Wells, E. F. Benson and Algernon Blackwood to offer a variety of voices.

The sub-genre of insect horror literature is one which has naturally been associated with "the exotic" and tropes of expeditions and exploration to places where stranger fauna can be found. As a result, some of the stories use words such as "natives", "savages" and "Oriental" to refer to characters and draw on contemporary, and now outdated, literary stereotypes such as the "old Indian" wise man, the "swarthy" Arab guide and "slow-witted Indians". These mummy and jungle stories are predominantly written from a Western European or white American perspective, and while the vocabulary used may exemplify the arrogance or ignorance of explorers and landowners, portrayals of indigenous and non-white characters may make for uncomfortable reading. The texts speak of different attitudes towards race and "civilization" at the time they were written—some, such as Jane G. Austin's story—more than one-hundred-and-fifty years ago.

Two of our earlier tales inspired by Ancient Egypt include bejewelled insects coming to life to act as uncanny instruments of vengeance. This theme endures in Stephen Sommers' film of *The Mummy* (1998) starring Brendan Fraser, with its on-screen representation of flesh-eating scarabs wreaking havoc on behalf of their master when the sanctity of the tomb is breached. On numerous occasions in our collection insects are portrayed as murderous monsters or as ominous disease bringers destroying bodies and minds. The scientists who interact with insects are frequently characterized as unhinged, incapable of containing the results of experiments gone awry. Positioning insects as unruly test subjects exploits what social ecologist Stephen Kellert describes as the "radical 'autonomy' of invertebrates from human will and control".[4] In anthropocentric terms, they behave dangerously and unpredictably.

In several stories threateningly intelligent insects compete with humans to take control of a defined territory or even worse, of the whole planet. Here humans become just another food source, plummeting down the hierarchy of animals. In these later futuristic tales, the rise of the insects acts as a covert comment on man's mismanagement of his environment, a fatal error which enables insects to thrive, supersede humanity and establish themselves as the dominant species.

Much that is discomforting and disturbing about insects derives from negative connotations, some of which are primal fears and others culturally constructed, even irrational. This prompted us to include stories where insect weirdness takes a positive form, and where encounters with them are beneficial to humans. We are delighted to showcase stories by Olive Schreiner, Lafcadio Hearn and Arlton Eadie featuring bugs which, though still exhibiting strangeness or supernatural elements, are undeniably beneficent. We feel they play an indispensable role in balancing our collection, broadening the slippery concept of the Insect Weird to encompass oddness tinged with optimism. Discombobulation at the insect need not always stem from dread, though a sense of crawling horror is the emotion that pervades.

DAISY BUTCHER AND JANETTE LEAF

NOTES

1   Jeffrey A. Lockwood, *The Infested Mind: Why Humans Fear, Loathe and Love Insects* (Oxford & New York: Oxford University Press, 2013), p. 1.
2   Lockwood, p. 6.
3   Eric C. Brown, "Introduction", in *Insect Poetics*, ed. Eric C. Brown, (Minneapolis: University of Minnesota Press, 2006), pp. ix–xxiii (p. xi).
4   Stephen R. Kellert, "The Biological Basis for Human Values of Nature", in *The Biophilia Hypothesis*, ed. Stephen R. Kellert and Edward O. Wilson (Washington DC: Island Press, 1993) pp. 57–58.

THE SPHINX

Edgar Allan Poe

Edgar Allan Poe (1809–1849) was born Edgar Poe in Boston, Massachusetts and was a prolific poet, story writer, essayist and journalist best known for the macabre tone of his work. After Poe's father abandoned the family and his mother died of pulmonary tuberculosis in 1811, Poe became orphaned at a young age. As an adult, Poe was cast out by his foster family (the Allans) and turned to a career in journalism. He married his thirteen-year-old cousin, Virginia Clemm, but she soon became chronically unwell until she eventually died in 1847. The deadly diseases and chronic illnesses that devastated his loved ones had a profound effect on his work which is particularly evident in his Insect Weird tale "The Sphinx".

"The Sphinx" was published in the January 1846 issue of *Arthur's Ladies Magazine* and, like "Some Words with a Mummy" (1845), is influenced by Ancient Egypt. Poe's titular sphinx does not take on the traditional, woman-lion-bird hybrid form but a more insectile anatomy of a death's head moth. Appropriately, as the first in our collection, this iconic weird insect, complete with its skull-like markings, inspires the image on our front cover. Poe's brief tale is set against the backdrop of a ravaging cholera epidemic, and is narrated by a man who, falling into an "abnormal gloom" believes he sees a monstrous insect crawling over the countryside. The story's themes explore disease, *trompe-l'oeil*-induced terror, magnification and distortion. Insect and deadly illness become conflated, and the narrator believes both are coming to claim him.

uring the dread reign of the Cholera in New York, I had accepted the invitation of a relative to spend a fortnight with him in the retirement of his *cottage ornée* on the banks of the Hudson. We had here around us all the ordinary means of summer amusement; and what with rambling in the woods, sketching, boating, fishing, bathing, music and books, we should have passed the time pleasantly enough, but for the fearful intelligence which reached us every morning from the populous city. Not a day elapsed which did not bring us news of the decease of some acquaintance. Then, as the fatality increased, we learned to expect daily the loss of some friend. At length we trembled at the approach of every messenger. The very air from the South seemed to us redolent with death. That palsying thought, indeed, took entire possession of my soul. I could neither speak, think, nor dream of any thing else. My host was of a less excitable temperament, and, although greatly depressed in spirits, exerted himself to sustain my own. His richly philosophical intellect was not at any time affected by unrealities. To the substances of terror he was sufficiently alive, but of its shadows he had no apprehension.

His endeavours to arouse me from the condition of abnormal gloom into which I had fallen, were frustrated in great measure, by certain volumes which I had found in his library. These were of a character to force into germination whatever seeds of hereditary superstition lay latent in my bosom. I had been reading these books without his knowledge, and thus he was often at a loss to account for the forcible impressions which had been made upon my fancy.

A favourite topic with me was the popular belief in omens—a belief which, at this one epoch of my life, I was almost seriously disposed to defend. On this subject we had long and animated discussions—he maintaining the utter groundlessness of faith in such matters.—I contending that a popular sentiment arising with absolute spontaneity—that is to say without apparent traces of suggestion—had in itself the unmistakeable elements of truth, and was entitled to as much respect as that intuition which is the idiosyncrasy of the individual man of genius.

The fact is, that soon after my arrival at the cottage, there had occurred to myself an incident so entirely inexplicable, and which had in it so much of the portentous character, that I might well have been excused for regarding it as an omen. It appalled, and at the same time so confounded and bewildered me, that many days elapsed before I could make up my mind to communicate the circumstance to my friend.

Near the close of an exceedingly warm day, I was sitting, book in hand, at an open window, commanding, through a long vista of the river banks, a view of a distant hill, the face of which nearest my position, had been denuded, by what is termed a land-slide, of the principal portion of its trees. My thoughts had been long wandering from the volume before me to the gloom and desolation of the neighbouring city. Uplifting my eyes from the page, they fell upon the naked face of the hill, and upon an object—upon some living monster of hideous conformation, which very rapidly made its way from the summit to the bottom, disappearing finally in the dense forest below. As this creature first came in sight, I doubted my own sanity—or at least the evidence of my own eyes; and many minutes passed before I succeeded in convincing myself that I was neither mad nor in a dream. Yet when I describe the monster (which I distinctly saw, and calmly surveyed through the whole period of its progress), my readers, I fear, will feel more difficulty in being convinced of these points than even I did, myself.

Estimating the size of the creature by comparison with the diameter of the large trees near which it passed—the few giants of the forest which had escaped the fury of the land-slide—I concluded it to be far larger than any ship of the line in existence. I say ship of the line, because the shape of the monster suggested the idea—the hull of one of our seventy-fours might convey a very tolerable conception of the general outline. The mouth of the animal was situated at the extremity of a proboscis some sixty or seventy feet in length, and about as thick as the body of an ordinary elephant. Near the root of this trunk was an immense quantity of black shaggy hair—more than could have been supplied by the coats of a score of buffaloes; and projecting from this hair downwardly and laterally, sprang two gleaming tusks not unlike those of the wild boar, but of infinitely greater dimension. Extending forward, parallel with the proboscis, and on each side of it was a gigantic staff, thirty or forty feet in length, formed seemingly of pure crystal, and in shape a perfect prism:—it reflected in the most gorgeous manner the rays of the declining sun. The trunk was fashioned like a wedge with the apex to the earth. From it there were outspread two pairs of wings—each wing nearly one hundred yards in length—one pair being placed above the other, and all thickly covered with metal scales; each scale apparently some ten or twelve feet in diameter. I observed that the upper and lower tiers of wings were connected by a strong chain. But the chief peculiarity of this horrible thing, was the representation of a *Death's Head*, which covered nearly the whole surface of its breast, and which was as accurately traced in glaring white, upon the dark ground of the body, as if it had been there carefully designed by an artist. While I regarded this terrific animal, and more especially the appearance on its breast, with a feeling of horror and

EDGAR ALLAN POE

awe—with a sentiment of forthcoming evil, which I found it impossible to quell by any effort of the reason, I perceived the huge jaws at the extremity of the proboscis, suddenly expand themselves, and from them there proceeded a sound so loud and so expressive of wo, that it struck upon my nerves like a knell, and as the monster disappeared at the foot of the hill, I fell at once, fainting to the floor.

Upon recovering, my first impulse of course was to inform my friend of what I had seen and heard—and I can scarcely explain what feeling of repugnance it was, which, in the end, operated to prevent me.

At length, one evening, some three or four days after the occurrence, we were sitting together in the room which I had seen the apparition—I occupying the same seat at the same window, and he lounging on a sofa near at hand. The association of the place and time impelled me to give him an account of the phenomenon. He heard me to the end—at first laughed heartily—and then lapsed into an excessively grave demeanour, as if my insanity was a thing beyond suspicion. At this instant I again had a distinct view of the monster—to which, with a shout of absolute terror, I now directed his attention. He looked eagerly—but maintained that he saw nothing—although I designated minutely the course of the creature, as it made its way down the naked face of the hill.

I was now immeasurably alarmed, for I considered the vision either as an omen of my death, or, worse, as the fore-runner of an attack of mania. I threw myself passionately back in my chair, and for some moments buried my face in my hands. When I uncovered my eyes, the apparition was no longer apparent.

My host, however, had in some degree resumed the calmness of his demeanour, and questioned me very vigorously in respect to the conformation of the visionary creature. When I had fully satisfied him on this head, he sighed deeply, as if relieved of some intolerable burden, and went on to talk, with what I thought a cruel calmness of various points of speculative philosophy, which had heretofore formed subject of discussion between us. I remember his insisting very especially (among other things) upon the idea that a principal source of error in all human investigations, lay in the liability of the understanding to under-rate or to over-value the importance of an object, through mere mis-admeasurement of its propinquity. "To estimate properly, for example," he said, "the influence to be exercised on mankind at large by the thorough diffusion of Democracy, the distance of the epoch at which such diffusion may possibly be accomplished, should not fail to form an item in the estimate. Yet can you tell me one writer on the subject of government, who has ever thought this particular branch of the subject worthy of discussion at all?"

He here paused for a moment, stepped to a bookcase, and brought forth one of the ordinary synopses of Natural History. Requesting me then to exchange seats with him, that he might the better distinguish the fine print of the volume, he took my arm chair at the window, and, opening the book, resumed his discourse very much in the same tone as before.

"But for your exceeding minuteness," he said, "in describing the monster, I might never have had it in my power to demonstrate to you what it was. In the first place, let me read to you a school boy account of the genus *Sphinx*, of the family *Crepuscularia*, of the order *Lepidoptera*, of the class of *Insecta*—or insects. The account runs thus:

"'Four membranous wings covered with little coloured scales of a metallic appearance; mouth forming a rolled proboscis, produced by an elongation of the jaws, upon the sides of which are found the rudiments of mandibles and downy palpi; the inferior wings retained to the superior by a stiff hair; antennae in the form of an elongated club, prismatic; abdomen pointed. The Death's-headed Sphinx has occasioned much terror among the vulgar, at times, by the melancholy kind of cry which it utters, and the insignia of death which it wears upon its corslet.'"

He here closed the book and leaned forward in the chair, placing himself accurately in the position which I had occupied at the moment of beholding "the monster."

"Ah, here it is!" he presently exclaimed—"it is reascending the face of the hill, and a very remarkable looking creature, I admit it to be. Still, it is by no means so large or so distant as you imagined it; for the fact is that, as it wriggles its way up this hair, which some spider has wrought along the window-sash, I find it to be about the sixteenth of an inch in its extreme length, and also about the sixteenth of an inch distant from the pupil of my eye!"

THE BLUE BEETLE: A CONFESSION

A. G. Gray, Jun.

Little if anything is known of A. G. Gray, Jun., not even the author's full name or gender, though the "Jun." suffix suggests he was a man. "The Blue Beetle: A Confession" appeared in *The Train: A First Class Magazine* (January 1857). The founder and editor of this literary monthly was Edmund Yates, a friend of Charles Ludwig Dodgson, otherwise known as Lewis Carroll. Carroll's poem "Solitude" appeared in the March 1856 edition of *The Train*, and is thought to be the first occasion on which he used his pseudonym in print. Since the contributors to Yates' previous publication numbered his friends and associates, it seems likely Gray moved in the same circles as Yates and Carroll.

"The Blue Beetle: A Confession" is told in the first person by an unnamed alchemical scientist who aspires to solve the mystery of the creation of life and falls foul of his own hubris. There are marked similarities to Mary Shelley's *Frankenstein* (1818) in that both tales involve the ruination of an experimental scientist's life by his tampering with the natural order of things. Frankenstein's conception of his monster is as a "vile insect". Gray's narrator inadvertently creates a literal "loathsome beetle", which he deems a "vile abortion". Although externally beautiful, the "large scarabæus of perfect shape and of a deep blue transparent colour" makes a menacing ticking sound which presages death. The juxtaposition of the titular insect with the subtitle immediately alerts the reader to the fact the beetle is linked to a sinful act.

ay after day, and night after night, did I brood over the great discovery which I thought was about to be opened up to me. I had long had a belief in the progressive development of creation; I believed that it was still possible to find the speck—the germ from which I could raise up a perfectly organized living being. I felt a new and strange pleasure in believing that the mystery of creation was now solved,—that from the first inorganic atom which had received the force of life all other created beings had slowly, gradually, regularly advanced, up to the period in which I lived.

The power of creation—the secret of life, was my goal. My belief was, that the force of life might be given to this inorganic atom. My books were those of the alchemists. With what wild delight I hailed the writings of Geber, of Albertus Magnus, of Arnold de Villeneuve, Heidenburg of Tritheim, Raymond Lully, and Bernard of Treves. I believed in the alchemists. I struggled through the intricacies of their hidden language; their experiments in search of gold I passed over, wonderful as they were, and strangely as they opened my mind to the real truth. I repeated all their experiments on life force, and substantiated every fact I read. My laboratory was perfectly furnished; my days were spent there, and often entire nights. My mind was absorbed in the great truth I was bringing to light.

The confined air of my laboratory at length affected my health; a change was absolutely necessary. I struggled against the idea of removing for some time, and often left my little wife with the tears standing in her deep blue eyes, after she had unsuccessfully implored me to leave London for a short while. Dear Annie! And yet I loved her! Heavens, to think that I—, but I must proceed with my story as it occurred.

We went to the North of Northumberland to stay with my old friend C——, who had frequently asked us to come on previous occasions. We were received warmly; and, as it was winter time, we had plenty of occupation.

A few brisk runs with the county fox-hounds almost made me forget my laboratory. The weather at length changed, first to severe frost with snow, and then to a complete thaw. The dismal north-east wind shrieked through the leafless trees, and drove torrents of sleet splashing against the old-fashioned windows.

Tired of hoping, and weary of grumbling, I was driven to take refuge in C——'s library. After a long search for something interesting, I came upon a little brown volume bound with two dingy metal clasps. On opening its dark and discoloured pages, I found that it was written in French manuscript. A hurried glance showed me that the work was on alchemy, a translation from the Arabic. All my former hopes returned in an instant. I pored over the pages of my newly obtained treasure till late on in the evening—heedless of the impatience of my friends, who, after several useless attempts to draw me away, at last left me to my book and self... The secret, then, was now mine; here, in this old neglected book, I had found a ground-work for my exertions. All the truths I had collected, all the experiments I had made, bore me out. I saw what had prevented others, in ancient times, from carrying out their designs. They knew not the life-giving power; the wonders of electricity had not then been discovered. Vaguely hinted at and darkly guessed at in their works, I saw them groping their way in mist and uncertainty: but I,—I was surrounded by the light of science. Wonderful, mysterious truths broke upon my mind. My whole method and plan of operations stood out clearly before me. A resistless force urged me to commence my scheme instantly. I must leave for London that very night.

I found my wife and friends retiring to rest. I told them my intention of starting for town immediately. Remonstrance and entreaty were of no avail, and in less than an hour I had reached the train at the neighbouring railway station, and was hastening through the stormy night towards London. The train seemed to drag slowly through the darkness, but about noon next day I arrived at my house.

Without rest I commenced my operations; late at night I had nearly completed them; and, worn out in body and mind, I threw myself on the floor to sleep, lulled by the subdued sound of my furnace, which moaned and muttered like an unhappy spirit.

Early in the morning, after a feverish sleep, I rose tired and un-refreshed, and began to complete the last portion of my arrangements. This was to prepare the liquid from which the beings to whom I had to impart life were to spring. On account of the experiments made in my late studies I had all the ingredients ready in my laboratory. I poured the mixture then carefully into a large silver trough. The liquid was perfectly limpid and of a beautiful blue colour, probably on account of a salt of copper entering largely into its composition.

And now I prepared my batteries, and soon afterwards the electric agent was applied. To my astonishment no decomposition took place,—the liquid remained clear and beautifully blue. Thus it remained for some hours. I hung over it in breathless expectation; the only change apparently being that the colour seemed deeper and purer.

Night came on, and the electric fluid still quietly streamed into the liquid. By accident, in adjusting one of the wires, I dashed a few drops from the trough on to the floor. There was a hissing sound as they fell, and as they touched the ground they burst into flame.

This I extinguished, and then applied myself to observing closely the contents of the vessel, for I knew that a great change had taken place in their constitution. I removed the light to a distance, fearing lest it should ignite the vapours which were now rising from the surface. On returning in the dark I found strange flashes of light circling in the interior of the fluid; these gradually became brighter till I was enabled to see every object in the room clearly by their radiance.

Subtle fumes also were rising from the surface. On inhaling these fumes at first I felt faint, but the sensation passed away. The perfume now was delicious—it was heavenly; I drank it in like nectar. I gazed upon the coruscating surface, and a delirious ecstasy seemed to pervade my whole being; delicious streams of music fell softly on my ears, and shadowy forms of ineffable beauty floated in the air around me. Suddenly an insane desire took possession of me: I longed to seize the silver vessel and quaff the deep blue poison. I stretched out my hands with a cry of joy—and then... I recovered at last from a fever which had kept me insensible for a week. It was some days before I could get any explanation of how I came to be in my own bed-room, with my little wife attending to my every want, her little hands ever busy, and her eyes beaming with love and tenderness.

Gradually the details of my late occupation dawned upon my memory. I imagined I perceived the subtle odour diffusing itself through the chamber, and shuddered as I lay back on my pillow. A feeling of remorse came over me when I thought of my design. I felt as if I had intruded where man should fear to tread, and I felt a gratification in thinking that my designs had been frustrated.

One morning, when the physician said that I was able to bear the news, I was told that one of the domestics, hearing a scream on that fearful night, had forced open the door of the laboratory. A strange, overpowering perfume, he said, at first drove him back, but rushing in a second time, he found me lying insensible on the floor.

With breathless eagerness I asked if any of the apparatus in the room had been touched? No, nothing had been touched; the windows had been opened to allow the poisonous vapours to disperse; the doors had then been locked and had never been opened since. A weight seemed removed from my mind—I would instantly go down and destroy all that remained of my strange experiment.

I was still too weak: three or four days passed over, and then I was able to go down stairs. With trembling hands and beating heart (why I could not tell) I turned the key and entered the laboratory alone. Every thing remained as I had left it a fortnight before.

There stood the ponderous batteries, long since worked out; there loosely hung the copper connecting wires covered with green rust. The silver trough was tarnished and dim, but everything stood as I had left it.

The interior of the trough was coated with metallic copper, while the solution had almost entirely evaporated: there was still a small quantity of liquid at the bottom, covered with thick, opal-tinted mould.

On looking closely at this mould-covered residue, I noticed a peculiar irregularity, or rather regularity in its surface. There were five little heaps or hillocks in regular arrangement—one at each angle of a square, and one in the centre—exactly like *the five-side of a gaming die.* These heaps were of such equal size and uniform shape that I could not attribute their presence to chance. I supposed that electricity had so acted upon the particles of the solution as to make them take up their present position.

I examined the mould under the microscope, and found it to be a fungus of a peculiar kind, but, in removing some more of the mould with a glass rod, I happened to touch one of the little heaps, and found under it a small blue crystal of cubic form, and under each of the other three angular hillocks I found a similar crystal. On removing the mould from the centre hillock I found what, at first, I thought was a circular mass of the same crystalline substance; but imagine my surprise and horror when I saw the mass begin to struggle among the liquid, and, clearing away the silky needles of the mould, disclose to my view a large scarabæus of perfect shape, and of a deep blue transparent colour.

A feeling of terror filled my mind. Whence had come this strange creature? Whence came the power with which he stretched out his antennæ, drew the blue case-covers from his back, and cleared the mould from his filmy wings? Could this be the result of my researches—my days of toil, my nights of unrest? A beetle! I strove to laugh, but the attempt failed, and my heart sank within me with a strange foreboding. At this moment, from the interior of the trough arose a peculiar sound—like the rapid ticking of a clock, although louder, and with a metallic tinkle in it—it was the same sound as that produced by the "death-tick" beetle.

As soon as the sound died away I looked once more at the creature: he was half in and half out of the liquid, and evidently as yet unable to fly. The prominent desire in my mind was to destroy the insect, for his unearthly sounds and the strange flashing of his bead-like eyes made me tremble with a vague terror. However, I overcame the feeling, and determined to let him live for a few days.

Early the next morning I visited the laboratory, but, on looking into the silver vessel, I was unable to detect any traces of the scarabæus. Puzzled and annoyed, I began to inspect the room, when I suddenly heard the ominous "death-tick," and after a few preliminary flights round the room, the beetle alighted upon the rim of the trough. A ray of sunlight glancing in fell upon him; his colour was exquisite—a rich deep cerulæan blue, he seemed a living sapphire, and would have been beautiful but for his loathsome form.

I had brought a piece of sugar with me, which I thought might please the taste of my new favourite. I placed it on the bench near— he flew directly towards it and settled upon it, but, as if dissatisfied, a moment afterwards he flew back to the rim of the trough. I heard a low whine at my feet, and looking down, saw my wife's little dog, "Lalette." I threw the rejected sugar towards her, and soon heard her crunching it up in her little jaws. Shortly afterwards I left the room, and as I closed the door, louder than ever I heard the sound of the "death-tick."

I was engaged out of doors during the day, and in the evening my wife's first question was, whether I had seen "Lalette" that day? I then remembered that he had been in the laboratory with me in the morning, and fancying that she must be locked in, I went to the door, and, opening it, called her by name. There was no movement or response; but as I called again, something whirred past me in the air and dashed out into the hall. I felt certain that my beetle had escaped. Shutting the door hastily, I rushed back for a light. On re-entering the laboratory I could neither see nor hear anything of the beetle; but in the middle of the floor, exactly where I had left her in the morning, poor "Lalette" was lying dead.

Some portions of the sugar were still lying beside her—she had been poisoned. Once more before leaving I sought diligently for the beetle, but no trace was to be found; "Lalette" was a great favourite, and my poor wife was inconsolable. I told her the dog must have picked up some poison in my room; and with promises of a new canine favourite soon her grief calmed down.

All that night an indefinable horror took possession of me. When I thought of that living sapphire being at large in the house, a firm belief possessed me that "Lalette" had been killed by that poisonous insect. All that night he haunted my dreams; several times I started from slumber, thinking I heard that unearthly death-tick. I determined in my feverish sleeplessness to search every nook and corner of the house, on the morrow. Somehow I felt at times that my existence, my destiny, was bound up in the life of this hideous insect.

Reproaches seemed spoken to me, in one dream of that long night, that I had created a living poison, and sent it out into the world. I shuddered and awoke. The words seemed burnt upon my brain. Could I ever forget them. Listen!

Next morning I heard that one of the domestics, a young pretty girl of nineteen years, was ill. Three days afterwards she died. The doctors said it was heart disease. One of them, a sententious old empiric, said the only peculiarity of the case was a strange mark upon the girl's breast. A pang shot through my whole frame. A mark! What mark! What was it like? By a mysterious perception I knew that this mark concerned me. But how? I soon knew. On the cold white breast of the corpse were *five blue spots*, arranged like the spots on the *five-side of a die*. Controlling my emotion as best I could, I locked myself in my own room, and, burying my face in my hands, cried, in agony— "Accursed beast! this is thy work; the blood of an innocent being is on my hands!" My brain seemed whirling round, and every attempt to collect my thoughts was in vain. The infernal creature—my creature!—had murdered this young girl, and how knew I where he would stop? One thing was plain; my wife and the whole household must be removed immediately. Seizing a pen, I hurriedly wrote to C——, and explaining, as best I could, the unexpected visit of my wife, I went up to the station and saw her start by the first train to the North. The corpse of the young girl was removed by her friends in the afternoon, and the other servants were despatched to their respective homes.

I was left alone in the house all that long, lonely night. I waited in each room listening for that fearful death-tick. Never lover waited more anxiously for a loving whisper from loved lips than I for that hideous sound. But, save the hushed murmur of the mighty city, and the clang of the slow hours as they passed, and the beating of my own heart, all was silence. I searched all that night, and the next day; aye! and the next day, and the next, but no vestige of the loathsome creature could I find. On the fourth day came a letter from my wife. My friend C——was ill; he was sinking fast, and wished to see me.

Locking-up my house—not without some dread—I journeyed northward to C——'s house. As I drove up the long avenue in the afternoon, I thought the old mansion had a mournful gloom brooding over it. My heart was depressed—a presentiment of evil hung about me. I could not cast it off. The tearful face of the servant who admitted me added to my mournful forebodings.

I found C——in bed, dying. Dying! The first glance showed me that his days were numbered. A sickly smile of welcome played over his features as I approached him; but it almost instantly changed for a look of intense suffering. I asked what the particular symptoms of his illness were. The medical man in attendance tried to explain the malady, but left me painfully impressed with the idea that he was entirely ignorant of the disease. I had turned to speak to some of the family who were in the room, when I was startled by a piercing cry of agony from the bed.

C——was sitting up in bed, his wan face distorted with pain; he was grasping his neck with his white nervous hands. "My throat is on fire!" he shrieked. "It burns, it burns! Water! for the love of heaven! a drop of water!" Trembling, I held a tumbler of water to his lips; he had scarcely tasted it when he dashed the glass from my hands to the floor, exclaiming,—"Devil! I did not ask for vitriol—give me water—water!" As he said this he tore open the neck of his dressing-gown. Merciful heavens! could I believe my eyesight? There was the fatal mark. There—even among the purple distended veins which interlaced like strong cords around his neck—I could see it. *Five blue spots arranged like the five-side of a die!* The room swam before my eyes, and the word "Murderer!" seemed ringing in my ears... When I recovered, C——was dead. My agitation had been attributed to grief at my friend's death; no one had noticed the cursed mark but myself. The members of the family were absorbed in grief; my wife strove to soothe and solace them; but such work was not for me. I gave myself up to my own frightful reflections.

The creature had then found his way to this remote place; how I knew not, nor did I ever know. It was enough for me to know that he was there. My oldest, truest friend was dead, and a happy home had been rendered wretched, and through me! Through this cursed creation of mine. Why had I not obeyed the first impulse, and killed him as he lay in the mould in the silver trough?

I wandered out into the night; my mind was all in desolate confusion. It was a lovely night—the sky glimmered with stars, and the full moon rose as I walked with uneven steps under the trees. I threw myself down on the wet grass and wept like a child. Soon the soft shimmer of the moonlight broke out into full radiance, and bathed the whole country in a flood of beautiful light. The gentleness of the scene after a time impressed me. I became calmer, and reflected on my position. "If the creature is here, he must be hunted down." I dare not tell the household; there was guilt and blood on my conscience. They would deem me mad, I thought. Then, again, I thought that the excitement of the last few days, together with my late illness, might have produced the effect of an optical illusion—that there was no mark. This conviction strengthened, I turned again to the house.

The servant who opened the door started when he saw my altered appearance, matted hair, and wet disorderly dress. But I asked calmly to be shown to the room where the body of C——was lying. I went in alone. Need I tell the result?—the fearful mark was there, and stood out brightly against the cold white skin.

Every corner of the room I searched, but no trace of the fiendish beast was there. After some time spent in this vain search I left the room, and gained my wife and her friends below. They were shocked at my changed appearance. I sat apart, moody and silent. A heavy suffocating cloud of presentiment overpowered me—I felt that my cup was not yet filled, but that, when filled, I should have to drink it to its bitter—bitter dregs. We separated to retire to rest; but, though few of us expected to sleep, no sooner had I laid my head on the pillow than I fell asleep—a dull heavy sleep—as dreamless and almost as breathless as that of the corpse in the next chamber. I do not know how long I had slept, when I awoke suddenly with an unaccountable feeling of terror.

How dark the room is getting—put your ear closer to my mouth—I feel faint with speaking loud—but I must tell you all.

I awoke, and, seemingly, close by my ear!—loud and distinct—I heard the death-tick! My hands clenched till the nails penetrated the flesh when I knew he was within my reach—close by my ear! Heaven help me if I do not crush the creature now!

The moonbeams poured in through the windows and filled the room with a mysterious light. The rays struck across the pillows of the bed and fell softly on the up-turned face of my little wife. She slumbered peacefully; but on her snowy brow, glittering as blue as Heaven itself, was the loathsome beetle! With one blow I struck him from her face, and then leaped from the bed. I saw his glittering jewel-like form upon the ground—I seized it and crushed it in my hands—a fierce pain shot up my arm—my blood seemed changed to molten lead. The agony was excruciating, I dropped the vile abortion; he flew from me, and, dashing through the glass of the window, disappeared into the moonlight night.

My story is well nigh told. You know—you know how my wife sickened and—died. But listen! you did not see the blue mark upon her white brow.

How dark the room is—and how slowly my heart is beating. Look at this arm—here!—above the elbow, there is the death-brand. *Five blue spots arranged like the spots on a die*. I have but an hour to live. You know my secret... Let me rest.

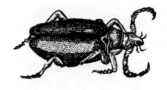

THE MUMMY'S SOUL

Anonymous

Written anonymously in 1862, "The Mummy's Soul" is the earliest known mummy curse tale as we know it and was published in the May issue of *The Knickerbocker; or New York Monthly Magazine*, a New York-based periodical running from 1833–1865. Washington Irving, under the pen-name Geoffrey Crayon, became a regular contributor to the magazine. The magazine soon established itself as a reputable publication. Edgar Allan Poe even praised its founder and editor, Charles Fenno Hoffman, for giving *The Knickerbocker* a respectable tone and character while it was under his control. Based on the content of *The Knickerbocker Magazine*, its readership seems to have been interested in articles on beautiful American scenery as well as articles on foreign lands, far-off lives and traditions. Nature and Environmentalism were prominent within the magazine and the "Oregon Trail" by Francis Parkman, one of the outstanding American historians of the nineteenth century, ran as a serial from April 1847 to July 1848. Another claim to fame for *The Knickerbocker* was that it published the first "Why did the chicken cross the road?" joke in March 1847.

Although the author of "The Mummy's Soul" is unknown, it is possible to speculate they may have been female since many anonymous submissions were thought to have come from women, and subsequent curse tales were definitely written by women. "The Mummy's Soul" shares themes with the work of Edgar Allan Poe such as torment, the gothic domestic space and entrapment. More uniquely though, the story features an insect which serves as an extension of the female mummy herself and as a harbinger of disease. The protagonist details how the insect becomes an unrelenting nightmare in his own home as it harasses him with its gruesome proboscis, and haunts him and his wife with the melodic singing of its wings.

t was high noon, and fresh, luxuriant life without, and the darkness of mid-night and the dead, within this Egyptian tomb, hollowed out of the heart of the Libyan chain of mountains. Two hundred feet above me, massive ruins, half-buried beneath the yellow, glittering sands of the desert, were revealed as the skeleton of a city of gigantic wonders. Now, Thebes was not so desolate. The sculptured faces of colossi gazed with stern, tearless eyes over the waste, as if in mockery of the frailty of contemporary creations. Around me were mummies, sculptures, and rough paintings on the walls. Life and death here touched each other, and were identified by the reality of mutual existence. A humanity of forgotten ages, by its ashes preached sermons of profoundest truths in stupendous charnel-houses. Yet I asked myself, in a spirit of unbelief of such truths, if the oracles of Egyptian mythology spoke falsely, when they asserted, that the soul, after three thousand years of pilgrimage to other shrines, would reinvest the bodies of the dead with new life?

A startled bat flew in and out of an empty tomb; and an angry scorpion clicked his armour-plates, as he crept along the ledge of one of the crypts above me. A faint puff of air from the passage filled my nostrils with the sickening effluvia of mummies, and scattered the dust from the carvings of the pillar. I was in a casket of Death, and the jewels were mummies. Dead for centuries, yet alive in every thing but life; lacking only a breath of that life to cast off the swathing-cloths, and confront me! The thought of seeing them step from the tomb, in the hideousness of such a resurrection, made me shudder.

Yet, if their doctrine of a renewal of life after thirty centuries, were to prove true, there might at any moment be a resurrection, and a consequent paroxysm of terror on my part. What if I should be attacked, as I threaded intricate passages in this birth-place of antique horrors, by mobs of these resurrected Egyptians, infuriated by the sacrilege of my presence?

The mere idea of encountering their shrivelled forms in deadly struggle, and wrestling for victory with entwined limbs, while their crisp hair, odorous of the crypt, brushed my face; all these foolish promptings of an imagination, excited by my strange surroundings, together with a shuffling noise in a distant passage, caused me to drop my torch, and rush to the entrance of the tomb, where I stood quivering with fright, not knowing which way to turn. Fortunately, Ferraj, my guide, was the comer; else, in the darkness and sickening solitude, I should have become mad.

The tomb in which I stood had been discovered the previous day. It consisted of one large chamber with heavy arches, a massive pillar in the centre, and with three tiers of niches on each side; the fronts being ornamented with outline paintings of a brilliant red colour. The ponderous carvings of the pillar were merely heavy lines of sculpture, with no delicacy of outline, no airy gracefulness to mar the effectiveness of their stupendous symmetry. Every curve and straight line on pillar and tablet was harsh, rigid, and even cruel in its expression of power. The rough granite had been carved, in many cases, into crude and intricate delineations of human pageantry, by the ready skill of the patient artist. Yet, the hands that had cut and painted, day after day, in the service of cunning priest or mourning relative, had dropped the chisel and the brush thousands of years before, leaving outlines of works to be memorials of undeveloped grandeur.

Many of the niches in the tiers had been despoiled of their contents. One only remained untouched; upon its tablet was painted, in rich colours, a lotus-flower, broken at the blossom. There was no inscription upon the tomb to designate its occupant; no legendary engraving of his or her life's events. The cement around the edges of the tablet was as hard as the rock in which the tomb was cut. A half-hour's labour with a crow-bar had but meagre result; so I placed a quantity of powder under the lower edge of the stone, where a small cavity had been made with the bar. There was a hissing noise as the fire ran up the fuse, followed by a dull sound of explosion, that was immediately hushed and smothered by the dead silence of the passages without. The slab with its painting fell to the ground, and was shattered.

Within the niche thus opened was a mummy-case, containing a mummy, bandaged from head to foot in fine linen, and lying upon a bed of crumbling flowers. I reproached myself, in a sorrowful, musing mood, for such a sacrilege, when I found it was the body of a woman. But a sickening, musty odour from the corpse spread its subtle essences throughout the chamber, and stealing to the brain intoxicated it. I seemed to see, in this momentary inebriation of the senses, the body of this mummy snap its cerements, and slowly recede through the rocky walls, which closed not after it; while it floated, in plain sight, down a passage, in the mountain, bordered by rows of tombs, one above another. And out of these graves of stone stretched bandaged arms of tawny-skinned mummies, whose fingers vainly clutched at the phantom, as, motionless in features and limbs, it glided down the terrible aisle, and was lost in the gloom.

The agony of the vision was over. My forehead was covered with a cold perspiration, and my eyes ached with the fierce heat that had created the appalling vision; while white flames of light seemed, now and then, to mingle with the darkness of the corridor.

I looked behind me. Ferraj sat cowering upon the ground, with his hands covering his face.

"Ferraj!"

"Howadji! Brave Sidi! did you not see the body move and motion with its hands? Did it move away into the darkness?" he cried, seizing my hand.

"Of course not, you foolish fellow. Is it not there in the case? It is impossible for the dead to come to life."

I laughed feebly to put him in good spirits; but he was not at all reassured, and I noticed that, while we remained in the tomb, he stood at a distance from the mummy, holding his torch like a sword, as if to parry a blow from unseen hands.

In profound awe, and with a delicate touch, I unwrapped the face of the body. A woman's features, black and shrivelled, were revealed. I was startled—even sickened—at the hideous revelation. For an instant I had forgotten my situation, and its surroundings, and remembered only an occasion when I turned back the coffin-lid, and gazed for the last time upon the face of my dead sister. I thought, in my reverie over this mummy, of a lovely face, and fair features, like marble. Imagination had never conjured up so shocking a vision. But my zeal as an antiquary suppressed delicate dreams and disagreeable realities. This woman might have been handsome in the era in which she existed; she was, perhaps, considered as the possessor of great beauty. She was very short, slight, with a low forehead; the cheek-bones were high, but not prominent, and the nose delicate and small; the eyes, the windows to a woman's soul, were closed in a sleep of centuries. Her hair was black, curled, and somewhat faded. Her mouth was small, exquisitely formed, and the lips were devoid of any heaviness of curve to mark the tincture of Ethiopian blood. But the dark, parchment-like skin, wrinkled and rough, made me loathe the corpse, and to wonder at the love that thus burned out beauty, by slow consuming fires of subtle chemistry; and laid away the shell of the soul, that it might once more be reinvigorated with a life that in its wanderings had animated beast, bird, or insect, and acquired strength at each succeeding transmigration. As I unwrapped the long bandages from the breast, a strong gust of wind rushed from the desert into the dim crypts of the mountains. It flared the expiring torches, scattered dust from pillar and niche, and caused the mummy to crumble into a nauseous powder, that half-choked me with its subtle essence of humanity. From a mass of beads and shreds of cloth, I picked out a stone *scarabæus*, on whose back was graven many minute hieroglyphics. I succeeded in translating the following: "*Three thousand years hence, a new life.*" So the prophecy had been refuted, and dust returned to dust, I said to myself. But the doubt whether the resurrection predicted would not reform this dust into a re-created body, intruded itself, and strengthened the imagination, which hoped it would be so.

In the crypt, at the head of the body, I found a tiny vase of green translucent stone, of antique form, embellished with exquisitely carved devices. From either side sprang a serpent, which extended upward with light, graceful curves, until with its hideous fangs it indented the delicate rim of the vase. It was so fragile that it seemed as if a touch from the most careful fingers would crush it to atoms. I accidentally inverted it, and there fell upon the floor a quantity of light, fine ashes, and an insect of enormous size. It lay upon the ground, at my feet, with outstretched wings. Ferraj stooped down, and taking it in his hand, gazed upon it for a minute, his lips quivering, and his hand trembling so much that his torch almost fell to the ground.

"*Efrit! Efrit!* a foul devil!" he shouted, and cast the thing from him into the remains of the mummy. Picking it up, I examined it carefully, but with an indescribable loathing, that seized me whenever I saw the vile thing.

It was a fly, six inches long, with a head the size and shape of a pea; and appeared like a globule of liquid silver. Its small white eyes sparkled with the brilliancy of a diamond, and projected slightly from the head. The body was elastic, and of a bright golden colour, encircled at regular distances with bands of green. Its long, delicate, many-jointed legs were adorned with a fine yellow hair. Its wings were broad sheets of beauty—traceries of golden lines, shadows of deep blackness—gorgeously embellished, where veins of silver hue tinged the edges, with a net-work of marvellous loveliness. These labyrinths of delicate colours so merged into one another that the eye wearied in striving to find where one hue ended and another commenced. The brilliancy of colour had not been dimmed by the death of the insect, but was revealed in all its glory. From the sharp-pointed tips of these wonderful wings hung tiny tassels of finest hair, filled with the dust in which it had been buried. Notwithstanding its diversity of colours, and wondrous construction, it was hideously deformed; for springing out of the very centre of the front of its head, lay coiled a fine elastic antenna of blood-red colour. Upon seeing it, my admiration changed to disgust. A shudder of terror ran over me when, with a sharp click, the extended antenna slipped from my fingers, and struck the head. Ferraj had stood apart from me during this examination; but when he saw my movement, and heard the sharp sound as the coil flew back, he uttered a low moan.

The remarkable elasticity of the insect convinced me that it had been embalmed in the vase in a fluid, long before evaporated. The ashes might or might not have formed a part of an embalming mixture.

Every thing about the insect was flexible and moist, as if life had just gone out. But I could not conjecture its use when alive, or what it symbolized when dead.

The insect fascinated me, not simply by its gorgeous variety of colours, not by any hitherto unknown peculiarity of structure, nor by the brilliant appearance of its dimmed eyes, but as a whole; even the loathsome helmet upon its head, was an essential in the fascination. I hated myself for yielding to the feeling that in after-days grew into an intense passion, and a pride in the possession of so wonderful a creation.

I gathered one or two handfuls of the mummy's dust, and put them, with the fly, into the vase, and left the tomb, dispirited—overcome by the sensations experienced, and the discoveries I had made. I had not the heart to farther prosecute my investigation among the tombs, and almost immediately departed for America.

I often exhibited my mementoes to friends; the ladies, acknowledging the wondrous magnificence of the insect, almost invariably declared it to be the most treacherous thing they had ever seen, and inveighed most bitterly against a judgment that selected such abortions, as mementoes of my sojourn in Egypt.

But my wife—my young and beautiful good angel—became terribly fascinated with this insect. I did not discover this slavery of her mind, until after many months; even then, by becoming suddenly cognizant of having found it in her hands upon many occasions, it occurred to me that she might be enthralled by this creature. When I accused her of it, she burst into tears, and acknowledged the truth of my accusation; saying, in a piteous, apologetic strain, "that the fascination of the pretty thing was so irresistible, and at the same time reminded her so strongly of my long absence in foreign countries, that she could not avoid dwelling in thought upon the strange scenery and discoveries that had kept me from her, and of contemplating the only memento of such an absence." Then, for the first time, I told her of the occurrences in the tomb. When I had concluded, she clasped her pretty little hands, and said: "Fred, this insect attracts me as it attracts you; only that with my submission to its thraldom is allied a premonition, that it will work me a fearful injury. I have repelled the idea again and again, but it always returns. I strive to be philosophical, and treat it as a frenzy, but there is no relief."

Thereafter, in company, we used to pass hours in contemplating the antipathetic features of this fly, and in conjecturing what part it acted in the economy of nature, when it winged the air among people whose existence was almost forgotten. These examinations intoxicated our imaginations, by the antiquity and mystery surrounding the object of our investigation. We clung more to each other by reason of our servility to this incomprehensible influence of the fly. We were not unhappy, but simply uneasy; never striving, after a couple of months, to throw off our bondage.

If this were the termination of the history, I would weep for joy. But it is at this particular point of time that the insect, hitherto quiet, plays its active part in a tragedy to which there is no parallel.

One evening, in making an experiment, I had occasion to use a mixture of ammonia and ether, and had prepared it in a saucer, when I was suddenly called from the house, leaving the compound upon the table, in the dish. When I returned, late in the evening, I ascertained that a servant had emptied the contents of the saucer into a vase. It never occurred to me to ask what vase she meant; as there were several in the room, it surely was in one of them, and I gave no thought to the matter. The bed-room opened into the study; the two rooms were separated by a partition of lath and plaster, and the door at night always stood open.

About half-past twelve o'clock, my sleep was broken in a quiet, unaccountable way, that is often the precursor of danger. Every faculty was fresh and keen, and unusually active. Listening, my ear suddenly caught a faint sound of music, whose delicate strains floated softly toward me from a corner of the bed-room; then, with the rapidity of lightning, there burst upon me a delicious, maddening flow of measure after measure of passionate symphonies. They flowed in from the study, and beat the stagnant air to-and-fro, until every particle became a bell that tinkled sweetest melody. This music was so sweet, yet so fierce; so gentle in its cadences, yet so vigorous in its utterances; so peaceful, yet so thrilling, that the room trembled with the reverberations. A delicious languor possessed me. There was a profound silence for a minute. Then, just above my face, there was another outbreak of this wild melody; these chiming echoes.

My wife moaned, and in her restlessness, her hand fell upon my face.

My thoughts had been so absolutely controlled by the weird, soulless music, that the touch frightened me; it was as if a hand had been put forth from the thick darkness, and laid upon my forehead. But the alarm, soon repulsed by calm reason, was succeeded by another shock, less sharp and sudden, but more lasting, and full of subtle terrors and keen agony. The hand of my wife was dry, feverish and shrunken, as if a quick, consuming fever had burned out its freshness, and left beneath the parchment-like skin, the hot ashes of its previous beauty.

She moaned feebly, when I passionately called her name. I pressed my lips to her face; it was as terrible as her hand. Alarmed at her incomprehensible silence, and at the swift, silent change manifest to my touch, I lighted the candle.

She was lying upon her side, looking at me with eyes so senseless in expression, so devoid of life or brilliancy in their idiotic fixedness, that the unexpected, terrible transformation, more grievous because of its hopelessness, touched my heart like the keen edge of a knife. I wept.

As I moaned and cried in my hopeless agony, her rough, hot hand once more rested upon my face, as if to express, feebly though it were, her sympathy for my affliction; though she could not appreciate the bitterness of my agony, she comprehended, dreamily without doubt, that a sorrow had fallen upon me.

With a cry of joy at this manifestation of her intense love, I clasped her in my arms; but the hope that had suddenly sprung up in my heart was cruelly crushed to death, for she lay in my arms a passive, undemonstrative being, with swift pulsations of the hot blood that scorched the delicate skin, until it was like fine parchment.

But while I was suffering most intensely, while my brain grew delirious under this desolation of my love—this mysterious, maddening affliction—I heard, with inexpressible fear, the wild, varying music. My wife trembled violently when she heard the clear ringing notes. Every second was affecting her appearance, developing a woman whose features were shrivelled and brown; the eyes, once animated by holiest love, were cold, passionless, and fixed in a soulless gaze. She lost all volition, and sunk into a dreadful apathy. *In every thing but form and face, she resembled the mummy in the tomb.* Hitherto my mind had been paralysed by terror and grief. Now it was recovering from its shock. I implored my wife to tell me the cause of her illness, to speak to me; and I put my ear close to her lips, to catch the faintest whisper. But the musical hum in the study was the only sound I heard. Frantic with the thought that my delay might hasten her death, I summoned a physician, who, after much delay, dare not prescribe. Another one was sent for; he had never heard or read of so strange a case. He prescribed brandy to stimulate the blood, which was fast becoming sluggish, and said that he could do no more.

It was after he had gone that, in bending over my wife, I saw several small spots of blood upon the pillow. Back of her left ear was found a spot where the skin was a little broken, as if by the prick of a pin, and from which blood slowly oozed. I was still stooping over her, and the servants were chafing her hands and feet, and giving the stimulant, when suddenly the mysterious music thrilled the air. My wife shuddered at the sound, and the women rested from their labour, to gaze upon each other in wonderment and alarm.

Taking a light from the stand, I passed into the study, closing the door after me. I had not removed my hand from the knob, when, with a whizzing noise, a large object, hot as a coal of fire, struck my face; and being beaten off, rose and fluttered hither and thither against the high ceiling. In amazement I recognized this assailant, this musician, this exuder of sweet sounds. It was the Insect. Its body, like glistening gold and flashing emerald, was distended to its full proportions; its great tasselled wings beat the air, until it frothed into unearthly music; its eyes, sparkling like diamonds, seemed the prisons of a thousand tiny fires, burning with a steady flame; its antenna was outstretched, and felt nervously along the white ceiling, leaving small red dots as indices of its touch. The loathsome thing flew from point to point as I pursued. It easily eluded the missiles I cast at it, and suddenly disappeared through the ventilator.

I picked up from the table the little green vase, in which the resurrected insect had been kept, and found that it was nearly full of the mixture I had left in the saucer. By the agency of these liquids vigorous life had been created in the body of the embalmed insect. That I did not comprehend the principle of this resurrection, through the instrumentality of such subtle materials, was not my fault. The insect was alive, and its place in the vase filled by fluids in which it must have been immersed—I accepted the facts as they were presented.

And the insect lived on human blood! As my eye glanced along the ceiling, the red dots thereon were a revelation of the cause of my wife's suffering; and were proofs of the injection into her veins of a subtle poison, to dry up her blood and parch the fair skin. The full extent of my sorrow, past and future, passed before my straining eyes, like a terrible vision; it shook me as the wind beats a blade of dried grass. I returned to the bed-side of my wife, as a man blasted by the bitterest sorrow, and sharpest agony of the soul. Eternal misery chained me, like a felon, to ghastly horrors; while Imagination decked my future with gloomy robes, and bid me hope only for death, as life would be full of vivid phantasms to blight the most joyous moments.

To love a woman as passionately as I loved my wife, and hold her in one's arms as the last great change of life gradually develops; to feel the beatings of the heart diminish, to see the gasps for breath, to look into the eyes soon to close forever, and read in them the love they look back into yours, are the saddest of duties to the dying. But how terrible the anguish, when the eyes are fixed in an idiotic stare, their light forever extinguished, and the loved one, unconscious of your maddening grief, your piteous, unavailing love, is released by Death from her unhappy life! My wife changed but little in appearance after that memorable night. Her body became emaciated; the skin became black, and hot to the touch; the eyes were half-closed, and their light hidden. She would lie in my arms, at the window, for hours; and, with her cheek pressed closely to my breast, just over my aching heart, would imitate the sweet sounds that had been made by the insect's wings. She never spoke; nor did she evince the slightest consciousness of my presence. Oftentimes she fiercely pressed her hands upon her head, as if it suffered intolerable pain. In my lamentable helplessness, I could do nothing but support her in my arms, and calmly endure the awful agony of the sight.

Since the night of its disappearance, I had not heard the insect. I cared not whither it had flown, so that it left me in peace. But one afternoon, when the rain was falling in broad sheets, while sitting as usual at the window, my wife lying in my arms, the hated music sounded, faint and low, in the partition separating the study from the bed-room. The strains aroused my wife from her apathy. She raised herself up, repeated them in all their variations, and as she ended, she quickly turned her face toward me, and threw her arms around my neck. There followed a sudden, convulsive gasping for breath, and a short, feeble moan. The arms unclasped, and my wife was dead.

*

My wife was buried, and I was a monomaniac. My only thought, the only thing for which I cared to live, was, in what manner I might seize and destroy the insect—the cause of all my sorrow. I tore down a large part of the partition, in which it was last heard, but was unsuccessful in my search. I was in despair. I sat for hours at the breach I had made in the wall, listening intently for the slightest sound; but none was heard, and I had come to believe that the insect had crept through some crevice into the chimney, and flown away.

The wall had not been repaired when, one night, in a pleasant stupor, I heard sweet music close to my ear, and felt cool air, and then a sharp stinging pain, lasting only for a second. The low, plaintive music soothed my brain. A delicious languor possessed me. For an instant the sublime solitude of the grave, with musical silence awed my soul. Then, with a noise like the distant cries of a vast army, there rushed upon me a scorching wind and monstrous phantasms.

I lay upon the sand before the front of the grand temple of Abou Simbal, with its three colossal statues hewn out of the mountain, sitting in a majestic agony of silence, watching the Nile, with their staring eyes of stone, as they have watched it for three thousand years. The desert laves them with its billows of sand, half-submerging their huge limbs in its yellow flow, half-revealing their stupendousness, while it contrasts the solemn grey of the rocks and statues with the gleaming of the swift river. I hear voices sounding in the inner temple, where sit the gods in gloomy darkness, where sacrifices were made and agonies endured. As I listen, the magnificent temple dissolves in the soft twi-light, and the sublime idea of Sesostris shadows my soul like a cloud.

Palm-trees and shattered columns! Philae and Isis and Osiris! Mecca of a people of stupendous wonders! Island of beautiful ruins and lovely desolation! The great black rocks inclosing it smoothed their jagged edges, and the moon-light trembled in its avenues, and lingered in the courts of its temples, as the darkness in which I wandered over a great desert plain, was parted by the heavenly vision. One glimpse of its magnificent beauty, and the gloomy blackness gathered and swung to-and-fro—the proscenium to a revelation of exquisite loveliness.

Once again, as in by-gone days, I wandered among the majestic ruins of Karnac. Masses of rock carved into graceful shapes stopped my way. Architraves of noble temples, fragments of fallen columns, made me sigh at their downfall. I walked down the avenue of sphinxes, amid mutilated colossi and rudely-sculptured columns, half-buried in the glittering sands of the desert. I lingered in the great halls of temples of stupendous size, where light and darkness struggled for superiority; and the imagination shrunk to nothingness, as it essayed to compass the magnificence of dead Thebes, whose gigantic skeleton lay unburied upon the desert. I was lost in the forest of columns of the grand hall at Karnac, and shivered with supernatural terror beside the granite statues at the entrance to the temple at El Uksorein. I hungered and thirsted in my journeys among these shreds of ancient grandeur, and my soul asked for relief, for terror itself had become colossal. And amid this rubbish of dead cities, oppressed by the very magnitude of desolation, my soul cried for relief. But the hot sun poured down its hottest rays, the monstrous obelisks hid me from the cool, refreshing wind, and vast walls threatened to crush me under their broad surfaces of hieroglyphics. In my agony, I dug a shallow grave in the sand, and hid myself therein, and let the sun pierce it with its rays, and sloughing stone to descend upon it—but I slept.

Suddenly, in my fitful slumber, surrounded by these well-remembered scenes, there shivered the air, shrilly and clearly, a sound that thrilled every nerve in my body, and echoed in my brain, until the air seemed a tumult of piercing chords, that racked the sensitive nerves, and pealed upon the fastidious ear until it was deafened. Vibration after vibration of sound overwhelmed me with its powerful utterances. I rise from my grave and listen for their source. The faint glow of the rising sun steals down the rough sides of the Libyan mountains, and the lordly river sweeps past on its unending journey. Once, twice, thrice, sounds the shrill note; and the fabled Memnon, as gigantic as if it still sat upon its carved throne, upon the western plain of ruined Thebes, strides toward me, falls upon and mangles me. I am stung by thousands of quick, sharp pains; my body burns with their fires. The music grows fainter and is still. Thick darkness overwhelms me, and I unavailingly buffet its noiseless waves.

*

The memory of the disease that tortured my mind and body during the month succeeding my visions, is rendered prominent by an illusion as painful as it was enduring. I believed that my wife, swathed in linen, aromatic of rich gums and spices, that poisoned the air with their heavy fragrance, sat at my bed-side in all the hideous blackness of her transformation; that she clasped my hand in hers, and gazed into my aching eyes with the blank idiotic stare which had characterized the final stage of her disease.

I did not doubt the reality of the vision; nor would my mind be disabused of its belief by cunning stratagems of kindly-disposed physicians. The close communion of souls, existing between living beings, was thus continued when one of them was dead. The agony of this companionship was, at first, exceedingly acute. My delirium added nothing to the happiness of this intercourse, and detracted nothing from its terrors. I was continually reminded of the mummy and the insect, and all the incidents connected with their discovery.

Day and night saw no change in the position of my wife, sitting silently at my bed-side. My head weighed me down, as if it were a mountain—a quiet Vesuvius of dormant horrors. My slumbers were infrequent, short and unquiet, full of visions of monstrosities in repose.

A month passed replete with these torments, and I fell into a deep sleep that continued for fifty hours. When I awoke, my consciousness of external things, much enfeebled to be sure, had returned. But the vigour of the mind was forever gone. I could think but slowly, and my conclusions were very imperfect. A lagging, slow-consuming fever, flowed in my veins, and my limbs had been shorn of their strength, and their quickness of movement was lost.

The condition in which I had been found by the servant, and the fatal drops of blood from the wound behind the ear, surely indicated the cause of my suffering, as identical with the cause that had killed my wife. If my many hopes had been blighted, my ambitions crushed, my heavy sorrows made still more heavy, and the swift running current of my life turned backward by the mysterious agency of this terrible insect, there yet flourished and thrived by their extinction a bitter hatred of the cause. Although my brain was dulled in its acuteness of perception, and my body was parched with a fierce unnatural heat that burned the skin into large wrinkles, and scorched the fair complexion to a tawny hue, yet I hoped and planned and lived only to destroy the insect, whose music I could now and then hear in the wall, and from which place of concealment the fiendish thing seldom ventured.

One day, in an unusually dejected mood, I entered my study, closed the door and sat down. In an instant, I heard the music of the insect, above my head; and looking up, saw it clinging to the chandelier, near the ceiling. A sense of ineffable happiness possessed me for several minutes. I thought of all I had suffered since I found the fly in the Egyptian tomb. The minute details of this life of strange catastrophes, culminating in my own sickness, were quickly reviewed. I watched the insect as it clung to the iron pipe of the chandelier, and fluttered its great wings; they fanned delirious music into existence, but I was not charmed; its eyes glistened in all their brilliancy, but I was not fascinated. Suddenly the long legs of the creature loosened their clasp, and it dropped like lead almost upon my upturned face; but before I could strike, it had risen to the ceiling.

It was not an unequal contest that followed this attack. The insect, eluding with ease my furious blows, struck me many times in the face with its antenna, but without penetrating the skin. I struck at it with books, with sticks, and with my fist, as it circled around or above me and fanned my face with its musical wings. Its eyes, with the cold brilliancy of a diamond, were ever on the watch; and at the slightest motion I made, the insect would rise or fall in its circlings. When at last, panting, disheartened at my failure to wound or kill it, I was about to yield in despair; the insect, likewise fatigued, settled down upon the

ANONYMOUS

top of my book-case. The sight revived me, and I seized the nearest missile; it was the vase in which I had found the insect. My enemy was rising when I threw the vase. There was a sound like the shattering of glass; the wall was splashed with blood and the mixture in the vase; there fell upon the floor, with the pieces, the stone *scarabœus*, and the insect. With an exclamation of joy, I picked up these, and went into the bed-room, where a fire was burning in the grate.

So strongly did I loathe the insect which, bruised, and bleeding my blood, wound his trembling antenna around my fingers, and thrust against them with its strong legs, that without a moment's hesitation, I cast it into the flames.

I heard a wail, like the cry of a woman in agony, and the study-door closed with a loud noise, as the insect was speedily consumed by the fire. With its death expired the flames. A sudden fear of something terrible about to be seen, or to happen, made me shudder. I looked at the graven stone in my hand, and at nothing else. I read, as of yore: "Three thousand years hence, a new life." A year or more had passed since I had thought of the prophecy that now flashed upon me at a time of all others to be avoided; for the reminiscences of the Egyptian tomb ought to have perished with the insect in the purifying fire. The unnatural strength that had sustained me through the conflict with my enemy, had gone, and left me weakened by exertion and excitement. My limbs shook, my head throbbed with acute pain, and my tongue was parched. I arose to leave a room whose atmosphere was pregnant with terrors that I breathed, and whose every nook and corner, the breached partition, and the dead ashes in the grate, too strongly reminded me of scenes and incidents I wished to have forgotten.

O my GOD! In a chair behind me sat the mummy of the tomb, alive, watching me with its small cunning eyes, as it tried to free one of its hands from the decaying cerements. It was the mummy I had found, not the one that crumbled into dust before the breath of a pure desert wind. It motioned me with its disengaged hand back to my seat, and strove to stand and oppose my passage, as with a cry of horror I rushed from the room. The cool air and the passing crowds on the street, soon restored me to a calmer mind; and ashamed of my terror, I returned to the bed-room that I might prove the falsity of my illusion. I opened the door and looked in. The mummy had drawn its chair close to the grate, and was gathering from it white ashes—the remains of the burned insect. The old terror, that ever bided in my soul, crept into my reasonings, and confounded my judgment. With a despairing cry, I frantically locked the door, and fled from the house to wander up and down the streets, until long after mid-night.

She is still in my bed-room, and I am trying to starve her to death. I can not sell the house. One or two particular friends, who wished to purchase, when I told them of the occupant of the study, and, to prove the truth of my assertions, bade them look through the key-hole, looked upon me with white, terror-stricken faces, and fled from the house. The consequence of such a revelation to a stranger would be worse, and cause rumours to be circulated prejudicial to my reputation. So I have concluded that the only manner to rid myself of this living incubus is to kill her by starvation. I have no pity, no heart. The possession of so terrible a creature is worse than murder deliberately committed.

I have boarded up all the windows, and discharged the servants, living alone with my burden.

Having partly overcome my fear, I have occupied a room next the study; and in the quiet of the night, I can hear the woman moving about the room in a slow movement; now and then she sings such strange, unnatural tunes, that in my fear I am compelled to leave the house for several hours.

It seems as if she would never die, for it is nine days since she made her appearance. The other day, when in the parlour listening to an unusual, grating sound in the study, such as I had not before heard there, some plastering fell from the wall separating the rooms, upon the floor. The Form, the Death in Life, was endeavouring to *break through!* I promptly collected building materials, and made the wall three feet thick. I worked night and day—I secured it.

Those are her *dying* groans. But whither—oh! whither! out into what new life goes that undying Egyptian soul? And *I?* Shall I be linked through eternity by a terrible destiny of unknown mystery, whirling through what Hermes Trismegistus of Thebes calls "the downward-borne elements of GOD?"*

And I too am dying. But a few hours she and I will again know in clearness and in truth the meaning of the words which Sothus wrote on the painted stone in the valley of Memphis, "wherein appeared, in but few letters, all the lore of life, and of the soul, and of after-days, and of the eternal flood."

Free! My will still moves the dead hand which pens these lines, but I hover afar over it like a star. Out into Eternity!

---

*   HERMES, *Poemander*, lib. I.

AFTER THREE
THOUSAND YEARS

Jane G. Austin

Jane Goodwin Austin (1831–1894) was a writer and historical novelist born in Worcester, Massachusetts. She was the daughter of Isaac Goodwin, a lawyer and antiquarian, and Elizabeth (Hammatt) Goodwin who became a fairly successful poet in her own right. After her father died, Austin moved to Boston with her mother and received a private education which led to her taking a great interest in her family history. She began to write stories surrounding the lives of her Pilgrim ancestors. After a hiatus to raise a family, she resumed her writing career and published stories in leading periodicals such as *Harper's Magazine*, the *Atlantic Monthly*, *Putnam's Magazine*, *Emerson's Magazine*, and the *Galaxy*. She lived in Concord, Massachusetts for a short time where she formed friendships with literary greats such as Louisa May Alcott, Ralph Waldo Emerson and Nathaniel Hawthorne. Aside from her numerous short stories, Austin wrote over twenty books and was working on another at the time of her death. Perhaps best known for her fairy-tale collections such as *Fairy Dreams; or, Wanderings in Elf Land* (1859), she was also an accomplished Gothic writer as "After Three Thousand Years" demonstrates. While Austin does not receive the same recognition as her literary friends, she is certainly a writer who is worthy of wider study.

Austin's mummy curse tale was published in *Putnam's Monthly Magazine of American Literature* in July 1868, a year prior to Louisa

May Alcott's "Lost in a Pyramid or, The Mummy's Curse". While Alcott's tale features a sinister plant that enacts the curse, Austin's story surrounds an unnerving scarab necklace. The necklace features phosphorescent gold beetles linked on a chain which is loose enough for them to wriggle about almost as if they were alive. As events unfold, Marion is warned never to wear the eerie necklace which was taken from the neck of a Pharaonic princess. While "The Mummy's Soul" features an active, mobile predator, Austin's insect threat is more of a bejewelled parasite. Like other mummy curse stories, Austin's tale teases out the colonial anxiety surrounding the plundering of Egypt in the nineteenth century as archaeologists are represented as arrogant trespassers.

"o you remember the last request you made of me, when we parted in Paris, you to return homeward, and I to bury myself in the tombs of the Pharaohs?" asked Vance, the latest lion of Eastern travel, of Marion Harleigh, as he took her out to dinner at Madame Belletoile's.

"Perfectly. I asked you to bring me some personal ornament from the mummy of a princess," replied the young lady with *sang-froid*.

"And you promised to wear it, remember," pursued Vance, maliciously watching for the pallor that did not come.

"Exactly, I promised to wear it, and I am ready to keep my promise. Did you bring me the opportunity?"

"Could I have ventured to present myself before you without it?" replied the traveller, with smiling courtesy.

"And what is it?"

"May I come tomorrow, and offer it?"

"I shall be very glad to see you."

The next morning, at twelve o'clock, Vance rang at the door of Mr Peter Harleigh's fine town-mansion, and, upon inquiring for Miss Harleigh, was shown at once to the drawing-room, graced by that young lady's presence. She came to meet him with outstretched hand.

"Welcome home!" said she, a little more earnestly, perhaps, than she would have spoken to Professor Byzantium, who also returned to New York from Eastern travel, by the Persia.

Millard Vance held the hand she offered, long enough to dart the piercing glance of his hazel eyes deep into the heart of the young girl, and then, releasing it, said softly,

"You are kind; but I have no home, you must remember."

"You should interpret the word more widely, and feel that your native land is enough for home, and your country-men and women enough for family, at least in the present," said Marion, hating herself for the blush she could not restrain. Turning hastily, she added,

"This is Mr Vance, Juliette. My cousin, Miss Randolph, Mr Vance."

A little figure rose from the great arm-chair where she had been almost buried, and bowed smilingly in answer to the stately bow of the traveller. Then she seated herself upon the sofa beside Marion, and unconsciously offered her misty golden curls, pure complexion, and sweet blue eyes, in contrast to her cousin's trained and statuesque brunette beauty.

Vance, studying the two without looking at either, found it impossible to award the palm to either, and gave both credit for arranging a contrasting tableau—a manœuvre for which Juliette was as yet too innocent, and Marion too proud.

After ten minutes, Vance drew a little Indian casket from his pocket and placed it in Miss Harleigh's hand.

"There is the Pharaonic spoil you have kindly allowed me to bring for you," said he.

Marion opened the box, and uttered a little cry of surprise. It appeared filled with golden beetles sparkling with phosphorescent gleams. Immediately she closed the lid upon them, and looked up into Vance's laughing face.

"They will not harm you; they are securely chained," said he, opening the case as it lay upon Marion's lap, and taking from it a necklace of golden scarabæi, with diamond eyes and green enamelled wings. Each insect was linked to each by a tiny chain, but so loosely as to admit of perfect freedom of movement. The necklace was clasped by a medal of burnished gold deeply graven with certain symbols or characters, not easily to be deciphered even as to form.

"Oh, the darling, lovely, odd thing!" exclaimed Juliette Randolph, while Vance lightly swung the glittering toy from his finger; but Marion turned pale, and slightly shivered.

"Where did it come from, Mr Vance?" asked she.

"From the neck of a Pharaonic princess, as you desired that it should," returned Vance, watching with boyish zest the effect of his announcement.

"Oh, tell us all the story, please, Mr Vance!—how you got it, and how she looked, and all," pleaded Juliette, settling herself in the sofa-corner with the impatient delight of a child about to listen to a fairy-tale.

Vance looked at her appreciatively, then suffered his regard to linger for a moment upon the proud, dark eyes Marion Harleigh had almost unconsciously fixed upon his own, before he gayly answered:

"Oh, yes; we travellers are but too happy in finding audience for our adventures, you know; and this one in a manner belongs with the necklace. I wintered upon the Nile last year, partly, no doubt, for my own pleasure, but partly, as I hope you will not refuse to believe, Miss Harleigh, in the hope of fulfilling your commission more certainly than a mere passing visitor could have done; for a new mummy is not to be met with every day, even upon the Nile; and I promised, you will remember, to take the ornament you were so kind as to ask for, directly from the person of its original possessor. My inquiries, bribes, false hopes, and opportunities of allowing myself to be cheated in the neatest possible manner, were unlimited; so also was my patience and my faith in its final reward. That faith was justified upon the day when my dragoman mysteriously introduced into the cabin of the Sphynx a rascally-looking Arab calling himself Sheikh of El Kab, the village off which we lay, and who offered for a compensation to conduct the illustrious lord, of whom he had heard as desirous of opening a new tomb, to the door of one discovered only a few days previously by himself and his son, who had resolved to sell their secret to the magnificent nobleman 'Inglis,' instead of to their own government, to whom it properly belonged.

"After hearing this story, I quietly remarked to my friend the Sheikh that I had been so many times imposed upon by the same account, and had lost so much time, patience, and money in consequence, that I had resolved to revenge myself upon the very next impostor for all that I had suffered at the hands of his fraternity, and that it was but fair to give him timely warning that I intended keeping to my resolution, and to offer him the chance of reconsidering his proposition.

"Without any pretence of being hurt in his feelings or wounded in his honour—pretences at which I should have only laughed—my Sheikh repeated his assertion that the tomb he mentioned was, and had been for ages, fast sealed, and that, from its situation and certain characters wrought upon the stone closing its door, he had no doubt it contained the remains of some person of consequence. Beyond this he knew nothing and professed nothing, and stipulated that, in all events, he was to receive a certain sum for admitting me to the tomb, let the results be what they might. Should they prove considerable, of course the reward was to be augmented.

"Rather impressed, after all, with the fellow's apparent honesty, I acceded to his terms, and that night, accompanied only by my two servants, I met him just outside the village, and followed to the catacombs perforating like the cells of a honey-comb the sandstone cliffs behind the town. The scene was wild enough, and more picturesque than you get even in the new Park, ladies; and, were I an artist either in words or colours, I would give it you with all the accessories of swarthy

Arabs in snow-white drapery and turbans, flashing torches, gloomy subterranean passages, sculptured walls, and paintings yet glowing with all the richness of the original colour. Sparing this, however, I will merely say that the old Sheikh proved himself a man of his word, and even 'builded better than he knew;' for the tomb whose door he had discovered hidden behind the pile of bones and dust half-filling an outer tomb, rifled ages ago, had never been opened, to all appearance, since it was first sealed up, perhaps three thousand years ago."

"Three thousand years!" softly exclaimed Juliette Randolph, opening her great blue eyes. "Has the world lasted more than three thousand years, Mr Vance?"

Miss Harleigh's downcast eyes glittered impatient scorn; but Vance smiled with the indulgence rarely refused by men to a pretty woman's ignorance, while he replied,

"For perhaps four times three thousand years, Miss Randolph, woman's beauty and man's devotion have enacted upon this earth of ours the same old-new story that makes it today so beautiful and fresh, to fresh and beautiful eyes."

A little quivering smile emphasized the look not yet died out of Miss Harleigh's haughty eyes; but Juliette, blushing like a rose, lifted her innocent gaze to meet the meaning Vance rather looked than spoke, and then she said,

"But the story, Mr Vance."

"Yes, the story. We penetrated the tomb at last, although not without much difficulty and hard work, for the cement was like stone, and the stone like—well, like stone itself. At last, however, we stood within the little chamber beside the single sarcophagus it contained. At the head lay, upon a sculptured pedestal, a lamp burned dry, but with the wick still clinging to the lip, and, at the foot, an exquisite vase of alabaster, three feet high.

"We lost no time, for the adventure was not without its peril had we been discovered by the Turkish authorities in opening the sarcophagus, and in removing the innumerable folds of mummy-cloth swathing the occupant by the expeditious means of slitting the whole series from neck to heel with a sharp knife, and turning it back like the covers of a box. Within lay a slight, elegant figure, very dark in colour, as mummies nearly always are, but retaining sufficient beauty of outline, both in face and form, to prove to my mind that a rare loveliness of the days gone by lay before me, neither preserved nor quite destroyed; and in my heart I wished that the too careful love that had laid it here had rather given that beautiful form to Nature, who would in those three thousand years have produced and reproduced from that germ, flowers enough to beautify the whole earth.

"But Miss Randolph's eyes are exclaiming, 'The story! the story!' and I return, contritely. This mummy, I had expected, would be richly decorated with amulets and ornaments, for such was the rule in the interment of women of the higher class among the Egyptians; but, to my surprise, there was absolutely no ornament about it, with the exception of the necklace you now hold, and a small square box or reliquary of gold suspended from it, and containing a bit of parchment inscribed with a brief hieroglyphic sentence. Carefully removing these, I folded the cerements once more about the silent figure, replaced the cover of the sarcophagus, and left my Pharaonic princess to resume the slumber so rudely disturbed. Let us hope that no evil dream connected with her lost necklace has marred her rest."

Vance ended smilingly; and Marion, who had listened with the utmost intentness, although never raising her eyes, suddenly looked at him, demanding,

"And what was written on the slip of parchment, Mr Vance?"

"Hieroglyphics."

"But they can be read by modern science," replied Marion, a little impatiently.

"Yes; and the parchment, with an impression from the clasp of the necklace, is now in the hands of the man best qualified to decipher them, of all our cryptic scholars. I left them with him last night, and am to learn his decision today. You shall know it almost as soon as I."

"Thanks," said Marion, breathing a little more freely. "It would be horrible to me to have a three-thousand-year-old secret hung like a millstone about my neck, if I could never hope to solve it."

"Then you will wear the necklace?" asked Vance, smiling down upon her, for he had risen to take leave.

"Certainly. Shall you be at Mrs Lane's tonight?"

"May I hope to meet you there?"

"We are going, and I shall wear the necklace of scarabæi, with many thanks to the giver."

"It is not a gift; it is a commission. You sent for it by me, as you send to Paris through your *modiste* for a new dress. It is a debt."

"Indeed!" exclaimed Marion, a little superbly. She had walked beside Vance the length of the drawing-room, and now stood near the door, out of ear-shot from the sofa.

"Yes," replied Vance, pausing in his leave-taking, and slowly adding,

"The price is already fixed. Do you wish to know it?"

"Perhaps I should know it before accepting the necklace. It may be beyond my means," said Marion, struggling for an indifferent look and tone.

"I think not—I hope not. I cannot tell you now what that price is,—but you will wear the necklace tonight?"

"Yes," murmured Marion, and felt glad to see him go.

"What a splendid man, Marion dear! And he knows such a quantity! One really feels quite ashamed of ignorance beside him," prattled little Juliette; and her cousin, with a lingering, unfathomable smile upon her lips, made some vague reply, and hid the true answer in her heart.

That evening, at nine o'clock, came an imperative ring at the Harleigh door, and a message earnestly requesting Miss Harleigh to see Mr Vance for one moment on important business.

In ten minutes she came down to him, superb in gold-coloured silk and black lace, but without ornaments.

"Your business is very urgent, then, Mr Vance," said she, a little haughtily.

"Thank God!" murmured Vance, staring at her regal neck and shoulders.

"For what? That you have some important business at last?" asked Marion Harleigh, one of the women who instinctively resent, even upon the man they love, the attempt to reconcile them to lure and jess. It was upon one of the profoundest truths of feminine nature that the mythologists founded their fable of Atalanta, of the sleeping princess—yes, of the Sphynx herself. He who approaches such a woman's heart with intent to win, must wholly subdue it, or she will turn upon him and slay him with her eyes for daring to make the attempt.

But Vance was too engrossed to note the antagonism so flattering to his vanity which had replaced Miss Harleigh's ordinary suavity.

"You have not put on the necklace!" exclaimed he at last.

"I was interrupted before my toilet was complete," said Marion.

"I can never be sufficiently thankful. I went from here to call upon the *savant* whom I mentioned this morning. He had gone out—as I afterward discovered, had gone to find me. I remained down-town,

66

and finally dined at Delmonico's with a friend. On my way home I called once more upon the *savant*, whose first words were—

"'Have you parted with that necklace?'

"I said that I had presented it to the lady for whom it was procured.

"'She will not wear it?' exclaimed he.

"'She has promised to do so tonight,' said I.

"'Great Heaven! You have killed her, man!' thundered he, and then went on to show me the translation of the hieroglyph taken from the breast of the mummy. It was—

"'See me, the beloved of a king. I scorned him for a lesser love, and thus I lie.'

"Upon the clasp of the necklace were engraved the words,

"'The gods who give life, also take it.'

"In some way that infernal (beg pardon, but I could not help it) necklace was the cause of that unhappy woman's death. Probably it is poisoned, and I—I brought it to you, and urged you to wear it—for my sake!"

His emotion was as unfeigned as it was evident; and Marion Harleigh forgot even her antagonism—forgot the danger she had escaped, and drooped her happy eyes, lest her lover should read them too easily.

But a lover reads his lady's eyes even through the lids, and, five minutes later, Millard Vance had presented Miss Harleigh with a girdle in place of the rejected necklace—a girdle formed of his own right arm; and she, her pride forgotten, submitted to its tender compulsion, nestled close to his heart, and even yielded her lips to his kiss, as meekly as the simplest country maiden could have done.

What wonder that Marion forgot then, or afterward, to repeat to any one the half-revealed secret of the necklace hidden in the depths of her well-stocked jewel-box?

The winter passed, and the spring, and Mr Harleigh took his daughter, the niece who was to him almost another daughter, and the good-natured elderly cousin who matronized them, to the little cottage by the sea where they spent always a portion of the year.

Vance went also, finding quarters in a farmhouse close at hand, and spending all his time with the two girls. Marion, now that she had time to think and to command herself, was the most capricious and shyest of *fiancées*; and poor Vance never knew from day to day if he should be permitted to quietly lay his homage at her feet, or if he must watch to see it spurned, ridiculed, or rejected. Seldom, indeed, could he obtain a *tête-à-tête*, and not unfrequently Marion declined altogether to see him, pleading, today a severe headache, tomorrow a dressmaker, the next day an imperative engagement in town, compelling her to leave with her father in the morning, not to return until his return at night.

In all his sufferings, at first poignant, but, alas! as time went on more endurable, from these various caprices and desertions, Vance found comfort always awaiting his acceptance in the pitying eyes and tremulous smile of Juliette Randolph, who, single-hearted darling that she was, could never understand how her cousin found pleasure in tormenting thus the man she loved—and such a man!

"Perhaps she does not love me, Juliette," suggested Vance, in disconsolate reply to this wonder, naively expressed on one occasion.

"Not love you, Millard! Why, of course she does! How could she—" began the child, and there stopped, blushing like the dawn.

Vance, a master in heart-lore as in books, finished the sentence, read the blushing face, and his own grew suddenly pale. Then his gloomy eyes wandered across the sea to the horizon-line, and rested there so long, that Juliette, who had as yet guessed neither his secret nor her own, gayly asked of what he was dreaming.

"I was thinking what a pity I came home last winter," said Vance simply.

"Oh, don't talk like that! Marion will be well tomorrow, and perhaps gay and bright. And on those days, you know, you do not wish that you had not come home," said Marion's cousin, with a smile as tender as it was arch.

Vance glanced at her, then away, and, leading her back to the house, excused himself from entering, and spent half the night pacing up and down the beach with the wild sea breaking whitely at his feet.

"I must have an explanation with Marion; and, unless she will consent to an early marriage, I shall leave this for some time. I will travel again, or—"

But if the night brings counsel, it also puts to sleep and benumbs the counsel that came before; and when, next morning, Vance found his lady-love genial, beautiful, and even affectionate, he said nothing of the explanation or the journey, and the day went on as many a day had gone before.

And other days, and weeks, and months, while still the little party lingered at the shore, held by the warm, dry autumn days, as sweet as summer, and even richer in their gorgeous beauty.

And still the explanation had not come; and still Vance lingered; and still Juliette, the simple, loving child, all innocently sought to soothe the wounds inflicted by her haughty cousin, and all unconsciously gathered poison to herself from the wound she sought to heal.

At last there came a day when Marion, suddenly arraigning her own heart for judgment, found it guilty of hypocrisy, ingratitude, cruelty, and all uncharitableness toward the one creature upon earth for whose sake life was worth the living. She stood aghast at the record placed by memory before eyes too long and too wilfully blinded, and then took a resolve in strict accordance with her fault. As the sin had been a sin of pride, so the reparation was born of a profound and sweet humility,—child of pride wedded to love.

"I will go to him this moment," whispered Marion, "and, telling him how dearly, how wholly I love him, I will beg forgiveness for my fault, and, if he wishes still to take me all to himself, I will—"

So, on the moment she went. It was the night of the full moon, the harvest-moon, and all earth and ocean lay glowing and quivering in a bath of golden splendour. From the woods and fields came rich autumnal odours, and from over the sea, sighing breaths of a dying tropic breeze,—night-birds and insects on the one hand, the long waste of dreaming waves sliding up the sands, and breaking in music, upon the other.

Marion stopped, to raise her face to heaven.

"Thank God for life, for this beautiful world, and for love," murmured she, and then went smiling on.

Her light feet made no noise upon the sand; the moon and the wind threw her long shadow and the rustling of her draperies behind her; and so she came all unconsciously along the beach to the spot where Vance and Juliette sat in the deep recess of a hollowed cliff.

Hearing her lover's voice, Marion paused. She could not speak indifferently to him just then, nor could she say what was in her heart to other ears than his. She hesitated, wondering how to act, but soon wondered no more, for Vance spoke again in answer to words which Marion did not hear.

"You do comfort me, darling; who else?" asked he passionately, and Marion, turned to stone as she stood, knew, as if she had seen it, the embrace and kiss that accompanied the words.

Then Juliette murmured sobbingly,

"Oh, Millard, you must not—you ought not! It is Marion whom you love, and she loves you. Let me go away from both of you—and die."

"No, you shall stay with me, and live," cried Vance, ardently. "She does not love me now, if she ever did. Has not she been trying to prove how little she cares for me ever since we came here? And I—oh, darling, it is a simple, trusting, loving heart like yours that a man should give his own for. Marion is a splendid woman—a woman of grand intellect, passions, and possibilities; but you, Juliette, you are the dove whose nest is in my heart. Come to me, doveling—come to your home forever! Trust me; you have the right, and Marion will never suffer."

Then, in the pause that followed, she turned, and went her way, careless if she were seen and heard, or not. Turning her back upon the man that had wooed her to her doom, she saw her shadow stretching black and ominous along her path, and set her feet within it at every step. The dreaming sea, no longer whispering of love and hope, moaned wearily among its grasses; the sighing wind brought an odour of decay from the woods and fields, of chill unrest from the distant sea. The sands, that had seemed the golden dust of Pactolus, were of a sudden filled with flints and shards. All nature showed a change, and yet nowhere was change like that in the heart Marion Harleigh carried home from the little journey she had made to find her love.

The next morning Vance was awakened in the early dawn by the farmer's wife, who, standing at his bedside, laid a letter in his hand.

"It was brought by the Squire's man. He said you was to have it last night, but it was so late when he got here that we was all a-bed, and so he called again first thing this morning and made me come right up with it."

"Yes, thank you. That will do, Mrs Brown," said Vance, who, holding the unopened letter, had turned of a sudden numb and chill, with a horrible, indefinite foreboding.

So soon as he was alone, he tore open the envelope with fingers almost too impatient and too tremulous to reach their object.

It contained the slip of parchment Marion had begged of him soon after their engagement, and a sheet of paper exhaling the violet perfume Marion loved, and with Marion's monogram at the top. It brought him this message:

"Your friend did not interpret the hieroglyph aright. This is my reading:

"'Behold me, who fancied myself the beloved of a king among men. He scorned me for a lesser love, and thus I lie.'"

In ten minutes Vance, with death at his heart, was on his way to her who thus summoned him. The early morning was fresh and sweet and delicate in its beauty as a young girl's first dream of love, but Vance knew it no more than Cain, who fled from the wrath of God and the eyes of man with a brand upon his brow.

Arrived at the cottage, and finding only the servants astir, he ordered Marion's maid to go and ask if she could see him in half an hour.

The woman went, and, when her shrill shriek rang through the house, one listener at least was neither startled or doubtful of its meaning.

Striding up the stair, and past the frightened servant who ran to call her master, he entered the chamber alone, and stood beside the bed where lay his mistress, royal in death. She had dressed herself in the bridal robes, given her only a few days previously by her doting father, and magnificent in silk and lace and embroidery of oriental pearls. The bridal veil, fastened to her glorious coronal of hair, swept down at either side, but no flowers encircled it, or lay upon, the quiet bosom, or were clasped in the icy fingers. No flower, no jewel, no ornament of any description entered into that strange bridal toilet, save such as formed part of the dress itself, and a necklace of golden scarabæi about the throat.

With a groan, such as the rack might at last wring from the strongest heart, Vance bent to examine this necklace, which had, as the merest glance showed, undergone some strange transformation.

Strange, indeed! The beetles, no longer mere toys and images, appeared to have suddenly assumed life, and the power attributed to them by the men who worshipped them as gods. Standing erect upon the myriad legs hitherto folded unobserved beneath their bodies, with open wings, and upraised antennæ, with their diamond eyes flashing and glittering in the first ray of the rising sun, the creatures appeared so fearful and so unearthly that Vance drew back a pace in terror from the sight. Recovering his manhood almost instantly, however, he snatched at the necklace with the shrinking hate of human nature in presence of the fiend, and would have torn it from its resting-place, although too late, for its work was done. But with a strange, new thrill of horror, he found the effort in vain. Each of these thread-like legs ended in a minute claw, and each of these claws, fastened deep in the flesh beneath, held to its prey, still warm beneath its deadly grasp.

The household, alarmed and wondering, were by this time flocking into the room; but Vance, turning upon them a pallid face, and strained, blood-shotten eyes, begged to be left yet a moment alone with the corpse of his promised wife. Only the father remained; and Vance, leading him to the bed, pointed at what lay there, saying, in a hard, cold voice,

"She dressed herself in these robes as a girl would naturally like to do, and she put this necklace about her neck. It was poisoned, as I told her when I gave it her, and warned her not to use it. She forgot my warning, and placed it about her throat, meaning, perhaps, to wear it as my gift when we should stand before the altar. I warned her, but she did not heed, and—there she lies."

Peter Harleigh, shrewd and crafty man of the world, looked long and earnestly into the face of his son-in-law, then into the face of the corpse, hardly sterner, hardly whiter, than that of the man; and at last he said,

"There is a mystery, but I do not care to fathom it, lest I hate the man my daughter loved. The story you tell will answer. Go, now, and leave me with my dead."

"I will take this; it is my right," said Vance, plucking away the necklace. Beneath it lay a livid band encircling the throat, and composed, as a close examination showed, of innumerable points or dots; but, even as they looked, this faded slowly from the surface, and, an hour later, the skin had become smooth and white as it had ever been.

No one saw Vance after this, until he stood with her father and cousin beside Marion Harleigh's open grave. When the services were ended, and the mourners, save themselves, dispersed, he turned to these two, and simply said,

"Good-by. You will not see me again."

Juliette, uttering a faint moan, turned away; then, tottering, fell in a swoon like death.

Her uncle, pointing to her prostrate body, sternly met the eyes of the miserable man who stood staring gloomily before him, and said,

"Not her too, surely! Is not one enough?"

"If Juliette will marry me, you may set the day for yourself," said Vance, desperately.

"One year from tomorrow, if Juliette still wishes. Let my girl lie one year, one little year, in her grave first, and then her claims shall give way to those of the living," replied the old man bitterly; and Vance—

"One year from tomorrow I will come back. Then, if Juliette will marry me, she shall."

The year came round, and, with it, Vance. Juliette, who loved, and could not comprehend him, was ready to accept the sacrifice he offered instead of a heart, and they were married.

She is happy in her nursery and in her household, and she worships and deceives in a thousand little ways the husband she fears as much as she loves.

And he? Of his inner life we do not speak; of the outer let this fact suffice: where no eye but his own ever sees it, he hides a little Indian casket containing the Egyptian necklace. The scarabæi, no longer excited by contact with warm human flesh, lie in the quiescent state we first saw them, but the venom remains, the power remains; and Vance, looking at them, fancies often that they are but the outward symbols of the avenging memories that gnaw and sting his heart forever.

A DREAM OF WILD BEES

Olive Schreiner

Olive Emilie Albertina Schreiner (1855–1920) was born in the Eastern Cape of Africa, the ninth of twelve children of missionary parents. She was named after three older brothers who died before she was born. When Schreiner was nine, her youngest sister also died, which profoundly affected her. She is best known as the author of *The Story of an African Farm* (1883), rich in insect imagery. It was originally published under the pseudonym Ralph Iron in honour of Ralph Waldo Emerson as Emerson's philosophy, along with that of Henry David Thoreau, was a strong influence on Schreiner's understanding of nature. She travelled to England to embark on a medical career, but had to abandon nursing and midwifery due to ill health. In her circle of women writers at that time was the future author of anthropomorphized animals, Beatrix Potter. In 1895 Schreiner gave birth to a daughter who died only hours later, and she also experienced several miscarriages. Such sad events in her life lend a poignancy to her story of a pregnant woman visited by beneficent insects.

"A Dream of Wild Bees" first appeared in *The Woman's World* Vol. 2 (1889), and is inextricably intertwined with female authorship and magazine readership. It tells of insects native to the African bush appearing to the mother-to-be and offering gifts to her unborn child, only one of which she can choose to accept. It is analogous to an adult fairy-tale. The bees are primarily rendered strange by the woman's subconscious thoughts. Their weirdness resides both in their ability to communicate with her, and to embody powers transferable to the baby in her womb.

mother sat alone at an open window. Through it came the voices of the children as they played under the acacia-trees, and the breath of the hot afternoon air. In and out of the room flew the bees, the wild bees, with their legs yellow with pollen, going to and from the acacia-trees, droning all the while. She sat on a low chair before the table and darned. She took her work from the great basket that stood before her on the table: some lay on her knee and half covered the book that rested there. She watched the needle go in and out; and the dreary hum of the bees and the noises of the children's voices became a confused murmur in her ears, as she worked slowly and more slowly. Then the bees, the long-legged wasp-like fellows who make no honey, flew closer and closer to her head, droning. Then she grew more and more drowsy, and she laid her hand, with the stocking over it, on the edge of the table, and leaned her head upon it. And the voices of the children outside grew more and more dreamy, came now far, now near; then she did not hear them, but she felt under her heart where the ninth child lay. Bent forward and sleeping there, with the bees flying about her head, she had a weird brain-picture; she thought the bees lengthened and lengthened themselves out and became human creatures and moved round and round her. Then one came to her softly, saying, "Let me lay my hand upon thy side where the child sleeps. If I shall touch him he shall be as I."

She asked, "Who are you?"

And he said, "I am Health. Whom I touch will have always the red blood dancing in his veins; he will not know weariness nor pain; life will be a long laugh to him."

"No," said another, "let me touch; for I am Wealth. If I touch him material care shall not feed on him. He shall live on the blood and sinews of his fellow-men, if he will; and what his eye lusts for, his hand will have. He shall not know 'I want.'" And the child lay still like lead.

And another said, "Let me touch: I am Fame. The man I touch, I lead to a high hill where all men may see him. When he dies he is not forgotten, his name rings down the centuries, each echoes it on to his fellows. Think not to be forgotten through the ages!"

And the mother lay breathing steadily, but in the brain-picture they pressed closer to her.

"Let me touch the child," said one, "for I am Love. If I touch him he shall not walk through life alone. In the greatest dark, when he puts out his hand he shall find another hand by it. When the world is against him, another shall say, '*You and I.*'" And the child trembled.

But another pressed close and said, "Let me touch; for I am Talent. I can do all things that have been done before. I touch the soldier, the statesman, the thinker, and the politician who succeed; and the writer who is never before his time, and never behind it. If I touch the child he shall not weep for failure."

About the mother's head the bees were flying, touching her with their long tapering limbs; and, in her brain-picture, out of the shadow of the room came one with sallow face, deep-lined, the cheeks drawn into hollows, and a mouth smiling quiveringly. He stretched out his hand. And the mother drew back, and cried, "Who are you?" He answered nothing; and she looked up between his eyelids. And she said, "What can you give the child health?" And he said, "The man I touch, there wakes up in his blood a burning fever, that shall lick his blood as fire. The fever that I will give him shall be cured when his life is cured."

"You give wealth?"

He shook his head. "The man whom I touch, when he bends to pick up gold, he sees suddenly a light over his head in the sky; while he looks up to see it, the gold slips from between his fingers, or sometimes another passing takes it from them."

"Fame?"

He answered, "Likely not. For the man I touch there is a path traced out in the sand by a finger which no man sees. That he must follow. Sometimes it leads almost to the top, and then turns down suddenly into the valley. He must follow it, though none else sees the tracing."

"Love?"

He said, "He shall hunger for it—but he shall not find it. When he stretches out his arms to it, and would lay his heart against a thing he loves, then, far off along the horizon he shall see a light play. He must go towards it. The thing he loves will not journey with him; he must travel alone. When he presses somewhat to his burning heart, crying 'Mine, mine, my own!' he shall hear a voice—'Renounce! renounce! this is not thine!'"

"He shall succeed?"

He said, "He shall fail. When he runs with others they shall reach the goal before him. For strange voices shall call to him and strange lights shall beckon him, and he must wait and listen. And this shall be the strangest: far off across the burning sands where, to other men, there is only the desert's waste, he shall see a blue sea! On that sea the sun shines always, and the water is blue as burning amethyst, and the foam is white on the shore. A great land rises from it, and he shall see upon the mountain-tops burning gold."

The mother said, "He shall reach it?"

And he smiled curiously.

She said, "It is real?"

And he said, "What *is* real?"

And she looked up between his half-closed eyelids, and said, "Touch."

And he leaned forward and laid his hand upon the sleeper, and whispered to it, smiling; and this only she heard—"*This shall be thy reward—that the ideal shall be real to thee.*"

And the child trembled; but the mother slept on heavily and her brain-picture vanished. But deep within her the antenatal thing that lay here had a dream. In those eyes that had never seen the day, in that half-shaped brain was a sensation of light. Light—that it never had seen. Light—that perhaps it never should see. Light—that existed somewhere.

And already it had its reward—the Ideal was Real to it.

OLIVE SCHREINER (Ralph Iron)

THE MOTH

H. G. Wells

Herbert George Wells (1866–1946) was born in Kent, the son of a former domestic servant and a shopkeeper. Wells apprenticed as a draper, pupil-teacher, and chemist, but his life arguably pivoted on his winning a scholarship to study biology under T. H. Huxley. Huxley was nicknamed "Darwin's Bulldog", coined the phrase "survival of the fittest", and was a formative influence on Wells. Wells was awarded a BSc in zoology from the University of London in 1890. His storytelling is informed by scientific terminology, and the plot of "The Moth" is shaped by his familiarity with the competitive struggle to determine superiority.

"The Moth" is one of Wells' earlier fictional endeavours appearing in *Pall Mall Gazette* in March 1895 as "A Moth—Genus Novo", but re-titled as "The Moth" in *The Country of the Blind and Other Stories* (1911) from which this reprinting is taken. It narrowly precedes publication of *The Island of Dr Moreau* (1896) and *The Invisible Man* (1897) both of which like "The Moth" contain unhinged scientists. "The Moth" concerns the bitter academic feud between two entomologists involving the destruction of Pawkins' professional reputation by Hapley, which results in Hapley being shunned by a fickle scientific community. Hapley is subsequently haunted by a new species of moth bearing a marked physical resemblance to his deceased, erstwhile rival. The weird insect operates as a reincarnated soul, agent of vengeance, and embodiment of monomania. It exposes entomological obsessiveness tipping over into insanity.

robably you have heard of Hapley—not W. T. Hapley, the son, but the celebrated Hapley, the Hapley of *Periplaneta Hapliia*, Hapley the entomologist.

If so you know at least of the great feud between Hapley and Professor Pawkins, though certain of its consequences may be new to you. For those who have not, a word or two of explanation is necessary, which the idle reader may go over with a glancing eye, if his indolence so incline him.

It is amazing how very widely diffused is the ignorance of such really important matters as this Hapley-Pawkins feud. Those epoch-making controversies, again, that have convulsed the Geological Society are, I verily believe, almost entirely unknown outside the fellowship of that body. I have heard men of fair general education even refer to the great scenes at these meetings as vestry-meeting squabbles. Yet the great hate of the English and Scotch geologists has lasted now half a century, and has "left deep and abundant marks upon the body of the science." And this Hapley-Pawkins business, though perhaps a more personal affair, stirred passions as profound, if not profounder. Your common man has no conception of the zeal that animates a scientific investigator, the fury of contradiction you can arouse in him. It is the *odium theologicum* in a new form. There are men, for instance, who would gladly burn Professor Ray Lankester at Smithfield for his treatment of the Mollusca in the Encyclopædia. That fantastic extension of the Cephalopods to cover the Pteropods... But I wander from Hapley and Pawkins.

It began years and years ago, with a revision of the Microlepidoptera (whatever these may be) by Pawkins, in which he extinguished a new species created by Hapley. Hapley, who was always quarrelsome, replied by a stinging impeachment of the entire classification of Pawkins.* Pawkins in his "Rejoinder"† suggested that Hapley's microscope was as defective as his power of observation, and called him an "irresponsible meddler"—Hapley was not a professor at that time. Hapley in his retort,‡ spoke of "blundering collectors," and described, as if inadvertently, Pawkins' revision as a "miracle of ineptitude." It was war to the knife. However, it would scarcely interest the reader to detail how these two great men quarrelled, and how the split between them widened until from the Microlepidoptera they were at war upon every open question in entomology. There were memorable occasions. At times the Royal Entomological Society meetings resembled nothing so much as the Chamber of Deputies. On the whole, I fancy Pawkins was nearer the truth than Hapley. But Hapley was skilful with his rhetoric, had a turn for ridicule rare in a scientific man, was endowed with vast energy, and had a fine sense of injury in the matter of the extinguished species; while Pawkins was a man of dull presence, prosy of speech, in shape not unlike a water-barrel, over conscientious with testimonials, and suspected of jobbing museum appointments. So the young men gathered round Hapley and applauded him. It was a long struggle, vicious from the beginning and growing at last to pitiless antagonism. The successive turns of fortune, now an advantage to one side and now to another— now Hapley tormented by some success of Pawkins, and now Pawkins

---

*　"Remarks on a Recent Revision of Microlepidoptera." *Quart. Journ. Entomological Soc.*, 1863.

†　"Rejoinder to certain Remarks," etc. *Ibid.* 1864.

‡　"Further Remarks," etc. *Ibid.*

outshone by Hapley, belong rather to the history of entomology than
to this story.

But in 1891 Pawkins, whose health had been bad for some time,
published some work upon the "mesoblast" of the Death's Head
Moth. What the mesoblast of the Death's Head Moth may be does
not matter a rap in this story. But the work was far below his usual
standard, and gave Hapley an opening he had coveted for years. He
must have worked night and day to make the most of his advantage.

In an elaborate critique he rent Pawkins to tatters—one can fancy
the man's disordered black hair, and his queer dark eyes flashing as
he went for his antagonist—and Pawkins made a reply, halting, inef-
fectual, with painful gaps of silence, and yet malignant. There was no
mistaking his will to wound Hapley, nor his incapacity to do it. But
few of those who heard him—I was absent from that meeting—realized how ill the man was.

Hapley got his opponent down, and meant to finish him. He followed with a simply brutal attack upon Pawkins, in the form of a paper
upon the development of moths in general, a paper showing evidence
of a most extraordinary amount of mental labour, and yet couched
in a violently controversial tone. Violent as it was, an editorial note
witnesses that it was modified. It must have covered Pawkins with
shame and confusion of face. It left no loophole; it was murderous in
argument, and utterly contemptuous in tone; an awful thing for the
declining years of a man's career.

The world of entomologists waited breathlessly for the rejoinder
from Pawkins. He would try one, for Pawkins had always been game.
But when it came it surprised them. For the rejoinder of Pawkins was
to catch influenza, proceed to pneumonia, and die.

It was perhaps as effectual a reply as he could make under the circumstances, and largely turned the current of feeling against Hapley.

The very people who had most gleefully cheered on those gladiators became serious at the consequence. There could be no reasonable doubt the fret of the defeat had contributed to the death of Pawkins. There was a limit even to scientific controversy, said serious people. Another crushing attack was already in the press and appeared on the day before the funeral. I don't think Hapley exerted himself to stop it. People remembered how Hapley had hounded down his rival, and forgot that rival's defects. Scathing satire reads ill over fresh mould. The thing provoked comment in the daily papers. This it was that made me think that you had probably heard of Hapley and this controversy. But, as I have already remarked, scientific workers live very much in a world of their own; half the people, I dare say, who go along Piccadilly to the Academy every year, could not tell you where the learned societies abide. Many even think that research is a kind of happy-family cage in which all kinds of men lie down together in peace.

In his private thoughts Hapley could not forgive Pawkins for dying. In the first place, it was a mean dodge to escape the absolute pulverization Hapley had in hand for him, and in the second, it left Hapley's mind with a queer gap in it. For twenty years he had worked hard, sometimes far into the night, and seven days a week, with microscope, scalpel, collecting-net, and pen, and almost entirely with reference to Pawkins. The European reputation he had won had come as an incident in that great antipathy. He had gradually worked up to a climax in this last controversy. It had killed Pawkins, but it had also thrown Hapley out of gear, so to speak, and his doctor advised him to give up work for a time, and rest. So Hapley went down into a quiet village in Kent, and thought day and night of Pawkins, and good things it was now impossible to say about him.

At last Hapley began to realize in what direction the preoccupation tended. He determined to make a fight for it, and started by trying to read novels. But he could not get his mind off Pawkins, white in the face and making his last speech—every sentence a beautiful opening for Hapley. He turned to fiction—and found it had no grip on him. He read the "Island Nights' Entertainments" until his "sense of causation" was shocked beyond endurance by the Bottle Imp. Then he went to Kipling, and found he "proved nothing," besides being irreverent and vulgar. These scientific people have their limitations. Then unhappily, he tried Besant's "Inner House," and the opening chapter set his mind upon learned societies and Pawkins at once.

So Hapley turned to chess, and found it a little more soothing. He soon mastered the moves and the chief gambits and commoner closing positions, and began to beat the Vicar. But then the cylindrical contours of the opposite king began to resemble Pawkins standing up and gasping ineffectually against check-mate, and Hapley decided to give up chess.

Perhaps the study of some new branch of science would after all be better diversion. The best rest is change of occupation. Hapley determined to plunge at diatoms, and had one of his smaller microscopes and Halibut's monograph sent down from London. He thought that perhaps if he could get up a vigorous quarrel with Halibut, he might be able to begin life afresh and forget Pawkins. And very soon he was hard at work in his habitual strenuous fashion, at these microscopic denizens of the way-side pool.

It was on the third day of the diatoms that Hapley became aware of a novel addition to the local fauna. He was working late at the microscope, and the only light in the room was the brilliant little lamp with the special form of green shade. Like all experienced microscopists, he kept both eyes open. It is the only way to avoid excessive fatigue. One eye was over the instrument, and bright and distinct before that was the circular field of the microscope, across which a brown diatom was slowly moving. With the other eye Hapley saw, as it were, without seeing. He was only dimly conscious of the brass side of the instrument, the illuminated part of the table-cloth, a sheet of note-paper, the foot of the lamp, and the darkened room beyond.

Suddenly his attention drifted from one eye to the other. The table-cloth was of the material called tapestry by shopmen, and rather brightly coloured. The pattern was in gold, with a small amount of crimson and pale blue upon a greyish ground. At one point the pattern seemed displaced, and there was a vibrating movement of the colours at this point.

Hapley suddenly moved his head back and looked with both eyes. His mouth fell open with astonishment.

It was a large moth or butterfly; its wings spread in butterfly fashion!

It was strange it should be in the room at all, for the windows were closed. Strange that it should not have attracted his attention when fluttering to its present position. Strange that it should match the table-cloth. Stranger far that to him, Hapley, the great entomologist, it was altogether unknown. There was no delusion. It was crawling slowly towards the foot of the lamp.

"New Genus, by heavens! And in England!" said Hapley, staring.

Then he suddenly thought of Pawkins. Nothing would have maddened Pawkins more… And Pawkins was dead!

Something about the head and body of the insect became singularly suggestive of Pawkins, just as the chess king had been.

"Confound Pawkins!" said Hapley. "But I must catch this." And looking round him for some means of capturing the moth, he rose slowly out of his chair. Suddenly the insect rose, struck the edge of the lampshade—Hapley heard the "ping"—and vanished into the shadow.

In a moment Hapley had whipped off the shade, so that the whole room was illuminated. The thing had disappeared, but soon his practised eye detected it upon the wall-paper near the door. He went towards it poising the lamp-shade for capture. Before he was within striking distance, however, it had risen and was fluttering round the room. After the fashion of its kind, it flew with sudden starts and turns, seeming to vanish here and reappear there. Once Hapley struck, and missed; then again.

The third time he hit his microscope. The instrument swayed, struck and overturned the lamp, and fell noisily upon the floor. The lamp turned over on the table and, very luckily, went out. Hapley was left in the dark. With a start he felt the strange moth blunder into his face.

It was maddening. He had no lights. If he opened the door of the room the thing would get away. In the darkness he saw Pawkins quite distinctly laughing at him. Pawkins had ever an oily laugh. He swore furiously and stamped his foot on the floor.

There was a timid rapping at the door.

Then it opened, perhaps a foot, and very slowly. The alarmed face of the landlady appeared behind a pink candle flame; she wore a night-cap over her grey hair and had some purple garment over her shoulders. "What *was* that fearful smash?" she said. "Has anything—" The strange moth appeared fluttering about the chink of the door. "Shut that door!" said Hapley, and suddenly rushed at her.

The door slammed hastily. Hapley was left alone in the dark. Then in the pause he heard his landlady scuttle upstairs, lock her door, and drag something heavy across the room and put against it.

It became evident to Hapley that his conduct and appearance had been strange and alarming. Confound the moth! and Pawkins! However, it was a pity to lose the moth now. He felt his way into the hall and found the matches, after sending his hat down upon the floor with a noise like a drum. With the lighted candle he returned to the sitting-room. No moth was to be seen. Yet once for a moment it seemed that the thing was fluttering round his head. Hapley very suddenly decided to give up the moth and go to bed. But he was excited. All night long his sleep was broken by dreams of the moth, Pawkins, and his landlady. Twice in the night he turned out and soused his head in cold water.

One thing was very clear to him. His landlady could not possibly understand about the strange moth, especially as he had failed to catch it. No one but an entomologist would understand quite how he felt. She was probably frightened at his behaviour, and yet he failed to see how he could explain it. He decided to say nothing further about the events of last night. After breakfast he saw her in her garden, and decided to go out and talk to reassure her. He talked to her about beans and potatoes, bees, caterpillars, and the price of fruit. She replied in her usual manner, but she looked at him a little suspiciously, and kept walking as he walked, so that there was always a bed of flowers, or a row of beans, or something of the sort, between them. After a while he began to feel singularly irritated at this, and to conceal his vexation went indoors and presently went out for a walk.

The moth, or butterfly, trailing an odd flavour of Pawkins with it, kept coming into that walk, though he did his best to keep his mind off it. Once he saw it quite distinctly, with its wings flattened out, upon the old stone wall that runs along the west edge of the park, but going up to it he found it was only two lumps of grey and yellow lichen. "This," said Hapley, "is the reverse of mimicry. Instead of a butterfly looking like a stone, here is a stone looking like a butterfly!" Once something hovered and fluttered round his head, but by an effort of will he drove that impression out of his mind again.

In the afternoon Hapley called upon the Vicar, and argued with him upon theological questions. They sat in the little arbour covered with briar, and smoked as they wrangled. "Look at that moth!" said Hapley, suddenly, pointing to the edge of the wooden table.

"Where?" said the Vicar.

"You don't see a moth on the edge of the table there?" said Hapley.

"Certainly not," said the Vicar.

Hapley was thunderstruck. He gasped. The Vicar was staring at him. Clearly the man saw nothing. "The eye of faith is no better than the eye of science," said Hapley awkwardly.

"I don't see your point," said the Vicar, thinking it was part of the argument.

That night Hapley found the moth crawling over his counterpane. He sat on the edge of the bed in his shirt sleeves and reasoned with himself. Was it pure hallucination? He knew he was slipping, and he battled for his sanity with the same silent energy he had formerly displayed against Pawkins. So persistent is mental habit, that he felt as if it were still a struggle with Pawkins. He was well versed in psychology. He knew that such visual illusions do come as a result of mental strain. But the point was, he did not only *see* the moth, he had heard it when it touched the edge of the lampshade, and afterwards when it hit against the wall, and he had felt it strike his face in the dark.

He looked at it. It was not at all dreamlike, but perfectly clear and solid-looking in the candle-light. He saw the hairy body, and the short feathery antennæ, the jointed legs, even a place where the down was rubbed from the wing. He suddenly felt angry with himself for being afraid of a little insect.

His landlady had got the servant to sleep with her that night, because she was afraid to be alone. In addition she had locked the door, and put the chest of drawers against it. They listened and talked in whispers after they had gone to bed, but nothing occurred to alarm them. About eleven they had ventured to put the candle out, and had both dozed off to sleep. They woke up with a start, and sat up in bed, listening in the darkness.

Then they heard slippered feet going to and fro in Hapley's room. A chair was overturned, and there was a violent dab at the wall. Then a china mantel ornament smashed upon the fender. Suddenly the door of the room opened, and they heard him upon the landing. They clung to one another, listening. He seemed to be dancing upon the staircase. Now he would go down three or four steps quickly, then up again, then hurry down into the hall. They heard the umbrella stand go over, and the fanlight break. Then the bolt shot and the chain rattled. He was opening the door.

They hurried to the window. It was a dim grey night; an almost unbroken sheet of watery cloud was sweeping across the moon, and the hedge and trees in front of the house were black against the pale roadway. They saw Hapley, looking like a ghost in his shirt and white trousers, running to and fro in the road, and beating the air. Now he would stop, now he would dart very rapidly at something invisible, now he would move upon it with stealthy strides. At last he went out of sight up the road towards the down. Then, while they argued who should go down and lock the door, he returned. He was walking very fast, and he came straight into the house, closed the door carefully, and went quietly up to his bedroom. Then everything was silent.

"Mrs Colville," said Hapley, calling down the staircase next morning, "I hope I did not alarm you last night."

"You may well ask that!" said Mrs Colville.

"The fact is, I am a sleep-walker, and the last two nights I have been without my sleeping mixture. There is nothing to be alarmed about, really. I am sorry I made such an ass of myself. I will go over the down to Shoreham, and get some stuff to make me sleep soundly. I ought to have done that yesterday."

But half-way over the down, by the chalk-pits, the moth came upon Hapley again. He went on, trying to keep his mind upon chess problems, but it was no good. The thing fluttered into his face, and he struck at it with his hat in self-defence. Then rage, the old rage—the rage he had so often felt against Pawkins—came upon him again. He went on, leaping and striking at the eddying insect. Suddenly he trod on nothing, and fell head-long.

There was a gap in his sensations, and Hapley found himself sitting on the heap of flints in front of the opening of the chalk-pits, with a leg twisted back under him. The strange moth was still fluttering round his head. He struck at it with his hand, and turning his head saw two men approaching him. One was the village doctor. It occurred to Hapley that this was lucky. Then it came into his mind with extraordinary vividness, that no one would ever be able to see the strange moth except himself, and that it behoved him to keep silent about it.

Late that night, however, after his broken leg was set, he was feverish and forgot his self-restraint. He was lying flat on his bed, and he began to run his eyes round the room to see if the moth was still about. He tried not to do this, but it was no good. He soon caught sight of the thing resting close to his hand, by the night-light, on the green table-cloth. The wings quivered. With a sudden wave of anger he smote at it with his fist, and the nurse woke up with a shriek. He had missed it.

"That moth!" he said; and then, "It was fancy. Nothing!"

All the time he could see quite clearly the insect going round the cornice and darting across the room, and he could also see that the nurse saw nothing of it and looked at him strangely. He must keep himself in hand. He knew he was a lost man if he did not keep himself in hand. But as the night waned the fever grew upon him, and the very dread he had of seeing the moth made him see it. About five, just as the dawn was grey, he tried to get out of bed and catch it, though his leg was afire with pain. The nurse had to struggle with him.

On account of this, they tied him down to the bed. At this the moth grew bolder, and once he felt it settle in his hair. Then, because he struck out violently with his arms, they tied these also. At this the moth came and crawled over his face, and Hapley wept, swore, screamed, prayed for them to take it off him, unavailingly.

The doctor was a blockhead, a just-qualified general practitioner, and quite ignorant of mental science. He simply said there was no moth. Had he possessed the wit, he might still, perhaps, have saved Hapley from his fate by entering into his delusion, and covering his face with gauze, as he prayed might be done. But, as I say, the doctor was a blockhead, and until the leg was healed Hapley was kept tied to his bed, and with the imaginary moth crawling over him. It never left him while he was awake and it grew to a monster in his dreams. While he was awake he longed for sleep, and from sleep he awoke screaming.

So now Hapley is spending the remainder of his days in a padded room, worried by a moth that no one else can see. The asylum doctor calls it hallucination; but Hapley, when he is in his easier mood, and can talk, says it is the ghost of Pawkins, and consequently a unique specimen and well worth the trouble of catching.

THE CAPTIVITY OF
THE PROFESSOR

A. Lincoln Green

Virtually nothing is known of A. Lincoln Green. The author's name
calls to mind the colour worn by Robin Hood and his Merry Men
and may well be a pseudonymous link to the writer's location. "The
Captivity of the Professor" is one of only two texts attributed to Green,
with the other being a prescient dystopian novel about a virulent pandemic: *The End of an Epoch*. Both were published by Blackwoods in
1901 with the short story appearing in *Blackwood's Edinburgh Magazine*
in February 1901.

"The Captivity of the Professor" tells of an entomologist taken
prisoner by highly evolved Amazonian ants and how he becomes their
slave, entertainer and experimental test subject. In this predicament,
his planned paper to the scientific community on "Recent Advances
in Entomology" acquires ironic meaning. The weird story challenges
both academic hubris and man's certainty he stands at the hierarchical
apex of animals. For the ants there seems little distinction between
the Professor, his fellow primate captive the capuchin, and the howler
monkey against whom he is obliged to compete. The Professor's scientific specialism lends veracity to his observations on the behaviour
of the insects who control and monitor him, and whose weirdness
lies in their extreme intelligence. They prefigure the "uplifted" ants
of Clifford Simak's *City* (1952) where in one scenario artificially
enhanced ants take over the entire world.

ust after I was nominated for the Presidency of the British Association at Glasgow, I determined if possible to obtain some new facts concerning the "agricultural" and the leaf-cutting (or *saüba*) ants of Brazil. The subject I had chosen for my inaugural address was "Recent Advances in Entomology," and I knew that the scientific world would, upon this important occasion, look to me for something more than a mere repetition of comparatively stale matter.

When Reinhardt returned from the Upper Amazons bringing with him such an astonishing collection of insects new to science, he informed me that the southern and more humid part of the La Montana region was extraordinarily prolific in ant-life, and there still remained several hundred square miles among the eastern foothills of the Andes which had never been explored by naturalists.

I therefore determined to visit this region; and (to be brief) crossed the Atlantic, and made a quick and uneventful river journey to Barra, where the Rio Negro joins the Amazons. Barra, as many of my readers will doubtless recollect, is a town made historical by Bates and Wallace, and is situated nearly a thousand miles from the mouth of the great Brazilian river. Here I was fortunate enough to find a small trading steamer which was about to start for the Jurua, a large stream which enters the Amazons from the southward about six hundred miles higher up. In this way I travelled almost as far as Caranary, on the Jurua; where, owing to the dangerous state of the rapids, I was obliged to leave the steamer and proceed by canoe.

Fortunately I was able to obtain a crew of six stalwart river Indians, who agreed to paddle me as far as Cigano. They were, I believe, members of the once prosperous Passé tribe spoken of by Humboldt and Bates; and they not only proved excellent canoe-men, but possessed a fair knowledge of Portuguese. At Cigano I was unfortunately compelled to engage another crew of Indians belonging to a lower and more primitive race; for I could not persuade my civilized and docile Passés to accompany me any farther.

At length, by pushing up a tributary stream called the Jagara (which, although wider than the Thames at Kingston, I cannot find marked on any map), I approached an unexplored district not far from the spot where the boundary-lines of Brazil, Bolivia, and Peru all run together. I now found myself among the foothills of the Andes, and in a densely wooded country abounding in new birds, plants, and insects to a bewildering degree. As we advanced the atmosphere became more and more humid, until it was almost as much charged with moisture as a Russian bath. It was no longer possible to keep sugar or salt in a crystalline condition, and even black gunpowder, when exposed to the air, turned to a semi-liquid paste.

Here I procured a number of valuable specimens, and gathered many novel and interesting facts. Although my time was getting rather short, I decided, before returning, to penetrate this fascinating and fruitful region as far as possible. When we had got some fifty miles up the Jagara my crew of Bura Indians (who were yellow-skinned, stolid savages, apparently akin to the Botocudos), although apparently not afraid of hard poling and paddling up the swift shallow stream, or of the heavy work involved by frequent *portages*, showed a strong disinclination to going farther. At length, when I directed them to turn up a narrow creek entering the stream from the westward, they stolidly ignored my wishes, and persisted in keeping the canoe close to the opposite bank, giving me to understand that there was some great and mysterious danger to be feared in the region on the western side of the Jagara. In answer to my demand for particulars, the natives informed me (chiefly by means of the *lingua geral* and Indian sign-language) that they were very much afraid of certain beings of minute size who inhabited this district, and who were in the habit of capturing and holding in cruel bondage any human trespassers on their domain. From the gestures of my crew I gathered that these supposed supernatural beings were somewhat akin to our European fairies or brownies; and the chief spokesman apparently wished me to believe that, although such terrible fellows, they were no bigger than a moderate-sized ant!

Of course I tried to reason these ignorant, superstitious savages out of such a nonsensical belief. In this I was quite unsuccessful; and at length, being irritated by their stupid obstinacy in refusing to do what I wished, I rated them well as cowards, and even resorted to threats of personal chastisement. As this had no effect, beyond making them extremely sullen, I got into the small and light *piragua* which we towed behind our large canoe, and telling the Indians to make a camp and wait for me on the "safe" side of the Jagara, I proceeded to paddle towards the little creek which I had determined to explore.

I am fairly at home in a canoe, and as I was provided with a double "paradox" gun, a sharp and heavy *machete*, a mosquito-net, a good waterproof blanket, and a knapsack containing provisions and other necessaries, I resolved to push up this small tributary of the Jagara as far as I could before sunset, to spend the night on its banks, and to return to the main stream next morning. My chief purpose in doing this was to convince my superstitious and timid crew that there was no real danger to be apprehended in the region I proposed to visit.

I had not gone far up the streamlet before I came to a succession of small cascades, and had to make repeated *portages*; which, owing to the tangled state of the tropic vegetation on both banks, taxed my strength pretty severely.

As I advanced the route became somewhat easier, and the tropical vegetation around me grew more and more luxuriant. In places the whole air seemed full of the most wondrous flowers, of all hues and sizes, pendent like miniature Chinese lanterns from the network of vines and *lianas* crossing the stream overhead, among which hundreds of sparkling humming-birds and glowing multitudes of butterflies continually flitted and hovered.

At length I reached a spot of such extravagant beauty that I rested on my paddle, almost wondering whether I had wandered into dreamland. I was in a clear circular pool at the foot of a magnificent waterfall, and shut in all around by the dense, tropical forest. In front of me festoons of splendid orchids hung from the lace-work of creepers which lined both sides of the cascade, while to and fro between them glittering bunches of humming-birds, of inconceivable brilliancy of hue, darted in front of the white veil of falling water; so that it seemed as if some ambushed *genii* among the flowers on either bank were pelting one another with handfuls of blazing rubies, emeralds, amethysts, opals, and diamonds!

Many of these exquisite winged jewels, especially those with a dazzling topaz lustre on their breasts, came and hovered near me; and I noticed that each had upon its slender bill, or among its delicate head-feathers, a curious white speck or projection, like a fragment of spray from the fall. So entranced was I at the marvellous, fairyland vision before me, that I paid but little attention to this curious fact, and, indeed, the bewildering and incredible loveliness of my surroundings made me lose all count of time as completely as if I had been bemused by haschish.

At length when I approached the shore on the right-hand side of the stream in order to carry my canoe above the waterfall, I was surprised to observe a narrow white pathway in the forest, which came right down to the water's edge. This, together with the surrounding foliage, seemed at first to be thronged with small ants, yet as soon as the prow of the *piragua* grounded, every insect disappeared as if by magic.

I hauled the canoe ashore, and, carrying my gun and other baggage, I strolled up the mysterious path (which was about two feet wide) to see if it led to the stream above the fall. It seemed to be paved with firm white cement, almost as hard as porcelain, and was as smooth and level as a cycle track.

Suddenly, from the forest recesses round about me, there burst forth a chorus of bird-music which made me look at my watch; for I had learned by experience that this was Nature's vesper-song, indicating the near approach of sunset. I had not recovered my surprise at the lateness of the hour when the light began to fade, and I knew that in ten minutes darkness would be upon me. At the moment I had just reached a small opening in the forest, where the white cemented path widened out into a kind of paved circular space about twenty feet in diameter, surrounded by smooth tree trunks and densely tangled foliage. This dry and open spot struck me as a convenient camping-place, so I leaned my gun against a tree, unslung my other burdens, and placed them upon the ground.

Just as I did so, a beetle of the *longicorn* variety, about the size of a common cockroach but of a blood-red colour, darted from a recess among the roots of the tree against which I had leaned my gun, and ran past me across the white open space with astonishing speed. In a trice I snatched up my butterfly-net, for I saw that this beetle was something quite new to science, more especially as its long, reversed antennæ, where they met over its back, seemed joined by a white nodular projection. Although I got my net over it more than once, it succeeded in making its escape into the bushes, owing to its marvellous agility.

After the beetle had disappeared, however, I noticed that the odd white excrescence which I had observed upon its back, between its reversed antennæ, had become displaced, and was entangled in the green muslin of my net. On looking at this object more closely I was surprised to find that it was an extremely curious ant, quite different from anything I had ever seen before. Its body was white, and had a smooth glistening appearance almost exactly like the surface of a wax vesta, while its head was of a delicate pink, its antennæ bright red, and its lustrous compound eyes of a rich violet or purple. This new and most interesting ant (which was evidently neither an *eciton* nor a *saüba*) was about nine millimetres long. Its thin white limbs were peculiarly delicate and fragile in appearance, and presented a marked contrast to those of the common ants of Brazil.

But by far the most extraordinary feature about it was its pink head, which, when compared with its body, appeared to be of enormous dimensions. The light was failing so rapidly that I could not make use of my Coddington lens; but I saw that the cephalic enlargement seemed to be chiefly, or wholly, due to an abnormal development of the anterior ganglion or brain, and not to a mere overgrowth of the mandibles, or of any part of the chitinous helmet, as is commonly the case when the head of an ant seems disproportionately large. Moreover, when I touched it, the skin of this strange, defenceless ant, instead of feeling hard and hornlike, seemed to be almost as soft as that of a human being.

Needless to say I handled so precious a specimen with extreme gentleness and care while I examined it. As it made no attempt to escape, I let it rest upon my open palm, and, so far from appearing terrified at its position, it turned its velvet-like compound eyes towards my face, and seemed to take stock of me in a calm and philosophical manner which was not a little diverting. I now noticed that one of its antennæ, which appeared to have been injured at some time, was cocked upwards and backwards, so that it bore a resemblance to a red feather in a cap. This gave the insect's countenance (and when I use the word "countenance" I speak advisedly, for its front aspect had something the appearance of a human face with a bulging overgrown forehead) a peculiarly waggish yet Mephistophelean look, which, especially when the little creature seemed to nod its head knowingly in response to a like movement on my part, was extremely comical.

Every moment the gloomy shadows around me were growing deeper, and fearing lest my valuable specimen might escape, in spite of its deficient powers of locomotion, I placed it, together with a fresh green leaf, in a ventilated celluloid box with a glass cover. This I enclosed in my aluminium botanical case, taking care that the metal catch was securely fastened.

It had now become almost dark, and I was extremely tired after my exertions in ascending the stream; so, after a hasty supper of biscuits, washed down by a draught of whisky-and-water from my flask, I stretched my mosquito-tent over its collapsible bamboo framework and crept into it. After striking a light and finding every opening secure, I wrapped my waterproof blanket around me, pillowed my head upon my knapsack, and was soon fast asleep.

II

In spite of the strangeness of my position I slept soundly for several hours, and dreamed that I was delivering my inaugural speech before the British Association at Glasgow. This speech, I may remark, had been occupying my thoughts a good deal during my journey, and I had not only noted down many telling phrases which had occurred to me from time to time, but had already learned by heart an elaborate and impressive peroration.

In my dream I thought I was about to utter this crowning part of my Presidential Address, when a certain rival entomologist—who shall be nameless—maliciously changed himself into a red howler monkey, and set up a series of such hideous and deafening yells that, although I raised my voice to its very highest pitch, no one paid the least heed to what I was saying.

Aroused by this distressing nightmare, I shifted my position some-what, noticing as I did so that the forest glade was full of brilliant fireflies, and that a continual stream of these tiny lantern-bearers seemed circling round and round me, so as to form a kind of halo above the spot where I lay. Oddly enough, this fact brought comfort to my dream-lacerated feelings (it must be remembered that I was but half awake), and, after watching the mazy curves of light for a short time, I again slept soundly.

When I reawoke my feet felt uncomfortably cold, and on tossing aside my waterproof blanket I found to my surprise that they were naked, although I had lain down in my stout shooting boots and a pair of coarse woollen stockings. Everything near me was drenched with dew, and a tropic morning mist, which clung closely to the ground and bushes, obscured all surrounding objects. As I disengaged myself from the mosquito-curtain, which had somehow become a good deal torn and damaged during the night, the first ray of sunshine gleamed down the forest path by which I had entered the clearing. I now noticed that around my bare feet were a number of very large ants, which were marching to and fro like soldiers on guard. They were bluish-grey in colour, and nearly an inch long, and their enormous jaws, which were shaped like a pair of pincers, looked so formidable that I involuntarily drew up my naked feet. It now became evident that my boots had been totally destroyed during the night, for upon the white ground just beyond my feet were a few shreds of tough sole leather and a litter of brass eyelet holes and rusty iron nails. While I puzzled over this unpleasant fact, the ground-mist grew rapidly thinner under the influence of the warm tropic sunlight, and I suddenly became aware that, with the exception of a clear space on either side of me, the whole arena was thronged with innumerable ants. Unlike the one I had captured, they were mostly dark brown in colour, and extremely active. All of them seemed hurrying to and fro as if engaged in some important business. Fearing lest I had fallen among a marauding army of large *ecitons* which might prove as dangerous as the terrible "Black Leopard" driver ants which I had encountered in Central Africa, I determined to make a hasty retreat to my canoe. But, on glancing round at my belongings, which of course I did not wish to leave behind me, I found that the warrior ants, which I could now see were gigantic representatives of a species all the members of which possess most formidable stings, had drawn closer to my bare feet, and were standing on the alert with their pincers open in a threatening manner. This made me pause, and while I was looking about me, and reckoning my chances of reaching the canoe without getting seriously injured, I noticed a kind of open lane among the busy multitudes of workers.

Along this opening there came a procession of such an extraordinary kind that I thought I must again be dreaming, for it was made up of active longicorn beetles, similar in many respects to the one I had seen the night before, *each of which carried upon its back a tallow-coloured ant with a large pink head, purple eyes, and bright scarlet antennæ!*

As this long procession drew near I saw that it had emerged from another white pathway in the forest, nearly at right angles to that by which I had entered the open circle.

I now observed that a tiny rampart, about an inch high, and made of some white earthy substance, had been built completely round me, and that the crowds of dark-coloured ants—which seemed to be composed of three or four quite distinct species—were bringing materials to add to its height.

The cavalier ants (for so henceforth I will call them) rode over this rampart without difficulty, and formed up in a circle just inside; so that I found myself enveloped by a large squadron of these extraordinary, beetle-riding creatures. The ant which had headed the procession now advanced to the guards about my feet as if to confer with them, and, on observing it closely, I saw that one of its conspicuous red antennæ was tilted backwards over its head. This made me glance at my aluminium botanical case, where I had bestowed the specimen I had captured the night before. Surely enough, in spite of its secure metal catch, the case was wide open, as also was my celluloid collecting-box.

"Surely," thought I, tugging desperately at my dishevelled forelock, "I must still be asleep and dreaming!"

And indeed, to tell the truth, from that day up to the present moment I have again and again had doubts as to whether my incredible experiences in the tropics were actual, or merely part of some feverish and interminable dream.

I have, I believe, a fair amount of courage; but there was something so strange and disquieting in the methodical tactics of these ants, that I abandoned all thoughts of trying to save my goods, and prepared to make a dash for the river (which was not more than forty yards off), hoping that I might clear the cordon of warriors before they could do me harm.

Vain hope! I had barely braced my muscles to spring up and run for it, when the soldier ants, all acting together as if by word of command, dug their pincers into my unprotected feet and humped their slate-coloured backs as if about to sting. Involuntarily I leaped up, but only to fall back again, writhing and sick with unspeakable agony—agony

I can compare with nothing except the fearful and paralysing throes of *angina pectoris!* Although the worst of the pain soon passed off, all my strength and resolution seemed to have ebbed away as utterly as if I had received some mortal wound.

As I lay still, faint and sweating, with my eyes closed, I felt something soft and tremulous gripping my right fore-finger, and, on glancing up, I looked into the round frightened eyes of a small and very lean monkey.

As far as I could tell it was a "brown capuchin" monkey, a kind very commonly seen in Europe. This creature and I seemed to be alone within the tiny rampart, for, to my unspeakable relief, both the warrior ants and the troop of beetle-riders appeared to have withdrawn. A pink-and-white speck on the little capuchin's furry "hood," close to where it joined the wrinkled face, now attracted my attention. It was a cavalier ant. Could it be that this monkey was being ridden, and directed, by one of these marvellous creatures?

He went on tugging nervously at my finger, making a plaintive chirruping noise meanwhile, and every now and then he glanced backwards towards the forest path by which the mounted procession had come. After doing this for several minutes he left me, and ran a little way towards this path, glancing back at me over his shoulder, then returned, and pulled impatiently at the edge of my coat.

As I watched him it became more and more plain that his movements were to a great extent regulated by the tiny ant upon his head; for whenever he turned this insect seemed to sway sideways and tug at the hair, exactly as a stage-driver braces himself when turning an unruly team.

By-and-by, just as it dawned upon me that I was expected to follow the monkey, the little meagre beast gave a kind of chattering screech, and scampered off a few paces, as if in mortal fear of some object behind me. Although evidently wishing to run away, he suddenly stopped, exactly as a shying horse stops when controlled by a strong-armed rider. On following the monkey's terrified gaze, I saw that the dreadful soldier-ants had again crossed the rampart from the rear, and were coming slowly towards me with open jaws. As I rose hastily to my feet, the little capuchin jumped towards me once more, and gave a frantic tug at my trousers. Casting a nervous glance at my enemies, I started to follow him without more ado, and was greatly relieved to find that I could walk. No sooner had I moved forward than a wide lane opened among the throng of working ants, while the squadron of beetle-riders, advancing with extraordinary swiftness, again surrounded me, this time acting as an escort.

One last thought of escape flashed through my mind as soon as I discovered that my most formidable enemies were no longer close to my heels. But no sooner had I turned my head towards the river path than a large blue dragon-fly, which must have been nearly six inches long, swooped downwards from somewhere above, and hovered so near my face as to touch me with its vibrating, iridescent wings. I started with mingled surprise and terror. Seated just behind its head was a pink-and-white cavalier, while on the blue metallic scales of its body three enormous soldier-ants stood in a row, and reached towards me with their pincer-like mandibles.

It was enough! I followed the little monkey submissively along the narrow white path through the forest!

After we had proceeded some fifty yards, we came to an open clearing, which must have been about an acre in extent. It was dotted all over with small white domes about the size of a water-melon, which I afterwards found were the nests of the cavaliers, and certain of their numerous insect servants. These nests were connected by a network of white cemented paths, between which were dense patches of seed-bearing grass (which I afterwards found to be a kind of "ant-rice") about as high as my knees. In the centre of the clearing was a small grove, or orchard, of banana-trees, and when my guide had led me through this, I found on the other side of it what looked like half-a-dozen round white hillocks, but which turned out to be huts built of fine cement. The largest of these was about six feet six inches in height, and the smallest about a yard. The ground about this group of huts was paved like the paths, and quite level, the whole being encircled by a raised edging or rampart about three inches high. My guide stopped close to the largest hut, which had a round hole in the side just large enough for a man to creep through. After standing upright for an instant before this opening, he bobbed down and ran in on all-fours, glancing back at me as he did so, as if to give me a hint to follow his example. While I stood hesitating, the dragon-fly, with its accursed crew, darted round behind me, and I suddenly felt a bump and a buzz against the nape of my neck. With a shudder—and almost a shriek—I dropped down upon my hands and knees, and shuffled through the opening.

As soon as I was inside, and had turned round to make sure that none of the terrible warriors had entered with me, I beheld the little white cavaliers, which were drawn up in a semicircle round the doorway, dismount from their beetles, and advance almost to the entrance of the hut. Here they broke up into groups, and behaved in a manner which irresistibly reminded me of human beings discussing some exciting topic. They waved their antennæ at one another, every now and then pointing them towards the hut as if exchanging ideas about my appearance, and the exciting circumstances of my capture.

On the arrival of another body of cavalier-ants, the first comers seemed eager to tell them the news; and my little cock-horned ex-captive, who apparently was playing the part of chief showman, repeatedly led parties of new-comers to the doorway of the hut, and apparently gave them much instructive and amusing information.

One frequent and very odd manœuvre puzzled me at first a good deal. I noticed, every now and then, that two or three cavaliers, while engaged in animated converse, would suddenly depress their red antennæ, hoist their white hindquarters into the air, and flourish their posterior pair of legs in an excited and highly ridiculous fashion. After watching this curious proceeding repeatedly, I arrived at the remark-able conclusion that it amounted to "ant laughter," or, at any rate, was the cavalier-ants' way of expressing applause, or extreme interest, at what they learned.

If this interpretation be correct, my late captive—and, alas! I must add, my future taskmaster—was undoubtedly something of a wag; for no sooner did he jerk his unmutilated antenna towards me, and begin to "talk," than his hearers, with one consent, would all lower their pink heads to the ground, lift their tallowy latter ends on high, and kick convulsively for several seconds.

III

This must have gone on for an hour or more, and as fresh mounted ants were continually arriving, a great crowd of them had meanwhile assembled in front of the hut. By-and-by the monkey, apparently prompted by his rider, who still maintained its seat upon his head, crept out of the doorway. I was about to follow him, when he turned, as if to push me back, and at the same moment the dragon-fly darted down and effectually barred my egress. Shortly afterwards the monkey returned with a couple of ripe bananas, which he placed before me on the clean floor of the hut. Feeling very hungry, I at once began to strip one of the bananas, and this act evidently caused great excitement among the crowd of lookers-on. All their scarlet antennæ became motionless, and every pair of purple compound eyes was turned intently towards me. When I devoured the first banana in a couple of bites, there seemed to be a kind of thrill of suppressed excitement among the crowd of spectators, and then every pink head was lowered to the ground, and the whole throng became a mass of pallid abdomens and furiously gesticulating legs.

I had just eaten my second banana when I was startled by a muffled, growling sound, which appeared to come from just behind the hut. Shortly afterwards a huge male jaguar passed across the paved surface in front of me, and disappeared down one of the narrow paths leading into the forest. None of the white ants took any notice of him; but I could distinctly see a blue soldier-bearing dragon-fly hovering above his head. Could it be that a large and formidable beast of prey such as this was kept in captivity by these extraordinary insects? The capuchin monkey did not seem very much upset by the sight of his hereditary foe, although he was evidently somewhat relieved when the jaguar was gone.

The bananas had only served to awaken my hunger, and I was wondering whether I should be obliged to subsist on such unsatisfying fare, when I saw a long procession of large brown worker-ants swarming over the three-inch rampart. As they came near I noticed that each ant was carrying something in its jaws. The little monkey, again acting as if under direction, ran to one of the neighbouring banana-trees, and tore off a fragment of a leaf about as large as a sheet of foolscap paper. This he placed upon the floor of the hut, just as the leaders of the new procession arrived. During the next ten minutes a continual stream of brown worker-ants (which seemed to belong to several common South American species) entered the hut and deposited their burdens upon the banana-leaf, until the heap must have contained a pound or more of buff-coloured granules, which had very much the appearance of coarse farina made from the root of the manioc. I wondered what this could all mean, and sat staring at the pile upon the leaf for some time after the last of the burden-bearers had departed. Apparently the cavaliers were watching me with close attention, as if questioning what I would do next. At length, again following the example of the little monkey, I took up some of the granules in my hand and tasted them.

What this stuff was I have not the least idea; but I found it not only exceedingly palatable, but very sustaining. The granules were somewhat soft, and of a sweet nutty flavour, which nevertheless reminded me somewhat of truffles. I found that, when I squeezed a handful of them together, they cohered into a mass, or cake, which was much more convenient to eat without any implements than the separate grains. In a short time I had finished the whole supply, and also another banana which was brought me by the little capuchin. By the time my hunger was appeased by the novel and excellent food which I had eaten, the feeling of faintness which I had experienced ever since I had been stung by the soldier-ants had disappeared entirely.

While marvelling at the extraordinary intelligence of the cavalier-ants, which apparently possessed a fair knowledge both as to the quality and the amount of nourishment required by a human being, I began to regard my captivity almost as a joke. I had then not the least doubt that, ere long, I should find some way of outwitting my custodians and of escaping to my canoe.

After seeing me fed, and apparently manifesting no little interest and amusement at the sight, the crowd of beetle-riders dispersed. I noticed, however, that a strong guard of soldier-ants was parading the top of the rampart, and once, when I attempted to put my head out of the doorway, I found the dragon-fly still on guard. My small tutor nestled down against me and went to sleep, and I now noticed that the cavalier-ant no longer occupied its place upon his head.

After being thus left alone for about a couple of hours, a mounted troop, headed by my cock-horned acquaintance, again drew up before the hut. The little ape at once went to the doorway and crouched down, as if making obeisance to its masters, and at the same instant a tiny humming-bird, which seemed to carry two or three cavaliers perched upon its topaz-coloured crest, darted down and settled for a moment on the capuchin's head. As the bird flew off again I noticed that a pink-and-white ant had again taken its position among the hair just above the monkey's forehead.

The little creature now seized my finger again, as if to drag me out of the hut, and this time, having learned that such hints were best obeyed promptly, I followed without demur. The cavaliers rode around me as before on their swiftly running beetles, and that accursed dragon-fly again hovered menacingly just over my head. As we were entering a narrow pathway between two dense walls of vegetation, I was appalled to see a huge jaguar advancing towards me along this very track. Being quite defenceless, my first instinct was to run away; but I had scarcely faced about when the dragon-fly came buzzing against my nose, so that I distinctly felt the points of one of the soldiers' long mandibles.

It will convey some idea as to the unreasoning terror inspired by an attack of these fearful insects when I say that I spun round and faced the jaguar again without an instant's hesitation!

The little monkey had drawn himself close to the edge of the path, but I could see that he was trembling in every limb. The jaguar came to a standstill about six feet from me, then crouched down and snarled. I could easily have blown his brains out, if I had had my "paradox" gun; but, alas! it stood some sixty yards off in the forest. At this moment I felt something nipping my right heel, and on glancing downwards I was startled to find a score or so of soldier-ants close behind me and advancing in a threatening manner. Forgetful of all else, I took a spring into the air, and tumbled right upon the top of the jaguar!

What happened during the next few seconds I could hardly tell. The brute uttered a series of the most awful roars and yells, and I was aware of being rolled about like a football and of receiving a number of cuffs and scratches in various parts of my body. Fortunately the scuffle ended as quickly as it began, and I got up, greatly relieved at finding that I had not been seriously injured. On glancing around I saw the jaguar's tail vanishing into one of the smaller huts, while, for some reason or other, my escort of cavaliers were all tumbling pell-mell off their beetles and standing head-downwards upon the path, while their white hinder extremities, which were hoisted on high, appeared seized with uncontrollable agitation.

After recovering from this strange epileptic seizure, the cavalier-ants remounted, and the poor little monkey, which seemed almost as much shaken as I was by the encounter, again started on in front.

By-and-by we came to a cultivated patch of ground where, apparently, the "ant-rice" had recently been cleared away. Half the little rectangular field—which was about forty feet across—had the appearance of having been roughly ploughed up. My attention was now drawn to a number of objects moving slowly across this piece of ground, and I soon saw that they were armadillos. There were six of them, and they seemed to be advancing in line, diligently scratching up the soil with their powerful digging-claws. Just above them hovered several large dragon-flies, each of which apparently carried a cavalier-ant and several armed warriors. No sooner had we reached the scene of operations than the little monkey snatched up a stick, went behind the armadillos, and began to act as if he were digging the ground. Another heavy stick, which appeared to have been gnawed to a sharp point by the chisel-like teeth of a porcupine, coypu, or some other large rodent animal, lay just in front of me, and, as the dragon-fly seemed becoming rather demonstrative, I lost no time in following the monkey's lead.

I soon saw that the little ape only made a mere pretence of working; and, as it was very hot, and I felt somewhat done up and languid after my recent trying experiences, I was tempted to follow his bad example, and take things easily. Our place, it appeared, was just behind the gang of armadillos, and it seemed to be expected of us that we should dig up the ground to a somewhat greater depth. After lazily prodding the soil for a few minutes, my small companion gave a sudden shriek of alarm, scampered back to the place where we had started work, and commenced digging the ground over again with desperate energy. I was wondering what had influenced him, when a topaz humming-bird came whirring towards us, bearing on its back my cock-horned ex-captive and a strong patrol of slate-coloured warriors. It settled on my head for an instant, and when it flew off again I saw that two at least of the big stinging ants had been left behind. My first instinct was to bring my hand to my head and endeavour to brush these horrible creatures away; but a slight admonitory nip made me pause in terror, and give up all thoughts of rebellion. Forthwith, with trembling knees, I joined my fellow-captive, and began to dig away at the ground with all my might.

It was, alas, abundantly plain that our new taskmaster would stand no shirking. He kept his aerial mount humming round our ears all the time, so we dug away as if for our lives, until all the earth scratched up by the armadillos was thoroughly turned over. Fortunately the soil was very light and loose, and the sky somewhat overcast, otherwise the fatigue of digging in such a climate would have nearly killed me.

When we had done, our strict overseer mercifully removed the guards from my head and went sailing away out of sight; and my little companion, who seemed sadly exhausted and depressed, led me to a spring of clear water which broke out in the middle of the banana-grove. After drinking freely, and washing my face and hands, I felt somewhat better both in mind and body, and was able to eat another pile of the granular food, which I found awaiting me in my quarters.

During the remainder of the day, although not allowed to leave the hut, I was left to my own devices, and spent most of my time resting flat upon my back, trying to realize my strange position, and making many plans of escape. I could not help dwelling upon the caustic irony of fate in placing a man who had been acknowledged by the whole scientific world as the foremost living authority on ants, in such a position as that in which I now found myself.

It was plain that these marvellous cavaliers excelled all other insects in intelligence, to an even greater degree than man excels all his fellow-mammals. Apparently they had not only turned to their own use, and improved upon, practically all the special primitive instincts and habits of other ants, but had also greatly enhanced the more valuable qualities (from their own point of view) of most of their domesticated breeds. I had seen amongst their crowds of slaves unusually large and perfect specimens of nearly every species of ant in South America. Probably these useful varieties had been bred by the cavaliers for many generations, for all appeared to yield them instinctive obedience, and to require scarcely any supervision. The cavaliers had, moreover, succeeded in taming and breeding, for certain special purposes, many other insects, such as the fireflies, dragon-flies, and swift, smooth-running beetles. In addition to this, they seemed to have a good understanding as to the kind of service which such diverse creatures as men, monkeys, rodents, armadillos, and humming-birds could render them. Why they kept such a useless beast as a jaguar in captivity was to me at that time a complete puzzle. I was inclined at first to think that they were prompted by scientific motives, or the mere vanity of possession; but afterwards I received ample proof that here, as in most other matters, they had a shrewd eye to business.

As was to be expected—seeing that the mental attributes of all insects must be more akin to their own than those of birds and mammals—they seemed to have obtained a much greater ascendancy over the former than over the latter. Most of their invertebrate servants appeared to do their bidding as a matter of course, without coercion or any special guidance; whereas I and other warm-blooded captives were always treated as stupid or untrustworthy creatures, which required to be strictly watched, restrained, and generally superintended.

At the approach of nightfall I made up my mind to make my escape in the darkness. But, just as the sun began to sink behind the Andes, a large luminous spider, which spun his web with astonishing rapidity, fixed a curtain over the entrance of my hut. On surveying this web carefully, I found that several threads from its outer side stretched upwards to a number of white nodular projections, about as big as a walnut, which I had already observed just above the doorway. Each of these I now found to my disgust to be a hollow guardroom, garrisoned by several big stinging ants, which would, of course, be able to drop down instantly upon any one disturbing the web.

On testing the walls of the hut elsewhere, I found them so firm and solid that there was not the least chance of my breaking through. I afterwards came to the conclusion that the white cement used for building and paving purposes was manufactured by captive hordes of termites which lived underground; but that the actual building operations were performed by true ant-slaves, similar to those I had seen at work in the forest. Be this as it may, both pavements and buildings were as hard as marble, with a fine porcelain-like surface.

I passed a restless night, brooding over my strange position. Although visited every half-hour or so by a night patrol of cavaliers, which, riding upon large fireflies, sailed in through a small opening in the spider's web and did their round with soldier-like precision, I was quite unmolested during the hours of darkness.

Moreover, although mosquitoes seemed both hungry and plentiful in this region, I was quite free from their attacks until the moment when I regained my liberty. This I believe to have been due to the presence of my spider *concierge* or of the soldier-bearing dragon-flies which were always hovering near my head in the day-time—it being a well-known fact in the tropics that all insects of the gnat tribe give these hereditary foes as wide a berth as possible.

IV

It would be a long and tedious narrative if I were to tell all the incidents of my captivity in detail; so having described the events of the first day, I will henceforth record only some of my more noteworthy experiences among these extraordinary ants.

As a rule, my life was exceedingly monotonous. Every morning, after being fed, I was set to work at something where my height, strength, and power of using sticks and other tools proved valuable to the ant-community. After several days of digging in the ant-rice fields, I was employed in clearing out rotten leaf-mould from some cave-like underground chambers. These had originally been filled by the *saübas*, or leaf-cutting ants, in the service of the cavaliers, and had evidently formed hot-beds for growing edible fungi. On this occasion I managed to wound my right hand rather badly with a splinter, and was extremely apprehensive lest the cock-horned ant should think I was shirking, and have me severely punished. But, strange to relate, my master,—for so henceforth I must call him,—after examining my wound with a good deal of attention, had the splinter plucked out by a soldier-ant (whose forceps-like jaws seemed made on purpose), and then gave me an hour's holiday. Afterwards he was kind enough to find me a lighter job; and for the rest of that day I stood, with a cane in my left hand, as foreman over a strong excavating gang of armadillos.

Early during my second week, and before despair had completely robbed me of initiative, I thought I saw a chance of escape. I had noticed that, when the night-guard was set, and before the first round of the firefly-borne inspectors, some of the big stinging ants would swarm down upon the floor of the hut and clear up any remains of my supper. Although they usually came cautiously, and in detachments, they seemed to have such a weakness for the granular material upon which I was fed, that it occurred to me to turn the fact to my advantage. For if, during the night, I could once lure all of them from the doorway, I could make a dash for freedom before they could do me any hurt. After one or two vain attempts to entice them *en masse* from their post of duty, I remembered a time-honoured plan of corrupting military morals which has often proved effective in the hands of prisoners—and novelists.

I had carefully preserved the contents of my spirit-flask for special emergencies, and one moonless night I determined to see if I could make my guards drunk by saturating some of my granular food with whisky. The scheme succeeded to admiration. No sooner was it dark than a company of soldier-ants climbed down to the floor, and in less than five minutes they were all too tipsy to return. By-and-by the first detachment was followed by a second. These also, after showing some indignation at the disgraceful state of their comrades, sampled my "Ancient Scotch"—and fell likewise into a state of scandalous intoxication.

After making quite sure that there were none left guarding the doorway, I lost not a minute in plunging through the tough spider's web, and hurrying towards the river as fast as the darkness would allow.

I believe that all would have gone well if I had not met the firefly patrol just as I crossed the three-inch rampart, about ten yards from the hut. It consisted of about a dozen mounted cavaliers, six of which forthwith accompanied me in my flight, while the rest separated, and darted off hither and thither.

As I hurried along the narrow track the little illuminated riders kept up with me, three on each side of my face. Their vigilance and excitement made them sit up like jockeys, and as they sped along I thought I could see the hind-legs of each cavalier working furiously against its firefly's body, like the spurred heels of a horseman.

Alas! I had barely entered the bush on the farther side of the clearing when I heard some large creature rushing along an adjoining forest-path, and as I emerged into the open space where I was first captured, I found myself confronted by the jaguar! Just then a brilliant firefly came whizzing down the dark narrow glade like a white-hot rifle-bullet, and directly I saw that it carried my redoubtable cock-horned master, I knew that the game was up. Instantly the jaguar, which previously had seemed to hesitate, sprang at me, knocked me down, and rolled me this way and that with his powerful paws. Then he suddenly drew back, like a sheep-dog which had been called off by the shepherd. As soon as I had recovered my breath, I picked myself up and slunk back to my quarters, thoroughly cowed and submissive. The jaguar sniffed at my dilapidated trousers, and growled horribly all the way, and I knew full well that at any moment, if my custodian gave him the order, he would tear me to pieces.

I now no longer speculated why the cavalier-ants kept this enormous jaguar. His business, like that of a sheep-dog or cattle-dog, was to chase and punish any of his mammalian fellow-servants who attempted to break away.

It is needless to say that I felt miserably cast down at the result of this effort to regain my freedom.

Probably no mere verbal statement would bring home to my readers the disastrous moral consequences of my condition as a slave among the cavalier-ants. After the startling novelty of my adventure had worn off, and I had endured several such defeats as the foregoing, my prevailing mental state was one of frantic and futile rage at finding all my human strength and intelligence, all my scientific knowledge and attainments, and all my experience of life generally, of absolutely no avail, either in helping me to escape, or in preventing my being treated by these imperious insects "as a horse or a mule which have no understanding."

In the same way, I suppose, a wild elephant finds his vast strength and natural wisdom, and all the wonderful fund of forest lore which he has gathered during half a century, entirely valueless when he is caught and subjugated by men.

Ere long this state of bitter exasperation alternated with fits of lethargic despair, during which the grosser and more grovelling animal instincts seemed to be supplanting all other springs of action. Latterly there were times when this shameful lapse into mere tame-animalism sent me forth to my labour like a working ox, prompted only by threats of near punishment or by the desire to fill my belly.

V

On the morning following my failure to escape, I found a large assembly of cavaliers formed up in a semicircle in front of my dwelling. Inside this semicircle, and placed in a row close to the doorway, were the delinquent guards, still, seemingly, in a state of helpless intoxication. Shortly afterwards a procession of black working ants, headed by an overgrown *saüba* with curiously distorted, scissor-like jaws, arrived upon the scene. This insect, apparently after a brief interview with my master—who advanced without dismounting from his high-bred longicorn—ran to each of the prostrate criminals in turn and expeditiously nipped off all their heads. After the executioner had done his duty, some of the dingy worker-ants carried the carcasses away; and henceforth a double detachment of slate-coloured warriors (which I found to be absolutely incorruptible) occupied the guardrooms at night. The only punishment I myself suffered was a temporary deprivation of my pleasant granular food. For three days I had to subsist upon bananas and about a quart of gritty millet-like seeds, which I found to be nothing like so nourishing as the mysterious provender which I have already described.

I may state here that whenever, in the opinion of my masters, I became obstreperous, this was the result; and latterly, strange to say, the fear of being deprived of my regular diet (of which I had become extremely fond) influenced my behaviour more than anything else.

The cavaliers, as is the way with most ruling castes, seemed to spend a good deal of time in recreation. In this, and in their evident possession of a sense of humour, and of well-developed powers of hearing (concerning which I shall have more to say presently), they differ widely from all other species of ants. Some of my most humiliating experiences were traceable to these facts; for at times I was compelled to shout, sing, and to go through various absurd performances for their pleasure. While I was a comparative novelty the mere sight of me seemed to suffice. They would come and watch me in crowds, and, on the first occasion when I undressed in their presence, the act seemed to afford them a vast deal of amusement, which they manifested in the odd fashion I have already described. After this I frequently had to take off all my ragged clothes at the command of my master when he brought parties of friends to look at me.

An even more abasing experience awaited me somewhat later, when, having chanced to skip and jump about in a somewhat agile manner when my bare feet were threatened by the horrible stinging-ants, I was made to repeat the performance over and over again for the entertainment of the assembled cavaliers. In fact, these diabolical insects taught me to "dance" by almost precisely the same methods that civilized showmen resort to when training performing elephants.

At the end of the first month a great trouble befell me in the tragic death of my poor little fellow-slave and tutor. I fear that my capture by the cavalier-ants proved a sad misfortune to this frail and gentle monkey. He had, I think, been in captivity for a long time, for he understood the ways and wishes of his masters in a wonderful manner. This fact, and his apparent kinship with mankind, probably caused our masters to appoint him as my guide and exemplar (just as a young setter or sheep-dog is set to work with an old one which knows its business), and as the interpreter of their wishes to my crude untutored mind. Hence, unhappily, he was made to do regular work in the fields and elsewhere—which, as any one who understands ape-nature will know, was to him an absolutely intolerable burden. Recognizing this, I did my best to spare him whenever possible, and I believe he repaid my good intentions with real gratitude and love.

One sultry morning, when I had a bad headache, I had great difficulty in understanding some new piece of work connected with the dam which the cavaliers had erected to enlarge a forest pool where they kept their tame coypus and capybaras. After trying in many ways to bring the matter within the scope of my comprehension, my poor little schoolmaster seemed worried out of his wits; and at length, in a spasm of frantic rage at my thick-headedness, he flung himself down upon the ground, accidentally squashing the soft-bodied master-ant which was seated upon his head.

It so happened that a large crowd of cavaliers was present at the time, and the sensation caused by this unhappy accident was very great. Both I and the wretched little capuchin were marched forthwith back to our quarters, where we waited, in considerable trepidation, to learn what would happen next.

Half an hour later a great concourse of cavaliers and warriors lined the three-inch rampart, and, as soon as they were in their places, an armed dragon-fly came buzzing into the hut, and drove the trembling monkey out into the open. Here, before my eyes, he was pounced upon and torn to pieces by the jaguar! This act of hateful injustice to my innocent friend and colleague so filled me with unthinking rage that I rushed out, all unarmed as I was, to take vengeance on the executioner. But I had scarcely taken three strides when several dragon-flies with their armed riders dashed at me like hawks, and a second later I was writhing upon the ground in such unspeakable torment that I wished that the jaguar would kill me also!

Henceforth my position was worse than ever; and, owing to the depression I felt at the loss of my only friend and companion, the mental and moral degeneration which I have already spoken of proceeded more rapidly than before.

Next morning, when I received the signal to go forth to my work, a truculent drab soldier-ant, apparently of a different species from any that I had hitherto seen, was placed by my master just above my bald forehead, where he sat, throughout the day, like a mahout upon an elephant, and prodded me viciously with his mandibles when he considered that I was not doing my best.

I think that all of those who know my character will readily under-stand that I did not sink into a state of idiotic despair without a struggle to retain my manhood and my reason. When alone I would frequently talk to myself, and recite poetry, and even elementary school lessons which I had learned by rote (such as the Latin and Greek declensions and the Multiplication Table), for the sake of reminding myself that I had once been a civilized human being. At times, when brought very low, I would raise my voice and shout as loudly as possible, in order to create a greater impression upon my failing intellect.

On one occasion when I felt very sick and feeble, after three days of punishment diet for insubordination, and almost demented through being unmercifully harassed and bullied by my master, who kept repeating some order which I could not in the least comprehend, I managed to pull myself to the hut-door in sheer desperation, and began bawling my own name at the very top of my voice—adding to it the whole string of degrees and honourable titles which have been conferred upon me by learned bodies all over the civilized world.

This recital, I was astonished to observe, seemed to make quite a sensation among the cavalier-ants, who immediately assembled in great crowds in front of my dwelling, and not only gave me a command to repeat the whole programme, but greeted my most strenuous vocal efforts with epileptic spasms of applause.

I was immediately rewarded by being allowed to sup upon my favourite provender: but, alas! I found that I had established a prec-edent; and henceforth, if I failed to shout or sing very loudly for some ten minutes after being brought in from the fields, I got nothing but a few handfuls of gritty millet which I could scarcely swallow.

Before long, however, this form of entertainment seemed to pall upon the cavaliers, who, I found, were exceedingly fickle; and I am ashamed to confess that I could not help feeling some chagrin at the waning of my popularity.

VI

On the whole, my physical health remained fairly good, and indeed seemed to improve somewhat as my mind became more clouded; otherwise I could not possibly have stood the heavy work which I was made to do in the fields and the forest. One saving circumstance was that the extreme dampness of this region shortened my hours of labour. It rained nearly every other day, and my masters had a strong objection to being out in the wet. They seemed to know instinctively when rain was coming, and would then hurry me back to my quarters at once, while they themselves took refuge in their little dome-like palaces.

Before I sank into a state of complete mental inertia, I felt a strong wish to investigate the internal economy of these "nests." This desire, however, was not gratified until I had practically ceased to take an intelligent interest in my surroundings. One morning, after a hurricane had torn through the neighbouring forest, I was led forth to repair damages, and found that a large branch of a tree had knocked away one side of the round, porcelain mansion inhabited by my cock-horned chief. I could see that the interior was made up of a bewildering labyrinth of chambers, with pearly semi-transparent walls; but otherwise I did not add to my knowledge of my master's domestic economy.

Although I have fallen into the habit of using the masculine gender when speaking of the ant whose special property I seemed to be—chiefly because there was something essentially virile and masterful in the character of this extraordinary insect—I have no reason for believing that all the cavaliers which I saw were not true amazons, as is the case with the active members of other ant communities.

During the last fortnight of my captivity my state of mental hebetude several times gave place to a kind of mild delirium, although I was not conscious of any fever. At such times I would sometimes imagine myself back at Oxford, and would commence discoursing on scientific subjects, under the momentary impression that I was lecturing to my class.

While moping stupidly in my hut one brilliant sunny afternoon after returning from labour, I was surprised to see a considerable number of mounted cavaliers advancing towards me. In their midst was some strange object which I could not at first make out, but which, when the procession drew near, I found to be a small and active rattlesnake, bearing upon its back a score or so of white-bodied ants somewhat different from any that I had seen before.

Although similar in many respects to the cavaliers, these insects evidently belonged to a distinct species or variety, for their enormous, bulging heads were tinted light blue; while their antennæ were, for the most part, of a brilliant ultra-marine. I soon noticed also that they differed considerably from the cavaliers in manner, being much more restless and excitable. When about two feet from my hut door the whole concourse dismounted; and when the visitors had to some extent satisfied their curiosity as to my appearance, my master, who seemed to be engaged in an animated discussion with one of the visitors (which chanced to have its antennæ tinted respectively of an Oxford and Cambridge blue) gave me an order to sing.

By this time I readily understood such commands as this, and had learned by painful experiences that no excuse would be accepted. I therefore without delay put my head out of the opening and shouted "Rule Britannia" at the very top of my voice. I began almost as mechanically as a phonograph, but when I came to the words *"Britons never, never, never shall be slaves!"* I suddenly realized my position, faltered, and broke down.

Upon this my master and his cavalier friends seemed greatly disconcerted, while the blue-headed strangers were so overcome with derisive "laughter" that they all turned head-over-heels and lay kicking helplessly upon their backs.

After a while the discussion was renewed between my master and the ant with Oxford-and-Cambridge antennæ; and, while watching them, I felt a sudden conviction that these ill-bred snake-riding ants had come to buy me from the cavaliers. In spite of the misery of my position, I dreaded being handed over to such unprepossessing insects; for, to tell the truth, I had formed a very low opinion of their character. They had nothing of the suavity and ease of manner which distinguished the cavaliers, but rather put me in mind of a lot of vulgar pushing commercials out for a holiday.

By-and-by the two parties seemed to arrive at some agreement, for the cavaliers remounted their swift beetles and escorted their blue-headed visitors (which, when scrambling on to their loathsome conveyance, strongly resembled a gang of rowdy trippers boarding an excursion train) along one of the paths leading into the forest.

VII

Next morning, at daybreak, I found the whole settlement astir, and that a general migration of the cavaliers seemed to be taking place towards the river. After receiving an unusually liberal breakfast I was placed in charge of my drab mahout and taken towards the forest arena where all my troubles began. My master, who hovered round me on an exquisite white humming-bird—which he only rode on state occasions—seemed to be looking me over with a critical eye, and he more than once gave my rider a hint to make me pull myself together, hold up my head, and step out more briskly.

This, perhaps, should have confirmed my previous suspicions that I was being driven to market; but, curiously enough, it had a very different effect upon my mind.

I have already said that I had recently been subject to attacks of mild delirium, during which I quite forgot my present lamentable circumstances, and thought myself back in the post of honour which I had occupied at home. As I strode along the narrow forest pathway, with my shoulders squared and my chin well up, it suddenly seemed to me that I was passing amid a crowd of admiring people at Glasgow while making a dignified approach towards the Presidential Chair. Automatically I began, below my breath, to rehearse parts of the speech which I had prepared for that great occasion.

As soon as I entered the open space, however, the startling novelty of the scene before me brought my mind back from its wanderings. The little arena was thronged with innumerable cavaliers, who not only occupied a high, terraced rampart, which had been erected all around the paved clearing like the tiers of an amphitheatre, but crowded every point of vantage among the leafy walls above. In fact, only the smooth, columnar tree-trunks which encircled the open space, and a few of the larger branches overhead, were left unoccupied. All else was tinted pink and white by the enormous throng of cavaliers, so that the foliage looked like an apple orchard in full blossom.

I had scarcely taken my appointed place in the centre of the ring when a procession appeared through one of the narrow glades in the forest which surpassed anything I had seen before.

A score or more of huge serpents, most of them pythons or anacondas over twenty feet long, came sliding, two or three abreast, into the opening, like trains entering some great London terminus. Their backs were blue and white with dense crowds of demonstrative (I had almost said "noisy") snake-riders; and these enormous cargoes of excursionists were followed by numerous smaller parties, mounted on rattlesnakes, coral snakes, whip snakes, and nearly every kind of serpent represented in South America.

For a while I seemed to be standing on a small island surrounded by a writhing sea of snakes; yet, knowing well that the whole business was being arranged by my potent masters, I felt scarcely any alarm, but found myself vaguely wondering where room was to be found for this vast influx of visitors; for the open-air theatre seemed crowded to its fullest capacity.

The two leading boa-constrictors wriggled straight to the nearest tree and coiled themselves spirally around it, one above the other, thus making, as it were, a number of galleries for about ten feet up the trunk. Most of the other large pythons followed their example, while all the smaller serpents swarmed up the trees and creepers surrounding the open space, and in a few minutes were arranged in a series of marvellous hanging bridges—all densely crowded with spectators—which completely festooned the forest walls.

I was so much taken up with watching this astounding spectacle that I did not notice certain tamed animals which the snake-riding ants had brought with them until I smelt a most unpleasant smell, and suddenly discovered, close to my side, a gaunt and very large howler monkey. This beast seemed quite undisturbed by my presence, and was sitting at its ease upon the white ground scratching its mangy, rufous flanks in an extremely diligent manner.

I found also that the cavaliers had just brought into the arena two of their best working teams of armadillos; while, sprawling on the ground close beside them, was a miserable three-toed sloth, which had lost half its hair and appeared to be in the last stages of consumption.

Almost before the newcomers were settled in their places I was made to stand on one side, while the armadillos and the sloth, after being placed in the middle of the ring, were carefully inspected by my cock-horned chief and his Oxford-and-Cambridge visitor. It was fairly plain that certain negotiations were in progress, but I could scarcely believe that my masters would be so silly as to swap both their best teams of trained and well-fed armadillos for a moribund, three-toed sloth.

Apparently, however, in commercial matters the cavaliers were no match for the bustling blue-heads; for shortly afterwards the whole herd of armadillos was driven off in the direction from whence the visitors had come, while the wretched sloth, attended by an armed dragon-fly, crawled away, slowly and painfully, towards the cavalier settlement.

On glancing around I noticed that the majority of the ants, which had hitherto shown but little interest in what was going on in the arena, seemed settling down in their places, like a music-hall audience on the announcement of some popular "turn."

I was now led to the centre again, and made to go down on my hands and knees cheek by jowl with the evil-smelling howler, which was about as large as a collie dog. It seemed as if I were about to be bartered away like the armadillos, and the fears which I had felt during the first visit of the snake-riders were now greatly increased, for the starved and neglected condition of their wretched "pets" showed only too plainly that they were far worse masters than cavaliers. Yet, in spite of the incident which I had just witnessed, I still had some hope that the obvious difference in exchange-value between myself and a sullen and mangy red howler would prove a bar to any such transaction. In this the event showed that I was woefully out of my reckoning, and that in my estimate of my own intrinsic worth I was altogether at sea.

Shortly after my mahout had made me go down on all-fours, side by side with the disgusting monkey, a fresh wave of delirium must have swamped my mind; for I remember declaring this attitude to be an altogether unprecedented one for the delivery of a Presidential Address!

I was partially aroused by a small dragon-fly buzzing against my lips—which was the recognized signal when my master desired me to shout or sing. Still prompted by the insane fancy that I was facing a scientific audience, I at once commenced to recite my carefully prepared oration; and, at the same moment, the brute of a monkey began howling like a whole menagerie of jackals.

It seemed for a while that the hideous nightmare fancy, already spoken of, had become true in fact. In my present waking delirium I thought I was indeed addressing the British Association at Glasgow, and that my most prominent scientific rival was attempting to howl me down.

Those who have been partially under the influence of intoxicating drugs will know that for some time after most of the faculties are overcome, and are wandering in the maddest mazes, there still seems to remain one critical atom of sanity in the innermost mental chamber which is perfectly aware of the real state of the case. In like manner, I knew,—in a sense—where I was; and what (Heaven help me!) I was doing.

Moreover, an electric flash of recollection told me that this was the very day when, had I been able to return, I should be in reality delivering my Presidential Address to the British Association at Glasgow! Yet so transitory was this lucid interval, that I did not cease raising my voice more and more, in order to make my peroration heard above a hideous crescendo of yelps from the obscene beast beside me.

But, alas! the vocal apparatus of a big howler monkey enables him to defy competition from any living thing! My chances could scarcely have been worse if I had backed myself in a roaring match against the eternal thunders of Niagara!

Suddenly my voice cracked under the intolerable strain. I instantly recovered my sober senses, and came to a full stop; while the monkey's triumphant howls rose louder and louder, to a stupendous and deafening *finale*.

At this the cavaliers seemed to be in a state of the utmost consternation (I am inclined to think that there were some heavy bets on the result), while all the blue-heads gave way to unseemly somersaults of laughter. It was only too plain that their scraggy and abominable ape— which had again seated himself upon the ground, and was engaged in strenuous entomological researches among his frowzy red hair—was acknowledged my victor in the contest.

Although sick with shame and fury, I had a momentary feeling of relief at the thought that these keen low-bred snake-riders would now refuse to trade.

But I had soon a new and graver cause for apprehension. My master, whose quivering antennæ told of intense irritation and chagrin, suddenly dashed off on his white humming-bird towards the cavaliers' clearing. For a few minutes both I and the vast concourse of spectators waited in suspense; then a sudden "sensation" quivered through the whole assembly. He had been to fetch the jaguar!

On emerging from the forest-path this hideous brute stopped, and stood blinking and licking his jaws on the farther side of the opening. In the meantime an eager debate seemed to have been started among one section of the cavaliers, and several deputations advanced to interview my master.

It seemed to me that a large number of them were pleading for my life; and I noticed that many of these kept pointing their scarlet antennæ towards the path leading to the river.

The jaguar began switching his barred tail to and fro against his hollow flanks, and growled more and more impatiently during the debate; while my master flew round from tier to tier on the rampart, and from gallery to gallery among the trees, as if taking the sense of the meeting. I believe that all the brutal snake-riders without exception urged him to let me be killed, but happily he seemed to treat their demonstrations with aristocratic contempt.

By-and-by, during an animated conference with several of the leading cavaliers, he evidently made some amusing proposal which was hailed with general approbation. Soon afterwards my mahout guided me to the very tree against which I had leaned my gun when I camped in this fatal spot. The ant-carrying snakes which encircled this tree hissed horribly as I drew near, but unwound themselves and moved away at my master's special request. I then saw that my double-barrelled "paradox" gun was still where I had placed it, although red with rust and almost hidden by a creeper. My mahout gave me a signal to bend forward, so I seized hold of the muzzle and managed to drag it forth, recollecting as I did so that on landing I had loaded both barrels with some waterproof ball-cartridges which I had had specially prepared before visiting this humid region.

Fortunately the locks, which had been well soused with hot petroleum and wrapped in a greasy cloth, were less corroded than the barrels.

While I was examining the gun my master's white humming-bird settled for a moment upon my forehead, and then hovered in front of my eyes, showing me that my mahout had been taken away. On glancing towards the river, I found that the line of guards had disappeared, and that the path was as clear as when I had first traversed it.

Scarcely had I noted these facts when the jaguar ceased growling and twitching his tail, and came creeping upon his belly across the clearing, with his eyes aflame with the lust for blood.

In another instant I had raised the gun and pulled both triggers. A stunning explosion knocked me backwards against the tree, and a blinding flame leaped right into my face. The choked left barrel had burst just beyond my fingers; but, in spite of all, one bullet had flown true! The jaguar was writhing on his back in the middle of the arena, and besmearing the white porcelain-like pavement with brains and blood from his shattered skull!

For some minutes I stood rooted to the spot, with no more power to plan or move than the forest trees about me; and I think that the sight I then saw impressed me more than anything else during my living nightmare in the forest. In spite of the terrific flash and detonation, and the death-struggles of the enormous jaguar in their very midst, the valiant cavaliers were all standing upon their heads in convulsions of laughter at the episode!

When their spasms had partially subsided, the spell which held me motionless was broken by the sight of a dozen huge soldier-ants, which came charging towards my naked feet from beyond where the jaguar was lying.

Without another thought I wheeled round and bolted down the path like a rabbit.

My little dug-out *piragua* still lay, tight and uninjured, upon the white pathway just above the pool. As I launched it, and pushed off, a white humming-bird suddenly poised itself in front of my face; and alone upon its snowy crest sat my tiny pink-headed master. This marvellous insect seemed to look me straight in the eyes for a few seconds, then he waved his unmutilated antenna in a friendly way, bobbed his Mephisthophelean visage, as if bidding me *bon voyage*, and whirred off into the forest.

I have no recollection as to how I descended the swollen rivulet; but a great shout greeted me as I swept out into the broad Jagara, and I saw several light canoes darting to meet me from the opposite bank. I was too dazed and idiotic to be surprised or to understand the speech of an aged white-haired Indian who took my *piragua* in tow and jabbered eagerly to me in Portuguese as he paddled across the rapid stream.

I was taken to an Indian village amid the forest on the farther bank, where I was nursed with the utmost kindness; but nearly a week passed before I could understand my aged rescuer, although I had acquired a fair knowledge of Portuguese. When I made my first attempt to give some account of my experiences, and told the old Indian about my cock-horned captive, who afterwards became my master, he crossed himself fervently.

"Ah, senhor!" he exclaimed with a shiver, "him I know well. Sixty years ago he was my master also. Ah, he is a great and terrible *piaché!* Surely he is the very devil!"

"What!" I cried, "have you also been a slave among the cavalier-ants?"

"Yes, senhor," replied he gravely. "When I was a youth they held me in bondage for two months: then they seemed to get tired of me, and gave me scarcely any food; and at last they dismissed me from their service. When your crew of the Buras came to my village and told me that you had ventured into that forbidden country and had not come back, I said, 'They will, perhaps, get tired of him also in about two months. Let us make a camp on the safe side of the Jagara and wait for him.'"

THE DREAM OF AKINOSUKE AND BUTTERFLIES

Lafcadio Hearn

Patrick Lafcadio Hearn (1850–1904) was born on the Ionian island of Lefkada to an Irish army surgeon and illiterate Greek mother whose marriage contract was annulled for lack of a signature. As a youth in Dublin, he was abandoned by both of his parents in turn and became the ward of his great-aunt, who sent him to a French Catholic school, then St Cuthbert's seminary in what is now Durham University. While there, a mishap caused an eye infection which permanently impaired his vision. Consequently, he always carried a magnifying glass, a tool with which he could inspect the minutiae of insect life. Aged nineteen he arrived moneyless in the United States where he worked as a reporter in Cincinnati and married an African-American woman. The union was deemed illegal for being in contravention of anti-miscegenation laws in Ohio. Hearn then transferred to New Orleans, Martinique, and finally to Japan where he married the daughter of a samurai, became a Japanese citizen and remained for the rest of his life.

In Japan, Hearn gathered material on local lore and eerie legends, inspiring his historically significant *Kwaidan: Stories and Studies of Strange Things*, from which "The Dream of Akinosuke" and "Butterflies" are taken. "The Dream of Akinosuke" essentially describes the interspecies marriage of man and ant. Weirdness consists in the manipulation of the ratio between human and insect, and the transposition of pre-industrial

Japanese culture to the ants' nest. The self-contained extract from "Butterflies" is taken from "Insect Studies" in *Kwaidan*, the other two insects subject to Hearn's philosophical contemplations being ants and mosquitoes. The legend tells of a butterfly soul travelling between realms to reunite lost lovers after death, both a weird conceit and an instance of positive, supernatural insect imagery.

THE DREAM OF AKINOSUKE

n the district called Toïchi of Yamato province, there used to live a gōshi named Miyata Akinosuké... [Here I must tell you that in Japanese feudal times there was a privileged class of soldier-farmers,—free-holders,—corresponding to the class of yeomen in England; and these were called gōshi.]

In Akinosuké's garden there was a great and ancient cedar-tree, under which he was wont to rest on sultry days. One very warm afternoon he was sitting under this tree with two of his friends, fellow-gōshi, chatting and drinking wine, when he felt all of a sudden very drowsy,—so drowsy that he begged his friends to excuse him for taking a nap in their presence. Then he lay down at the foot of the tree, and dreamed this dream:—

He thought that as he was lying there in his garden, he saw a procession, like the train of some great daimyō, descending a hill near by, and that he got up to look at it. A very grand procession it proved to be,—more imposing than anything of the kind which he had ever seen before; and it was advancing toward his dwelling. He observed in the van of it a number of young men richly apparelled, who were drawing a great lacquered palace-carriage, or *gosho-guruma*, hung with bright blue silk. When the procession arrived within a short distance of the house it halted; and a richly dressed man—evidently a person of rank—advanced from it, approached Akinosuké, bowed to him profoundly, and then said:—

"Honoured Sir, you see before you a *kérai* [vassal] of the Kokuō

141

of Tokoyo.* My master, the King, commands me to greet you in his august name, and to place myself wholly at your disposal. He also bids me inform you that he augustly desires your presence at the palace. Be therefore pleased immediately to enter this honourable carriage, which he has sent for your conveyance."

Upon hearing these words Akinosuké wanted to make some fitting reply; but he was too much astonished and embarrassed for speech;—and in the same moment his will seemed to melt away from him, so that he could only do as the *kérai* bade him. He entered the carriage; the *kérai* took a place beside him, and made a signal; the drawers, seizing the silken ropes, turned the great vehicle southward;—and the journey began.

In a very short time, to Akinosuké's amazement, the carriage stopped in front of a huge two-storeyed gateway (*rōmon*), of Chinese style, which he had never before seen. Here the *kérai* dismounted, saying, "I go to announce the honourable arrival,"—and he disappeared. After some little waiting, Akinosuké saw two noble-looking men, wearing robes of purple silk and high caps of the form indicating lofty rank, come from the gateway. These, after having respectfully saluted him, helped him to descend from the carriage, and led him through the great gate and across a vast garden, to the entrance of a palace whose front appeared to extend, west and east, to a distance of miles. Akinosuké was then shown into a reception-room of wonderful size and splendour. His guides conducted him to the

---

* This name "Tokoyo" is indefinite. According to circumstances it may signify any unknown country,—or that undiscovered country from whose bourn no traveller returns,—or that Fairyland of far-eastern fable, the Realm of Hōrai. The term "Kokuō" means the ruler of a country,—therefore a king. The original phrase, *Tokoyo no Kokuō*, might be rendered here as "the Ruler of Hōrai," or "the King of Fairyland."

place of honour, and respectfully seated themselves apart; while serving-maids, in costume of ceremony, brought refreshments. When Akinosuké had partaken of the refreshments, the two purple-robed attendants bowed low before him, and addressed him in the following words,—each speaking alternately, according to the etiquette of courts:—

"It is now our honourable duty to inform you... as to the reason of your having been summoned hither... Our master, the King, augustly desires that you become his son-in-law;... and it is his wish and command that you shall wed this very day... the August Princess, his maiden-daughter... We shall soon conduct you to the presence-chamber... where His Augustness even now is waiting to receive you... But it will be necessary that we first invest you... with the appropriate garments of ceremony."*

Having thus spoken, the attendants rose together, and proceeded to an alcove containing a great chest of gold lacquer. They opened the chest, and took from it various robes and girdles of rich material, and a *kamuri*, or regal headdress. With these they attired Akinosuké as befitted a princely bridegroom; and he was then conducted to the presence-room, where he saw the Kokuō of Tokoyo seated upon the *daiza*,† wearing the high black cap of state, and robed in robes of yellow silk. Before the *daiza*, to left and right, a multitude of dignitaries sat in rank, motionless and splendid as images in a temple; and Akinosuké, advancing into their midst, saluted the king with the

---

* The last phrase, according to old custom, had to be uttered by both attendants at the same time. All these ceremonial observances can still be studied on the Japanese stage.

† This was the name given to the estrade, or dais, upon which a feudal prince or ruler sat in state. The term literally signifies "great seat."

triple prostration of usage. The king greeted him with gracious words, and then said:—

"You have already been informed as to the reason of your having been summoned to Our presence. We have decided that you shall become the adopted husband of Our only daughter;—and the wedding ceremony shall now be performed."

As the king finished speaking, a sound of joyful music was heard; and a long train of beautiful court ladies advanced from behind a curtain, to conduct Akinosuké to the room in which his bride awaited him.

The room was immense; but it could scarcely contain the multitude of guests assembled to witness the wedding ceremony. All bowed down before Akinosuké as he took his place, facing the King's daughter, on the kneeling-cushion prepared for him. As a maiden of heaven the bride appeared to be; and her robes were beautiful as a summer sky. And the marriage was performed amid great rejoicing.

Afterwards the pair were conducted to a suite of apartments that had been prepared for them in another portion of the palace; and there they received the congratulations of many noble persons, and wedding gifts beyond counting.

Some days later Akinosuké was again summoned to the throne-room. On this occasion he was received even more graciously than before; and the King said to him:—

"In the southwestern part of Our dominion there is an island called Raishū. We have now appointed you Governor of that island. You will find the people loyal and docile; but their laws have not yet been brought into proper accord with the laws of Tokoyo; and their customs have not been properly regulated. We entrust you with the duty of improving their social condition as far as may be possible; and We desire that you shall rule them with kindness and wisdom.

All preparations necessary for your journey to Raishū have already been made."

So Akinosuké and his bride departed from the palace of Tokoyo, accompanied to the shore by a great escort of nobles and officials; and they embarked upon a ship of state provided by the king. And with favouring winds they safely sailed to Raishū, and found the good people of that island assembled upon the beach to welcome them.

Akinosuké entered at once upon his new duties; and they did not prove to be hard. During the first three years of his governorship he was occupied chiefly with the framing and the enactment of laws; but he had wise counsellors to help him, and he never found the work unpleasant. When it was all finished, he had no active duties to perform, beyond attending the rites and ceremonies ordained by ancient custom. The country was so healthy and so fertile that sickness and want were unknown; and the people were so good that no laws were ever broken. And Akinosuké dwelt and ruled in Raishū for twenty years more,—making in all twenty-three years of sojourn, during which no shadow of sorrow traversed his life.

But in the twenty-fourth year of his governorship, a great misfortune came upon him; for his wife, who had borne him seven children,—five boys and two girls,—fell sick and died. She was buried, with high pomp, on the summit of a beautiful hill in the district of Hanryōkō; and a monument, exceedingly splendid, was placed above her grave. But Akinosuké felt such grief at her death that he no longer cared to live.

Now when the legal period of mourning was over, there came to Raishū, from the Tokoyo palace, a *shisha*, or royal messenger. The *shisha* delivered to Akinosuké a message of condolence, and then said to him:—

"These are the words which our august master, the King of Tokoyo, commands that I repeat to you: 'We will now send you back to your own people and country. As for the seven children, they are the grandsons and the granddaughters of the King, and shall be fitly cared for. Do not, therefore, allow your mind to be troubled concerning them.'"

On receiving this mandate, Akinosuké submissively prepared for his departure. When all his affairs had been settled, and the ceremony of bidding farewell to his counsellors and trusted officials had been concluded, he was escorted with much honour to the port. There he embarked upon the ship sent for him; and the ship sailed out into the blue sea, under the blue sky; and the shape of the island of Raishū itself turned blue, and then turned grey, and then vanished forever... And Akinosuké suddenly awoke—under the cedar-tree in his own garden!...

For the moment he was stupefied and dazed. But he perceived his two friends still seated near him,—drinking and chatting merrily. He stared at them in a bewildered way, and cried aloud,—

"How strange!"

"Akinosuké must have been dreaming," one of them exclaimed, with a laugh. "What did you see, Akinosuké, that was strange?"

Then Akinosuké told his dream,—that dream of three-and-twenty years' sojourn in the realm of Tokoyo, in the island of Raishū;—and they were astonished, because he had really slept for no more than a few minutes.

One gōshi said:—

"Indeed, you saw strange things. We also saw something strange while you were napping. A little yellow butterfly was fluttering over

146

your face for a moment or two; and we watched it. Then it alighted on the ground beside you, close to the tree; and almost as soon as it alighted there, a big, big ant came out of a hole, and seized it and pulled it down into the hole. Just before you woke up, we saw that very butterfly come out of the hole again, and flutter over your face as before. And then it suddenly disappeared: we do not know where it went."

"Perhaps it was Akinosuké's soul," the other gōshi said;—"certainly I thought I saw it fly into his mouth... But, even if that butterfly *was* Akinosuké's soul, the fact would not explain his dream."

"The ants might explain it," returned the first speaker. "Ants are queer beings—possibly goblins... Anyhow, there is a big ant's nest under that cedar-tree.":...

"Let us look!" cried Akinosuké, greatly moved by this suggestion. And he went for a spade.

The ground about and beneath the cedar-tree proved to have been excavated, in a most surprising way, by a prodigious colony of ants. The ants had furthermore built inside their excavations; and their tiny constructions of straw, clay, and stems bore an odd resemblance to miniature towns. In the middle of a structure considerably larger than the rest there was a marvellous swarming of small ants around the body of one very big ant, which had yellowish wings and a long black head.

"Why, there is the King of my dream!" cried Akinosuké; "and there is the palace of Tokoyo!... How extraordinary!... Raishū ought to lie somewhere southwest of it—to the left of that big root... Yes!—here it is!... How very strange! Now I am sure that I can find the mountain of Hanryōkō, and the grave of the princess.":...

In the wreck of the nest he searched and searched, and at

last discovered a tiny mound, on the top of which was fixed a water-worn pebble, in shape resembling a Buddhist monument. Underneath it he found—embedded in clay—the dead body of a female ant.

BUTTERFLIES

ost of the Japanese stories about butterflies appear, as I have said, to be of Chinese origin. But I have one which is probably indigenous; and it seems to me worth telling for the benefit of persons who believe that there is no "romantic love" in the Far East.

Behind the cemetery of the temple of Sōzanji, in the suburbs of the capital, there long stood a solitary cottage, occupied by an old man named Takahama. He was liked in the neighbourhood, by reason of his amiable ways; but almost everybody supposed him to be a little mad. Unless a man take the Buddhist vows, he is expected to marry, and to bring up a family. But Takahama did not belong to the religious life; and he could not be persuaded to marry. Neither had he ever been known to enter into a love-relation with any woman. For more than fifty years he had lived entirely alone.

One summer he fell sick, and knew that he had not long to live. He then sent for his sister-in-law, a widow, and for her only son,—a lad of about twenty years old, to whom he was much attached. Both promptly came, and did whatever they could to soothe the old man's last hours.

One sultry afternoon, while the widow and her son were watching at his bedside, Takahama fell asleep. At the same moment a very large white butterfly entered the room, and perched upon the sick man's pillow. The nephew drove it away with a fan; but it returned immediately to the pillow, and was again driven away, only to come back a third time. Then the nephew chased it into the garden, and across the garden, through an open gate, into the cemetery of the neighbouring temple. But it continued to flutter before him as if unwilling to be driven further, and acted so queerly that he began to wonder whether it was really a butterfly, or a *ma.*[*] He again chased it, and followed it far into the cemetery, until he saw it fly against a tomb,—a woman's tomb. There it unaccountably disappeared; and he searched for it in vain. He then examined the monument. It bore the personal name "Akiko," together with an unfamiliar family name, and an inscription stating that Akiko had died at the age of eighteen. Apparently the tomb had been erected about fifty years previously: moss had begun to gather upon it. But it had been well cared for: there were fresh flowers before it; and the water-tank had recently been filled.

On returning to the sick room, the young man was shocked by the announcement that his uncle had ceased to breathe. Death had come to the sleeper painlessly; and the dead face smiled.

The young man told his mother of what he had seen in the cemetery.

"Ah!" exclaimed the widow, "then it must have been Akiko!"...

"But who was Akiko, mother?" the nephew asked.

The widow answered:—

"When your good uncle was young he was betrothed to a charming girl called Akiko, the daughter of a neighbour. Akiko died of consumption, only a little before the day appointed for the wedding; and her promised husband sorrowed greatly. After Akiko had been buried, he made a vow never to marry; and he built this little house

---

[*]   An evil spirit.

beside the cemetery, so that he might be always near her grave. All this happened more than fifty years ago. And every day of those fifty years—winter and summer alike—your uncle went to the cemetery, and prayed at the grave, and swept the tomb, and set offerings before it. But he did not like to have any mention made of the matter; and he never spoke of it... So, at last, Akiko came for him: the white butterfly was her soul."

CATERPILLARS

E. F. Benson

Edward Frederic Benson (1867–1940) was the fifth of six children. His parents were Edward Benson, headmaster of Wellington College, later Archbishop of Canterbury, and Mary (Minnie) Sidgwick. Minnie, younger sister of the moral philosopher, Henry Sidgwick, was described by the Prime Minister, William Gladstone as "the cleverest woman in Europe". Her talented children inherited her intelligence, as well as her defiance of heterosexual constraints. Benson was educated at Marlborough and Kings College Cambridge where he became a member of the Chit-Chat club at which M. R. James would read ghostly stories by candlelight. In the wake of the trials of Oscar Wilde, he shared a villa in Capri with the aesthete, John Ellingham Brooks. Benson was a prolific and versatile writer in multiple genres including biography, the atmospheric ghost story, humorous novel, children's literature, and skating short story. He was an athletic man and represented England at figure skating.

Benson is most widely known for the lightly satiric "Mapp and Lucia" series, in which the esoteric character of Emmeline (Lucia) Mapp is said to be a spoof of the top-selling novelist Marie Corelli. "Caterpillars" comes earlier in his writing career and was published in *The Room in the Tower and Other Stories* (1912) by Mills & Boon before the firm began specializing in romance fiction. It clearly takes inspiration from Benson's time on Capri as it is a first-person narrative of an encounter with supernatural insects occupying an Italian villa like an infestation. These crab-footed, large and faintly luminous caterpillars are unusual in our anthology in being insects still in their larval stage. Unnerving as they are as a host of crawling grubs, a further part of their menace consists in what they may metamorphose into.

saw a month or two ago in an Italian paper that the Villa Cascana, in which I once stayed, had been pulled down, and that a manufactory of some sort was in process of erection on its site. There is therefore no longer any reason for refraining from writing of those things which I myself saw (or imagined I saw) in a certain room and on a certain landing of the villa in question, nor from mentioning the circumstances which followed, which may or may not (according to the opinion of the reader) throw some light on or be somehow connected with this experience.

The Villa Cascana was in all ways but one a perfectly delightful house, yet, if it were standing now, nothing in the world—I use the phrase in its literal sense—would induce me to set foot in it again, for I believe it to have been haunted in a very terrible and practical manner. Most ghosts, when all is said and done, do not do much harm; they may perhaps terrify, but the person whom they visit usually gets over their visitation. They may on the other hand be entirely friendly and beneficent. But the appearances in the Villa Cascana were not beneficent, and had they made their "visit" in a very slightly different manner, I do not suppose I should have got over it any more than Arthur Inglis did.

The house stood on an ilex-clad hill not far from Sestri di Levante on the Italian Riviera, looking out over the iridescent blues of that enchanted sea, while behind it rose the pale green chestnut woods that climb up the hillsides till they give place to the pines that, black in contrast with them, crown the slopes. All round it the garden in the luxuriance of mid-spring bloomed and was fragrant, and the scent of magnolia and rose, borne on the salt freshness of the winds from the sea, flowed like a stream through the cool vaulted rooms.

On the ground floor a broad pillared *loggia* ran round three sides of the house, the top of which formed a balcony for certain rooms of the first floor. The main staircase, broad and of grey marble steps, led up from the hall to the landing outside these rooms, which were three in number, namely two big sitting-rooms and a bedroom arranged *en suite*. The latter was unoccupied, the sitting-rooms were in use. From these the main staircase was continued to the second floor, where were situated certain bedrooms, one of which I occupied, while from the other side of the first-floor landing some half-dozen steps led to another suite of rooms, where, at the time I am speaking of, Arthur Inglis, the artist, had his bedroom and studio. Thus the landing outside my bedroom at the top of the house, commanded both the landing of the first floor, and also the steps that led to Inglis' rooms. Jim Stanley and his wife, finally (whose guest I was), occupied rooms in another wing of the house, where also were the servants' quarters.

I arrived just in time for lunch on a brilliant noon of mid-May. The garden was shouting with colour and fragrance, and not less delightful after my broiling walk up from the *marina*, should have been the coming from the reverberating heat and blaze of the day into the marble coolness of the villa. Only (the reader has my bare word for this, and nothing more), the moment I set foot in the house I felt that something was wrong. This feeling, I may say, was quite vague, though very strong, and I remember that when I saw letters waiting for me on the table in the hall I felt certain that the explanation was here: I was convinced that there was bad news of some sort for me. Yet when I opened them I found no such explanation of my premonition: my correspondents all reeked of prosperity. Yet this clear miscarriage of a presentiment did not dissipate my uneasiness. In that cool fragrant house there was something wrong.

I am at pains to mention this because to the general view it may explain that though I am as a rule so excellent a sleeper that the extinction of my light on getting into bed is apparently contemporaneous with being called on the following morning, I slept very badly on my first night in the Villa Cascana. It may also explain the fact that when I did sleep (if it was indeed in sleep that I saw what I thought I saw) I dreamed in a very vivid and original manner, original, that is to say, in the sense that something that, as far as I knew, had never previously entered into my consciousness, usurped it then. But since, in addition to this evil premonition, certain words and events occurring during the rest of the day, might have suggested something of what I thought happened that night, it will be well to relate them.

After lunch, then, I went round the house with Mrs Stanley, and during our tour she referred, it is true, to the unoccupied bedroom on the first floor, which opened out of the room where we had lunched.

"We left that unoccupied," she said, "because Jim and I have a charming bedroom and dressing-room, as you saw, in the wing, and if we used it ourselves we should have to turn the dining-room into a dressing-room and have our meals downstairs. As it is, however, we have our little flat there, Arthur Inglis has his little flat in the other passage; and I remembered (aren't I extraordinary?) that you once said that the higher up you were in a house the better you were pleased. So I put you at the top of the house, instead of giving you that room."

It is true, that a doubt, vague as my uneasy premonition, crossed my mind at this. I did not see why Mrs Stanley should have explained all this, if there had not been more to explain. I allow, therefore, that the thought that there was something to explain about the unoccupied bedroom was momentarily present to my mind.

The second thing that may have borne on my dream was this.

At dinner the conversation turned for a moment on ghosts. Inglis, with the certainty of conviction, expressed his belief that anybody who could possibly believe in the existence of supernatural phenomena was unworthy of the name of an ass. The subject instantly dropped. As far as I can recollect, nothing else occurred or was said that could bear on what follows.

We all went to bed rather early, and personally I yawned my way upstairs, feeling hideously sleepy. My room was rather hot, and I threw all the windows wide, and from without poured in the white light of the moon, and the love-song of many nightingales. I undressed quickly, and got into bed, but though I had felt so sleepy before, I now felt extremely wide-awake. But I was quite content to be awake: I did not toss or turn, I felt perfectly happy listening to the song and seeing the light. Then, it is possible, I may have gone to sleep, and what follows may have been a dream. I thought anyhow that after a time the nightingales ceased singing and the moon sank. I thought also that if, for some unexplained reason, I was going to lie awake all night, I might as well read, and I remembered that I had left a book in which I was interested in the dining-room on the first floor. So I got out of bed, lit a candle, and went downstairs. I went into the room, saw on a side-table the book I had come to look for, and then, simultaneously, saw that the door into the unoccupied bedroom was open. A curious grey light, not of dawn nor of moonshine, came out of it, and I looked in. The bed stood just opposite the door, a big four-poster, hung with tapestry at the head. Then I saw that the greyish light of the bedroom came from the bed, or rather from what was on the bed. For it was covered with great caterpillars, a foot or more in length, which crawled over it. They were faintly luminous, and it was the light from them that showed me the room. Instead of the sucker-feet of ordinary caterpillars they had rows of pincers like crabs, and they moved by grasping what they lay on with their pincers, and then sliding their bodies forward. In colour these dreadful insects were yellowish-grey, and they were covered with irregular lumps and swellings. There must have been hundreds of them, for they formed a sort of writhing, crawling pyramid on the bed. Occasionally one fell off on to the floor, with a soft fleshy thud, and though the floor was of hard concrete, it yielded to the pincer-feet as if it had been putty, and, crawling back, the caterpillar would mount on to the bed again, to rejoin its fearful companions. They appeared to have no faces, so to speak, but at one end of them there was a mouth that opened sideways in respiration.

Then, as I looked, it seemed to me as if they all suddenly became conscious of my presence. All the mouths at any rate were turned in my direction, and next moment they began dropping off the bed with those soft fleshy thuds on to the floor, and wriggling towards me. For one second a paralysis as of a dream was on me, but the next I was running upstairs again to my room, and I remember feeling the cold of the marble steps on my bare feet. I rushed into my bedroom, and slammed the door behind me, and then—I was certainly wide awake now—I found myself standing by my bed with the sweat of terror pouring from me. The noise of the banged door still rang in my ears. But, as would have been more usual, if this had been mere nightmare, the terror that had been mine when I saw those foul beasts crawling about the bed or dropping softly on to the floor did not cease then. Awake now, if dreaming before, I did not at all recover from the horror of dream: it did not seem to me that I had dreamed. And until dawn, I sat or stood, not daring to lie down, thinking that every rustle or movement that I heard was the approach of the caterpillars. To them and the claws that bit into the cement the wood of the door was child's play: steel would not keep them out.

But with the sweet and noble return of day the horror vanished: the whisper of wind became benignant again: the nameless fear, whatever it was, was smoothed out and terrified me no longer. Dawn broke, hueless at first; then it grew dove-coloured, then the flaming pageant of light spread over the sky.

The admirable rule of the house was that everybody had breakfast where and when he pleased, and in consequence it was not till lunch-time that I met any of the other members of our party, since I had breakfast on my balcony, and wrote letters and other things till lunch. In fact, I got down to that meal rather late, after the other three had begun. Between my knife and fork there was a small pill-box of cardboard, and as I sat down Inglis spoke.

"Do look at that," he said, "since you are interested in natural history. I found it crawling on my counterpane last night, and I don't know what it is."

I think that before I opened the pill-box I expected something of the sort which I found in it. Inside it, anyhow, was a small caterpillar, greyish-yellow in colour, with curious bumps and excrescences on its rings. It was extremely active, and hurried round the box, this way and that. Its feet were unlike the feet of any caterpillar I ever saw: they were like the pincers of a crab. I looked, and shut the lid down again.

"No, I don't know it," I said, "but it looks rather unwholesome. What are you going to do with it?"

"Oh, I shall keep it," said Inglis. "It has begun to spin: I want to see what sort of a moth it turns into."

I opened the box again, and saw that these hurrying movements were indeed the beginning of the spinning of the web of its cocoon. Then Inglis spoke again.

"It has got funny feet, too," he said. "They are like crabs' pincers. What's the Latin for crab? Oh, yes, Cancer. So in case it is unique, let's christen it: 'Cancer Inglisensis.'"

Then something happened in my brain, some momentary piecing together of all that I had seen or dreamed. Something in his words seemed to me to throw light on it all, and my own intense horror at the experience of the night before linked itself on to what he had just said. In effect, I took the box and threw it, caterpillar and all, out of the window. There was a gravel path just outside, and beyond it, a fountain playing into a basin. The box fell on to the middle of this.

Inglis laughed.

"So the students of the occult don't like solid facts," he said. "My poor caterpillar!"

The talk went off again at once on to other subjects, and I have only given in detail, as they happened, these trivialities in order to be sure myself that I have recorded everything that could have borne on occult subjects or on the subject of caterpillars. But at the moment when I threw the pill-box into the fountain, I lost my head: my only excuse is that, as is probably plain, the tenant of it was, in miniature, exactly what I had seen crowded on to the bed in the unoccupied room. And though this translation of those phantoms into flesh and blood—or whatever it is that caterpillars are made of—ought perhaps to have relieved the horror of the night, as a matter of fact it did nothing of the kind. It only made the crawling pyramid that covered the bed in the unoccupied room more hideously real.

After lunch we spent a lazy hour or two strolling about the garden or sitting in the loggia, and it must have been about four o'clock when Stanley and I started off to bathe, down the path that led by the fountain into which I had thrown the pill-box. The water was shallow and clear, and at the bottom of it I saw its white remains. The water had disintegrated the cardboard, and it had become no more than a few strips and shreds of sodden paper. The centre of the fountain was a marble Italian Cupid which squirted the water out of a wine-skin held under its arm. And crawling up its leg was the caterpillar. Strange and scarcely credible as it seemed, it must have survived the falling-to-bits of its prison, and made its way to shore, and there it was, out of arm's reach, weaving and waving this way and that as it evolved its cocoon.

Then, as I looked at it, it seemed to me again that, like the cater-pillar I had seen last night, it saw me, and breaking out of the threads that surrounded it, it crawled down the marble leg of the Cupid and began swimming like a snake across the water of the fountain towards me. It came with extraordinary speed (the fact of a caterpillar being able to swim was new to me), and in another moment was crawling up the marble lip of the basin. Just then Inglis joined us.

"Why, if it isn't old 'Cancer Inglisensis' again," he said, catching sight of the beast. "What a tearing hurry it is in."

We were standing side by side on the path, and when the caterpil-lar had advanced to within about a yard of us, it stopped, and began waving again, as if in doubt as to the direction in which it should go. Then it appeared to make up its mind, and crawled on to Inglis' shoe.

"It likes me best," he said, "but I don't really know that I like it. And as it won't drown I think perhaps—"

He shook it off his shoe on to the gravel path and trod on it.

All afternoon the air got heavier and heavier with the Sirocco that was without doubt coming up from the south, and that night again I went up to bed feeling very sleepy; but below my drowsiness, so to speak, there was the consciousness, stronger than before, that there was something wrong in the house, that something dangerous was close at hand. But I fell asleep at once, and—how long after I do not know—either woke or dreamed I awoke, feeling that I must get up at once, *or I should be too late*. Then (dreaming or awake) I lay and fought this fear, telling myself that I was but the prey of my own nerves disordered by Sirocco or what not, and at the same time quite clearly knowing in another part of my mind, so to speak, that every moment's delay added to the danger. At last this second feeling became irresistible, and I put on coat and trousers and went out of my room on to the landing. And then I saw that I had already delayed too long, and that I was now too late.

The whole of the landing of the first floor below was invisible under the swarm of caterpillars that crawled there. The folding doors into the sitting-room from which opened the bedroom where I had seen them last night, were shut, but they were squeezing through the cracks of it, and dropping one by one through the keyhole, elongating themselves into mere string as they passed, and growing fat and lumpy again on emerging. Some, as if exploring, were nosing about the steps into the passage at the end of which were Inglis' rooms, others were crawling on the lowest steps of the staircase that led up to where I stood. The landing, however, was completely covered with them: I was cut off. And of the frozen horror that seized me when I saw that, I can give no idea in words.

Then at last a general movement began to take place, and they grew thicker on the steps that led to Inglis' room. Gradually, like some hideous tide of flesh, they advanced along the passage, and I saw the foremost, visible by the pale grey luminousness that came from them, reach his door. Again and again I tried to shout and warn him, in terror all the time that they would turn at the sound of my voice and mount my stair instead, but for all my efforts I felt that no sound came from my throat. They crawled along the hinge-crack of his door, passing through as they had done before, and still I stood there making impotent efforts to shout to him, to bid him escape while there was time.

At last the passage was completely empty: they had all gone, and at that moment I was conscious for the first time of the cold of the marble landing on which I stood barefooted. The dawn was just beginning to break in the Eastern sky.

Six months later I met Mrs Stanley in a country house in England. We talked on many subjects and at last she said:

"I don't think I have seen you since I got that dreadful news about Arthur Inglis a month ago."

"I haven't heard," said I.

"No? He has got cancer. They don't even advise an operation, for there is no hope of a cure: he is riddled with it, the doctors say."

Now during all these six months I do not think a day had passed on which I had not had in my mind the dreams (or whatever you like to call them) which I had seen in the Villa Cascana.

"It is awful, is it not?" she continued, "and I feel, I can't help feeling, that he may have—"

"Caught it at the villa?" I asked.

She looked at me in blank surprise.

"Why did you say that?" she asked. "How did you know?"

Then she told me. In the unoccupied bedroom a year before there had been a fatal case of cancer. She had, of course, taken the best advice and had been told that the utmost dictates of prudence would be obeyed so long as she did not put anybody to sleep in the room, which had also been thoroughly disinfected and newly white-washed and painted. But—

AN EGYPTIAN HORNET

Algernon Blackwood

Algernon Henry Blackwood (1869–1951) was born in Kent and educated at Wellington College. His home life was characterized by
his father's repressive Evangelicalism, which Blackwood shunned in
favour of Buddhism, occultism and theosophical pantheism. He had a
chequered career which encompassed working as a dairy farmer and
hotelier in Canada, bartender, model and violin teacher in New York,
and journalist for the *New York Times*. On returning to England, he
began writing ghost or occult stories which he would subsequently
narrate on the radio, and during the First World War he worked
as an undercover agent. He was a member of The Ghost Club and
The Hermetic Order of the Golden Dawn along with his contemporary, the author of fantasy and supernatural horror, Arthur Machen.
Blackwood's short story collection, *Incredible Adventures* (1914) was
heralded as a prime example of the weird, and the exquisite detail
with which he creates an oddly unnerving atmosphere is evident in
"An Egyptian Hornet" published the year afterwards.

"An Egyptian Hornet" is a whimsical tale first published in the
popular American Midwest publication, *Reedy's Mirror* (19 March 1915)
and again in *Day and Night Stories* (1917). It is a third person anecdote
about the Reverend James Milligan's bathroom encounter with a
"formidable insect" which has the potential for extreme aggression.
In the mundane, domestic space where Milligan performs his most
personal acts, something of a battle of wills takes place between the

naked man and the huge hornet as each sizes the other up. Violation is ever imminent, and much of the weirdness of the insect lies in the anthropomorphized view of it as evil by the religious man.

he word has an angry, malignant sound that brings the idea of attack vividly into the mind. There is a vicious sting about it somewhere—even a foreigner, ignorant of the meaning, must feel it. A hornet is wicked; it darts and stabs; it pierces, aiming without provocation for the face and eyes. The name suggests a metallic droning of evil wings, fierce flight, and poisonous assault. Though black and yellow, it sounds scarlet. There is blood in it. A striped tiger of the air in concentrated form! There is no escape—if it attacks.

In Egypt an ordinary bee is the size of an English hornet, but the Egyptian hornet is enormous. It is truly monstrous—an ominous, dying terror. It shares that universal quality of the land of the Sphinx and Pyramids—great size. It is a formidable insect, worse than scorpion or tarantula. The Rev. James Milligan, meeting one for the first time, realized the meaning of another word as well, a word he used prolifically in his eloquent sermons—devil.

One morning in April, when the heat began to bring the insects out, he rose as usual betimes and went across the wide stone corridor to his bath. The desert already glared in through the open windows. The heat would be afflicting later in the day, but at this early hour the cool north wind blew pleasantly down the hotel passages. It was Sunday, and at half-past eight o'clock he would appear to conduct the morning service for the English visitors. The floor of the passage-way was cold beneath his feet in their thin native slippers of bright yellow. He was neither young nor old; his salary was comfortable; he had a competency of his own, without wife or children to absorb it; the dry climate had been recommended to him; and—the big hotel took him in for next to nothing. And he was thoroughly pleased with himself, for he was a sleek, vain, pompous, well-advertised personality, but mean as a rat. No worries of any kind were on his mind as, carrying sponge and towel, scented soap and a bottle of Scrubb's ammonia, he travelled amiably across the deserted, shining corridor to the bathroom. And nothing went wrong with the Rev. James Milligan until he opened the door, and his eye fell upon a dark, suspicious-looking object clinging to the window-pane in front of him.

And even then, at first, he felt no anxiety or alarm, but merely a natural curiosity to know exactly what it was—this little clot of an odd-shaped, elongated thing that stuck there on the wooden frame-work six feet before his aquiline nose. He went straight up to it to see—then stopped dead. His heart gave a distinct, unclerical leap. His lips formed themselves into unregenerate shape. He gasped: "Good God! What is it?" For something unholy, something wicked as a secret sin, stuck there before his eyes in the patch of blazing sunshine. He caught his breath.

For a moment he was unable to move, as though the sight half fascinated him. Then, cautiously and very slowly—stealthily, in fact—he withdrew towards the door he had just entered. Fearful of making the smallest sound, he retraced his steps on tiptoe. His yellow slippers shuffled. His dry sponge fell, and bounded till it settled, rolling close beneath the horribly attractive object facing him. From the safety of the open door, with ample space for retreat behind him, he paused and stared. His entire being focused itself in his eyes. It was a hornet that he saw. It hung there, motionless and threatening, between him and the bathroom door. And at first he merely exclaimed—below his breath—"Good God! It's an Egyptian hornet!"

Being a man with a reputation for decided action, however, he soon recovered himself. He was well schooled in self-control. When people left his church at the beginning of the sermon, no muscle of his face betrayed the wounded vanity and annoyance that burned deep in his heart. But a hornet sitting directly in his path was a very different matter. He realized in a flash that he was poorly clothed—in a word, that he was practically half naked.

From a distance he examined this intrusion of the devil. It was calm and very still. It was wonderfully made, both before and behind. Its wings were folded upon its terrible body. Long, sinuous things, pointed like temptation, barbed as well, stuck out of it. There was poison, and yet grace, in its exquisite presentment. Its shiny black was beautiful, and the yellow stripes upon its sleek, curved abdomen were like the gleaming ornaments upon some feminine body of the seductive world he preached against. Almost, he saw an abandoned dancer on the stage. And then, swiftly in his impressionable soul, the simile changed, and he saw instead more blunt and aggressive forms of destruction. The well-filled body, tapering to a horrid point, reminded him of those perfect engines of death that reduce hundreds to annihilation unawares—torpedoes, shells, projectiles, crammed with secret, desolating powers. Its wings, its awful, quiet head, its delicate, slim waist, its stripes of brilliant saffron—all these seemed the concentrated prototype of abominations made cleverly by the brain of man, and beautifully painted to disguise their invisible freight of cruel death.

"Bah!" he exclaimed, ashamed of his prolific imagination. "It's only a hornet after all—an insect!" And he contrived a hurried, careful plan. He aimed a towel at it, rolled up into a ball—but did not throw it. He might miss. He remembered that his ankles were unprotected. Instead, he paused again, examining the black and yellow object in safe retirement near the door, as one day he hoped to watch the world in leisurely retirement in the country. It did not move. It was fixed and terrible. It made no sound. Its wings were folded. Not even the black antennæ, blunt at the tips like clubs, showed the least stir or tremble. It breathed, however. He watched the rise and fall of the evil body; it breathed air in and out as he himself did. The creature, he realized, had lungs and heart and organs. It had a brain! Its mind was active all this time. It knew it was being watched. It merely waited. Any second, with a whiz of fury, and with perfect accuracy of aim, it might dart at him and strike. If he threw the towel and missed—it certainly would.

There were other occupants of the corridor, however, and a sound of steps approaching gave him the decision to act. He would lose his bath if he hesitated much longer. He felt ashamed of his timidity, though "pusillanimity" was the word thought selected owing to the pulpit vocabulary it was his habit to prefer. He went with extreme caution towards the bathroom door, passing the point of danger so close that his skin turned hot and cold. With one foot gingerly extended, he recovered his sponge. The hornet did not move a muscle. But—it had seen him pass. It merely waited. All dangerous insects had that trick. It knew quite well he was inside; it knew quite well he must come out a few minutes later; it also knew quite well that he was—naked.

Once inside the little room, he closed the door with exceeding gentleness, lest the vibration might stir the fearful insect to attack. The bath was already filled, and he plunged to his neck with a feeling of comparative security. A window into the outside passage he also closed, so that nothing could possibly come in. And steam soon charged the air and left its blurred deposit on the glass. For ten minutes he could enjoy himself and pretend that he was safe. For ten minutes he did so. He behaved carelessly, as though nothing mattered, and as though all the courage in the world were his. He splashed and soaped and sponged, making a lot of reckless noise. He got out and dried himself. Slowly the steam subsided, the air grew clearer, he put on dressing-gown and slippers. It was time to go out.

Unable to devise any further reason for delay, he opened the door softly half an inch—peeped out—and instantly closed it again with a resounding bang. He had heard a drone of wings. The insect had left its perch and now buzzed upon the floor directly in his path. The air seemed full of stings: he felt stabs all over him; his unprotected portions winced with the expectancy of pain. The beast knew he was coming out, and was waiting for him. In that brief instant he had felt its sting all over him, on his unprotected ankles, on his back, his neck, his cheeks, in his eyes, and on the bald clearing that adorned his Anglican head. Through the closed door he heard the ominous, dull murmur of his striped adversary as it beat its angry wings. Its oiled and wicked sting shot in and out with fury. Its deft legs worked. He saw its tiny waist already writhing with the lust of battle. Ugh! That tiny waist! A moment's steady nerve and he could have severed that cunning body from the directing brain with one swift, well-directed thrust. But his nerve had utterly deserted him.

Human motives, even in the professedly holy, are an involved affair at any time. Just now, in the Rev. James Milligan, they were quite inextricably mixed. He claims this explanation, at any rate, in excuse of his abominable subsequent behaviour. For, exactly at this moment, when he had decided to admit cowardice by ringing for the Arab servant, a step was audible in the corridor outside, and courage came with it into his disreputable heart. It was the step of the man he cordially "disapproved of," using the pulpit version of "hated and despised." He had overstayed his time, and the bath was in demand by Mr Mullins. Mr Mullins invariably followed him at seven-thirty; it was now a quarter to eight. And Mr Mullins was a wretched drinking man—"a sot."

In a flash the plan was conceived and put into execution. The temptation, of course, was of the devil. Mr Milligan hid the motive from himself, pretending he hardly recognized it. The plan was what men call a dirty trick; it was also irresistibly seductive. He opened the door, stepped boldly, nose in the air, right over the hideous insect on the floor, and fairly pranced into the outer passage. The brief transit brought a hundred horrible sensations—that the hornet would rise and sting his leg, that it would cling to his dressing-gown and stab his spine, that he would step upon it and die, like Achilles, of a heel exposed. But with these, and conquering them, was one other stronger emotion that robbed the lesser terrors of their potency—that Mr Mullins would run precisely the same risks five seconds later, unprepared. He heard the gloating insect buzz and scratch the oilcloth. But it was behind him. *He* was safe!

"Good morning to you, Mr Mullins," he observed with a gracious smile. "I trust I have not kept you waiting."

"Mornin'!" grunted Mullins sourly in reply, as he passed him with a distinctly hostile and contemptuous air. For Mullins, though depraved, perhaps, was an honest man, abhorring parsons and making no secret of his opinions—whence the bitter feeling.

All men, except those very big ones who are supermen, have something astonishingly despicable in them. The despicable thing in Milligan came uppermost now. He fairly chuckled. He met the snub with a calm, forgiving smile, and continued his shambling gait with what dignity he could towards his bedroom opposite. Then he turned his head to see. His enemy would meet an infuriated hornet—an Egyptian hornet!—and might not notice it. He might step on it. He might not. But he was bound to disturb it, and rouse it to attack. The chances were enormously on the clerical side. And its sting meant death.

"May God forgive me!" ran subconsciously through his mind. And side by side with the repentant prayer ran also a recognition of the tempter's eternal skill: "I hope the devil it will sting him!"

It happened very quickly. The Rev. James Milligan lingered a moment by his door to watch. He saw Mullins, the disgusting Mullins, step blithely into the bathroom passage; he saw him pause, shrink back, and raise his arm to protect his face. He heard him swear out aloud: "What's the d—d thing doing here? Have I really got 'em again—?" And then he heard him laugh—a hearty, guffawing laugh of genuine relief—"It's *real!*"

The moment of revulsion was overwhelming. It filled the churchly heart with anguish and bitter disappointment. For a space he hated the whole race of men.

For the instant Mr Mullins realized that the insect was not a fiery illusion of his disordered nerves, he went forward without the smallest hesitation. With his towel he knocked down the flying terror. Then he stooped. He gathered up the venomous thing his well-aimed blow had stricken so easily to the floor. He advanced with it, held at arm's length, to the window. He tossed it out carelessly. The Egyptian hornet flew away uninjured, and Mr Mullins—the Mr Mullins who drank, gave nothing to the church, attended no services, hated parsons, and proclaimed the fact with enthusiasm—this same detestable Mr Mullins went to his unearned bath without a scratch. But first he saw his enemy standing in the doorway across the passage, watching him—and understood. That was the awful part of it. Mullins would make a story of it, and the story would go the round of the hotel.

The Rev. James Milligan, however, proved that his reputation for self-control was not undeserved. He conducted morning service half an hour later with an expression of peace upon his handsome face. He conquered all outward sign of inward spiritual vexation; the wicked, he consoled himself, ever flourish like green bay trees. It was notorious that the righteous never have any luck at all! That was bad enough. But what was worse—and the Rev. James Milligan remembered for very long—was the superior ease with which Mullins had relegated both himself and hornet to the same level of comparative insignificance. Mullins ignored them both—which proved that he felt himself superior. Infinitely worse than the sting of any hornet in the world: he really *was* superior.

THE BLUE COCKROACH

Christopher Blayre

Christopher Blayre is the pseudonym of Edward Heron-Allen (1861–1943). Allen was born in London, educated at Harrow, but chose not to go to university. Despite this, he was in many respects a polymath, and books in his own name include subjects such as violin making and palmistry. He was embraced by London's literati including Oscar Wilde and his wife Constance, reading their palms, analysing handwriting, and offering to cast the horoscope of their son, Cyril. Allen was a member of the Society for Psychical Research, and, for his work on marine zoology he was elected a Fellow of the Royal Society in 1919. He was also a gifted Persian scholar and translated *The Rubaiyat of Omar Khayyam*. Around 1920 his stories of fantasy and horror began to appear under the pseudonym of Christopher Blayre, the "Sometime Registrar" of the fictional Cosmopoli University.

"The Blue Cockroach" is a paper supposedly deposited by the Professor of Applied Chemistry at Cosmopoli and appears in *The Purple Sapphire and Other Posthumous Papers* (1921). Framed in this way, as if told by a reputable source, the story takes on an air of authenticity. It repeats Gray's trope of a weird insect made stranger by vivid blue colouration, but compared to the blue scarab, the cockroach is associated with psychic disturbance rather than death or disease. The hallucinogenic visions it transmits may be a defence mechanism or accidental by-product rather than a sinister form of aggression;

however, cockroaches are a rapidly reproducing species. Where there is one, there may come a multitude.

ora was responsible—the Dora who punctuated her name after the manner of the plural of Mouse as affected by Civil Engineers. D.O.R.A. Primarily responsible that is to say; for this is a story of one of the very few instances of that *Ersatz*, which devastated Germany during the Late Unpleasantness, but of which our more favoured Nation suffered but few aggressions.

From another point of view perhaps the responsibility lies with Itha and Armorel. They are the imperious nieces of the Professor of Applied Chemistry in the University of Cosmopoli. Itha was twelve at the time, and Armorel eight, but, having no wife to rule him with a rod of iron, the Professor had, by the dire progression of a process for which he was unable to account, gradually become as a slave beneath their ferule, and in the most meagre days of Dora's sumptuary regulations Itha and Armorel had demanded Bananas.

Well, Bananas were at that moment as Snakes in Iceland—apparently, and many a rebuff did the Professor endure from "proud young Porters" at Stores whence of old he had been accustomed to supply his nieces' demands.

Of course the Professor ought to have been married. So ought Pamela, but the youth of the Professor had been spent, not only in consuming the midnight oil and other illuminants, but in abstract researches into their nature, composition, and adaptations. He was an acknowledged authority on Coal-tar Products, Inverted Sugars, and their derivatives commercial and prophylactic. Pamela had waited; and she had waited too long. By the time the Professor had become a Member of Council of the Chemical, and a Fellow of the Royal

Societies he was a confirmed bachelor, and Pamela had reached the age which used to be labelled in their series of photographs of Celebrities (female) by the *Strand Magazine* as "Present Day." They corresponded at long, and met at longer, intervals, when Pamela, growing fragrant with the fire of forgotten suns, like a Winter Pear, came up from Wiltshire in a spirit of revolt against the limitations of the Provincial Milliner.

In the meagre days above referred to, Pamela was in town, and the Professor, rather grudging the expenditure of time involved, had bidden her to lunch with him at the Imperial. A visit to Kings-way, in search of chemical glass, had the result that his way back to the Imperial lay through Covent Garden Market, at that time a dreary vista of empty windows and derelict packing cases, where erstwhile the fruits of distant lands had been wont to overflow in polychromatic luxuriance. But in one of the windows lay a small bunch—a "hand" they call it—of home-sick and weary Bananas, and the Professor remembered the grey reproachful eyes of Itha and Armorel, who could never believe that he could possibly fail them if he really made an effort.

He went in. An adolescent representative of an Ancient Race— who had escaped conscription—received him with scarcely inquisitive apathy.

"Are those the only Bananas you have?" asked the Professor.

"And all we are likely to," replied the Merchant elliptically.

"I am in trouble," said the Professor. "I have a little niece who is eagerly desirous of Bananas—and she is very delicate," he added as a mendacious afterthought, blushing as he thought of Itha in a dilapidated Scout uniform perched in the highest branches of a tree, or careering along the sands "bareback" on a repatriated Army remount. "Do you think you could help me?"

The Adolescent Oriental looked him over with a scrutiny which became, in the end, sympathetic. Perhaps he had a niece—or something—and understood.

"Bill!"

A subterranean noise as though the dirty floor were in labour, and from a square hole in the planks at their feet half a human being emerged. This was evidently part of Bill—a sinister figure, mid-way between Phil Squod and Quilp. A vision of strabismus and a fustian cap.

"Could you find this gentleman a hand or two of Bananas out of that case?—you know."

Disappearance of the upper half of Bill, a sound of rending timbers, and presently his reappearance with two "hands"—beautiful golden Bananas, and the nether portion of his person.

"Beauties," remarked Bill, "come yesterday."

"How much?" inquired the Professor.

When he recovered he saw himself, mentally, a poorer, but a better man. The Merchant was delivering a lecture upon the economics of War, and the iniquities of Dora. And as he turned the "hand" over, that its excellence might act as an anæsthetic to the operation of extraction, there ran out upon the counter the Blue Cockroach.

Unconsciously the Professor—like the Poet in the Den of the Scarabee—recoiled, but no Scarabee was there to murmur without emotion "*Blatta*." But Bill was there.

"Ah!" said he, "I've seen *him* before—queer things we get sometimes in the cases—lizards—snakes—and whatnot. Once I found a Monkey. Jolly little beggar—he was all right, lived on the fruit. We used to take them to the live-beast place at the end. Shut up now."

"Don't you ever get bitten—or stung?"

"No—we're careful. This fellow's harmless."

It was a most lovely beast. In shape and size identical with the cockroaches which stray among one's brushes on board ship, and architecturally indistinguishable from the larger members of the Kitchen family, the Blue Cockroach was clad in a pure, pale azure, as if a cunning artificer in enamels had fashioned it, and had given to its surface a texture of the finest smooth velvet. Its long antennæ waved inquiringly back and forth, its tiny eyes sparkled black with crimson points, and then it began to run. The Professor caught it in his hand as it toppled from the edge of the counter.

It bit him.

A curious sickening little puncture like the nip of an earwig. A sensation of heat, and then of cold that ran all over him, and Bill and the Merchant grew nebulous—and waved about. The Professor had never fainted in his life, but he said to himself "This is how they must feel." In a moment it was over. He had shaken off the insect, and true to the scientific instinct he took out of his pocket one of the corked tubes he had just acquired, and drove the Blue Cockroach into it.

"One of the fellows at the Museum may like to have it," he said.

The Merchant shrugged his shoulders. A boot-heel, not a corked tube, seemed to him to be the appropriate climax to the Odyssey of the Blue Cockroach. For some inexplicable reason, however, he reduced the price he had quoted from the limits of Chimaera to within the bounds of Extravagance, and the Professor went upon his way, the Bananas in his hand and the Blue Cockroach in his pocket.

A tiny point on his right palm showed where the insect had attacked him, but beyond that the incident was closed.

As he proceeded along Coventry Street, the Professor became aware of a great calm—an undefined happiness. He had regarded his appointment with Pamela more in the light of a kindly duty than as an occasion for pleasurable anticipation, but now he suddenly found himself looking forward to their meeting with a keen sense of curiosity and satisfaction. It was too long since they met last. He felt sure she would have come to town sooner had he expressed a wish in that direction in his letters. What a handsome creature she had been when he was a student! What a shame it was that she had never married. The Professor found himself quietly wondering why—if—whether?

"I am fifty-four," said he to himself. But he smiled frowningly—or frowned smilingly.

"She's a wonderful woman!" was his first thought as she rose to greet him from the big chair in the vestibule. Indeed Pamela seemed younger than he remembered her to have looked a year ago. She seemed to radiate that impression of delicate strength and ultra-feminine self-reliance which constitutes the undefinable charm of many middle-aged spinsters.

Their lunch was delightful. Pamela seemed as though she were starting fresh. The Professor seemed to have shed his professorial armour, and to have become once more a human being. He entertained her with descriptions of his war activities, no longer as of yore skimming over the subject, but letting her into the secret chamber of his ambitions, his aspirations, his work. When a man of the Professor's intellectual eminence exerts himself to charm, the charm is dangerously subtle. An element of flattery pervades the exercise, which is—or should be—irresistible. Pamela did not resist—she had never been called upon to resist, and was not going to begin now. Thirty years fell away, as time wasted in sleep. It is not a disagreeable admission—indeed there is a curious emotional joy predominant, when two people who should have been lovers find themselves saying in their hearts "What fools we have been!"

By the time that the arrival of coffee and cigarettes had cleared away the last barriers which had erected themselves upon their voyage of re-discovery, the Professor was virtually identifying Pamela with his life-work.

"It is not all explosives and bacteriology," he confided to her. "I have been at work upon substitutes for sugar, and I have found one which will be a god-send to the people who properly detest saccharine. I have brought here a little tube of my finished article. It has all the sweetening properties of the finest cane sugar. Will you try it?"

Of course she would. If it had been a dangerous poison she would have gladly offered herself as a martyr to Science—his Science.

"You need not be afraid of it. It is not only a wonderful sweetener—it is also a powerful prophylactic. It acts like an atoxyl that would kill with extraordinary rapidity any pathogenic organisms in the system. I look forward to trying it as a remedy for Sleeping Sickness, Yellow Fever—any of the tropical diseases carried by insects which inject death-dealing bacteria—trypanosomes—into our blood by their bites. My dear"—she quivered—"I believe I hold here one of the greatest discoveries that has ever been made in prophylactic medicine!"

They sweetened their coffee—each with a tiny pellucid crystal.

"It is just like real sugar," she said dreamily, "not harsh like saccharine. My dear"—his eyes grew narrower—"I do believe you are right. I am so proud of you." She ended with a little contented sigh which was half a laugh, and looked round the restaurant, which was by this time gradually becoming empty, and wondered whether anyone else there looked out upon their worlds with so supreme a sensation of satisfaction and fulfilment as she. What fools they had been!

The Professor also finished his coffee and leaned back in his chair, looking round the room with a sudden sensation of discomfort. He had just thought again of the Blue Cockroach—the reason he had thought of it was that he had suddenly experienced, as it were, a return of the sensation which came over him at the moment it bit him. It was, however, only momentary, though, casually glancing at his hand, it seemed as if the little puncture were more visible than it had been.

And then a remarkable thing happened. He turned again to Pamela and saw her with new—or rather with old—eyes. He found her eyes fastened upon him with a mingled expression of apprehension and curiosity—and as he returned her gaze—she blushed vividly. He felt strangely uncomfortable, and without any conscious volition on his part he found himself going rapidly over in his mind their conversation of the previous hour. It was surely waste of time to orate for an hour to this dull but worthy person, upon a subject which could have no interest for her and of which she could not possibly understand a single word. He was dissatisfied with himself, and naturally blamed her vaguely for his dissatisfaction and discomfort.

"Well!" he said, "it has been very pleasant seeing you again, Pamela. We must—er—not let it be so long again—before—" His stereotyped phrases lost themselves in embarrassed silence.

He asked for the bill. It seemed to him rather excessive. However, just for once...

Pamela had not ceased looking at him. She was puzzled; it seemed to her as if a newly opened door had been quietly but relentlessly shut in her face. The Professor certainly had aged a good deal since she saw him last; she had not noticed it before. An uncomfortable sensation crept over her that she had been expansive beyond warrantable limits with this grave grey man, and she felt a little hot under an impression that she had allowed the conversation to stray beyond what was quite seemly and decorous—at her age. She was rather relieved that he seemed in a hurry to get away. She had all an intelligent woman's horror of an anti-climax.

An hour later she was in the train. At that moment the Professor laid down his pen in his study and looked before him out of the window. The same thought struck both of them simultaneously.

"What fools we were!"

*"Now whether there be truth or no in that which the native Priests do aver, I know not, nor may I make more curious enquiry, but if it be indeed the fact that the sting of divers of their Flyes do engender Passions as of Love, Hate, and the like, then the matter is curious and worthy of enquiry, but such as I did make enquiry of did postpone me with shrewd cunning and avoiding answer, nor would they be come at to speak further upon it at that or any other time."** *

---

*   "The True Accompt of the Travels into Distant Lands of the learned Doctor Franzelius Bott, wherein many curious Customs and Wisdom of the Inhabitants are truly set down." (Leyden: 1614, p. 117.)

THE WICKED FLEA

J. U. Giesy

John Ulrich Giesy (1877–1947) was an American writer and physician who also wrote under the pseudonym Charles Dustin. He was a medical graduate of Starling Medical College in Columbus, Ohio and went on to publish prolifically in many popular pulp magazines such as *Argosy*, *Adventure* and *Weird Tales*. "The Wicked Flea" appeared in *Weird Tales'* October 1925 issue and is the last story published in Giesy's "Professor Zapt" series, which follows the exploits of Professor Xenophon Xerxes Zapt.

The character of Zapt appears to fit neatly into the eccentric scientist character as his experiments get out of hand, leading to the creation of several fleas of large size. One particular flea cannibalistically eats its fellows and is deemed "wicked." Ultimately, it escapes on its search for prey large enough to satiate its increased appetite. Unusually for a tale about a giant, blood-sucking parasite, there is a comical, more lighthearted tone overall than in our other stories. Historical examples of lice literature such as John Donne's "The Flea" (1633), Robbie Burns' "To a Louse" (1786) and Paul Pindar's *The Fleaiad, An Heroic Poem, with Notes* (1787) all feature satirical and comedic elements. While ideas of contagion, blood disease and vampirism are common for the flea, Giesy's tale exemplifies the flea's enduring legacy as a comedic literary device.

Big fleas have smaller fleas upon their backs to bite 'em.
And these in turn have smaller fleas, and so ad infinitum;
And larger fleas have larger fleas, and larger fleas to go on,
And these in turn have larger fleas, and larger fleas, and so on.

—JONATHAN SWIFT

hat," said Professor Xenophon Xerxes Zapt, the eminent investigator of the unknown in science, sometimes called "Unknown Quantity" Zapt, both from the line of his research, as well as the double X in his name; "is life?"

"Why—I don't know." Bob Sargent, fiancé of the professor's motherless daughter, Nellie, glanced from the record he was just removing from the phonograph in the living room of the Zapt home, to the little man, with greying mutton-chop whiskers, his body clad in the limp and comfortable if somewhat antiquated black alpaca coat he customarily wore about the house. "That is—I'm afraid I don't just appreciate the bearing of your question."

Xenophon Xerxes nodded. "I didn't expect you would." He continued to stare at the stalwart young attorney through the heavy lenses before his near-sighted eyes. "And you are not alone in your lack of comprehension, Robert. Nowadays the rising generation seems to consider life as something akin to that form of syncopated phonetic vibration commonly denominated—jazz."

"Well—possibly." Sargent slipped the record into the cabinet. "Does our music annoy you, professor?"

"That, Robert, is entirely aside from the point. Music is no more

187

than sound, and—er—sound is a form of vibration, as you are presumably aware. And"—Xenophon Xerxes paused as though to give weight to the ensuing climax—"so is life, Robert—so is life."

"Oh, yes, of course," Bob hastened to agree. "I see what you mean now. And if both sound and life are vibrations, isn't that possibly the reason jazz has enjoyed such a vogue? Isn't it possible that there is a difference in the rate of vibration, and that this particular form of music quickens the ratio of the human—"

"Exactly!" Xenophon Zapt rubbed his hands together. There were times when he did not wholly approve of the young man his daughter had declared she intended to marry, but now—he beamed. "God bless my soul, Robert—you surprise me. Really I am amazed to find your mental perceptions so active. Can you perhaps see where the established truism leads?"

"Why—naturally—I suppose it means jazz will have a long life."

"Jazz is merely an illustration," Xenophon Xerxes frowned. "It has nothing to do with the case. Given a hypothetical cause it should be possible to predicate a theoretical effect."

"The trouble is that theory doesn't always work out in practise," said Bob.

"Admitting that—the failures are indubitably due to some fallibility in the original premise, Robert. And—such things lend zest to the investigation of nature's laws."

Sargent turned his eyes to Nellie seated on the living room couch, with a handsome Persian Angora cat in her lap. He sighed. Once the professor got started, the best thing was to let him talk himself out. "You are—considering some serious life problem, then?" he remarked.

"All life is serious, Robert." The professor compressed his thin lips. "And facetiousness is not an inherent characteristic of my nature.

I am not prone to idly employ those variant vibratory fluctuations of the vocal organs, briefly designated speech."

"Certainly not, sir," Bob protested. "I meant that you had some application of the established relation between the correlated facts in mind."

"Goodness," said Nellie softly, with a twinkle in the blue eyes under her soft brown hair.

"Exactly." Xenophon Xerxes gave her a glance. "The word 'correlated' is well chosen, Robert. It is the correlation on which the whole matter hinges, in fact. Life being vibration, what, in your estimation, would be the effect of increasing the vibratory ratio, upon the phenomenon of cell multiplication we are in the habit of calling growth?"

"Why—er—," Bob lifted his gaze to the ceiling as though for inspiration; "possibly—if you increased your cell multiplication numerically as well as in rapidity, you might get a—a giant."

"Precisely." Professor Zapt nodded. "You not only *might*—you necessarily would. There are times, Robert, when I feel that were you to devote yourself to the endeavour you *might* develop a really excellent mind. But—no matter. Were one to apply this principle in the right direction he would almost certainly gain some interesting results. Take the ant or the flea, for example—what would be the result were either multiplied indefinitely in size?"

"Jazz," Sargent said out of an irrepressible sense of humour. "If you applied it to the flea, that is. They'd make everybody dance—"

"Bob!" Nellie cautioned, while her father put up a slender hand and stroked his whiskers as was his way when thinking deeply or annoyed.

Sargent subsided, and the professor, after a dignified interval, resumed: "I referred to an experimental application, rather than to one at large. Both insects are possessed of a remarkable proportionate strength. Were man endowed with an equivalent commensurate to his size, he could easily cover a league at a single leap."

"That would be as bad as the fairy story of the Seven League Boots, wouldn't it?" Nellie looked up smiling from tweaking one of the Angora's ears.

Xenophon Xerxes sniffed. Without deigning a reply he rose and passed from the room, disappearing up a stairway in the direction of the laboratory he maintained on the second floor of the house.

"And now he's mad again," Miss Zapt complained. "Bob, why can't you behave when he has something he wants to talk about?"

"Me?" Sargent protested with more vigour than grammatical correctness. "You were the one who mentioned fairy tales."

"But you made it worse. Anyway I don't care. Think of fleas as big as men—"

"I'd rather not. It sounds weird. I wonder how far it could jump."

"Oh—miles." Nellie smiled. "I s'pose I shouldn't have said that about the Seven League Boots, but—I could have done worse. You know that doggerel about fleas, don't you, Bob?"

"Can't say I do." Sargent shook his head. "But—almost any *doggerel* should harmonize with fleas."

Miss Zapt giggled. "'Big fleas have little fleas upon their backs to bite 'em. An' little fleas have littler fleas, and so—*ad infinitum*,'" she recited.

Bob nodded. "Just so: *ad infinitum*. Only this thing of your father's is the reverse. It's crescendo, rather than diminuendo. And that brings us back to music. Let's have a little more jazz."

II

"Bob," said Miss Zapt the next evening, "do you know what I saw Father doing this afternoon?"

"Rather not." Sargent grinned. "What was Father up to?"

"He was coaxing neighbour Brown's dog into our yard with a piece of meat, and then when the brute came over he took him into the garage."

"To hunt fleas!" Sargent sat down and eyed the little beauty before him. "Good Lord!"

"Bob!" Nellie's blue eyes widened swiftly.

"Sure!" Bob began to chuckle. "When your paternal ancestor get's an idea in his headpiece, Sweetness, the only way to get it out is to let it exhaust itself."

"But—you—you don't think he really means to try to—to—"

"Raise fleas? *Ad infinitum*," Bob harked back to her quotation of the previous evening. "Translated, *ad infinitum* means 'no end', as our English cousins put it. Sure! I think he means to do just that."

"But—if he brings them into the house!" All at once Xenophon Xerxes' lone heir appeared a trifle aghast.

"Oh—he'll keep 'em shut up somehow," Bob soothed.

"But—if they should get out! If they should get on Fluffy!"

There had been times past when the eminent investigator had not hesitated to make use of her cat during the enthusiasm incident upon some experiment, without Nellie's prior knowledge. And although thus far her pet had escaped any serious consequences, Miss Zapt never knew what might happen next. Because of that she knit her brows as she went on: "It would be just like him to expect me to let him use her as a—a sort of incubator for this monstrosity he thinks he's going to raise."

Bob shook his head. "Not very long if he succeeds. He'll have to keep the thing on a chain—"

"Bob!"

"Well—you never can tell about an *ad infinitum* flea. It's apt to hop off six or seven miles at a jump. He'll probably cage it and feed it on raw beef."

"Bob!"

"Or blood. He'll have to. If he gets anything like what he's after, rather than feeding off Fluffy in the ordinary sense it's more apt to chase her around the house."

"Bob—you're simply teasing, and I think you're—horrid." Miss Zapt wrinkled the end of her nose.

"As a matter of fact I don't know whether I am or not," said Bob. "I know it sounds ridiculous, but—"

"But imagine a weeny-teeny thing like a flea grown that big!"

"I'm trying to. It's an appalling thought. I can't imagine how he expects to bring the thing about." Sargent sighed.

"Neither can I. But he spent the whole morning in the laboratory."

"And in the afternoon he made gustatory advances to friend Brown's dog." Sargent chuckled again. "He was ready to start the job. Honey—that father of yours knows a lot about natural laws."

"But—this isn't natural!" Nellie protested. "How do you suppose a flea that size would look?"

"Not having considered the matter before, I'm hardly qualified to state—except that it would look like a flea in a telescope, I guess." Bob glanced toward a bookcase in the corner. "There's the encyclopedia—we might find a picture of the brute."

Nellie rose, and returned from the case with a good-sized volume. She began turning leaves. "Fl-Fle-a. Here it is."

Bob bent to inspect the paragraph on which her finger was resting. "'*Flea*—(entom.) An insect of the genus Pulex, remarkable for its agility and troublesome bite. The common flea is *Pulex irritans*,'" he read, and paused to stare at a small illustration of the object in question. "*Pulex irritans. Irritans* is Latin for 'irritating' or 'annoying.' *Pulex* is his family name. Seems appropriate all right. The irritating or annoying Pulex."

"The whole thing is annoying." Miss Zapt closed the book with considerable force. "Why under the sun do you suppose father wants to waste his time enlarging or magnifying—or whatever he intends doing—a thing like that?"

"At first glance there does seem a reason for some such question," Sargent smiled. "But—I presume it's the principle involved."

"But—what's the use?" Nellie's tone showed exasperation.

"Why—I don't know. Don't they train 'em? Seems to me I've heard of trained fleas. Now if he could raise about a dozen Pulexes the size of a mouse or a—rat—"

"Bob! Talk sense. A flea that large would be—dangerous. Didn't you read what it said about their bite?"

"Yes. Troublesome, my child. But—he might use 'em in a moral crusade. A dozen turned loose on the beaches would discourage one-piece bathing suits. Mermaids would need a suit of armour and a club. And if he'd stencil 'em with anti-vice badges—"

"Oh, well, go on and be funny if you want to! I think it's simply crazy," Nellie declared with an irritated laugh.

III

It was some ten days before Bob saw Miss Zapt again. A legal matter called him out of town the next morning, so suddenly that he said good-bye by telephone. Consequently, the next time they were together it was some time before their conversation turned on any topic save themselves. Then Nellie changed it rather abruptly:

"Well, you were right. Father is having me buy beef."

"Seems to agree with you," Sargent said, without taking his eyes from her face or his arm from about her waist.

"I'm not eating it, silly," she rejoined. "What's the use of being stupid? You know I mean you were right in saying he'd feed it to—those fleas."

"Oh! And how is the irritating Pulex—or Pulexes?" Bob grinned.

"I don't know. I haven't seen them, and I don't want to see them. But he's got them in the laboratory, and every morning I have to order meat. First it was one pound, then two, and yesterday four—"

"Four!" Bob erupted. "Four pounds of meat to feed fleas? Holy Smoke!"

Nellie sighed. "He takes it up there and that's all except that he's been quite excited the past few days, and spends all his time in the laboratory except when I call him to his meals. I don't believe he's slept much the last two nights."

"Hm-m-m!" Bob seemed suddenly lost in silent consideration of Nellie's statement.

"What's the matter, darling?" she asked all at once.

"Eh? I was thinking." Sargent flung up his head.

"And I wasn't speaking to you," Miss Zapt returned tartly. "What is it, Fluffy? What's the matter?"

Bob became aware of the Angora. She had slid into the room and was standing in the centre of the floor with a bushily expanded tail held very nearly erect. Her entire bearing was one of hesitation and doubt. She seemed vaguely disturbed.

For a moment after her mistress had spoken she made no move, and then, without warning, she sat down on her haunches and turned her head in an almost quizzical way in Nellie's direction.

"Meow!" She emitted a whimper between anathema and perturbed complaint, and began to quiver, finally lifting a hind leg toward her back in tentative fashion and discovering it would not reach. Yet instead of being returned to the floor that leg remained extended and commenced to twitch.

"Bob! She's going to have a fit!"

"Wait." Sargent laid a hand on Nellie's arm, while he regarded the cat out of speculative eyes. "Give her time to reach a conclusion."

"Time?" Miss Zapt's tone resented the suggestion. She advanced upon her pet.

And Fluffy drew back. In a series of amazingly rapid lurches she retreated like a poorly tuned motor thrown into the reverse, toppled all at once sidewise, became in an instant a wildly gyrating ball of long hair, head, tail and feet.

"Bob!" Nellie went to her knees beside the madly contorting body. "Telephone for a veterinary! Quick! Fluffy!" With a swoop of anxious arms she gathered the Persian to her breast, staggered to the couch and dropped down upon it. "Bob!"

"Wait," Sargent said for the second time. "I think I can do quite as much for Fluffy as a vet. Hasn't it dawned upon you yet, Sweetness?"

"What?"

"Fleas—or a flea perhaps. *Pulex irritans*. She couldn't reach it to scratch it and—it annoyed her. She's an irritated cat."

Miss Zapt sniffed very much as Xenophon Xerxes might have done in a similar instance. At the same time Bob's suggestion appeared to find weight with her, to judge by her expression. She dug slender fingers into Fluffy's hair in search of the possible cause of her actions. And Fluffy seemed actually pleased. She began purring gently—stretched.

A minute, two minutes passed. "I don't see it," said Miss Zapt.

"Well, keep it up anyway," Bob said. "It seems to soothe her."

Nellie turned actually angry eyes back to her quest. Of a sudden they focused intently. "Bob!"

"What?"

"I saw it. But it moved."

"It would." Sargent knelt beside girl and cat. He parted the pelt in investigation—revealed a darkly moving object, jammed down a thumb and finger and withdrew an object the size of an ordinary bean. "Got it," he announced and rose to obtain a better light on what he had found.

"What—is it?" Nellie joined him. "Woodtick?"

"No-o. It's a flea all right. Well—I'm darned." Sargent's accents were those of a slightly awed wonder. "It's an honest-to-goodness flea, but—Good Lord!" The blood-swollen body between his digits burst and left them stained.

"You've—killed it!" Nellie accused.

"Looks like it." Bob viewed the remains in rueful fashion. "Where's your father?"

"Up-stairs. Do you think it's—one of his?" Nellie's eyes were wide.

"Judging by its size. Come along."

Sargent started for the stairs. Nellie went with him. Outside the laboratory door they paused and Bob rapped.

"Well? Well?" Xenophon Xerxes replied in the tone of one not wishing to be disturbed.

"It's Sargent, professor," Bob called. "I've something that belongs to you, I fancy."

"You've what?" The laboratory door was jerked partly open and Xenophon Xerxes peered out.

Bob extended his hand with the dead flea upon it. "It was on Fluffy. It was disturbing her a good deal, and we caught it, and—it burst."

"Naturally. But—it doesn't matter, Robert." The professor drew the door farther open. "Come in—and I will show you a really interesting exhibit of the scientific application of modern knowledge applied to the metabolic processes, and the use of vitamins."

"You mean—you have—others?" Bob edged into the room behind Nellie.

"Of course." Xenophon actually beamed. "Did you imagine you had destroyed the only one? Not at all, Robert. Not at all. Here—" He led the way to a glass box pierced at each end by a metal bar from which wires led to a small electrical generator on an insulated table. "You can see how they are coming on."

"Ugh!" Nellie gave one glance and shuddered.

Bob stared out of suddenly narrowed eyes. Inside the glass were possibly a dozen of the insects even larger than the one he had found. They swarmed over a lump of raw beef. "Remarkable. I wouldn't have believed it possible," he said at length.

Xenophon Xerxes nodded. "Man stands today on the threshold of things undreamed in other years, Robert. Today we are beginning to lay hold upon an understanding of life forces, and hence the processes of life itself. Organic therapy, the study of endocrine glands, has done much. But even the endocrines are powerless to function unless given the substance with which to build. There has been a missing link in our knowledge. Then came the discovery of vitamins—the essential growth-producing elements of food—the—er—essence of food. It was the application of that knowledge I found essential in this experiment."

"But—I thought you said life was vibration?" Sargent seemed a trifle dazed.

"I did, Robert. I did. Life *is* vibration. But let me ask you—what maintains vibration once it is brought into manifestation?"

"Why—er—force. Do you mean—food?"

"Exactly!" Xenophon rubbed his thin hands together. "You're coming on, Robert, upon my word! Therefore in order to obtain the success I aimed at, it became necessary to raise a vibratory rate in the presence of a food excess, and at the same time supply the impulse for that food's use. The generator here furnishes the vibratory rate. The beef is the food—its juices. As you know, in all electrical devices there is a negative and a positive pole. The negative is the active—the change-producing. Current flows from negative to positive. Therefore in order to supply my third essential, that small sponge on the negative electrode you see entering the cage is soaked in water-soluble vitamins, which are carried by the vibratory current to become a part of the contained atmosphere. The hypothetical requirements being correctly deduced and furnished—the result—well, Robert, you can see the result for yourself."

"Rather." Bob turned his eyes to the cage again and started. "I say, professor—are those things getting larger? They look bigger—"

"They are growing, Robert." Xenophon Xerxes smiled. "Don't let that surprise you. Growth is a multiplication of cells. And since a cell in multiplying, reproduces itself—you will perceive that the ratio of increase is the square of the primary number. For that very reason it will soon become necessary to destroy all save the best developed specimen of the lot. Of course when I stop the current passing, the rapid development halts."

Sargent nodded. "It's a good deal like compound interest, isn't it?" he said a trifle vaguely.

"I trust you find it interesting, purely as a demonstration." Zapt eyed him in a suspicious manner.

"Oh, yes, indeed." Bob took a long, deep breath. "I never saw anything like it, in my life."

"Without wishing to seem egotistical, Robert," Zapt accepted the assurance quickly, "I feel that I am justified in the assertion that until I brought about the necessary correlation of environment, outside of what has been called from time to time a freak of nature, neither did anyone else."

"I should hope not," Nellie broke into the conversation. "If he did, he probably thought he was drunk."

Her father viewed her in tolerant silence. He put up a hand and stroked his greying whiskers. "And as a matter of fact, Robert," he remarked, transferring his gaze to the already amazing products of his endeavours, "I may add that the experiment is scarcely more than begun."

IV

With that statement Mr Robert Sargent most emphatically agreed on a later occasion, when, having apparently heard his voice below stairs, Professor Zapt came down in his flapping coat and a pair of carpet slippers and invited him up to inspect advanced results.

There was a childlike quality about the little scientist at times, in that he desired to exhibit the fruits of his labours, as Bob had learned in the past. And he judged that Xenophon Xerxes was handicapped in the present instance by Nellie's attitude toward what she frankly declared was an unwarranted interference with nature's designs as affecting insect life. Moreover he was genuinely curious to learn to what extent the professor had succeeded as he accompanied him back up-stairs. Nellie went along.

Xenophon Xerxes threw open the laboratory door with the hint of a flourish and jerked his hand at the glass cage Bob had seen before.

"There," said he, "is Pulex."

Sargent stared and caught his breath. Where before had been some dozen surprisingly large fleas, there was now but one. And that one was immense. It was monstrous—huge—a swollen, bloated, overgrown, Brobdingnagian extravaganza of a flea, that nearly filled the glass walls inside which it squatted, beneath a heavily weighted top.

"Call him Pulex, do you?" Bob began, and paused at Nellie's gasp.

He turned to her, found her gazing at the unbelievable inmate of the glass box with wide-open, pupil-stretched eyes. Her lips parted. "You mean—you've given—that thing—a name?" she faltered.

"Exactly. Pulex, my dear, from the entomological denomination derived from the Latin—*Pulex irritans*—genus *Pulex*—variety, *irritans*," Xenophon Xerxes announced.

Bob nodded. "Well—he looks irritable. Isn't he sort of cramped in that box?"

"Possibly," Zapt assented. "But you see, Robert, the process of growth has slowed the last two days. It is my opinion that development has about reached its limit."

"It's horrible." Nellie's face was white. "Bob—look at it—look at its—eyes. It—knows we're here," she chattered. "It's looking at us. It's terrible—wicked!"

"The wicked flea," Sargent said, smiling, as she paused with clicking teeth. "The wicked flea, and no man pursueth."

Miss Zapt broke into hysterical laughter. "The wicked—flea—and—no man—pur-su-eth! Oh, ha, ha, Bob! That's the best thing—you've said—in a month!"

Xenophon Xerxes stiffened before that outburst of what he plainly regarded as unseemly mirth. "Get her out of here, Robert," he directed.

"Take her down-stairs. Women have no scientific appreciation. They prefer an untimely humour."

"Come along, Honey Lamb Child, we'll fly while no wicked flea can pursue us," Sargent prompted and led her back down-stairs.

Once there she subsided upon the living room couch. "Oh, Bob! Did you—see Father's face?" she gasped.

Bob grinned and nodded. "He looked almost as irritable as Pulex," he said.

Nellie giggled. "Well—don't let's talk any more about it. I shouldn't have made him angry."

"All right," Bob agreed. Nor had he any intention of reverting to the subject when next he passed beneath the professor's roof.

Neither did he contemplate coming into contact with Xenophon Xerxes himself. The seclusion the eminent investigator had maintained during his experiment rather precluded that. Consequently it was with a feeling of distinct surprise that he found him puttering about the lower floor.

Furthermore, Zapt's demeanour was a thing calculated to attract attention, though he manifestly aimed at the reverse. His bearing, indeed, was that of a man in a state of mental unrest. He replied to Bob's greeting in absent-minded fashion, went over and moved a chair out of a corner, tilted it on its legs and set it back in place. Immediately afterward he left the room, and in five minutes he was back. He hung about, twiddling his fingers beneath the tail of his shapeless coat, until, seizing a moment when he fancied himself unobserved, he bent and glanced under the couch.

"Father!"

Xenophon straightened at the sound of Nellie's voice.

"What is the matter?"

"Nothing—er—that is, nothing." Xenophon went over and sat

down in his favourite chair beside a table loaded with scientific journals and books. He sighed. For possibly three minutes he sat with forehead furrowed into a frown of what might have been consideration. Then he bounced up and went into the hall. Sounds indicated his investigation of a closet where umbrellas and raincoats were stored.

Nellie glanced at Bob, rose and passed silently to the archway through which the hall was reached.

"Father—what are you hunting?" she asked.

Silence followed, punctuated by the closing of the closet door. Xenophon Xerxes joined her, re-entered the living room and regained his seat. For a moment he drummed on the table with nervous fingers. He cleared his throat.

"As a matter of fact," he announced at the end of possibly a minute, "Pulex has escaped."

"Pulex?"

"Escaped?"

Bob and Nellie spoke at once.

"Yes." The professor got up again. "It's really most annoying. I—I can only blame myself. Quite early this evening I fell into a doze while observing what I felt sure were the final hours of his growth. I—er—forgot to shut off the generator, connected with the cage. I can only presume that it continued to run and—er—Pulex became too large for the container. At all events it—burst. When I awoke it was in fragments and the—er—insect had disappeared."

"And," Nellie accused, "that's why you've been roaming around looking under things the last hour?"

"Yes, my dear," Xenophon Xerxes sighed. "I—er—confess I have been in hopes of coming across it—that it had—er—secreted itself. I've been intending to have it permanently mounted as a demonstration of—" He broke off at sounds of a commotion in the rear of the house, cocked his head as though seeking to appraise them, and then exclaimed: "God bless my soul! Perhaps—"

Without finishing the hypothetical conclusion, he started for the hallway.

Sargent and Nellie followed quite as a matter of course. The trio made their way to the rear, Xenophon Xerxes being the first to reach the kitchen and snap on a light.

His act revealed a remarkable sight.

Crouched on the floor was Pulex, and regarding him from a corner, half in terror and half in defiance, with every hair on her body in a state of furry excitement, was Nellie's cat.

"Fluffy!" Miss Zapt started forward to the rescue after a moment of breathless amaze.

"Hold on!" Bob swung her back, thrust himself before her, taking her task upon himself. He bore straight down on Pulex.

But Pulex did not wait. As Bob started he leaped.

"Catch him!" Xenophon lifted his voice in admonitory treble.

"Catch him yourself!" Sargent whirled. Pulex had leaped not from, but directly at him, and though he had ducked instinctively, a passing leg had rasped his cheek. As he turned, Pulex leaped again, missing him again as he dodged, and hit the farther wall with a heavy thud.

"Damn!" The expletive seemed jolted from Sargent's mouth.

Fluffy scampered between his legs, tripped him and sent him down to the floor with a bump.

"God bless my soul!" Xenophon Xerxes faltered. "The thing is— actually vicious. Did you notice that it seemed—inclined to attack you, Robert?"

"Yes." Bob scrambled up. "I noticed it." His eyes sought Pulex and found him squatted warily observant against a baseboard. "He's a wicked flea—but this time there's a man going to pursue him." He flung himself forward.

And Pulex exercised discretion. The kitchen window was open, and he lifted himself through it, butting headlong against a screen, tearing it loose along one edge and scrambling frantically through the resulting avenue of escape.

"God bless my soul!" said Xenophon Xerxes again. "I fear we've lost him, Robert."

"I don't know whether we have or not." Bob's blood was up. He dashed at the kitchen door and vanished through it.

Nellie joined him outside.

Zapt followed.

The three stood staring into the gloom of the back yard, faintly illuminated by the rays of a second quarter moon. There came presently to their ears a rasping, scratching sound from overhead.

Bob ran farther out and sought for its source. "There he is," he announced, and pointed to where Pulex was ambling sedately along the ridgepole of the house. As they watched, the fugitive gained the shadow of a chimney and disappeared.

"I'll get him out of that soon enough," Bob promised. "They can't stand water. Where's the hose?"

"I'll—bring it, Robert." Xenophon Xerxes hurried off, his coat tails flapping.

"Get a broom or a stick." Bob turned his glance to Nellie. "He'll jump when the water hits him. Be ready to swat him."

"Swat the flea," Nellie giggled and ran off to obtain the suggested means for so doing.

Zapt came back with the hose. He had turned on the water and thrust the nozzle into Sargent's hands.

Nellie reappeared with a broom and the handle of a mop.

Bob explained their purpose and Xenophon took the mop, stepping back from the wall of the house, with Nellie posted a short space from him.

"Now!" Bob lifted the stream of water against the chimney, and saw a dark object hurtle above him.

"Catch him!" he cried, turning toward Nellie and her father.

The hose turned with him. Its stream struck Xenophon Xerxes just below an uptilted chin.

"Professor!" Bob began in a tone of consternation.

"Ass!" The eminent investigator hurled his mopstick upon the ground and strode, dripping, into the house.

V

Officer Daniel McGuiness, patrolman of the district embracing the Zapt residence, rang in at the end of a round and gave ear to a question couched in the station sergeant's voice:

"Say, Mac, what sort of people are M. K. Brown and wife on Elm Street? Is the lady by any chance bugs?"

"Why," Danny frowned at the transmitter, "not thot I know of, sar-junt. For why do ye ask?"

"Well," the voice came back, "she called up a bit ago and wanted to know if we'd send out there. Said a flea chased her dog into the house."

"A—flea?" Danny steadied himself against the patrol box.

"That's what *she* said."

"Ut—chased her—dog?"

"Accordin' to th' lady."

"How big—was th' dog?"

There was a pause while Danny waited for an answer. When it

came its delay seemed explained by the sergeant's intention to make it sufficient:

"See here, McGuiness, don't get funny! Go find out what sort of hootch they're using, th' next time you pass their house."

"Yis, sor." Danny hung up, removed his helmet and scratched his head. Resuming his beat he turned over the amazing information he had just received—a flea—had chased—Brown's dog—into the house.

"It ain't possible," said Danny to himself. "It's been hot th' last few days, though. Maybe—anyway, when I git over there, I'll stop—though if there are any sich anymiles about th' place, 'tis more a job fer th' sanitary squad."

Wherefore, when he approached the Brown residence, he turned in from the street, mounted the front porch and set a heavy finger to a bell.

His summons was answered by Brown himself.

Danny knew him. "Good evenin', Misther Brown," he said. "Th' sar-junt was sayin' as how—maybe I'd better stop."

"Yes. Come in, McGuiness." Brown held the door wide.

Danny removed his helmet and followed into a room where Mrs Brown sat. He accepted a chair. "An' now just phawt was th' trouble?" he suggested. "Th' Sarge was sayin' somethin'—about a—about a—"

"About a flea," Mrs Brown declared in a tone of nervous excitement. "That is, it looked like a flea, except that it was so large. I never saw anything like it."

Danny nodded. "An'—ut chased—your dog?"

"Yes. He ran up on the porch and whimpered, and when Mrs Brown went to let him in, this thing was right behind him," Brown said.

"Th' dog's a little felly?"

"He's a full-grown Gordon setter."

"You seen ut yourself?" Danny looked Brown full in the eyes.

"Yes." They did not falter. "When Mrs Brown screamed I ran out to see what was wrong and there it was in the hall. Oh, I know it sounds crazy, McGuiness, but a man believes what he sees."

"Yis, sor—sometimes." Danny sniffed. It was almost as though he were seeking some definite odour.

And Brown noted the action. He laughed shortly. "Oh—I'm not drunk, McGuiness."

"Yis, sor—no, sor," Danny corrected himself quickly. "An' so this here—whatever ut was—follied th' dog inside?"

"It did."

"An' where is ut now?"

"It's gone. We didn't keep it as a pet. I tried to throw my coat over it, but it jumped back through the door."

"Oh, thin—ye druv it off." Danny rose. "Thot bein' th' case I don't see phawt I can do at prisint. If ye see anything more of it—of course—"

Mrs Brown spoke again. "I suppose it was foolish to report it. But—it was so strange—I thought somebody ought to know such a thing was at large. So—I rang up."

"Yis, ma'am," said McGuiness. "I'll report to th' sar-junt th' next toime I ring in, that I come over an'—"

He broke off at the sound of a feminine scream from the street, whirled quickly, clapped on his helmet and bolted out of the house.

He emerged to find a young woman clinging to the arm of a masculine companion and clattered heavily toward them.

"Phawt's th' matter?" he demanded, coming to a halt.

"I've—been bitten," the girl said in a gasping voice.

Danny eyed her escort in suspicious fashion. "Phawt was ut bit ye?" he asked.

"The—the—toad."

"Th'—toad?" Danny McGuiness stared. His words came like a belated echo at the end of an appreciable pause.

"Yes. At least I guess it was a toad. It hopped out, just as we were passing." The young woman released her escort's arm and faced Danny.

Danny considered. "It hopped out an' bit ye—how?" he asked at length.

"Why—with its mouth, I suppose."

"Th' toad did?" Danny was breathing deeply.

"Certainly." The girl's companion spoke for the first time. "See here, officer, what's the matter with you, anyway?"

Danny took a grip on his senses and his club. "There ain't anything th' matter with me, young felly," he averred. "Where was ut this here toad bit ye, ma'am?"

"Why, right here," the victim declared.

Danny nodded. "Yis, yis, but—whereabouts on—yerself?"

"Oh—why, on the ankle—just above the foot."

"'Tis the usual location of ankles." Danny nodded again. "An' afterwards—phawt did th' toad do after ut bit ye?"

"Just a minute, officer," the other man interrupted. "We were talking of a—"

"You were talkin' of a toad," said Danny gruffly.

"Yes. And there's no use in going at the matter as though it had been a holdup or a thug. It hopped out and bit Miss Grant and hopped off again down the road. Then you ran out and asked what had happened. That's all there is to it. Are you able to walk, dear?"

Miss Grant murmured an assent.

Her escort turned back to Danny.

"So now that you know all the details, if you don't mind, we'll proceed."

"Yis, sor." Danny drew back. "I run out because th' young lady screamed. An' phawt ye told me filled me wid surprise, because"—for the life of him he could not resist a parting shot, in view of the other man's manner—"'tis th' first toime I ever heard of a toad bite, by th' token that th' varmints haven't anny teeth. Good noight, sor. I hope ye git home all roight. Now if ut had been a flea—"

"A flea?" The other man eyed him, and all at once he laughed. "Officer, you've lost your sense of proportion. I saw it. It was as big as a—a scuttle of coal, at least."

"Yis, sor—'tis sort of dark along here." Danny watched the pair move off, before he removed his helmet and wiped his forehead with the back of a hand. "Phew!" He replaced the helmet. "Th' flea was big enough to chase th' kiyoodle an' th' toad was big as a hod o' coal. Somebody's lost their sinse of proportion, all roight, I guess." He resumed his sadly delayed patrol.

"'Tis a funny noight," he mused. "Dog-chasin' fleas, an' bitin' toads. Domned if ut *don't* sound home brewed. An' as for my sinse of proportion"—he gazed about him and chuckled—"iverything looks nacheral enough. Most loikely thim two was swateheartin' along an' th' poor toad hopped out an' seared her, an' she thought she was bit. Wimmen git funny notions, whin they're tuk suddint off their guard. As fer th' flea—beloike ut was somethin' th' fool dog treed."

But if Danny's line of argument satisfied him, what complacency he had evolved by the time he once more arrived at the end of his round was destined to receive a shattering jolt.

"McGuiness," the sergeant demanded, "what sort of a menagerie has broken out up there tonight? There's a man just come into th' emergency, says he was bitten in a taxicab."

"Bit-ten?" Danny faltered.

"Yes, bitten. Shut up and listen. He drove up there in a cab and went into a house. When he came out something was in the cab and bit him and jumped out of the window. He's got a wound on his leg and they're giving him anti-tetanic serum. He says he thinks it was a cat with hydrophobia—"

"A—a—cat?" McGuiness babbled.

"Yes. A cat—a mad cat. Understand? Now get busy and see what's broke loose. If you find anything—shoot it."

"Yis, sor." Danny was sweating from something besides the heat as he hung up.

"Howly Hiven!" he muttered as he closed the box with a slowness indicative of instinctive caution. "First ut was a flea—an' thin ut was a toad—an' now ut is a cat. Phawt th' divil *is* ut, I wonder—an' is ut wan thing or a menagerie loike th' sar-junt says? If ut is wan thing, how can ut be three things to wunst? I dunno, but 'tis surely somethin' or I've been overlookin' a bootleggin' joint. An' even so they ain't injectin' it intil folks in taxis. Thot felly has a wound."

Suddenly he tightened his grip on his stick, felt for his service weapon and started up the street with a newly acquired stealth.

"Shoot ut, th' sar-junt says. An' if I foind ut, begob I will. Maybe after ut's dead, we can foind out phawt ut is."

In such a frame of mind officer Daniel McGuiness once more approached Brown's house. Trees lined the street before it and Zapt's residence next door, their branches casting a chequering of shadow across the pavement. And as Danny advanced, peering intently about him—one of those shadowy patches—*moved*.

At least that is how it appeared, until closer inspection convinced him that some dark object was progressing along the sidewalk.

McGuiness came to a halt and stared. And even as he did so the thing crawled into a patch of light thrown by the corner arc lamp.

"Howly—Mither!" The words were no more than a startled gasp.

This was the most amazing sight in Officer McGuiness' life. Whatever the thing was, it was worthy of attention. It had an enormously bloated body, seemingly encased in a series of overlapping horny scales. And it dragged itself forward, mainly on a pair of grotesque legs that stuck up above its back, at the knees—or joints, or whatever one called them.

For a breath-taking moment Danny stood with an odd sensation as though the hair beneath his helmet was striving to push the latter off. Then his hand reached for his weapon. He was startled, amazed, dumbfounded, but not actually afraid. He had been told to shoot the thing if he came across it, and not for an instant did he doubt that he had met up with it. He drew the deadly service gun and aimed it. His hand steadied, centred the muzzle on the target.

"Bang!"

"What was that?" said Miss Zapt.

Bob Sargent frowned. "It sounded like a blowout—or a shot."

At the last word Nellie's blue eyes widened. "Bob! It was right in front of the house!" She ran to the door and through it to the porch.

"Good evenin', Miss Nellie," a voice she recognized as that of the policeman on night duty in their district called. "Don't ye be scared. 'Tis nuthin'! I just shot somethin' wid hydrophoby."

"With—what?" said Miss Zapt.

"I dunno. 'Twas a funny-lookin' son of th' divil, askin' yer pardin."

"Father! Bob!" Miss Zapt ran down the steps and out to the street.

Xenophon Xerxes, once more in dry garments, followed with Sargent. They caught up with her where she stood beside Officer McGuiness.

"The wicked flea. He's killed it," she said, pointing to a dark and motionless object at his feet.

"Flea?" Danny began and paused as though short of breath. "Was ut a flea, thin?"

"Yes. The wicked flea, and no man pursueth. Haven't you read your Bible, Mr McGuiness?" She laughed.

Danny nodded. "I hov thot. Th' wicked flea, an' no man pursueth." He put out a foot and pushed Pulex. "Sure thin—he looks wicked but—I've been pursuin' him half th' evenin'. An' by th' same token Missus Brown was roight in sayin' he chased her dog into th' house."

"God bless my soul!" Xenophon Xerxes exploded. "Did—did this—this insect do that, McGuiness?"

"'Tis phawt th' lady says, though till th' last few moments I've been misdoubtin' her word." Danny scowled.

"Marvellous!" The professor rubbed his hands. "Amazing! Ancestral instinct, perhaps. You see, he came off Brown's dog in the first place."

"He—phawt?" Danny dragged his glance from the body of Pulex. "Howld on, perfissor. D'ye mean to say this thing come offn th' dog?"

"Of course," Xenophon Xerxes nodded.

"Thin," said Danny with conviction, "sure I don't blame th' kiyoodle fer tryin' to escape him, wunst he had shook him off. Begorra—I—"

"Wait a bit, officer," Zapt interrupted. "Of course the creature was not originally so—large." He plunged into explanations.

Danny heard him in stolid silence. At the end he glanced once more at Pulex, removed his helmet and ran a finger about its dampened band. "An' ye raised him from—"

"A pup," Sargent interjected.

McGuiness gave him a glance. "You raised him from an ordinary little wan, perfissor?" he said in a tone of wonder.

"Exactly," said Xenophon Xerxes Zapt.

"An' he escaped you th' noight?"

"Yes. Precisely. He escaped."

"An' chased Brown's dog, an' bit a young wumman on th' ankle above her foot, an' a man in a taxicab—"

"What! What's that?" Xenophon Xerxes exclaimed. "Do you mean—"

Danny nodded. "Tis th' truth I'm tellin' ye, perfissor. 'Twas most loikely some of his ancestral instincts again. But th' sar-junt told me to kill ut, an I did so, an' whilst 'tis a raymarkable dimonstration, as I ain't denyin', I'm thinkin' that after all ut's small loss. Fleas of thot size—"

"I agree with you, McGuiness." Xenophon Xerxes thrust a hand into a pocket and withdrew a bit of crumpled paper to press it into Danny's unresisting fingers. "Here—is a trifle for your trouble. I do not regret your excellent marksmanship in the least. And I—er—appreciate your commendable fidelity to duty. As a matter of fact I intended giving it chloroform myself." He stooped and took up the carcass of Pulex. "Good-night, officer—good-night."

An hour later, and for the third time, Officer Daniel McGuiness approached the telephone box at the completion of his round. He yanked it open and jerked the receiver off the hook. "Give me th' sar-junt," he demanded and waited till he heard that officer's voice.

"'Tis McGuiness," he said then, "an' I've claned up my district. I found thot flea an' killed ut—"

"What's that?" The sergeant's voice was gruff. "McGuiness—talk sense."

"I'm talkin' sinse," Danny retorted. "Listen." Then he explained.

"Oh—Zapt," the sergeant made comment when he had finished. "Well—that accounts for it, I guess."

"It does," said Danny McGuiness. He hung up and banged shut the box.

THE MIRACLE OF THE LILY

Clare Winger Harris

Clare Winger Harris (1891–1968) was a prominent female author of early Science Fiction who gained success and won respect for her stories published in male-dominated pulp magazines such as *Amazing Stories*, *Weird Tales* and *Science Wonder Quarterly*. She was a firm favourite of readers and her short stories often featured strong female characters. Her work was praised by many critics and has been reprinted over the years. Recently, Harris was celebrated in a 2018 exhibition "Dreaming the Universe: The Intersection of Science, Fiction, & Southern California" at the Pasadena History Museum.

Harris's story "The Miracle of the Lily" was published in *Amazing Stories* in April 1928 and is set in a dystopian future where an epic battle between humans and oversized, intelligent insects has led to a shortage of food. The story spans a great length of time and documents insect uprising, human resistance, and resulting famine in the 40th century. As a prime example of female-authored hard Science Fiction, Harris's story posits the insect overlords as inter-planetary enemies who have also conquered Venus. This plague tale of giant insects focuses on the fight for human survival as mankind's ancestral land has become impossible to farm due to insect domination.

I

THE PASSING OF A KINGDOM

ince the comparatively recent resumé of the ancient order of agriculture I, Nathano, have been asked to set down the extraordinary events of the past two thousand years, at the beginning of which time the supremacy of man, chief of the mammals, threatened to come to an untimely end.

Ever since the dawn of life upon this globe, life, which it seemed had crept from the slime of the sea, only two great types had been the rulers; the reptiles and the mammals. The former held undisputed sway for eons, but gave way eventually before the smaller, but intellectually superior mammals. Man himself, the supreme example of the ability of life to govern and control inanimate matter, was master of the world with apparently none to dispute his right. Yet, so blinded was he with pride over the continued exercise of his power on Earth over other lower types of mammals and the nearly extinct reptiles, that he failed to notice the slow but steady rise of another branch of life, different from his own; smaller, it is true, but no smaller than he had been in comparison with the mighty reptilian monsters that roamed the swamps in Mesozoic times.

These new enemies of man, though seldom attacking him personally, threatened his downfall by destroying his chief means of sustenance, so that by the close of the twentieth century, strange and daring projects were laid before the various governments of the world with an idea of fighting man's insect enemies to the finish. These pests were growing in size, multiplying so rapidly and destroying so much vegetation, that eventually no plants would be left to sustain human life. Humanity suddenly woke to the realization that it might suffer the fate of the nearly extinct reptiles. Would mankind be able to prevent the encroachment of the insects? And at last man *knew* that unless drastic measures were taken *at once*, a third great class of life was on the brink of terrestrial sovereignty.

Of course no great changes in development come suddenly. Slow evolutionary progress had brought us up to the point, where, with the application of outside pressure, we were ready to handle a situation, that, a century before, would have overwhelmed us.

I reproduce here in part a lecture delivered by a great American scientist, a talk which, sent by radio throughout the world, changed the destiny of mankind but whether for good or for evil I will leave you to judge at the conclusion of this story.

"Only in comparatively recent times has man succeeded in conquering natural enemies; flood, storm, inclemency of climate, distance, and now we face an encroaching menace to the whole of humanity. Have we learned more and more of truth and of the laws that control matter only to succumb to the first real danger that threatens us with extermination? Surely, no matter what the cost, you will rally to the solution of our problem, and I believe, friends, that I have discovered the answer to the enigma.

"I know that many of you, like my friend Professor Fair, will believe my ideas too extreme, but I am convinced that unless you are willing to put behind you those notions which are old and not utilitarian, you cannot hope to cope with the present situation.

"Already, in the past few decades, you have realized the utter futility of encumbering yourselves with superfluous possessions that had no useful virtue, but which, for various sentimental reasons, you continued to hoard, thus lessening the degree of your life's efficiency by using for it time and attention that should have been applied to the practical work of life's accomplishments. You have given these things up slowly, but I am now going to ask you to relinquish the rest of them *quickly*, everything that interferes in any way with the immediate disposal of our enemies, the insects."

At this point, it seems that my worthy ancestor, Professor Fair, objected to the scientist's words, asserting that efficiency at the expense of some of the sentimental virtues was undesirable and not conducive to happiness, the real goal of man. The scientist, in his turn, argued that happiness was available only through a perfect adaptability to one's environment, and that efficiency *sans* love, mercy and the softer sentiments was the short cut to human bliss.

It took a number of years for the scientist to put over his scheme of salvation, but in the end he succeeded, not so much from the persuasiveness of his words, as because prompt action of some sort was necessary. There was not enough food to feed the people of the earth. Fruit and vegetables were becoming a thing of the past. Too much protein food in the form of meat and fish was injuring the race, and at last the people realized that, for fruits and vegetables, or their nutritive equivalent, they must turn from the field to the laboratory; from the farmer to the chemist. Synthetic food was the solution to the problem. There was no longer any use in planting and caring for food stuffs destined to become the nourishment of man's most deadly enemy.

The last planting took place in 2900, but there was no harvest, the voracious insects took every green shoot as soon as it appeared, and even trees, that had previously withstood the attacks of the huge insects, were by this time, stripped of every vestige of greenery.

The vegetable world suddenly ceased to exist. Over the barren plains which had been gradually filling with vast cities, man-made fires brought devastation to every living bit of greenery, so that in all the world there was no food for the insect pests.

II

MAN OR INSECT?

Extract from the diary of Delfair, a descendant of Professor Fair, who had opposed the daring scientist.

From the borders of the great state-city of Iowa, I was witness to the passing of one of the great kingdoms of earth—the vegetable, and I can not find words to express the grief that overwhelms me as I write of its demise, for I loved all growing things. Many of us realized that Earth was no longer beautiful; but if beauty meant death; better life in the sterility of the metropolis.

The viciousness of the thwarted insects was a menace that we had foreseen and yet failed to take into adequate account. On the city-state borderland, life is constantly imperilled by the attacks of well organized bodies of our dreaded foe.

(*Note*: The organization that now exists among the ants, bees and other insects, testifies to the possibility of the development of military tactics among them in the centuries to come.)

Robbed of their source of food, they have become emboldened to such an extent that they will take any risks to carry human beings away for food, and after one of their well organized raids, the toll of human life is appalling.

But the great chemical laboratories where our synthetic food is made, and our oxygen plants, we thought were impregnable to their attacks. In that we were mistaken.

Let me say briefly that since the destruction of all vegetation which furnished a part of the oxygen essential to human life, it became necessary to manufacture this gas artificially for general diffusion through the atmosphere.

I was flying to my work, which is in Oxygen Plant No. 21, when I noticed a peculiar thing on the upper speedway near Food Plant No. 3,439. Although it was night, the various levels of the state-city were illuminated as brightly as by day. A pleasure vehicle was going with prodigious speed westward. I looked after it in amazement. It was unquestionably the car of Eric, my co-worker at Oxygen Plant No 21. I recognized the gay colour of its body, but to verify my suspicions beyond the question of a doubt, I turned my volplane in pursuit and made out the familiar licence number. What was Eric doing away from the plant before I had arrived to relieve him from duty?

In hot pursuit, I sped above the car to the very border of the state-city, wondering what unheard of errand took him to the land of the enemy, for the car came to a sudden stop at the edge of what had once been an agricultural area. Miles ahead of me stretched an enormous expanse of black sterility; at my back was the teeming metropolis, five levels high—if one counted the hangar-level, which did not cover the residence sections.

I had not long to wait, for almost immediately my friend appeared. What a sight he presented to my incredulous gaze! He was literally covered from head to foot with the two-inch ants, that next to the beetles, had proved the greatest menace in their attacks upon humanity. With wild incoherent cries he fled over the rock and stubble-burned earth.

As soon as my stunned senses permitted, I swooped down toward him to effect a rescue but even as my plane touched the barren earth, I saw that I was too late, for he fell, borne down by the vicious attacks of his myriad foes. I knew it was useless for me to set foot upon the ground, for my fate would be that of Eric. I rose ten feet and seizing my poison-gas weapon, let its contents out upon the tiny black evil things that swarmed below. I did not bother with my mask, for I planned to rise immediately, and it was not a moment too soon. From across the waste-land, a dark cloud eclipsed the stars and I saw coming toward me a horde of flying ants interspersed with larger flying insects, all bent upon my annihilation. I now took my mask and prepared to turn more gas upon my pursuers, but alas, I had used every atom of it in my attack upon the non-flying ants! I had no recourse but flight, and to this I immediately resorted, knowing that I could outdistance my pursuers.

When I could no longer see them, I removed my gas mask. A suffocating sensation seized me. I could not breathe! How high had I flown in my endeavour to escape the flying ants? I leaned over the side of my plane, expecting to see the city far, far below me. What was my utter amazement when I discovered that I was scarcely a thousand feet high! It was not altitude that was depriving me of the life-giving oxygen.

A drop of three hundred feet showed me inert specks of humanity lying about the streets. Then I knew; *the oxygen plant was not in operation!* In another minute I had on my oxygen mask, which was attached to a small portable tank for emergency use, and I rushed for the vicinity of the plant. There I witnessed the first signs of life. Men equipped with oxygen masks, were trying to force entrance into the locked building. Being an employee, I possessed knowledge of the combination of the great lock, and I opened the door, only to be greeted by a swarm of ants that commenced a concerted attack upon us.

The floor seemed to be covered with a moving black rug, the corner nearest the door appearing to unravel as we entered, and it was but a few seconds before we were covered with the clinging, biting creatures, who fought with a supernatural energy born of despair. Two very active ants succeeded in getting under my helmet. The bite of their sharp mandibles and the effect of their poisonous formic acid became intolerable. Did I dare remove my mask while the air about me was foul with the gas discharged from the weapons of my allies? While I felt the attacks elsewhere upon my body gradually diminishing as the insects succumbed to the deadly fumes, the two upon my face waxed more vicious under the protection of my mask. One at each eye, they were trying to blind me. The pain was unbearable. Better the suffocating death-gas than the torture of lacerated eyes! Frantically I removed the head-gear and tore at the shiny black fiends. Strange to tell, I discovered that I could breathe near the vicinity of the great oxygen tanks, where enough oxygen lingered to support life at least temporarily. The two vicious insects, no longer protected by my gas-mask scurried from me like rats from a sinking ship and disappeared behind the oxygen tanks.

This attack of our enemies, though unsuccessful on their part, was dire in its significance, for it had shown more cunning and ingenuity than anything that had ever preceded it. Heretofore, their onslaughts had been confined to direct attacks upon us personally or upon the synthetic-food laboratories, but in this last raid they had shown an amazing cleverness that portended future disaster, unless they were checked at once. It was obvious they had ingeniously planned to smother us by the suspension of work at the oxygen plant, knowing that they themselves could exist in an atmosphere containing a greater percentage of carbon-dioxide. Their scheme, then, was to raid our laboratories for food.

III

LUCANUS THE LAST

A Continuation of Delfair's Account

Although it was evident that the cessation of all plant-life spelled inevitable doom for the insect inhabitants of Earth, their extermination did not follow as rapidly as one might have supposed. There were years of internecine warfare. The insects continued to thrive, though in decreasing numbers, upon stolen laboratory foods, bodies of human-beings and finally upon each other; at first capturing enemy species and at last even resorting to a cannibalistic procedure. Their rapacity grew in inverse proportion to their waning numbers, until the meeting of even an isolated insect might mean death, unless one were equipped with poison gas and prepared to use it upon a second's notice.

I am an old man now, though I have not yet lived quite two centu-ries, but I am happy in the knowledge that I have lived to see the last living insect which was held in captivity. It was an excellent specimen of the stag-beetle (*Lucanus*) and the years have testified that it was the sole survivor of a form of life that might have succeeded man upon this planet. This beetle was caught weeks after we had previously seen what was supposed to be the last living thing upon the globe, barring man and the sea-life. Untiring search for years has failed to reveal any more insects, so that at last man rests secure in the knowledge that he is monarch of all he surveys.

I have heard that long, long ago man used to gaze with a fearful fascination upon the reptilian creatures which he displaced, and just so did he view this lone specimen of a type of life that might have covered the face of the earth, but for man's ingenuity.

It was this unholy lure that drew me one day to view the captive beetle in his cage in district 404 at Universapolis. I was amazed at the size of the creature, for it looked larger than when I had seen it by television, but I reasoned that upon that occasion there had been no object near with which to compare its size. True, the broad-caster had announced its dimensions, but the statistics concretely given had failed to register a perfect realization of its prodigious proportions.

As I approached the cage, the creature was lying with its dorsal covering toward me and I judged it measured fourteen inches from one extremity to the other. Its smooth horny sheath gleamed in the bright artificial light. (It was confined on the third level.) As I stood there, mentally conjuring a picture of a world overrun with billions of such creatures as the one before me, the keeper approached the cage with a meal-portion of synthetic food. Although the food has no odour, the beetle sensed the man's approach, for it rose on its jointed legs and came toward us, its horn-like prongs moving threateningly; then apparently remembering its confinement, and the impotency of an attack, it subsided and quickly ate the food which had been placed within its prison.

The food consumed it lifted itself to its hind legs, partially supported by a box, and turned its great eyes upon me. I had never been regarded with such utter malevolence before. The detestation was almost tangible and I shuddered involuntarily. As plainly as if he spoke, I knew that Lucanus was perfectly cognizant of the situation and in his gaze I read the concentrated hate of an entire defeated race.

I had no desire to gloat over his misfortune, rather a great pity toward him welled up within me. I pictured myself alone, the last of my kind, held up for ridicule before the swarming hordes of insects who had conquered my people, and I knew that life would no longer be worth the living.

Whether he sensed my pity or not I do not know, but he continued to survey me with unmitigated rage, as if he would convey to me the information that his was an implacable hatred that would outlast eternity.

Not long after this he died, and a world long since intolerant of ceremony, surprised itself by interring the beetle's remains in a golden casket, accompanied by much pomp and splendour.

I have lived many long years since that memorable event, and undoubtedly my days here are numbered, but I can pass on happily, convinced that in this sphere man's conquest of his environment is supreme.

IV

EFFICIENCY MAXIMUM

In a direct line of descent from Professor Fair and Delfair,
the author of the preceding chapter, comes Thanor
whose journal is given in this chapter.

Am I a true product of the year 2928? Sometimes I am convinced that I am hopelessly old-fashioned, an anachronism, that should have existed a thousand years ago. In no other way can I account for the dissatisfaction I feel in a world where efficiency has at last reached a maximum.

I am told that I spring from a line of ancestors who were not readily acclimated to changing conditions. I love beauty, yet I see none of it here. There are many who think our lofty buildings that tower two and three thousand feet into the air are beautiful, but while they are architectural splendours, they do not represent the kind of loveliness I crave. Only when I visit the sea do I feel any satisfaction for a certain yearning in my soul. The ocean alone shows the handiwork of God. The land bears evidence only of man.

As I read back through the diaries of my sentimental ancestors I find occasional glowing descriptions of the world that was, the world before the insects menaced human existence. Trees, plants and flowers brought delight into the lives of people as they wandered among them in vast open spaces, I am told, where the earth was soft beneath the feet, and flying creatures, called birds, sang among the greenery. True, I learn that many people had not enough to eat, and that uncontrollable passions governed them, but I do believe it must have been more interesting than this methodical, unemotional existence. I can not understand why many people were poor, for I am told that Nature as manifested in the vegetable kingdom was very prolific; so much so that year after year quantities of food rotted on the ground. The fault, I find by my reading, was not with Nature but with man's economic system which is now perfect, though this perfection really brings few of us happiness, I think.

Now there is no waste, all is converted into food. Long ago man learned how to reduce all matter to its constituent elements, of which there are nearly a hundred in number, and from them to rebuild compounds for food. The old axiom that nothing is created or destroyed, but merely changed from one form to another, has stood the test of ages. Man, as the agent of God, has simply performed the miracle of transmutation himself instead of waiting for natural forces to accomplish it as in the old days.

At first humanity was horrified when it was decreed that it must relinquish its dead to the laboratory. For too many eons had man closely associated the soul and body, failing to comprehend the body as merely a material agent, through which the spirit functioned. When man knew at last of the eternal qualities of spirit, he ceased to regard the discarded body with reverential awe, and saw in it only the same molecular constituents which comprised all matter about him. He recognized only material basically the same as that of stone or metal; material to be reduced to its atomic elements and rebuilt into matter that would render service to living humanity, that portion of matter wherein spirit functions.

The drab monotony of life is appalling. Is it possible that man had reached his height a thousand years ago and should have been willing to resign Earth's sovereignty to a coming order of creatures destined to be man's worthy successor in the eons to come? It seems that life is interesting only when there is a struggle, a goal to be reached through an evolutionary process. Once the goal is attained, all progress ceases. The huge reptiles of preglacial ages rose to supremacy by virtue of their great size, and yet was it not the excessive bulk of those creatures that finally wiped them out of existence? Nature, it seems, avoids extremes. She allows the fantastic to develop for awhile and then wipes the slate clean for a new order of development. Is it not conceivable that man could destroy himself through excessive development of his nervous system, and give place for the future evolution of a comparatively simple form of life, such as the insects were at man's height of development? This, it seems to me, was the great plan, a scheme with which man dared to interfere and for which he is now paying by the boredom of existence.

The earth's population is decreasing so rapidly, that I fear another thousand years will see a lifeless planet hurtling through space. It seems to me that only a miracle will save us now.

V

THE YEAR 3928

The Original Writer, Nathano, Resumes the Narrative

My ancestor, Thanor, of ten centuries ago, according to the records he gave to my great grandfather, seems to voice the general despair of humanity which, bad enough in his times, has reached the *nth* power in my day. A soulless world is gradually dying from self-inflicted boredom.

As I have ascertained from the perusal of the journals of my forebears, even antedating the extermination of the insects, I come of a stock that clings with sentimental tenacity to the things that made life worth while in the old days. If the world at large knew of my emotional musings concerning past ages, it would scarcely tolerate me, but surrounded by my thought-insulator, I often indulge in what fancies I will, and such meditation, coupled with a love for a few ancient relics from the past, have led me to a most amazing discovery.

Several months ago I found among my family relics a golden receptacle two feet long, one and a half in width and one in depth, which I found, upon opening, to contain many tiny square compartments, each filled with minute objects of slightly varying size, texture and colour.

"Not sand!" I exclaimed as I closely examined the little particles of matter.

Food? After eating some, I was convinced that their nutritive value was small in comparison with a similar quantity of the products of our laboratories. What were the mysterious objects?

Just as I was about to close the lid again, convinced that I had one over-sentimental ancestor, whose gift to posterity was absolutely useless, my pocket-radio buzzed and the voice of my friend, Stentor, the interplanetary broadcaster, issued from the tiny instrument.

"If you're going to be home this afternoon," said Stentor, "I'll skate over. I have some interesting news."

I consented, for I thought I would share my "find" with this friend whom I loved above all others, but before he arrived I had again hidden my golden chest, for I had decided to await the development of events before sharing its mysterious secret with another. It was well that I did this for Stentor was so filled with the importance of his own news that he could have given me little attention at first.

"Well, what is your interesting news?" I asked after he was comfortably seated in my adjustable chair.

"You'd never guess," he replied with irritating leisureliness.

"Does it pertain to Mars or Venus?" I queried. "What news of our neighbour planets?"

"You may know it has nothing to do with the self-satisfied Martians," answered the broadcaster, "but the Venusians have a very serious problem confronting them. It is in connection with the same old difficulty they have had ever since interplanetary radio was developed forty years ago. You remember, that, in their second communication with us, they told us of their continual warfare on insect pests that were destroying all vegetable food? Well, last night after general broadcasting had ceased, I was surprised to hear the voice of the Venusian broadcaster. He is suggesting that we get up a scientific expedition to Venus to help the natives of his unfortunate planet solve their insect problem as we did ours. He says the Martians turn a deaf ear to their plea for help, but he expects sympathy and assistance from Earth who has so recently solved these problems for herself."

I was dumbfounded at Stentor's news.

"But the Venusians are farther advanced mechanically than we," I objected, "though they are behind us in the natural sciences. They could much more easily solve the difficulties of space-flying than we could."

"That is true," agreed Stentor, "but if we are to render them material aid in freeing their world from devastating insects, we must get to Venus. The past four decades have proved that we can not help them merely by verbal instructions."

"Now, last night," Stentor continued, with warming enthusiasm, "Wanyana, the Venusian broadcaster, informed me that scientists on Venus are developing interplanetary television. This, if successful, will prove highly beneficial in facilitating communication, and it may even do away with the necessity of interplanetary travel, which I think is centuries ahead of us yet."

"Television, though so common here on Earth and on Venus, has seemed an impossibility across the ethereal void," I said, "but if it becomes a reality, I believe it will be the Venusians who will take the initiative, though of course they will be helpless without our friendly cooperation. In return for the mechanical instructions they have given us from time to time, I think it no more than right that we should try to give them all the help possible in freeing their world, as ours has been freed, of the insects that threaten their very existence Personally, therefore, I hope it can be done through radio and television rather than by personal excursions."

"I believe you are right," he admitted, "but I hope we can be of service to them soon. Ever since I have served in the capacity of official interplanetary broadcaster, I have liked the spirit of good fellowship shown by the Venusians through their spokesman, Wanyana. The impression is favourable in contrast to the superciliousness of the inhabitants of Mars."

We conversed for some time, but at length he rose to take his leave. It was then I ventured to broach the subject that was uppermost in my thoughts.

"I want to show you something, Stentor," I said, going into an adjoining room for my precious box and returning shortly with it. "A relic from the days of an ancestor named Delfair, who lived at the time the last insect, a beetle, was kept in captivity. Judging from his personal account, Delfair was fully aware of the significance of the changing times in which he lived, and contrary to the majority of his contemporaries, possessed a sentimentality of soul that has proved an historical asset to future generations. Look, my friend, these he left to posterity!"

I deposited the heavy casket on a table between us and lifted the lid, revealing to Stentor the mystifying particles.

The face of Stentor was eloquent of astonishment. Not unnaturally his mind took somewhat the same route as mine had followed previously, though he added atomic-power-units to the list of possibilities. He shook his head in perplexity.

"Whatever they are there must have been a real purpose behind their preservation," he said at last. "You say this old Delfair witnessed the passing of the insects? What sort of a fellow was he? Likely to be up to any tricks?"

"Not at all," I asserted rather indignantly, "he seemed a very serious minded chap; worked in an oxygen-plant and took an active part in the last warfare between men and insects."

Suddenly Stentor stooped over and scooped up some of the minute particles into the palm of his hand—and then he uttered a maniacal shriek and flung them into the air.

"Great God, man, do you know what they are?" he screamed, shaking violently.

"No, I do not," I replied quietly, with an attempt at dignity I did not feel.

"Insect eggs!" he cried, and shuddering with terror, he made for the door.

I caught him on the threshold and pulled him forcibly back into the room.

"Now see here," I said sternly, "not a word of this to anyone. Do you understand? I will test out your theory in every possible way but I want no public interference."

At first he was obstinate, but finally yielded to threats when supplications were impotent.

"I will test them," I said, "and will endeavour to keep hatchlings under absolute control, should they prove to be what you suspect."

It was time for the evening broadcasting, so he left, promising to keep our secret and leaving me regretting that I had taken another into my confidence.

VI

THE MIRACLE

For days following my unfortunate experience with Stentor, I experimented upon the tiny objects that had so terrified him. I subjected them to various tests for the purpose of ascertaining whether or not they bore evidence of life, whether in egg, pupa or larva stages of development. And to all my experiments, there was but one answer. No life was manifest. Yet I was not satisfied, for chemical tests showed that they were composed of organic matter. Here was an inexplicable enigma! Many times I was on the verge of consigning the entire contents of the chest to the flames. I seemed to see in my mind's eye the world again over-ridden with insects, and that calamity due to the indiscretions of one man! My next impulse was to turn over my problem to scientists, when a suspicion of the truth dawned upon me. These were seeds, the germs of plant-life, and they might grow. But alas, where? Over all the earth man has spread his artificial dominion. The state-city has been succeeded by what could be termed the nation-city, for one great floor of concrete or rock covers the country.

I resolved to try an experiment, the far-reaching influence of which I did not at that time suspect. Beneath the lowest level of the community edifice in which I dwell, I removed, by means of a small atomic excavator, a slab of concrete large enough to admit my body. I let myself down into the hole and felt my feet resting on a soft dark substance that I knew to be dirt. I hastily filled a box of this, and after replacing the concrete slab, returned to my room, where I proceeded to plant a variety of the seeds.

Being a product of an age when practically to wish for a thing in a material sense is to have it, I experienced the greatest impatience, while waiting for any evidences of plant-life to become manifest. Daily, yes hourly, I watched the soil for signs of a type of life long since departed from the earth, and was about convinced that the germ of life could not have survived the centuries, when a tiny blade of green proved to me that a miracle, more wonderful to me than the works of man through the ages, was taking place before my eyes. This was an enigma so complex and yet so simple, that one recognized in it a direct revelation of Nature.

Daily and weekly I watched in secret the botanical miracle. It was my one obsession. I was amazed at the fascination it held for me—a man who viewed the marvels of the thirty-fourth century with unemotional complacency. It showed me that Nature is manifest in the simple things which mankind has chosen to ignore.

Then one morning, when I awoke, a white blossom displayed its immaculate beauty and sent forth its delicate fragrance into the air. The lily, a symbol of new life, resurrection! I felt within me the stirring of strange emotions I had long believed dead in the bosom of man. But the message must not be for me alone. As of old, the lily would be the symbol of life for all!

With trembling hands, I carried my precious burden to a front window where it might be witnessed by all who passed by. The first day there were few who saw it, for only rarely do men and women walk; they usually ride in speeding vehicles of one kind or another, or employ electric skates, a delightful means of locomotion, which gives the body some exercise. The fourth city level, which is reserved for skaters and pedestrians, is kept in a smooth glass-like condition. And so it was only the occasional pedestrian, walking on the outer border of the fourth level, upon which my window faced, who first carried the news of the growing plant to the world, and it was not long before it was necessary for civic authorities to disperse the crowds that thronged to my window for a glimpse of a miracle in green and white.

When I showed my beautiful plant to Stentor, he was most profuse in his apology and came to my rooms every day to watch it unfold and develop, but the majority of people, long used to business-like efficiency, were intolerant of the sentimental emotions that swayed a small minority, and I was commanded to dispose of the lily. But a figurative seed had been planted in the human heart, a seed that could not be disposed of so readily, and this seed ripened and grew until it finally bore fruit.

VII

EX TERRENO

It is a very different picture of humanity that I paint ten years after the last entry in my diary. My new vocation is farming, but it is farming on a far more intensive scale than had been done two thousand years ago. Our crops never fail, for temperature and rainfall are regulated artificially. But we attribute our success principally to the total absence of insect pests. Our small agricultural areas dot the country like the parks of ancient days and supply us with a type of food, no more nourishing, but more appetizing than that produced in the laboratories. Truly we are living in a marvellous age! If the earth is ours completely, why may we not turn our thoughts toward the other planets in our solar-system? For the past ten or eleven years the Venusians have repeatedly urged us to come and assist them in their battle for life. I believe it is our duty to help them.

Tomorrow will be a great day for us and especially for Stentor, as the new interplanetary television is to be tested, and it is possible that for the first time in history, we shall see our neighbours in the infinity of space. Although the people of Venus were about a thousand years behind us in many respects, they have made wonderful progress with radio and television. We have been in radio communication with them for the last half century and they shared with us the joy of the establishment of our Eden. They have always been greatly interested in hearing Stentor tell the story of our subjugation of the insects that threatened to wipe us out of existence, for they have exactly that problem to solve now; judging from their reports, we fear that theirs is a losing battle. Tomorrow we shall converse face to face with the Venusians! It will be an event second in importance only to the first radio communications interchanged fifty years ago. Stentor's excitement exceeds that displayed at the time of the discovery of the seeds.

Well it is over and the experiment was a success, but alas for the revelation!

The great assembly halls all over the continent were packed with humanity eager to catch a first glimpse of the Venusians. Prior to the test, we sent our message of friendship and good will by radio, and received a reciprocal one from our interplanetary neighbours. Alas, we were ignorant at that time! Then the television receiving apparatus was put into operation, and we sat with breathless interest, our eyes intent upon the crystal screen before us. I sat near Stentor and noted the feverish ardour with which he watched for the first glimpse of Wanyana.

At first hazy mist-like spectres seemed to glide across the screen. We knew these figures were not in correct perspective. Finally, one object gradually became more opaque, its outlines could be seen clearly. Then across that vast assemblage, as well as thousands of others throughout the world, there swept a wave of speechless horror, as its full significance burst upon mankind.

The figure that stood facing us was a huge six-legged beetle, not identical in every detail with our earthly enemies of past years, but unmistakably an insect of gigantic proportions! Of course it could not see us, for our broadcaster was not to appear until afterward, but it spoke, and we had to close our eyes to convince ourselves that it was the familiar voice of Wanyana, the leading Venusian radio broadcaster. Stentor grabbed my arm, uttered an inarticulate cry and would have fallen but for my timely support.

"Friends of Earth, as you call your world," began the object of horror, "this is a momentous occasion in the annals of the twin planets, and we are looking forward to seeing one of you, and preferably Stentor, for the first time, as you are now viewing one of us. We have listened many times, with interest, to your story of the insect pests which threatened to follow you as lords of your planet. As you have often heard us tell, we are likewise molested with insects. Our fight is a losing one, unless we can soon exterminate them."

Suddenly, the Venusian was joined by another being, a colossal ant, who bore in his fore-legs a tiny light-coloured object which he handed to the beetle-announcer, who took it and held it forward for our closer inspection. It seemed to be a tiny ape, but was so small we could not ascertain for a certainty. We were convinced, however, that it was a mammalian creature, an "insect" pest of Venus. Yet in it we recognized rudimentary man as we know him on earth!

There was no question as to the direction in which sympathies instinctively turned, yet reason told us that our pity should be given to the intelligent reigning race who had risen to its present mental attainment through eons of time. By some quirk or freak of nature, way back in the beginning, life had developed in the form of insects instead of mammals. Or (the thought was repellent) had insects in the past succeeded in displacing mammals, as they might have done here on earth?

There was no more television that night. Stentor would not appear, so disturbed was he by the sight of the Venusians, but in the morning, he talked to them by radio and explained the very natural antipathy we experienced in seeing them or in having them see us.

Now they no longer urge us to construct ether-ships and go to help them dispose of their "insects." I think they are afraid of us, and their very fear has aroused in mankind an unholy desire to conquer them.

I am against it. Have we not had enough of war in the past? We have subdued our own world and should be content with that, instead of seeking new worlds to conquer. But life is too easy here I can plainly see that. Much as he may seem to dislike it, man is not happy, unless he has some enemy to overcome, some difficulty to surmount.

Alas my greatest fears for man were groundless!

A short time ago, when I went out into my field to see how my crops were faring, I found a six-pronged beetle voraciously eating. No—man will not need to go to Venus to fight "insects."

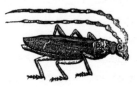

WARNING WINGS

Arlton Eadie

Born Leopold Leonard Eady (1886–1935), Arlton Eadie was an English Science Fiction writer. He published two serialized novels, *The Trail of the Cloven Hoof* (1934) and *The Carnival of Death* (1935) along with dozens of short stories on vampires, mummies, werewolves and phantoms. Eadie's "Warning Wings" was published in *Weird Tales* in September 1929. The magazine was founded in 1922 by J. C. Henneberger and J. M. Lansinger, and is considered one of the most influential publications for fantasy and Science Fiction. *Weird Tales* published works by well-known writers of Science Fiction and the Weird, such as H. G. Wells' "The Stolen Body" in November 1925 and H. P. Lovecraft's "The Call of Cthulhu" in February 1928.

Although Eadie tended to write monster fiction, and *Weird Tales* was well known for its horror, "Warning Wings" takes a different approach as a self-labelled "Ghost Tale of the Sea." The moth often suffers something of a bad reputation associated with death and decay, as can be seen in Edgar Allan Poe's "The Sphinx" (1846) and also in Bram Stoker's *Dracula* (1897). In these examples, Poe's moth is synonymous with a cholera epidemic while Stoker's serves as a messenger of evil. Although the Gothic tradition utilizes the moth as a bad omen, Arlton Eadie offers an alternative representation. Instead of bringing about doom and destruction, Eadie's moth uses its intelligence and ability to communicate for the good of mankind. "Warning Wings" is a significant entry to the anthology as it demonstrates the Insect Weird is not always on the topic of malevolent minibeasts and there are examples of benevolent bugs.

" teady, sir! Please don't do that."

Quietly as the words were uttered, their tone of urgent entreaty was such that I stopped dead and allowed my hand—already raised to crush the moth which had for the past half-hour been blindly dashing itself against the bulb of the electric table-lamp—to fall limply to my side. Surprised at the unexpected exclamation, and secretly somewhat amused at his evident concern for the life of the fluttering insect, I turned and faced the speaker.

He was a fresh arrival at the hotel, for his face was unfamiliar to me. Tall and broad-shouldered, with a neatly trimmed, pointed grey beard, his features tanned to that warm, even tone which only the sea can give—one does not need to spend many hours in the neighbourhood of the Southampton water-front before becoming accustomed to the type to which he belonged. Evidently he was an officer of one of the ocean liners which are to be counted by the score in the docks near by. There was a flicker of amusement in his keen grey eyes as he stepped forward in answer to my look of surprise.

"Seemingly this little wanderer of the night has incurred your displeasure," he observed, pointing to the moth which had now renewed its frantic dashes against the brightly lit globe.

"It seemed so determined to beat its life out that I thought it only kindness to end its misery," I shrugged.

The stranger shook his head slightly. "There is another way."

He stepped toward the lamp and after several attempts managed to catch the little creature between his cupped hands. Then, holding it

241

with infinite tenderness, he crossed to the open window and allowed it to flutter away into the summer night. As he turned, after shutting the window, I saw that he was regarding me with a queer little half smile.

"You may think it strange that I should take the trouble to preserve the life of an insect that another man would crush without a second thought," he said. "But I have a fondness for moths, especially of that particular kind. Oh, you mustn't run away with the idea that I'm a learned entomologist," he went on with a laugh. "As a matter of fact, I do not know the scientific name of the species, although its common designation is, I believe, the 'Ghost Moth'. No, sir, my action just now was purely sentimental. The sight of those tiny fluttering wings brought back the memory of a strange adventure which I had in mid-Atlantic, many years ago."

A far-away expression had crept into his eyes, only to vanish the next moment as he turned again to me and resumed briskly:

"If I tell you the story, it may serve for both explanation and excuse for my unwarrantable intrusion just now."

I hastened to assure him that no excuse was necessary; but at the same time I hinted rather strongly that I should be glad to hear the account of what had happened. To confess the truth, I was not a little curious to know why such a strong bond of sympathy existed between this clear-eyed matter-of-fact man of the world and the little white moth. Sailors' yarns are seldom uninteresting to a landsman, and occasionally they are true as well. Whether this one comes in the latter category I am unable to guarantee; but I can vouch for the fact that the teller of it did not look like a man who would gain any satisfaction from "twisting the ankle" of a casual stranger. As I listened to the story being told in his deep, earnest voice, glancing occasionally into the speaker's frank, bronzed face, I know that I believed every word of it.

*

"At the present time I am in command of the R. M. S. S."—he mentioned the name of a famous Atlantic flyer which had arrived at Southampton the previous day—"but at the time of which I am about to speak, some twenty years since, I was in charge of a smaller vessel belonging to the same line. I was a youngish man then—as liner-captains go—and she was my first command. But you must not imagine that I was nervous on that account, for I'd been in the ferrying trade ever since I'd taken my third-mate's ticket, and I flattered myself that I knew the 'lane' blindfold.

"I suppose it sounds strange to you when I speak of a 'lane' across the Western Ocean. If you talk about the sea to the average landsman, he conjures up a vision of 'the trackless deep,' a phrase which he has learnt from story-writers who have more poetical imagination than actual seagoing experience. True, there was a time when the shipmaster was left free to set his course by the most direct route from port to port, and especially was this so in the days when the competition between the different shipping companies led their captains to strain every nerve to secure the speed-record for their particular ships. But all that is changed now. With the furnaces of a modern liner eating up a ton of coal every one-and-a-half minutes—to say nothing of the food and wages bills mounting up—it is essential for the captain to maintain speed, and the man who takes a 43-000-tonner at twenty-five knots through the zone of drifting icebergs, and the fogs which lay over the Grand Banks in summer, is simply asking for trouble. Consequently two 'lanes' are marked out on his chart; the 'northern' and most direct sea-passage, to be followed when the icebergs are bound up by the Greenland winter and the fog zone off the Grand Banks is of smaller area; and the 'southern,' which is calculated to pass outside the limit to which the bergs drift before melting, and to avoid the larger fog area over the Banks. For the Southampton boats the course is set from the Lizard; those coming from Liverpool set theirs when they drop the Fastnet Light, off the southwest coast of Ireland; while those coming 'north about' through the Pentland Firth steer from a spot well to the nor'rad of the rocky islet of Rockall. And once the course is set, the helm is not shifted unless it is in response to a signal of distress.

"It is necessary for me to make these details quite clear in order for you to appreciate the position of difficulty in which I found myself during the particular voyage I am about to describe.

"It was June when we sailed from this port, so we were due to take the southern route. We stood down Channel until the Bishop Light was winking away on our starboard beam—it stands on an outlying reef of the Scilly Isles, and is the last beacon you pass sailing west—then the course was set 'West, three-quarters South,' which brought the ship into the usual summer route. A little over three days' steaming brought us into the neighbourhood of thirty-five degrees of longitude west of Greenwich. At this point our track met the track of the Liverpool and Queenstown boats, and, according to schedule, our bows were pointed farther south, which made our course 'West-South-West.' You must understand that I'm describing the track we followed twenty years ago. Since the *Titanic* disaster in 1912 the route has been altered, so that it now swings more to the southward until it reaches the same latitude as the Azores, after which it curves north again to New York.

"Well, we shifted our helm, as I have said, about one bell in the first watch (8:30 p. m. shore time), and shortly afterward I came off the bridge to turn in. I took a last look round before going below. It was one of those perfect nights which make passengers think that a sailor's life is all beer and skittles. The ship was threshing her way over the gentle swell with scarce a tilt showing on her long lines of decks; the stars shone bright in the cloudless sky; the slight following breeze was hardly strong enough to lift the drooping folds of the ensign at our stern. It seemed that on such a night the most nervous of new-fledged captains might sleep in peace. Certainly no thought of sudden and unexpected disaster was in my mind when I threw myself down on my cot to sleep.

"But for some unaccountable reason sleep would not come to me. I tossed restlessly from side to side; got up and opened the ports of my cabin; closed them again; tried the old trick of counting the steady beats of the throbbing propeller. But all in vain. In spite of my effort to overcome it, the sense of expectant wakefulness seemed to increase rather than diminish. At last I gave up the struggle, and, switching on the light, took a book from the rack and settled myself to read. It was then that I noticed for the first time a vague sound mingling with the familiar noises of the ship.

"At first it seemed nothing more than a soft intermittent tapping, but as I continued to listen I noticed that the same number of taps was repeated again and again. Subconsciously at first, but soon with awakened interest, I realized that the sounds fitted into certain letters of the Morse code. I laid the book aside and sat up, listening.

"*Tap-tap-tap—Tap... tap... tap—Tap-tap-tap.*

"I raised my eyes to the spot whence the sound proceeded and at once saw what was causing it. Attracted by the light, a tiny white moth had entered the porthole and was now fluttering frantically against the illuminated dial of the telltale compass that was fixed in the ceiling above my bed. The soft tapping had been caused by the creature dashing itself against the glass in its effort to reach the light within. I smiled to myself as I saw the commonplace explanation of the sounds which had so puzzled me; but at the same time I could not help being struck by the fact that the noise it was making was strangely like the Morse code.

"But I was in no mood to be kept awake by so trivial a thing. Picking the towel from the rack, I mounted on the cot and raised my hand to sweep the little creature out of existence, even as you were about to crush that other moth in this room a few minutes since. But just as I was about to strike, the moth's flutterings began afresh.

"*Tap-tap-tap—Tap... tap... tap—Tap-tap-tap.*

"I stood like a man turned to stone as the real meaning of this chance-spelt signal rushed upon me. It was 'S O S'—the sailors' call for help!

"Nor was this all. I had already noticed that the creature had come to rest in the same position every time it had finished the ninth stroke, but now I saw that its head was resting on the compass at almost exactly the same point where our present course lay. The difference was only a quarter of a point to the southward; that is to say, we were heading 'West-South-West,' whereas the course indicated by the moth was 'West-South-West, *quarter South*.'

"Even as I stood staring the signal was repeated. The light feathery wings beat the air once more; again came the three rapid taps, the pause, the three slower taps, another pause, and then the three final taps in quick succession. Again the creature alighted on the glass with its head resting on the same quarter-point of the compass.

"Now, I'm not naturally a superstitious man, but I don't mind admitting that I felt a very curious feeling stealing over me as I stood alone in that cabin and watched that little greyish-white insect spell out the signal which is never sent out unless a vessel be in dire straits, and then come to rest pointing so unerringly to a course so near our own. It was useless for me to try to persuade myself that it was pure coincidence; that the three fluttering taps might be the natural movements of the moth; that there might be something on the covering-glass of the compass which would account for the thing always seeking the same spot. Try as I might, I could not get it out of my head that the little moth was trying to tell me to shift my helm a quarter of a point to the south.

"Still, one does not act on impulse when in charge of an ocean liner, nor does one depart from the specified track without good cause. First of all I must make sure that my imagination was not playing a trick on me. I slipped on my uniform and quietly made my way aft to the First Officer's berth. McAndrew was a hard-headed and eminently practical Scot in whose sound common sense I felt I could trust in such a case as this. He was asleep, but his eyes snapped open the instant I laid my hand on his shoulder.

"'Anything wrong, sir?' he cried as he recognized me.

"'Not exactly,' I answered. 'But I want your advice on a little matter that's been troubling me a bit.'

"Mac looked a little surprised, but he was a good deal more so when I led the way to my cabin and pointed to the compass.

"'Why, it's naething but a wee bit moth,' he cried. 'They call them "ghaistie-flutters" up where I was born, them being white, ye see—'

"I interrupted him by holding up my hand.

"'Watch—and listen,' I said, purposely refraining from telling him what to expect in case it should unconsciously influence his judgment.

"As I spoke a slight movement began to agitate the soft, downy wings, and presently:

"*Tap-tap-tap—Tap... tap... tap—Tap-tap-tap.*

"McAndrew glanced round at me when the wings had become still.

"'If I'd ha' heard that on a wireless receiver I'd have thought I was listening to an "S O S",' he said slowly.

"'It's been rapping out the same three letters for the past half-hour,' I told him. 'And every time it has come to rest over the same point of the compass.'

"He craned his neck upward and I saw him start.

"'Guid preserve us!' he jerked out. 'The wee beastie is heading within a quarter of a point of our ain course!'

"I nodded silently, for the moth was again repeating its strange message.

"'West-South-West, quarter South,' I read as the frail wings ceased quivering. 'And I'm very much tempted to follow the new course.'

"He gave me a long, searching look before replying.

"'Yon is a matter aboot which nae mon can advise another, sir,' he said at length. 'It's something clean beyond the rules of seamanship and navigation. But speaking for myself, sir, if I were in command of this packet I'd shift my helm to the quarter where yon puir beastie seems trying to guide us.'

"I stood for a long while in thought after he had finished speaking. A young master mariner can make or mar his reputation on his first trip. I had been given the command over the heads of older and more experienced men, and I well knew that my conduct would be closely and jealously watched, and, if needs be, criticized. If I were to veer out of the usual track and ill came of it, I would be a marked man for the rest of my life—and I'd seen too many out-of-work shipmasters kicking their heels round the agents' offices not to know what *that* meant. On the other hand, there was the little white moth fluttering out the message that no sailor worth his salt can listen to unmoved, and pointing persistently to the south. I was not a man who loved taking chances, but—for good or ill—I determined to take one then.

"I turned briskly.

"'Pass the word to the quartermaster, Mr McAndrew,' I ordered. 'The course is "West-South-West, *quarter South*"!'

"'Quarter South it is, sir,' the old Scotsman returned, with glistening eyes. Then he raised his hand and touched his cap reverently.

'May the good Lord reward ye if ye're doing right—and may He help ye if ye're not!'

"He went out on the bridge, and a few seconds after I saw the 'lubberline,' which coincides with the head of the ship, veer round until it came abreast of the spot where the moth was resting, showing that we had swung on to the new course.

"Almost at the same moment, as though it knew that its mission had been accomplished, the little moth fell to the deck, quivered for an instant, and then was still for ever. I gently lifted the little dead messenger, placed it in an empty matchbox, and stowed it away in my locker. I have it still, and sometimes, when things go wrong and the world seems to be just a huge ant-hill of humanity ruled by blind chance and brute instincts, I take out that matchbox and look upon the tiny white moth that came to me in mid-Atlantic... and my faith is restored.

"For, thirty-six hours after changing course, we sighted the old *Rangoon*, outward-bound and crowded, and blazing from bridge to stern. Over a thousand souls lived to bless the change of course indicated by that little winged messenger, and among them was the lady who is now my wife...

"And that's why I have a tender spot in my heart for the little light-blinded creatures which flutter in out of the night."

BEYOND THE STAR CURTAIN

Garth Bentley

Garth Bentley (1903–1956) was an author, poet and editor who gradu-
ated from Northwestern University in Illinois. He worked on industrial
handbooks, was the founder of "International Council of Industrial
Editors" and also authored a handbook on *How to Edit an Employee
Publication* along with several poetry collections. Bentley's "Beyond
the Star Curtain" was published in *Wonder Stories*, an early American
pulp magazine which ran from 1929 to 1955. Being published in one of
the leading Science Fiction magazines allowed Bentley and his work
to be included in the impressive alumni of *Wonder Stories* along with
giants of the genre such as John Wyndham. Wyndham's story "The
Venus Adventure" would be published a year after "Beyond the Star
Curtain" in the May 1932 issue.

"Beyond the Star Curtain" is an imaginative tale following two
space travellers as they return to Earth after having miscalculated their
timelines. When they arrive back on their home planet, they find an
overgrown jungle filled with megaflora and fauna which they deduce
to be thousands if not millions of years in the future. The sheer variety
of insect species they encounter in the story creates intrigue as the
monstrous giants lurking in the oversized vines and mushrooms include
stick insects, beetles, fiendish ants and the menacing praying mantis.
Instead of setting the action on a mysterious far-off planet, Bentley's
space opera creates an uncanny, alien version of Earth, complete with
a damsel in distress for good measure. Bentley's prescient tale journeys

through an alternative, unfamiliar "Mother Earth" where humans are converted into insect prey, and could also serve as a comment on the dangers of climate change.

hrough the velvet darkness of interstellar space sped the ovoid vessel, its gigantic bulk hurtling, with almost inconceivable speed, toward the cloud-wrapped earth. The space ship—for such it was—seemed a veritable comet as it entered the boundaries of the solar system, gliding through the emptiness on the wings of its own accumulated momentum. Yet, large though it was, its bulk was dwarfed by the majesty of the outer ring, which illumined the blackness.

As it neared its destination, a series of quick, soundless explosions came from the tubes in the bow of the ship. Great streams of flame shot out into space, checking the momentum of the craft by the recoil of the explosions. It entered the upper air of the earth at a wide angle, the tubes spitting an unceasing cannonade. The outer hull—a thick alloy of beryllium steel and chromium—began to glow dully as it heated from the friction of the air.

Eventually the craft slowed its headlong pace and settled into a regular orbit about the planet. Many times it circled the giant ball in an ever-decreasing orbit as the speed gradually lessened. The glow faded from the outer shell, and at last it plunged through the thick, concealing bank of clouds into the lower regions of the atmosphere, sinking at last to rest on the earth's surface.

Inside the great egg-shaped ship, two men leisurely unstrapped themselves from the stout hammocks where they had lain since the deceleration of the ship's speed had begun. They seemed young men—in the late twenties or early thirties—judging from their smooth, clear cut features and strong athletic figures. Under the brief silken garments which both wore bulged muscles that told of unusual strength. Something about the set of their mouths, the square outlines of their chins and the levelness of their glances proclaimed both to be men of resolute and daring character, even as their well-shaped heads told of unusual intelligence.

Derek Porter, blond, English, and the elder of the two, turned to his companion with a pleasant grin.

"Well, Old Son, we are back on old Mother Earth again. How does it feel to you?"

"Fair enough," the other admitted. Verne Williams topped his partner's six feet by an inch or so. He was unmistakably American with his grey eyes and reddish-brown hair. "Wonder how long we've been gone?" he speculated, busying himself over the knobs and dials of the controls.

"Hard telling. Maybe ten years, maybe ten thousand. Who knows? But as soon as it gets light"—they had alighted on the shadowed half of the earth—"we can get out of this chariot and have a look around."

"One thing sure," Verne offered, "people won't believe half what we tell them about our trip. Not that I blame them, either," he added.

Nor would it be remarkable if the story of their adventures fell on sceptical ears, for they were returning from the strangest adventure man had ever undertaken. And this, in an age when man—newly conscious of his freedom from the grip of his native planet—had wandered about the solar system at will. But these two, in a ship far exceeding anything previously known in power and cruising radius and undreamed speed, had gone far beyond the boundaries of the solar system—beyond even the universe itself.

Toward the Southern Cross they had flown, seeking the answer to the riddle of the "Coal Sack"—that great dark pitch in the heavens where no stars shine and the blackness of empty space seems almost tangible. They had found it—a wide curtain of blackness, filling the heavens at that point for a space large enough to hide a dozen solar systems of greater size than their own. Through the curtain they had hurled their ship, through thick blackness in which the latent electricity and the cosmic rays of two impinging, tangent universes, intersecting at that point, struggled for supremacy, hurling back from their whirlpool of force even the light rays that sought to penetrate this cosmic veil.

The two earthlings in their man-made ship had won through at last. The ovoid, with the cumulative momentum of its long journey, plunged into the infinity of darkness, although the struggle in the black whirlpool threatened to disrupt the very atoms of it and the earthly intruders it bore. Their chronometers, their radio, the lights and even the greater portion of the controlling mechanism of the ship had been destroyed or warped and twisted out of all usefulness. It was only after great effort that they were able to continue, having repaired the latter after a fashion with the materials which were available.

Once beyond the "Coal Sack," they had found themselves in a new universe, a firmament of colourful, mighty suns, blazing with all the known hues and others that they could not name. Around many of the suns, swung great planets, circling at a leisurely, unhurried pace. As they glided through the placid heavens of the strange universe, they felt a pleasant lassitude creep over them. Their craft no longer hurtled through the sky at its former mad rate as it had before they had plunged into the maelstrom of darkness. Nor did there seem the need for speed.

They had landed on one of the strange planets, called by its own inhabitants Karaku, which encircled a great blue sun. Here they had found a pleasant and hospitable people, far different in physical and mental structure from the earthlings, but who had made them welcome.

On Karaku, with its habitable portion always toward the sun, there had been no time. The sun was always overhead and the period of the planet's rotation was so long that, though the Karakuans lived to fabulous ages, showing no changes as the "time" passed, there were none alive who knew when their world had last completed a trip around its orbit. So, having no means of measuring time, they did not measure it at all, but lived their placid uneventful lives completely oblivious of such a property. Nor did any but the earthling mourn the lack of measurements. Things moved so very slowly in this new universe that even the two strangers did not worry long about a thing that had no existence.

But the people of Karaku, although pleasant and intelligent, were not human beings, and the thoughts of the two men turned at last to the planet of their birth. In the timeless world they had no way of knowing whether they had been gone years or centuries. There had been no physical change in their bodies and they had drifted into the easy effortless life of Karaku. Although even their thoughts seemed to move slowly, at last they began to feel the desire to see creatures of their own kind. Eventually they took their leave of the hospitable planet, hurtled somehow through the dark veil and, after again repairing the damage to their controls, brought their craft at last to earth.

Derek, who had risen from the bunk where he had been indulging in a short nap, moved to the side of the ship and pressed his face to one of the fused quartz ports. For some time he stood looking out upon the scene, while Verne drowsed in his hammock, then at last he turned to his companion.

"It doesn't look like any place that I ever saw before," he remarked. "The sky is still hidden by the clouds but it's getting light enough to see things a bit. Suppose we start moving."

Verne rose from his perch and joined him. Outside the ship stretched a meadow of rank swamp grasses, reaching in places half-way up the side of the craft. Hemming them in on all sides stretched the dark green fronds of jungle growth. The tall trees, their tops like umbrellas, high in the air, were strange and unfamiliar. Some of them showed freshly broken tops where the space ship had ploughed its way in landing and already the broken edges of their trunks were beginning to blacken. Verne considered the landscape for some moments without speaking. Then he whistled shrilly.

"Say, Derek, you don't think we could have missed our aim and landed someplace else, do you? This looks a lot like Venus to me."

"It does that. But this is the earth, all right. Don't you remember the moon—just before we dived through the clouds? There's no mistaking Sister Luna among all the other moons of the universe."

"But there's no vegetation like this on earth," Verne protested, waving in the general direction of the port through which he had looked upon the strange pulpy trees, the tangled creepers and the fleshy fungus. "Not even in the jungles of the Amazon can you find stuff like that growing. And by rights we should be well up in the north temperate zone—somewhere on the North American continent."

Derek scratched his head.

"I'm afraid what you should have said," he replied slowly, "is that there was nothing like this growing on the earth while we lived here."

"What do you mean?" Verne asked anxiously. Something in the big Englishman's voice conveyed more than mere words could have done.

"How do you know how long we were gone? We spent our time on a strange planet in an entirely different universe, probably in a different time dimension or in one where time wasn't a dimension at all. We know it took us years to reach the black curtain and the lord knows how long to return from it; and how long we spent on Karaku? As far as we were concerned time stood still while we were there. Neither one of us seemed to get a day older after we broke through the dark spot. If you ask me, I think a good many thousand years have passed since we last saw earth. Perhaps millions."

"Impossible!"

"Maybe. But there's the fact that everything is relative—even time. My own opinion is that we passed through another dimension where time just didn't exist."

"But what makes you think we were away so long? The scenery?"

"Partly," Derek replied. "But most of all the stars. Remember the Big Dipper while we were snorting around the planet before landing? How it seemed to have been pressed all out of shape? Back in school they used to tell you that the stars in it are actually moving in different directions but that it would take a long time before the changes could be noticed. The fact that they have visibly changed position proves to me that a great many centuries have passed."

"Then," Verne remarked, only half realizing the import of his friend's statement, "that means everybody we ever knew or heard of has been dead for a long while."

"More than that," Derek replied grimly. "I'm only hoping we will still find human beings on the earth at all."

II

"No other people left on earth? Surely the human race cannot have disappeared entirely, granting even that a long time has passed." Verne was emphatic in his denial.

"Oh, I don't believe that the race would have died out of itself. But you can see for yourself the climatic changes that have taken place. The earth has evidently gotten much warmer, to judge from the tropical foliage; and if the change was sudden, whether it came from conditions in the centre of the earth or because—which is more likely—the earth has been drawn closer to the sun, humanity might have been wiped out before man's intelligence showed him a way to conquer his new environment. Or, if the change came gradually over a period of many thousands of years, humanity may have evolved in various ways to meet the new conditions. People may be nothing like the men and women we knew. Human beings may no longer exist."

"I still can't believe that we've been gone so long although all of the evidence points to your being right," Verne sighed. "Now that we're back it seems to me that it was only yesterday that we left."

"It does seem like it," Derek admitted. "While we were on Karaku we were under a different set of influences and time didn't count. But now we're on our own world and each day we get one day older for Father Time is back in the saddle and we'll have to get used to his hard riding. The fact that we sit here so contentedly philosophizing with a whole new planet to explore, proves that we haven't entirely shaken off the Karakuan influence. Let's get going."

He rose and strode over to the mechanism which controlled the doors.

"I'm going outside and see what it's like. Coming?"

"Sure. But wait a minute. I've been in jungles before and we'll need something besides our bare hands, particularly if we go far."

From a locker, Verne drew two of the strange metal swords that they had brought with them from Karaku, where the inhabitants—although essentially peaceful—considered a sword a necessary part of the costume. They were wicked looking weapons and could prove very useful where the vegetation was heavy. The long thin blades were broad at the top, tapering down toward the jewelled metal handles, and giving the appearance of long, thin inverted triangles. They were made of a metal unknown to earth, light as aluminium but able to shear through an inch plate of steel when wielded by strong men.

"They'll make pretty good machetes," Derek admitted. "Besides there's no telling what we may meet in a jungle like this. There may be snakes in those bushes."

Together they swung out through the outer door of the hull and jumped lightly to the thick spongy grass below. The humid, steamy atmosphere was like the interior of a Turkish bath. Even in their light garments, their bodies were drenched with perspiration before they had taken a dozen steps through the safe muggy turf. Verne bent low, examining the sod.

"Derek," he exclaimed. "Do you know what this is we're walking on? It's moss—moss a foot and a half thick!"

They came to the edge of the little clearing and plunged into the forest hacking their way with the razor-edged swords. It was a jungle unlike any with which they were familiar. In many ways it resembled the swamps of colourless growths that covered the twilight zones of Venus, yet the flora were more nearly akin to that of the old earth. The thick undergrowth of shrubbery was a weird mixture of plants grown unbelievably large. The occasional trees they came across were fighting a losing battle against unclean parasitic growths that covered almost every inch of the stems and branches, drawing their sustenance from the lifeblood of the trees. Great toadstools and mushrooms reared their umbrella tops on thick, fleshy stems to the height of trees. Giant lianas drooped and festooned themselves from the branches of weedy plants, incredibly tall. Slimy and evil smelling mould and dank moss covered the ground, and everywhere was the overpowering fetid smell of decaying vegetation.

It was only by the greatest effort that they attained their objective—a giant acacia tree upon a little knoll, that somehow seemed to have defied the choking grip of the parasites. Verne swung himself up into the branches and climbed steadily to the top. As far as the eye could see, the jungle stretched unbroken. Through the powerful K-glasses, he could see a purple haze, far to the north that seemed to promise the presence of mountains.

He began to descend, swinging himself rapidly down through the branches. Half-way down, his foot slipped from its hold on one of the stems. To save himself, he grasped the first thing at hand—a dead limb about the size of his arm. As it came away he felt barbed legs fasten themselves to his arms and his body as the limb—now very much alive—clung tenaciously to his clothing. Slipping, dropping from branch to branch, his clutching fingers trying vainly to grip the tree, he plunged with his antagonist to the ground below. The jointed horror, struggling but, like Verne, half-dazed, waved long antennae aimlessly in the air.

Derek, at whose feet Verne had fallen, leaped forward, his weapon poised carefully. The thing raised itself from the struggling man, a creature out of a drug-ridden nightmare. Derek's blade cut through the air with a vicious slash, and the horror, its body neatly severed, fell to one side, the long legs—unbelievably thin—kicking feebly.

Verne rose from the ground slowly.

"What was it, Derek?" he asked, shaking his head as if to clear his dazed brain by the gesture. "I slipped and grabbed hold of the nearest branch and then the next thing I knew the branch had pulled away and was fastened on to me with all kinds of arms and legs."

Derek was examining the dead monster with interest.

"Remember when you were a boy you used to see funny twig-like bugs on bushes and old trees? Walking sticks we called them. They were jointed just like a bamboo cane and when they were on a dead limb, you could hardly see them unless they took a notion to move. They were about the most perfect examples of natural camouflage among all living creatures."*

"Sure. I remember them. But the ones I used to see were only about three or four inches long while this one is almost five feet long and is as big around as my upper arm."

"This is probably the grand-daddy of them all, but there's no mistaking the breed. They are all harmless leaf-eaters." He paused and looked about him anxiously. "Do you know, Verne, I'm getting just a bit worried?"

"Why? This fellow's dead enough. And, as you said, his kind are harmless."

"I'm not worrying about him. He's done, and walking sticks aren't numerous even in a bug's paradise such as the world seems to have turned into. But if he could grow to such a size—what about the rest of the insect tribe?"

"Maybe he was just a freak—or some new species."

"Maybe. But while you were up there in the tree, I saw some queer looking birds flying around here—birds with six legs. One of them came close and instead of a bird it turned out to be an ordinary

---

* The ordinary U. S. variety is called *Diapheromera Femorata*. These insects belong to the phasmidae of the order of orthoptera.

ichneumon fly—the size of a cock pheasant. And—look up there—"
He broke off to point above the trees.

At first Verne thought it was a monoplane soaring high in the air.
There was the long slender body of the fuselage, the wide extended
wings. Then it swung lower and he saw it for what it was—a great
dragon fly, skimming the higher levels of the forest on its way back to
some stagnant pool in the depths of the jungle.

By common consent the two turned backward toward the plane.
They said little about the creatures they had seen. It was all too
incredible—this new climate of the earth's and its effect on the insect
kingdom. It would require time for their minds to become adjusted
to the new conditions. As they walked along over the way they had
come—where the rapidly growing fungus was already replacing the
growths they had cut from their path—Verne mentioned the mountains
he had seen through the glass.

"At least they looked like mountains," he said. "But from what I've
seen so far I wouldn't bet on it. They're several hundred miles away at
least. If we want to get to them we'd better take the ship. We couldn't
make more than five or six miles a day on foot."

"There weren't any signs of human habitations, were there? Towns,
houses or even smoke?"

"No. Not a sign. But this atmosphere is so thick and steamy that
the range of vision is pretty limited even with the glasses. Over to the
right of us I saw a place where a fog of mist was rising, but I'm pretty
sure it was only a swamp."

"Lord! what a fine homecoming," Derek grinned. "Remember how
we wondered what kind of an official reception we'd get from the
people in the old home town? And now look where we've landed! We
don't know where. We don't even know when. My vote is to go back
to Karaku. The people there weren't exactly humans but they were

better than bugs in a stinking swamp. Or we could get in the old tub and go cruising around until we find a planet peopled with humans."

"We may have to," Verne agreed. "But then we haven't enough power to take us to Karaku or to go cruising around. There's just about enough to get us out of the planet's range of attraction, with enough in the forward tubes to allow us to land somewhere safely. Venus would be our only hope and it's probably worse than this. It was bad enough in the old days with its slimy worms and dripping forests. And the people always gave me the shivers with their dead fishy eyes.

"Besides," he continued, "I can't believe that there aren't any human beings left on earth at all. The human race is pretty tenacious when it comes to surviving under all sorts of adverse conditions. I'm for hitting north towards those mountains. It's a cinch that if any people are left, they'd make for the polar bear country. Let's have a look anyway."

"It's all right with me," Derek agreed. "After we've come all this way to get back home, I think I'd just as soon have a little more of a look around. After all this may be only a dirty little patch on the earth's surface. If we can just get the ship up off the moss—and I think we can, even if we haven't got an incline—we can use minimum charges and coast along a bit until we spot your mountains."

They entered the ship together. In a few moments, from the lower stern tubes came explosions of flame and sharp detonations of sound. The great ovoid quivered and wrenched at the clinging moss. The air was black with weird and unknown insects, disturbed by the waves of unaccustomed sound, swarming up from the dank, green depths. The ship rose with a jerk, pitching and tossing as they manoeuvred it over the ground until the bow pointed northward. Then there was a sudden roar, the stern tubes belched smoke and flame, and the ship flashed in the air.

At minimum speed, the rocket ship swung northward in a series of great parabolas. Unequipped as it was with wings—except for the two stabilizing vanes on the sides of the craft—and lacking propeller or rudder, the two men were forced to depend entirely on the tubes to guide their vessel, as well as to propel it and keep it aloft. But when not at the controls, they found time to study the country as they passed over it.

It was an utterly strange land to both of them. Everywhere stretched the seemingly endless sea of rank vegetation, broken here and there by small bare patches or spurs of naked rock. Above them lay the thick blanket of clouds that shut off all sight of the sky and made a definite ceiling for the murky, humid atmosphere. Occasionally the forest gave way to broad rivers, sluggish and muddy, or to steamy, semi-stagnant lakes whose surface was often disturbed by uncouth, weird forms. Apparently the same power which had given added size to the insect world had also operated to the enlargement of those hideous simple-celled inhabitants of the warm pools, creatures which mark the boundary between the plant and animal kingdoms.

On some of the pools, they saw great water bugs, gliding over the surface like catamarans, and near all of them they saw the hordes of the great dragon flies. Large black flies and other strange winged folk rose in clouds from the fungus growths of the forests, disturbed by the flaming thunder of the tubes as each fresh discharge sent the ship on another stage of its curving flight.

In one spot they disturbed myriad bird grasshoppers, huge insects grown to the size of eagles, that blackened the air with their numbers as they rose from the strip of forest they had been devastating. Through the glasses, Verne—who was at one of the windows—could see plainly the blunt armoured heads and thoraxes, the powerful, jointed legs and the crushing mandibles, bathed in the dark brown secretion he had once called "terbacker juice" in the bygone days when he had captured their tiny cousins to bait his fish hooks.

They reached the mountains within a few hours and found them little more than rock hills, covered as was everything else by the dense vegetation. No sign of human habitation met their eye, but while they were looking for a place to bring the ship to rest, Derek saw—still farther north—a thin pencil of smoke. A short blast from the rockets and the falling ship again resumed its course. A few seconds later, the firing of the forward tubes brought it to an abrupt halt and it crashed into the under-brush bordering one of the small bare patches. Verne, thrown off his balance by the force of the landing, climbed to his feet rubbing his shoulder.

"Nice gentle way you have of landing this crate," he remarked in an injured tone. "That's twice in the same spot."

Derek turned away from the controls, grinning.

"This old lady wasn't built for a pleasure ship to go cruising about the planet. It was meant to head off in a straight line and keep going. Out there"—he waved a hand toward the clouds—"you can slow her up for a million miles or so ahead of your destination. Here we've got to stop in a hurry or we'd be half-way around the globe. Besides, the distance of that smoke was deceiving. I thought it was a lot farther away."

They left the ship and, swords in hand, started across the ground. The going was not easy through the thick moss but they finally reached the spot where the dying embers of the fire were sending out a few feeble flickers. It was an ordinary smudge of the type used to discourage the insect pests of the forest. But this was not the thing that most interested them—though the fire itself told of the presence of human beings. Two small tents made of a strange cloth interwoven with metal threads, stood close to the fire. With quickened steps they moved closer to inspect the tents for occupants when the humming silence of the jungle was broken by a shrill scream.

The two men stopped transfixed. It came again, a piercing shriek of terror. Feminine. And not far away. They turned and dashed in the direction from which the sound came, hacking their way through the tangled forest that sought to bar them. A third time they heard it, this time close by.

They redoubled their efforts and slashed through the last barrier into a second small clearing.

Three figures in the very centre of the space stood posed in an unforgettable tableau. There was a girl, young and pretty with her pale skin, and with her dark hair falling in a loose mass over her shoulders, shrinking back in terror. And there was a man, a white-haired man, who stood as if hypnotized, his hands gripping a long wooden spear, staring at the thing that confronted him.

It was this creature that drew their attention. It was huge—almost seven feet high. Wide delicate wings, pale green in colour, trailed like misty veils from the slender body which stood supported on four wiry legs. Its head, ratlike, except for the great insect eyes—out of all proportion to its other features—was a hideous caricature surmounting a thin neck. The two great forearms were hugged close to the breast, folded up in a perfect attitude of prayer. With its devout pose and the fairy, delicate wings, it seemed an angel from a weird green heaven come to serve the bidding of a bizarre deity of a far distant planet. It stood, its neck slightly bent over the supplicating forearms and its gaze on the petrified man before it. Derek grasped Verne's arm in a grip that hurt.

GARTH BENTLEY

"What is it, Derek?" the latter demanded. "It looks like a ghost."

"It's worse than a ghost. It's an insect devil, grown to a terrible size. A praying mantis. Come on!" He broke off and started across the clearing on a dead run, his sword gripped in his hand. Verne followed closely.

But their haste was in vain. Before they had crossed but a few yards a sudden transformation came over the green creature. From a praying angel it became an avenging devil with a suddenness that took the breath away. The wings spread to the fullest extent, standing up like parallel screens of transparent gauze. The end of the flexible abdomen began to curl and uncurl, swinging backwards and forwards between the four supporting legs with a swishing sound like the hiss of a gigantic puff adder. The upper portion of the slender body rose to its full height on the straddling under legs. The praying forearms opened wide in a horrible embracing gesture, the murderous barbs and the sharp claw-like talons outspread.

The two men shouted vainly to the doomed human, trying to break the spell the weird, terrible creature seemed to have cast upon him. He did not hear them or, if he heard, he did not heed their cries of warning, but continued to gaze spellbound into the blazing opal eyes of the creature's darting head.*

---

* There is much speculation among entomologists concerning the reason for the mantis' pose. Many naturalists believe that this blood-thirsty insect (*Mantis Religiosa*, of the otherwise vegetarian family, Orthoptera) possesses the power to hypnotize its prey and that the pose is a part of its hypnotic process: Crickets, which flee from the slightest sign of danger, will stand motionless while the creature kills them. The mantis is the insect tiger, attacking anything and devouring its prey alive. It frequently devours its own mate during the act of mating.

Then it struck. Quicker than thought the forelegs whipped forward, the sharp talons gripped the man and drew him ruthlessly to the green breast. He shrieked in terror as one barbed forearm held his body to the creature in a cruel crushing vice. The cruel head bent swiftly forward as the other forelimb bent the man's head downward. Then the narrow snout of the mantis buried itself in the taut neck of its victim, severing the nerve ganglions and crushing the vertebrae.

Totally ignoring the hysterical girl and the two men rushing toward her, the mantis prepared to enjoy its ghastly meal. Derek reached the creature first, stabbing wildly with his blade at the huge terror. He sheared through one of the under legs cleanly, his blade burying itself in the creature's soft abdomen. It dropped its victim and wheeled to meet this new attack, assuming its terrible fighting pose. Derek, looking into the creature's eyes, seemed to feel a queer paralysis creeping over him.

He saw the great forearms distended, raised to strike. But the creature was hampered greatly by the missing leg and the deep wound in the abdomen. Its movements were sluggish as it moved toward him. He tried to shake off the fascination of the peacock feather eyes, to break the spell that held him. He saw the creature towering above him. Then Verne was on the creature's flank, his sword swinging. A flash of cold metal and the mantis' head flew from its slender body.

Derek shuddered as the green spectre sank to the ground, close to the body of her former victim. The great wings still fluttered and the legs moved feebly, but the creature was undoubtedly dead. They turned from it to the girl who was sobbing over the body of the dead man.

III

Even in her grief at the death of her father, Loma was beautiful. Her dark eyes, veiled with a mist of tears, turned toward the two men as they approached her. Verne, hungry for the glimpse of a woman after so long a time among aliens, stared unashamedly and realized for the first time what had pulled him back across the reaches of space. Even Derek, hardened misogynist that he was, felt his heart warm to her in her sorrow. But the new conditions of earth seemed to have bred a stronger, less sentimental race. As if realizing the futility of her grief—or bowing to the inevitability of death—Loma soon dried her tears, crossed her father's arms upon his breast, picked up the thin javelin which he had carried, and rose to meet them.

"Who are you who have slain the green killer?" she asked, in a language, altered, greatly changed, but still recognizable as English.

They told her that they were two who had been very far away, visiting a far distant planet in another universe. They saw that their explanation meant little to the girl, and it was only when Derek waved his hand toward the heavens, telling her that they came from "beyond the clouds", that they made their meaning clear. A shadow of disbelief fluttered across her face, but she made no comment other than to thank them for delivering her.

It was not until long afterward that Verne learned that neither she nor her people, the pitiful remnant of America's once proud civilization, had any conception of the universe beyond the clouds. To them, the canopy which kept out the blazing rays of the sun was an impenetrable roof over a flat world. Only a few had ever seen the sun on the rare occasions when the clouds had parted for an instant. Then it had seemed the avenging destroyer from a world of fire, shrivelling the fungoid verdure, and sending suffocating clouds of vapour up from the swampy earth. None had ever seen a star or realized the cosmic wonders that once made the heavens a thing of beauty to earth's peoples.

"Where did you and your father come from?" Verne asked.

Loma motioned toward the northwest.

"They live far from here," she replied, "many marches through the jungle. My father heard of other peoples living to the south and we set out with a great expedition to locate them. We travelled for many days, but ill luck seemed always to attend us. One by one our men were lost in the depths of the swamps or fell in battle with the insects. Some were stricken with the shaking death* and as we had no medicine they did not last long. Finally there were none but my father, my brother and myself. While we rested by the fire which we had built in a glade not far from here, he vanished. When we lay down by the fire he was there and when we awoke he was gone, leaving no traces. I fear the killer got him, too."

"Perhaps he merely wandered away," Verne suggested. "We may be able to find him for you."

"Perhaps," she agreed, but they could see that she had few hopes.

"At least, we can take you back to your people," Derek promised. "You will have to show us the way."

"Come, then." She turned to lead the way back to the tents and the campfire.

"Wait a minute."

Verne could not bear to leave the body of the man where it lay. Derek joined him, and together they dug a shallow trench into which they placed the body reverently. Loma watched in open eyed wonder as they built a rough cairn of rocks over the grave.

---

* Malaria

"Do you not bury your dead?" Verne asked.

"No," she admitted. "We leave the bodies outside and—they vanish. Do they plant the dead in the earth in your city, which we sought so far?"

Loma had evidently ignored their own explanation of their origin and had identified them as members of the fabled colony her father had sought. Deciding that it would be useless to repeat their explanation, they continued to question her about her people and her city, while they ploughed their way between the fleshy stalks of the sulphur-tuft forest. The great hoods of the toadstools, towering forty and more feet above their heads, dripped moisture unceasingly. Occasionally they encountered the fetid, overpowering odour of the foul stinkhorn* and they made wide detours to avoid its thick, gigantic column. Going slowly it took them some time to cover the ground that the two men had forced their way through in such a hurry only a short time before.

They reached the spot where the fire had been burning, finding it almost out. The tents were torn and trampled and near them they found traces of great foot prints. From Loma's description, for she guessed the intruder that had wrecked the camp—they recognized the destroyer as a giant beetle, who finding the tents in his chosen line of march, had calmly demolished them. They were just a little thankful that they had not been present when the monster had appeared.

The space ship lay undisturbed where it had come to rest, half buried in the muck and soft mud beneath the thin crust of the turf. Loma cried out and drew back as she saw the great vessel, evidently mistaking it for a new and, therefore terrible, species of beetle. Only

---

* *Phallus Impudicus.*

after much coaxing would she even approach its sides, and both Derek and Verne had to go in and come out of the door a great many times before she would consent to follow them inside.

Once in the ship, however, her wonder changed to immediate delight at the dry and cosy interior. Her intensely practical mind immediately grasped its utility as living quarters, and she seemed to appreciate to the full the safety it offered. Places of sanctuary, it seemed, were few and far between in the world that she knew. There, every strange creature was an enemy, and man—ill equipped as he was to fight a ravaging nature that gave no quarter—had only survived by matching his cunning against the armoured and weaponed insects. From what she had told them they guessed that the people of her times lived in constant terror of the creatures which had inherited the world.

The steaming swamps, the fungus forests and the stagnant, scum-covered waters bred millions of hostile creatures, most of whom esteemed human beings as dainty tidbits. It was an insect-ridden world, a world where the works of man had vanished before the all-consuming dampness during the years when man had been too busy with the problem of survival, against ever-changing and always unfavourable conditions, to progress.

As a result, humanity had slipped a long way backward. The people lived precarious lives in the high caves they had hollowed out of the mountains. Cunning of the mass had given way to cunning of the individual. Except when danger threatened the home settlements, it was every man for himself—and a horrible fate awaited him who fell into the clutches of any of the carnivorous insects.

It was a terror-stricken Loma who first felt the quivering of the ship as Derek, at the controls, fired the forward rockets in an effort to escape the clinging tentacles of the mud which had gripped the nose of the ship. At last it shook itself free, and when it lay once more on an even keel the great stern tubes spoke and the ship lifted itself from the ground in a great swoop.

Once her fears were overcome, Loma accepted this new means of transportation with little difficulty. With true feminine logic, she felt no wonder at whatever the amazing minds of her companions might produce. After all, she reasoned, they were merely men, although rather good looking, especially the reddish-haired one. From time immemorial, woman has accepted the finest gifts man could devise as the portion justly due her—particularly if the man be her lover—without thought to the greatness or the strangeness of the gift.

To Loma, the great space ship which had struck awe in the hearts of the dwellers on strange planets, was merely a handy vehicle conveying her back to her own people, and she bothered little about the how or why of its origin and purpose. As she stood at Verne's side, watching the green country speed backward below them, her mind was far more occupied with the idea that her companion was very much in love with her, stranger though he was. And in her own way she was not at all displeased.

They had flown but a little while when there came an ominous sputtering from the rear tubes. Derek investigated and when he returned to the little cabin in the centre of the ship his face was very grave. Verne noticed his expression and drew him to one side.

"What's the matter, Derek?" he asked.

"The fuel. We're almost out of it. One more discharge of the rear tubes will exhaust our supply completely."

"How about the forward tubes?"

"They have only a little left and we will need that to slow us up in landing. Ploughing through this soupy atmosphere has taken an enormous quantity since we've had to fight both gravity and air resistance."

They were interrupted by a sudden shout from Loma, that sent them rushing forward to the window where she stood looking through the glasses.

"I think those are the hills where my people live," she cried pointing toward a distant line of purple.

Verne heaved a sigh of relief. The ovoid was already falling in the down curve of the arc and the flight would end in a few moments more. But they could easily make the rest of the way on foot. It could only be a matter of twenty-five or thirty miles, making due allowances for the deceptive qualities of the atmosphere.

Then the tubes gave a last coughing explosion and the ship began a long coasting fall to the ground. The forward tubes belched forth their blasts as the nose of the craft pointed to earth. Carefully gauged, the discharges slackened the ship's speed to a minimum and they made a safe landing on the soft moss.

Refreshed by a short sleep and food from the ship's larder, the three left the sanctuary of the vessel and began the long trek through the wilderness toward the mountain home of Loma's people. In the comparative cool of the dawn they made good time. Verne and Derek, with their keen cutlasses hacked away the impeding lianas and thick grasses and cut narrow paths through dense thickets of *calocera viscosa*, sprung to imposing heights from the rotting vegetation which covered the ground. Loma, armed with a light hand axe, helped as well as she was able. But before long, in the depths of the jungle, they were forced to slow down their pace.

Here great forests of bamboo-like growths, so thickly seeded that passage was impossible, often caused long and tedious detours. Great puff-balls,* fifty to one hundred feet in diameter frequently blocked their path, and after Verne had disgustedly slit one with his sword, releasing a choking cloud of spores, they found it best to give these mushroom monstrosities a wide berth.

All day they forced their way through the tangled undergrowth, pausing only for a meal of food they had brought with them from the ship. When the mellow twilight, lengthened because of the light diffused through the enclosing cloud banks, warned them of the near approach of night, they prepared to camp near the rock ruins of a limestone hill. Not even the rocks, it seemed, could long withstand the destroying damp. Erosion had taken its toll of even the hardest substances.

Underneath the projecting shoulder of the cliffs, they found some measure of protection against the voracious mosquitoes which rose as the heat of the day moderated. These insects, large as hawks and terrifying with the weird whirring of their wings, were a true menace to life. Only the fact that their natural enemies in the insect world had increased proportionately, while the warm-blooded men and animals from which they drew their food had almost died out, prevented them from over-running the earth. As it was, there were plenty of them.

Yet it was not long before they found these monsters vastly preferable to their diminutive ancestors. Though the mosquitoes were far more dangerous because of their increased size, one of them being able to drain the blood from a human being, the loud noise of their wings gave ample warning of their approach and their size made them easy targets for the sharp swords.

When the darkness had fallen and the day insects began to give place to the huge moths and night flying things, they retired to a light

---

*   *Lycoperdon Giganticum.*

sleep, leaving Verne on guard beside their fire. They were all thoroughly tired, for though they had come but a few miles, the labour had been exceedingly wearying. Derek had offered to stand the first watch, but Verne, knowing his partner had taken the brunt of the work during the day, would not hear of it.

He settled himself comfortably on a smooth boulder covered with moss and let his thoughts turn back to the old world he had known. But his day had not been an easy one and in spite of all his efforts, he found his eyelids drooping. He made a heroic effort to rouse himself but his eyes finally closed and he fell into a deep and profound sleep.

He awoke to find himself being lifted from the ground, his body held in a vice-like grip. He tried to move, to break away, and succeeded in loosing a cry which brought Derek and Loma to their feet in alarm. The moon had evidently arisen and its pale light, filtering through the clouds, made the scene light with a silvery, eerie radiance. He looked at his captor, twisting his neck about with difficulty, and saw a horny, horrible head, great eyes and two questing antennae waving above him. Giant mandibles held him in an unbreakable grip, though the pressure on his ribs was not altogether unbearable.

He saw Derek running toward him and saw him strike at the monster. The great head that held him dropped from the thorax and he fell heavily to the ground. The mighty jaws relaxed, and freeing himself from the grisly, misshapen head, he climbed to his feet and retrieved his sword. He saw the headless body of his late captor, its six legs contracting spasmodically as death claimed it.

Then he heard Derek call to him and he saw Loma and his friend surrounded by a ring of giant ants. The monstrous insects, fully six feet long and standing several feet high were attempting to get within the circle of his flailing sword.

*

Verne hesitated but a moment before throwing himself upon the nearest of the monsters. His sword sliced through the thick armoured body and the creature went down. The insects, intent only on reaching Derek and the girl, ignored Verne as he hacked at them from the rear, until only three of them were left. Verne with a quick thrust, severed the antennae from the head of the nearest one, who, deprived of the most important of its organs, immediately withdrew from the battle, stumbling aimlessly around as if entirely devoid of its senses. Verne made for the next one but the creature, as if realizing that the battle was lost, turned and scuttled away at high speed, just as Derek disposed of the last of his antagonists.

Together with Loma, the two men inspected their late adversaries. The black, gleaming bodies, many of them still squirming in the pale moonlight, were horrible in the extreme, like creatures out of some fantastic purgatory. They seemed perfect fighting machines, with their heavy horny bodies and the cruel thick mandibles, capable of crushing the humans to pulp. And the silent, cold ferocity with which they had attacked, the purposeful intentness of their fighting marked them the real rulers of this new existence.

"Wonder why the other one scrammed in such a hurry?" asked Verne as they turned from examining their victims.

It was Loma who answered.

"That ant went for help," she replied. "We have evidently stopped near a colony of them. It will come back with many others."

"Then we had better get somewhere else in a hurry," Derek decided. "There's no use sitting here waiting for trouble. Perhaps if we can get far enough away they will not pursue us."

But even as he spoke, they heard the coming of the ants. This time there were hundreds of them, approaching in regular formation. The two men held their swords ready and Loma, behind them, gripped the small axe.

"Looks like it's goodby, old fellow," Derek said quietly. "We can keep them off for a while, but..."

"Maybe," Verne admitted. "We can at least give them plenty of trouble. Hit for their antennae; they're helpless if anything happens to them." He grasped his sword tightly and took a few vicious cuts at the air.

Then the first wave of the attackers swept up to them and they had no time for conversation. They struck blindly, wounding, killing, maiming, but ever the ants pressed forward. And still more came from around the hillside. By sheer weight of the attack, the three were pressed back against the cliffs, pressed back until they no longer had room to swing their weapons but had to depend on short, chopping cuts that often glanced off the armoured heads of the insects. Then they felt great furry legs sweeping over them. Derek's arms were pinioned to his sides by the mandibles of a giant emmet and he saw its abdomen, with its needle-pointed stinger, curving toward his body. He felt a rapier-like pain shoot through him, heard a scream from Loma and Verne's voice cursing loudly. Then he was gone.

IV

He regained consciousness slowly, and found himself being carried rapidly over the ground by one of the ants. He tried to move his arms and legs but found them unresponsive. Out of the corner of his eye, for he could not turn his head, he could see Loma's fluttering draperies and he tried to call to her and found that he could make no sound. He did not see Verne but guessed that he could not be far away.

For some time they swung along, going uphill and down, over the tops of huge fungus growths and up the sides of unscalable boulders. He marvelled at his captor's ability to carry him so easily, without pausing to rest or shift the weight of so great a burden. Then he remembered, from an almost forgotten course in zoology, that if ants were the size of men they would be the strongest creatures on earth. And he marvelled the more that he and Verne and Loma had been able to withstand them for so long, as they had.

They came at last to where the path became a definitely marked road which led into the city of the ants. The great hills towered hundreds of feet in the air and covered acres of ground at their bases. Cone-shaped, the great bulks seemed far larger than any works of man, than any of the architectural wonders they had seen on far Karaku. The dwellings were roofed with stones,* giving them an appearance of solidity which he felt was entirely deserved. Nothing short of a severe earthquake could damage them.

They met numerous others of the great creatures coming from the communes, warriors, like those which had captured them, workers major and the tiny workers minor, setting out to forage food for the larvae, the nurses and the ant queens. No one showed the slightest curiosity toward the captives, nor was there any reception accorded the captors.

Occasionally a soldier stationed along the avenues challenged members of the party, and there was a great deal of gesticulating and rubbing of antennae, while the guard sought for the identifying odour of the communal hill. The challenges became more frequent as they approached the towering entrance, like the mouth of a huge cavern, at

---

* These ants had evidently evolved from the occidental ants found in western United States, which roof their hills with pebbles, stones, etc.

the base of the central dome. But always they pressed onward, and at last passed into the great corridor that led to the inside of the commune.

For a long time, or so it seemed to Derek, they were carried through the dark, stuffy corridors of the commune. As his eyes grew more accustomed to the semi-darkness, he could make out the bare walls of the avenue they were traversing, and the endless corridors intersecting it at regular intervals. A continual stream of workers passed them, going toward the outside.

They came to the store rooms, situated far below the surface of the ground. Here they were met by countless workers carrying eggs upward toward the higher cells of the mound, where the warmth of the outer air during the daylight hours might hasten the process of incubation. Derek marvelled that the great mandibles, capable as he well knew of a bone crushing grip, could carry the eggs with so gentle a pressure as to cause no damage to the delicate shells or their undeveloped inmates.

Then they came to the rooms where the "nurses" were caring for the queer, helpless larvae. Like human nurses in hospitals, these ant prototypes hovered over their charges, feeding them, changing their positions. They groomed the bodies of the larvae as well, licking them as a mother cat licks the fur of her kittens. In another huge cell, Derek caught a glimpse of a great-bellied queen mother surrounded by a horde of her worker attendants.

Deeper in the commune they came to other great rooms where workers and virgin queens were attending the fungus gardens. In still others of the subterranean chambers of the dwelling, he saw workers caring for the aphids—the domesticated cows of the ant world, great soft creatures who accepted their grooming with every evidence of pleasure.

At last they came to the tier of cells where the worker ants were busily engaged in storing food away. Into one of these the three ants with their unresisting burdens made their way. While Derek was speculating on the probable fate in store for them there, the three of them were unceremoniously dumped on the floor and rolled to one side. Thus their captors left them beside the bodies of huge beetles, hornets of great size, and other insects which had some how fallen into the clutches of the ants.

Here they lay helpless for a long time in the stench and smothering air of the dim roof, unmolested and, to all appearances, forgotten. They had become a part of the commune's emergency store of food and would remain there until needed. Seeing that Verne was awake, Derek called to him softly.

"Hurt, fellow?"

"No. But I can't move. What have they done to us?"

"Paralysed us with their stingers and laid us away in their icehouse until somebody gets hungry or the food supply runs low."

"Why don't they kill us and put us out of our misery?"

"Why should they care how miserable we are, even if it occurred to them to think of it at all? I imagine that they expected us to die from the effects of the stinging, but we were just paralysed. You forget that we're dealing with insects now. They don't think or reason any more than so many of the Karakuan robots. These bugs don't consider us enemies in the sense we think of the word. When they bumped into us we were pretty dangerous customers, it never occurred to them that we might not be worth the lives it would cost to get us. Their instinct told them to capture us and they did it. They would have kept after us until the last ant in the tribe was dead. But once they had us stored safely in the hill, they forgot us."

After a long while, during which he must have slept, Derek heard Loma calling to Verne.

"Verne," she called softly. "Oh Verne. I believe that I can move my arm."

"Yes," Verne answered. "I've been feeling little twinges in my legs for some time. How about you, Derek?"

Derek tried to move and was able to turn his head slightly.

"I believe that the poison is beginning to wear off," he replied. "Evidently it doesn't have a permanent effect on human beings, through our skins and our lungs. I imagine the stuff they shot into us was some kind of a formic acid compound and, while it might have been fatal, it won't have any permanent effects."

The time passed with a slowness that was maddening. To the three, unable to move about, it seemed that they had spent years as captives in the commune. But little by little they gained the use of their limbs. At first they found their bodies sluggish, hard to control, but as more time passed they were able to move about the chamber. As the paralysis left them, they began to feel the need for food and water. The men had brought a supply of concentrated food from the rocket, but it was only a question of time until they faced the alternative of starving or helping themselves to the ants' gruesome stores.

Their captors seemed to have had absolutely no curiosity concerning their strange garments or accoutrements. Nothing had been taken from them. Even the great swords, stained with the life fluid of the warriors had been left in the store room with them, clutched in the frozen grip of their paralysed fingers.

Once more in control of their bodies, the three began laying plans for escape. Verne, who seemed to love a good fight for its own sake, was all for a bold attempt to cut their way out of the commune. Derek, on the other hand, remembering the swarming thousands that filled the corridors between them and freedom, was in favour of more stealthy measures. Eventually his counsel prevailed and at length, swords ready, they prepared to leave the prison that had held them for so long.

The lower corridors were comparatively free from ants. The occasional workers, returning laden with food for the store rooms, they avoided by dodging into nearby corridors when possible. When they had no time for this, the worker was murdered in cold blood and the body placed in the nearest food chamber. Once or twice they met great males, the phenomenally stupid consorts of the ant queens. These were great hulking fellows, unable to distinguish friend or foe, dependent on the workers for their sustenance and lacking the fighting qualities of the workers and warriors. These were calmly ignored by the three fugitives.

For some time they wandered about the subterranean catacombs, hiding and fleeing and fighting. Yet always they made their way upward toward the light of day, and each succeeding hour of freedom gave them renewed confidence. Then one day they met their first warrior ant and the whole course of their plans was changed.

Derek was in the lead and he stopped suddenly as he came full upon a full-grown warrior turning from a side corridor. The ant halted abruptly and, as Derek held back, waiting for Verne to join him, the warrior examined him closely with great nearsighted eyes. All the time the questing antennae, where, as he knew, the ant's powerful sense of smell is located, went carefully over his body. Then as if reassured by the examination, the ant passed on, leaving Derek frozen with astonishment.

Verne and Loma who had waited, silent spectators of the meeting, for some hostile move on the part of the warrior, moved quickly to his side.

"Why didn't the ant attack you?" they asked breathlessly.

Derek shook his head. Then to their intense surprise, he burst into a ringing peal of laughter.

"I'm just thinking of the time we have wasted," he said. "If only I had remembered what every student of entomology knows, we would have been free before now. Ants depend almost entirely on their acute sense of smell and on the instincts that guide their every moment. They recognize their friends or enemies by smelling them, and we have been in this particular hill long enough to have soaked up some of the communal odour of this outfit. That ant may have thought I was a funny looking worker, but as long as her feelers told her I was all right, she believed them in preference to the evidence of her eyes."

He broke off, chuckling.

"All this time we have spent sneaking down corridors and hiding out was purely unnecessary," he continued. "Ants are the wonders of the insect world, marvels of industry and courage, and living in highly organized communities, but after all they are only insects and are ruled by instinct rather than intelligence. And whenever blind instinct meets intelligent reasoning, brains always win out. The very strength of the ants is, after all, their greatest weakness."

He grasped his astonished companions by the arms and moved off down the corridor.

"Come on. All we have to do is to walk boldly out of the hill and not an ant will disturb us."

The ease with which they made their way to the upper levels proved the truth of his assertions. The great majority of the ants they passed, busily engaged in the work of the commune, ignored them completely. An occasional soldier halted them momentarily, but always allowed them to pass undisputed. At last they met a file of workers, bound evidently for the outside, since they were empty handed.

The three humans attached themselves unobtrusively to the rear guard of the group and passed along the corridors henceforth unchallenged. It was a master stroke, for they might otherwise have wandered about the labyrinthian ways of the commune for a long lime. As it was, they noticed the avenues growing wider, until they found themselves in the broad main corridor, leading to the entrance. It was all they could do to keep from running ahead to the bright opening that marked the presence of light and fresh air. But they restrained this impulse, knowing that to give way to their desire would invite unwelcome attention on the part of the guards at the entrance.

Following the unconscious file of workers, they passed beyond the confines of the hill; and not until they were outside the limits of the community of stone-roofed mounds did they fall back and allow their guides to go on without them.

Many days later, days filled with almost miraculous escapes from death in many different forms, days of creeping across clearings and hewing their way through the jungle of ferns and fungus, they came to the upper end of a valley set well among the hills of the north. Here the fungus grew less luxuriantly, the undergrowth was less dense, and occasionally they found trace of once familiar plants. Loma, who was leading the way, halted and turned to her companions.

"We are nearing the valley with me? You will be welcome."

Her words were addressed to both of them, but her eyes were resting on Verne's face, pleading. With her family wiped out on the ill-fated expedition of which she was the sole survivor, there was little to call her back—although there were many young men in her village who had looked upon her in a way that told of love unspoken. If only, she thought, this young man with the reddish hair...

Verne caught her glance and smiled, his heart leaping within him.

"After all, why not, Derek?" he said, trying to make his tone appear casual. "There is no place else to go and they are probably the last remnants of our own people. We came clear across space to find them. There is no reason for not going on."

Derek nodded.

"Sure," he replied. "I imagine they are pretty primitive but then we can help them out considerably. Perhaps in time we can reclaim part of the land, drive off the insects and establish a new civilization. Perhaps we can even build space ships to carry them to another planet... We'll do a lot for them, won't we, partner?"

"Yeah."

Verne's voice was muffled, for his lips were pressed close to Loma's dark hair. Derek glanced at them and then turned away. He stood looking off down the valley that sheltered the remnants of earth's people, his mind busy with a golden dream of future empire. But Verne's thoughts were all of the present and the girl in his arms.

LEININGEN VERSUS THE ANTS

Carl Stephenson

Carl Stephenson (1893–19??) was born in Vienna and is the only author in this collection whose native language was not English. His year of death is usually given as 1954; however, doubt has been cast upon the accuracy of the date on the grounds of confusion with an American namesake. Stephenson founded his own publishing house, translated English and French works into German, and wrote satirical, parodic and critical books under the pseudonym of Stefan Sorel and under his own name.

Stephenson's short story was originally published in German as "*Leiningens Kampf mit den Ameisen*" in *Die Neue Linie* (*The New Line*) in 1937. It then appeared as "Leiningen Versus the Ants" in the December 1938 edition of *Esquire*. Other well-known contributors in the 30s include F. Scott Fitzgerald, John Steinbeck and Ernest Hemingway. Ordinarily for a foreign-language piece, the magazine would reference a translator. Since in this case it does not, the assumption is Stephenson translated himself. His tale of masculine heroics underpinned with simmering sexual tension in a hot climate fits perfectly with the gentleman's magazine environment. The story describes the plantation owner Leiningen leading his workers in a battle against an army of highly invasive and ingenious ants in the Amazon rainforest. It is a fight to the death. As individuals the ants are not oversized, it is their massed numbers working in concert that function as a vast, all-consuming and unstoppable macro-organism. In 1954 it was adapted into a film starring Charlton Heston and renamed *The Naked Jungle*. Entomological weirdness here lies not in any mythological past or dystopian future, not in any scientific experiment gone awry or in any fantastic manifestation, but in the normal colonizing behaviour of intelligent insects in the wild.

"nless they alter their course, and there's no reason why they should, they'll reach your plantation in two days at the latest."

Leiningen sucked placidly at a cigar about the size of a corn cob and for a few seconds gazed without answering at the agitated District Commissioner. Then he took the cigar from his lips and leaned slightly forward. With his bristling grey hair, bulky nose, and lucid eyes, he had the look of an ageing and shabby eagle.

"Decent of you," he murmured, "paddling all this way just to give me the tip. But you're pulling my leg, of course, when you say I must do a bunk. Why, even a herd of saurians couldn't drive me from this plantation of mine."

The Brazilian official threw up lean and lanky arms and clawed the air with wildly distended fingers. "Leiningen!" he shouted, "you're insane! They're not creatures you can fight—they're an elemental—an 'act of God'! Ten miles long, two miles wide—ants, nothing but ants! And every single one of them a fiend from hell; before you can spit three times they'll eat a full-grown buffalo to the bones. I tell you if you don't clear out at once there'll be nothing left of you but a skeleton picked as clean as your own plantation."

Leiningen grinned. "Act of God, my eye! Anyway, I'm not an old woman; I'm not going to run for it just because an elemental's on the way. And don't think I'm the kind of fathead who tries to fend off lightning with his fists, either. I use my intelligence, old man. With me, the brain isn't a second blindgut; I know what it's there for. When I began this model farm and plantation three years ago, I took into account all that could conceivably happen to it. And now I'm ready for anything and everything—including your ants."

The Brazilian rose heavily to his feet. "I've done my best," he gasped. "Your obstinacy endangers not only yourself, but the lives of your four hundred workers. You don't know these ants!"

Leiningen accompanied him down to the river, where the Government launch was moored. The vessel cast off. As it moved downstream, the exclamation mark neared the rail and began waving its arms frantically. Long after the launch had disappeared round the bend, Leiningen thought he could still hear that dimming, imploring voice. "You don't know them, I tell you! *You don't know them!*"

But the reported enemy was by no means unfamiliar to the planter. Before he started work on his settlement, he had lived long enough in the country to see for himself the fearful devastations sometimes wrought by these ravenous insects in their campaigns for food. But since then he had planned measures of defence accordingly, and these, he was convinced, were in every way adequate to withstand the approaching peril.

Moreover, during his three years as planter, Leiningen had met and defeated drought, flood, plague, and all other 'acts of God' which had come against him—unlike his fellow settlers in the district, who had made little or no resistance. This unbroken success he attributed solely to the observance of his lifelong motto: *The human brain needs only to become fully aware of its powers to conquer even the elements.* Dullards reeled senselessly and aimlessly into the abyss; cranks, however brilliant, lost their heads when circumstances suddenly altered or accelerated and ran into stone walls; sluggards drifted with the current until they were caught in whirlpools and dragged under. But such disasters, Leiningen contended, merely strengthened his argument that intelligence, directed aright, invariably makes man the master of his fate.

Yes, Leiningen had always known how to grapple with life. Even here, in this Brazilian wilderness, his brain had triumphed over every difficulty and danger it had so far encountered. First he had vanquished primal forces by cunning and organization, then he had enlisted the resources of modern science to increase miraculously the yield of his plantation. And now he was sure he would prove more than a match for the 'irresistible' ants.

That same evening, however, Leiningen assembled his workers. He had no intention of waiting till the news reached their ears from other sources. Most of them had been born in the district; the cry, 'The ants are coming!' was to them an imperative signal for instant, panic-stricken flight, a spring for life itself. But so great was the Indians' trust in Leiningen, in Leiningen's word, and in Leiningen's wisdom, that they received his curt tidings, and his orders for the imminent struggle, with the calmness with which they were given. They waited, unafraid, alert, as if for the beginning of a new game or hunt which he had just described to them. The ants were indeed mighty, but not so mighty as the boss. Let them come!

They came at noon the second day. Their approach was announced by the wild unrest of the horses, scarcely controllable now either in stall or under rider, scenting from afar a vapour instinct with horror.

It was announced by a stampede of animals, timid and savage, hurtling past each other; jaguars and pumas flashing by nimble stags of the pampas; bulky tapirs, no longer hunters, themselves hunted, outpacing fleet kinkajous; maddened herds of cattle, heads lowered, nostrils snorting, rushing through tribes of loping monkeys, chattering in a dementia of terror; then followed the creeping and springing denizens of bush and steppe, big and little rodents, snakes, and lizards.

Pell-mell the rabble swarmed down the hill to the plantation, scattered right and left before the barrier of the water-filled ditch, then sped onwards to the river, where, again hindered, they fled along its banks out of sight.

This water-filled ditch was one of the defence measures which Leiningen had long since prepared against the advent of the ants. It encompassed three sides of the plantation like a huge horseshoe. Twelve feet across, but not very deep, when dry it could hardly be described as an obstacle to either man or beast. But the ends of the 'horseshoe' ran into the river which formed the northern boundary, and fourth side, of the plantation. And at the end nearer the house and outbuildings in the middle of the plantation, Leiningen had constructed a dam by means of which water from the river could be diverted into the ditch.

So now, by opening the dam, he was able to fling an imposing girdle of water, a huge quadrilateral with the river as its base, completely around the plantation, like the moat encircling a medieval city. Unless the ants were clever enough to build rafts, they had no hope of reaching the plantation, Leiningen concluded.

The twelve-foot water ditch seemed to afford in itself all the security needed. But while awaiting the arrival of the ants, Leiningen made a further improvement. The western section of the ditch ran along the edge of a tamarind wood, and the branches of some great trees reached over the water. Leiningen now had them lopped so that ants could not descend from them within the 'moat'.

The women and children, then the herds of cattle, were escorted by peons on rafts over the river, to remain on the other side in absolute safety until the plunderers had departed. Leiningen gave this instruction, not because he believed the non-combatants were in any danger, but in order to avoid hampering the efficiency of the defenders. "Critical situations first become crises," he explained to his men, "when oxen or women get excited."

Finally, he made a careful inspection of the 'inner moat'—a smaller ditch lined with concrete, which extended around the hill on which stood the ranch house, barns, stables, and other buildings. Into this concrete ditch emptied the inflow pipes from three great petrol tanks. If by some miracle the ants managed to cross the water and reach the plantation, this 'rampart of petrol' would be an absolutely impassable protection for the besieged and their dwellings and stock. Such, at least, was Leiningen's opinion.

He stationed his men at irregular distances along the water ditch, the first line of defence. Then he lay down in his hammock and puffed drowsily away at his pipe until a peon came with the report that the ants had been observed far away in the south.

Leiningen mounted his horse, which at the feel of its master seemed to forget its uneasiness, and rode leisurely in the direction of the threatening offensive. The southern stretch of ditch—the upper side of the quadrilateral—was nearly three miles long; from its centre one could survey the entire countryside. This was destined to be the scene of the outbreak of war between Leiningen's brain and twenty square miles of life-destroying ants.

It was a sight one could never forget. Over the range of hills, as far as eye could see, crept a darkening hem, ever longer and broader, until the shadow spread across the slope from east to west, then downwards, downwards, uncannily swift, and all the green herbage of that wide vista was being mown as by a giant sickle, leaving only the vast moving shadow, extending, deepening, and moving rapidly nearer.

When Leiningen's men, behind their barrier of water, perceived the approach of the long-expected foe, they gave vent to their suspense in screams and imprecations. But as the distance began to lessen between the 'sons of hell' and the water ditch, they relapsed into silence. Before the advance of that awe-inspiring throng, their belief in the powers of the boss began to steadily dwindle.

Even Leiningen himself, who had ridden up just in time to restore their loss of heart by a display of unshakable calm, even he could not free himself from a qualm of malaise. Yonder were thousands of millions of voracious jaws bearing down upon him and only a suddenly insignificant, narrow ditch lay between him and his men and being gnawed to the bones 'before you can spit three times'.

Hadn't his brain for once taken on more than it could manage? If the blighters decided to rush the ditch, fill it to the brim with their corpses, there'd still be more than enough to destroy every trace of that cranium of his. The planter's chin jutted; they hadn't got him yet, and he'd see to it they never would. While he could think at all, he'd flout both death and the devil.

The hostile army was approaching in perfect formation; no human battalions, however well drilled, could ever hope to rival the precision of that advance. Along a front that moved forward as uniformly as a straight line, the ants drew nearer and nearer to the water ditch. Then, when they learned through their scouts the nature of the obstacle, the two outlying wings of the army detached themselves from the main body and marched down the western and eastern sides of the ditch.

This surrounding manœuvre took rather more than an hour to accomplish; no doubt the ants expected that at some point they would find a crossing.

During this outflanking movement by the wings, the army on the centre and southern front remained still. The besieged were therefore able to contemplate at their leisure the thumb-long, reddish-black, long-legged insects; some of the Indians believed they could see, too, intent on them, the brilliant, cold eyes, and the razor-edged mandibles, of this host of infinity.

It is not easy for the average person to imagine that an animal, not to mention an insect, can *think*. But now both the European brain of Leiningen and the primitive brains of the Indians began to stir with the unpleasant foreboding that inside every single one of that deluge of insects dwelt a thought. And that thought was: Ditch or no ditch, we'll get to your flesh!

Not until four o'clock did the wings reach the 'horseshoe' ends of the ditch, only to find these ran into the great river. Through some kind of secret telegraphy, the report must then have flashed very swiftly indeed along the entire enemy line. And Leiningen, riding—no longer casually—along his side of the ditch, noticed by energetic and wide-spread movements of troops that for some unknown reason the news of the check had its greatest effect on the southern front, where the main army was massed. Perhaps the failure to find a way over the ditch was persuading the ants to withdraw from the plantation in search of spoils more easily attainable.

An immense flood of ants, about a hundred yards in width, was pouring in a glimmering-black cataract down the far slope of the ditch. Many thousands were already drowning in the sluggish, creeping flow, but they were followed by troop after troop, who clambered over their sinking comrades, and then themselves served as dying bridges to the reserves hurrying on in their rear.

Shoals of ants were being carried away by the current into the middle of the ditch, where gradually they broke asunder and then, exhausted by their struggles, vanished below the surface. Nevertheless, the wavering, floundering hundred-yard front was remorselessly if slowly advancing towards the besieged on the other bank. Leiningen had been wrong when he supposed the enemy would first have to fill the ditch with their bodies before they could cross; instead, they merely needed to act as stepping stones, as they swam and sank, to the hordes ever pressing onwards from behind.

Near Leiningen a few mounted herdsmen awaited his orders. He sent one to the weir—the river must be dammed more strongly to increase the speed and power of the water coursing through the ditch.

A second peon was despatched to the outhouses to bring spades and petrol sprinklers. A third rode away to summon to the zone of the offensive all the men, except the observation posts, on the nearby sections of the ditch, which were not yet actively threatened.

The ants were getting across far more quickly than Leiningen would have deemed possible. Impelled by the mighty cascade behind them, they struggled nearer and nearer to the inner bank. The momentum of the attack was so great that neither the tardy flow of the stream nor its downward pull could exert its proper force; and into the gap left by every submerging insect, hastened forward a dozen more.

When reinforcements reached Leiningen, the invaders were half way over. The planter had to admit to himself that it was only by a stroke of luck for him that the ants were attempting the crossing on a relatively short front: had they assaulted simultaneously along the entire length of the ditch, the outlook for the defenders would have been black indeed.

Even as it was, it could hardly be described as rosy, though the planter seemed quite unaware that death in a gruesome form was drawing closer and closer. As the war between his brain and the 'act of God' reached its climax, the very shadow of annihilation began to pale to Leiningen, who now felt like a champion in a new Olympic game, a gigantic and thrilling contest, from which he was determined to emerge victor. Such, indeed, was his aura of confidence that the Indians forgot their stupefied fear of the peril only a yard or two away;

under the planter's supervision, they began fervidly digging up to the edge of the bank and throwing clods of earth and spadefuls of sand into the midst of the hostile fleet.

The petrol sprinklers, hitherto used to destroy pests and blights on the plantation, were also brought into action. Streams of evil-reeking oil now soared and fell over an enemy already in disorder through the bombardment of earth and sand.

The ants responded to these vigorous and successful measures of defence by further developments of their offensive. Entire clumps of huddling insects began to roll down the opposite bank into the water. At the same time, Leiningen noticed that the ants were now attacking along an ever-widening front. As the numbers both of his men and his petrol sprinklers were severely limited, this rapid extension of the line of battle was becoming an overwhelming danger.

To add to his difficulties, the very clods of earth they flung into that black floating carpet often whirled fragments towards the defenders' side, and here and there dark ribbons were already mounting the inner bank. True, wherever a man saw these they could still be driven back into the water by spadefuls of earth or jets of petrol. But the file of defenders was too sparse and scattered to hold off at all points these landing parties, and though the peons toiled like madmen, their plight became momently more perilous.

One man struck with his spade at an enemy clump, did not draw it back quickly enough from the water; in a trice the wooden haft swarmed with upward scurrying insects. With a curse, he dropped the spade into the ditch; too late, they were already on his body. They lost no time; wherever they encountered bare flesh they bit deeply; a few, bigger than the rest, carried in their hindquarters a sting which injected a burning and paralysing venom. Screaming, frantic with pain, the peon danced and twirled like a dervish.

Realizing that another such casualty, yes, perhaps this alone, might plunge his men into confusion and destroy their morale, Leiningen roared in a bellow louder than the yells of the victim: "Into the petrol, idiot! Douse your paws in the petrol!" The dervish ceased his pirouette as if transfixed, then tore off his shirt and plunged his arm and the ants hanging to it up to the shoulder in one of the large open tins of petrol. But even then the fierce mandibles did not slacken; another peon had to help him squash and detach each separate insect.

Distracted by the episode, some defenders had turned away from the ditch. And now cries of fury, a thudding of spades, and a wild trampling to and fro, showed that the ants had made full use of the interval, though luckily only a few had managed to get across. The men set to work again desperately with the barrage of earth and sand. Meanwhile an old Indian, who acted as medicine man to the plantation workers, gave the bitten peon a drink he had prepared some hours before, which, he claimed, possessed the virtue of dissolving and weakening ants' venom.

Leiningen surveyed his position. A dispassionate observer would have estimated the odds against him at a thousand to one. But then such an onlooker would have reckoned only by what he saw—the advance of myriad battalions of ants against the futile efforts of a few defenders—and not by the unseen activity that can go on in a man's brain.

For Leiningen had not erred when he decided he would fight elemental with elemental. The water in the ditch was beginning to rise; the stronger damming of the river was making itself apparent.

Visibly the swiftness and power of the masses of water increased, swirling into quicker and quicker movement its living black surface, dispersing its pattern, carrying away more and more of it on the hastening current.

Victory had been snatched from the very jaws of defeat. With a hysterical shout of joy, the peons feverishly intensified their bombardment of earth clods and sand.

And now the wide cataract down the opposite bank was thinning and ceasing, as if the ants were becoming aware that they could not attain their aim. They were scurrying back up the slope to safety.

All the troops so far hurled into the ditch had been sacrificed in vain. Drowned and floundering insects eddied in thousands along the flow, while Indians running on the bank destroyed every swimmer that reached the side.

Not until the ditch curved towards the east did the scattered ranks assemble again in a coherent mass. And now, exhausted and half numbed, they were in no condition to ascend the bank. Fusillades of clods drove them round the bend towards the mouth of the ditch and then into the river, wherein they vanished without leaving a trace.

The news ran swiftly along the entire chain of outposts, and soon a long scattered line of laughing men could be seen hastening along the ditch towards the scene of victory.

For once they seemed to have lost all their native reserve, for it was in wild abandon now they celebrated the triumph—as if there were no longer thousands of millions of merciless, cold, and hungry eyes watching them from the opposite bank, watching and waiting.

The sun sank behind the rim of the tamarind wood and twilight deepened into night. It was not only hoped but expected that the ants would remain quiet until dawn. But to defeat any forlorn attempt at a crossing, the flow of water through the ditch was powerfully increased by opening the dam still further.

In spite of this impregnable barrier, Leiningen was not yet altogether convinced that the ants would not venture another surprise attack. He ordered his men to camp along the bank overnight. He also detailed parties of them to patrol the ditch in two of his motor cars and ceaselessly to illuminate the surface of the water with headlights and electric torches.

After having taken all the precautions he deemed necessary, the farmer ate his supper with considerable appetite and went to bed. His slumbers were in no wise disturbed by the memory of the waiting, live, twenty square miles.

Dawn found a thoroughly refreshed and active Leiningen riding along the edge of the ditch. The planter saw before him a motionless and unaltered throng of besiegers. He studied the wide belt of water between them and the plantation, and for a moment almost regretted that the fight had ended so soon and so simply. In the comforting, matter-of-fact light of morning, it seemed to him now that the ants hadn't the ghost of a chance to cross the ditch. Even if they plunged headlong into it on all three fronts at once, the force of the now powerful current would inevitably sweep them away. He had got quite a thrill out of the fight—a pity it was already over.

He rode along the eastern and southern sections of the ditch and found everything in order. He reached the western section, opposite the tamarind wood, and here, contrary to the other battle fronts, he found the enemy very busy indeed. The trunks and branches of the trees and the creepers of the lianas, on the far bank of the ditch, fairly swarmed with industrious insects. But instead of eating the leaves there and then, they were merely gnawing through the stalks, so that a thick green shower fell steadily to the ground.

No doubt they were victualling columns sent out to obtain provender for the rest of the army. The discovery did not surprise Leiningen. He did not need to be told that ants are intelligent, that certain species even use others as milch cows, watchdogs, and slaves. He was well aware of their power of adaptation, their sense of discipline, their marvellous talent for organization.

His belief that a foray to supply the army was in progress was strengthened when he saw the leaves that fell to the ground being dragged to the troops waiting outside the wood. Then all at once he realized the aim that rain of green was intended to serve.

Each single leaf, pulled or pushed by dozens of toiling insects, was borne straight to the edge of the ditch. Even as Macbeth watched the approach of Birnam Wood in the hands of his enemies, Leiningen saw the tamarind wood move nearer and nearer in the mandibles of the ants. Unlike the fey Scot, however, he did not lose his nerve; no witches had prophesied his doom, and if they had he would have slept just as soundly. All the same, he was forced to admit to himself that the situation was now far more ominous than that of the day before.

He had thought it impossible for the ants to build rafts for them-selves—well, here they were, coming in thousands, more than enough to bridge the ditch. Leaves after leaves rustled down the slope into the water, where the current drew them away from the bank and car-ried them into midstream. And every single leaf carried several ants. This time the farmer did not trust to the alacrity of his messengers. He galloped away, leaning from his saddle and yelling orders as he rushed past outpost after outpost: "Bring petrol pumps to the south-west front! Issue spades to every man along the line facing the wood!" And arrived at the eastern and southern sections, he dispatched every man except the observation posts to the menaced west.

Then, as he rode past the stretch where the ants had failed to cross the day before, he witnessed a brief but impressive scene. Down the slope of the distant hill there came towards him a singular being, writhing rather than running, an animal-like blackened statue with a shapeless head and four quivering feet that knuckled under almost ceaselessly. When the creature reached the far bank of the ditch and collapsed opposite Leiningen, he recognized it as a pampas stag, covered over and over with ants.

It had strayed near the zone of the army. As usual, they had attacked its eyes first. Blinded, it had reeled in the madness of hideous torment straight into the ranks of its persecutors, and now the beast swayed to and fro in its death agony.

With a shot from his rifle Leiningen put it out of its misery. Then he pulled out his watch. He hadn't a second to lose, but for life itself he could not have denied his curiosity the satisfaction of knowing how long the ants would take—for personal reasons, so to speak. After six minutes the white polished bones alone remained. That's how he himself would look before you can—Leiningen spat once, and put spurs to his horse.

The sporting zest with which the excitement of the novel contest had inspired him the day before had now vanished; in its place was a cold and violent purpose. He would send these vermin back to the hell where they belonged, somehow, anyhow. Yes, but how, was indeed the question; as things stood at present it looked as if the devils would raze him and his men from the earth instead. He had underestimated the might of the enemy; he really would have to bestir himself if he hoped to outwit them.

The biggest danger now, he decided, was the point where the western section of the ditch curved southwards. And arrived there, he found his worst expectations justified. The very power of the current had huddled the leaves and their crews of ants so close together at the bend that the bridge was almost ready.

True, streams of petrol and clumps of earth still prevented a landing. But the number of floating leaves was increasing ever more swiftly. It could not be long now before a stretch of water a mile in length was decked by a green pontoon over which the ants could rush in millions.

Leiningen galloped to the weir. The damming of the river was controlled by a wheel on its bank. The planter ordered the man at the wheel first to lower the water in the ditch almost to vanishing point, next to wait a moment, then suddenly to let the river in again. This manœuvre of lowering and raising the surface, of decreasing then increasing the flow of water through the ditch, was to be repeated over and over again until further notice.

This tactic was at first successful. The water in the ditch sank, and with it the film of leaves. The green fleet nearly reached the bed and the troops on the far bank swarmed down the slope to it. Then a violent flow of water at the original depth raced through the ditch, overwhelming leaves and ants, and sweeping them along.

This intermittent rapid flushing prevented just in time the almost completed fording of the ditch. But it also flung here and there squads of the enemy vanguard simultaneously up the inner bank. These seemed to know their duty only too well, and lost no time accomplishing it. The air rang with the curses of bitten Indians. They had removed their shirts and pants to detect the quicker the upwards-hastening insects; when they saw one, they crushed it; and fortunately the onslaught as yet was only by skirmishers.

Again and again, the water sank and rose, carrying leaves and drowned ants away with it. It lowered once more nearly to its bed; but this time the exhausted defenders waited in vain for the flush of destruction. Leiningen sensed disaster; something must have gone wrong with the machinery of the dam. Then a sweating peon tore up to him:

"They're over!"

While the besieged were concentrating upon the defence of the stretch opposite the wood, the seemingly unaffected line beyond the wood had become the theatre of decisive action. Here the defenders' front was sparse and scattered; everyone who could be spared had hurried away to the south.

Just as the man at the weir had lowered the water almost to the bed of the ditch, the ants on a wide front began another attempt at a direct crossing like that of the preceding day. Into the emptied bed poured an irresistible throng. Rushing across the ditch, they attained the inner bank before the slow-witted Indians fully grasped the situation. Their frantic screams dumbfounded the man at the weir. Before he could direct the river anew into the safeguarding bed he saw himself surrounded by raging ants. He ran like the others, ran for his life.

When Leiningen heard this, he knew the plantation was doomed. He wasted no time bemoaning the inevitable. For as long as there was the slightest chance of success, he had stood his ground, and now any further resistance was both useless and dangerous. He fired three revolver shots into the air—the prearranged signal for his men to retreat instantly within the 'inner moat'. Then he rode towards the ranch house.

This was two miles from the point of invasion. There was therefore time enough to prepare the second line of defence against the advent of the ants. Of the three great petrol cisterns near the house, one had already been half emptied by the constant withdrawals needed for the pumps during the fight at the water ditch. The remaining petrol in it was now drawn off through underground pipes into the concrete trench which encircled the ranch house and its outbuildings.

And there, drifting in twos and threes, Leiningen's men reached him. Most of them were obviously trying to preserve an air of calm and indifference, belied, however by their restless glances and knitted brows. One could see their belief in a favourable outcome of the struggle was already considerably shaken.

The planter called his peons around him.

"Well, lads," he began, "we've lost the first round. But we'll smash the beggars yet, don't you worry. Anyone who thinks otherwise can draw his pay here and now and push off. There are rafts enough and to spare on the river and plenty of time still to reach 'em."

Not a man stirred.

Leiningen acknowledged his silent vote of confidence with a laugh that was half a grunt. "That's the stuff, lads. Too bad if you'd missed the rest of the show, eh? Well, the fun won't start till morning. Once these blighters turn tail, there'll be plenty of work for everyone and higher wages all round. And now run along and get something to eat; you've earned it all right."

In the excitement of the fight the greater part of the day had passed without the men once pausing to snatch a bite. Now that the ants were for the time being out of sight, and the 'wall of petrol' gave a stronger feeling of security, hungry stomachs began to assert their claims.

The bridges over the concrete ditch were removed. Here and there solitary ants had reached the ditch; they gazed at the petrol meditatively, then scurried back again. Apparently they had little interest at the moment for what lay beyond the evil-reeking barrier; the abundant spoils of the plantation were the main attraction. Soon the trees, shrubs, and beds for miles around were hulled with ants zealously gobbling the yield of long weary months of strenuous toil.

As twilight began to fall, a cordon of ants marched around the petrol trench, but as yet made no move towards its brink. Leiningen posted sentries with headlights and electric torches, then withdrew to his office, and began to reckon up his losses. He estimated these as large, but, in comparison with his bank balance, by no means unbearable. He worked out in some detail a scheme of intensive cultivation which would enable him, before very long, to more than compensate himself for the damage now being wrought to his crops. It was with a contented mind that he finally betook himself to bed where he slept deeply until dawn, undisturbed by any thought that next day little more might be left of him than a glistening skeleton.

He rose with the sun and went out on the flat roof of his house. And a scene like one from Dante lay around him; for miles in every direction there was nothing but a black, glittering multitude, a multitude of rested, sated, but none the less voracious ants: yes, look as far as one might, one could see nothing but that rustling black throng, except in the north, where the great river drew a boundary they could not hope to pass. But even the high stone breakwater, along the bank of the river, which Leiningen had built as a defence against inundations, was, like the paths, the shorn trees and shrubs, the ground itself, black with ants.

So their greed was not glutted in razing that vast plantation? Not by a long chalk; they were all the more eager now on a rich and certain booty—four hundred men, numerous horses, and bursting granaries.

At first it seemed that the petrol trench would serve its purpose. The besiegers sensed the peril of swimming it, and made no move to plunge blindly over its brink. Instead they devised a better manœuvre; they began to collect shreds of bark, twigs, and dried leaves and dropped these into the petrol. Everything green, which could have been similarly used, had long since been eaten. After a time, though, a long procession could be seen bringing from the west the tamarind leaves used as rafts the day before.

Since the petrol, unlike the water in the outer ditch, was perfectly still, the refuse stayed where it was thrown. It was several hours before the the ants succeeded in covering an appreciable part of the surface. At length, however, they were ready to proceed to a direct attack.

Their storm troops swarmed down the concrete side, scrambled over the supporting surface of twigs and leaves, and impelled these over the few remaining streaks of open petrol until they reached the other side. Then they began to climb up this to make straight for the helpless garrison.

During the entire offensive, the planter sat peacefully, watching them with interest, but not stirring a muscle. Moreover, he had ordered his men not to disturb in any way whatever the advancing horde. So they squatted listlessly along the bank of the ditch and waited for a sign from the boss.

The petrol was now covered with ants. A few had climbed the inner concrete wall and were scurrying towards the defenders.

"Everyone back from the ditch!" roared Leiningen. The men rushed away, without the slightest idea of his plan. He stooped forward and cautiously dropped into the ditch a stone which split the floating carpet and its living freight, to reveal a gleaming patch of petrol. A match spurted, sank down to the oily surface—Leiningen sprang back; in a flash a towering rampart of fire encompassed the garrison.

This spectacular and instant repulse threw the Indians into ecstasy. They applauded, yelled, and stamped, like children at a pantomime. Had it not been for the awe in which they held the boss, they would infallibly have carried him shoulder high.

It was some time before the petrol burned down to the bed of the ditch, and the wall of smoke and flame began to lower. The ants had retreated in a wide circle from the devastation, and innumerable charred fragments along the outer bank showed that the flames had spread from the holocaust in the ditch well into the ranks beyond, where they had wrought havoc far and wide.

Yet the perseverance of the ants was by no means broken; indeed, each set-back seemed only to whet it. The concrete cooled, the flicker of the dying flames wavered and vanished, petrol from the second tank poured into the trench—and the ants marched forward anew to the attack.

The foregoing scene repeated itself in every detail, except that on this occasion less time was needed to bridge the ditch, for the petrol was now already filmed by a layer of ash. Once again they withdrew; once again petrol flowed into the ditch. Would the creatures never learn that their self-sacrifice was utterly senseless? It really was senseless, wasn't it? Yes, of course it was senseless—provided the defenders had an *unlimited* supply of petrol.

When Leiningen reached this stage of reasoning, he felt for the first time since the arrival of the ants that his confidence was deserting him. His skin began to creep; he loosened his collar. Once the devils were over the trench there wasn't a chance in hell for him and his men. God, what a prospect, to be eaten alive like that!

For the third time the flames immolated the attacking troops, and burned down to extinction. Yet the ants were coming on again as if nothing had happened. And meanwhile Leiningen had made a discovery that chilled him to the bone—petrol was no longer flowing into the ditch. Something must be blocking the outflow pipe of the third and last cistern—a snake or a dead rat? Whatever it was, the ants could be held off no longer, unless petrol could by some method be led from the cistern into the ditch.

Then Leiningen remembered that in the outhouse near by were two old disused fire engines. Spry as never before in their lives, the peons dragged them out of the shed, connected their pumps to the cistern, uncoiled and laid the hose. They were just in time to aim a stream of petrol at a column of ants that had already crossed and drive them back down the incline into the ditch. Once more an oily girdle surrounded the garrison, once more it was possible to hold the position—for the moment.

It was obvious, however, that this last resource meant only the postponement of defeat and death. A few of the peons fell on their knees and began to pray; others, shrieking insanely, fired their revolvers at the black, advancing masses, as if they felt their despair was pitiful enough to sway fate itself to mercy.

At length, two of the men's nerves broke: Leiningen saw a naked Indian leap over the north side of the petrol trench, quickly followed by a second. They sprinted with incredible speed towards the river. But their fleetness did not save them; long before they could attain the rafts, the enemy covered their bodies from head to foot.

In the agony of their torment, both sprang blindly into the wide river, where enemies no less sinister awaited them. Wild screams of mortal anguish informed the breathless onlookers that crocodiles and sword-toothed piranhas were no less ravenous than ants, and even nimbler in reaching their prey.

In spite of this bloody warning, more and more men showed they were making up their minds to run the blockade. Anything, even a fight midstream against alligators, seemed better than powerlessly waiting for death to come and slowly consume their living bodies.

Leiningen flogged his brain till it reeled. Was there nothing on earth could sweep this devils' spawn back into the hell from which it came?

Then out of the inferno of his bewilderment rose a terrifying inspiration. Yes, one hope remained, and one alone. It might be possible to dam the great river completely so that its waters would fill not only the water ditch but overflow into the entire gigantic 'saucer' of land in which lay the plantation.

The far bank of the river was too high for the waters to escape that way. The stone breakwater ran between the river and the plantation; its only gaps occurred where the 'horseshoe' ends of the water ditch passed into the river. So its waters would not only be forced to inundate into the plantation, they would also be held there by the breakwater until they rose to its own level. In half an hour, perhaps even earlier, the plantation and its hostile army of occupation would be flooded.

The ranch house and outbuildings stood upon rising ground. Their foundations were higher than the breakwater, so the flood would not reach them. And any remaining ants trying to ascend the slope could be repulsed by petrol.

It was possible—yes, if one could only get to the dam! A distance of nearly two miles lay between the ranch house and the weir—two miles of ants. Those two peons had managed only a fifth of that distance at the cost of their lives. Was there an Indian daring enough after that to run the gauntlet five times as far? Hardly likely; and if there were, his prospect of getting back was almost nil.

No, there was only one thing for it, he'd have to make the attempt himself; he might just as well be running as sitting still, anyway, when the ants finally got him. Besides, there *was* a bit of a chance. Perhaps the ants weren't so almighty, after all; perhaps he had allowed the mass suggestion of that evil black throng to hypnotize him, just as a snake fascinates and overpowers.

The ants were building their bridges. Leiningen got up on a chair. "Hey, lads, listen to me!" he cried. Slowly and listlessly, from all sides of the trench, the men began to shuffle towards him, the apathy of death already stamped on their faces.

"Listen, lads!" he shouted. "You're frightened of those beggars, but you're a damn sight more frightened of me, and I'm proud of you. There's still a chance to save our lives—by flooding the planta-tion from the river. Now one of you might manage to get as far as the weir—but he'd never come back. Well, I'm not going to let you try it; if I did I'd be worse than one of those ants. No, I called the tune, and now I'm going to pay the piper.

"The moment I'm over the ditch, set fire to the petrol. That'll allow time for the flood to do the trick. Then all you have to do is to wait here all snug and quiet till I'm back. Yes, I'm coming back, trust me"—he grinned—"when I've finished my slimming-cure."

He pulled on high leather boots, drew heavy gauntlets over his hands, and stuffed the spaces between breeches and boots, gauntlets and arms, shirt and neck, with rags soaked in petrol. With close-fitting mosquito goggles he shielded his eyes, knowing too well the ants' dodge of first robbing their victim of sight. Finally, he plugged his nostrils and ears with cotton wool, and let the peons drench his clothes with petrol.

He was about to set off when the old Indian medicine man came up to him; he had a wondrous salve, he said, prepared from a species of chafer whose odour was intolerable to ants. Yes, this odour protected these chafers from the attacks of even the most murderous ants. The Indian smeared the boss's boots, his gauntlets, and his face over and over with the extract.

Leiningen then remembered the paralysing effect of ants' venom, and the Indian gave him a gourd full of the medicine he had adminis-tered to the bitten peon at the water ditch. The planter drank it down without noticing its bitter taste; his mind was already at the weir.

He started off towards the north-west corner of the trench. With a bound he was over—and among the ants.

The beleaguered garrison had no opportunity to watch Leiningen's race against death. The ants were climbing the inner bank again—the lurid ring of petrol blazed aloft. For the fourth time that day the reflection from the fire shone on the sweating faces of the imprisoned men, and on the reddish-black cuirasses of their oppressors. The red and blue, dark-edged flames leaped vividly now, celebrating what? The funeral pyre of the four hundred, or of the hosts of destruction?

Leiningen ran. He ran in long, equal strides, with only one thought, one sensation, in his being—he *must* get through. He dodged all trees and shrubs; except for the split seconds his soles touched the ground the ants should have no opportunity to alight on him. That they would get to him soon, despite the salve on his boots, the petrol on his clothes, he realized only too well, but he knew even more surely that he must, and that he would, get to the weir.

Apparently the salve was some use after all; not until he had reached half way did he feel ants under his clothes, and a few on his face. Mechanically, in his stride, he struck at them, scarcely conscious of their bites. He saw he was drawing appreciably nearer the weir—the distance grew less and less—sank to five hundred—three—two—one hundred yards.

Then he was at the weir and gripping the ant-hulled wheel. Hardly had he seized it when a horde of infuriated ants flowed over his hands, arms, and shoulders. He started the wheel—before it turned once on its axis the swarm covered his face. Leiningen strained like a madman, his lips pressed tight; if he opened them to draw breath...

He turned and turned; slowly the dam lowered until it reached the bed of the river. Already the water was overflowing the ditch. Another minute, and the river was pouring through the nearby gap in the breakwater. The flooding of the plantation had begun.

Leiningen let go the wheel. Now, for the first time, he realized he was coated from head to foot with a layer of ants. In spite of the petrol, his clothes were full of them, several had got to his body or were clinging to his face. Now that he had completed his task, he felt the smart raging over his flesh from the bites of sawing and piercing insects.

Frantic with pain, he almost plunged into the river. To be ripped and slashed to shreds by piranhas? Already he was running the return journey, knocking ants from his gloves and jacket, brushing them from his bloodied face, squashing them to death under his clothes.

One of the creatures bit him just below the rim of his goggles; he managed to tear it away, but the agony of the bite and its etching acid drilled into the eye nerves; he saw now through circles of fire into a milky mist, then he ran for a time almost blinded, knowing that if he once tripped and fell... The old Indian's brew didn't seem much good; it weakened the poison a bit, but didn't get rid of it. His heart pounded as if it would burst; blood roared in his ears; a giant's fist battered his lungs.

Then he could see again, but the burning girdle of petrol appeared infinitely far away; he could not last half that distance. Swift-changing pictures flashed through his head, episodes in his life, while in another part of his brain a cool and impartial onlooker informed this ant-blurred, gasping, exhausted bundle named Leiningen that such a rushing panorama of scenes from one's past is seen only in the moment before death.

A stone in the path... too weak to avoid it... the planter stumbled and collapsed. He tried to rise... he must be pinned under a rock... it was impossible... the slightest movement was impossible...

Then all at once he saw, starkly clear and huge, and, right before his eyes, furred with ants, towering and swaying in its death agony, the pampas stag. In six minutes—gnawed to the bones. God, he *couldn't* die like that! And something outside him seemed to drag him to his feet. He tottered. He began to stagger forward again.

Through the blazing ring hurtled an apparition which, as soon as it reached the ground on the inner side, fell full length and did not move. Leiningen, at the moment he made that leap through the flames, lost consciousness for the first time in his life. As he lay there, with glazing eyes and lacerated face, he appeared a man returned from the grave. The peons rushed to him, stripped off his clothes, tore away the ants from a body that seemed almost one open wound; in some places the bones were showing. They carried him into the ranch house.

As the curtain of flames lowered, one could see, in place of the illimitable host of ants, an extensive vista of water. The thwarted river had swept over the plantation, carrying with it the entire army. The water had collected and mounted in the great 'saucer', while the ants had in vain attempted to reach the hill on which stood the ranch house. The girdle of flames held them back.

And so, imprisoned between water and fire, they had been delivered into the annihilation that was their god. And near the farther mouth of the water ditch, where the stone mole had its second gap, the ocean swept the lost battalions into the river, to vanish for ever.

The ring of fire dwindled as the water mounted to the petrol trench, and quenched the dimming flames. The inundation rose higher and higher: because its outflow was impeded by the timber and underbrush it had carried along with it, its surface required some time to reach the top of the high stone breakwater and discharge over it the rest of the shattered army.

It swelled over ant-stippled shrubs and bushes, until it washed against the foot of the knoll whereon the besieged had taken refuge. For a while an alluvium of ants tried again and again to attain this dry land, only to be repulsed by streams of petrol back into the merciless flood.

Leiningen lay on his bed, his body swathed from head to foot in bandages. With fomentations and salves, they had managed to stop the bleeding, and had dressed his many wounds. Now they thronged around him, one question in every face. Would he recover? "He won't die," said the old man who had bandaged him, "if he doesn't want to."

The planter opened his eyes. "Everything in order?" he asked.

"They're gone," said his nurse. "To hell." He held out to his master a gourd full of a powerful sleeping-draught. Leiningen gulped it down.

"I told you I'd come back," he murmured, "even if I am a bit streamlined." He grinned and shut his eyes. He slept.

ALSO AVAILABLE

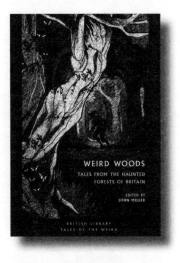

'But foliage surrounded him, branches blocked the way; the trees stood close and still; and the sun dipped that moment behind a great black cloud. The entire wood turned dark and silent. It watched him.'

Woods play a crucial and recurring role in horror, fantasy, the gothic and the weird. They are places in which strange things happen, where it is easy to lose your way. Supernatural creatures thrive in the thickets. Trees reach into underworlds of pagan myth and magic. Forests are full of ghosts.

Lining the path through this realm of folklore and fear are twelve stories from across Britain, telling tales of whispering voices and maddening sights from deep in the Yorkshire Dales to the ancient hills of Gwent and the eerie quiet of the forests of Dartmoor. Immerse yourself in this collection of classic tales celebrating the enduring power of our natural spaces to enthral and terrorise our senses.

ALSO AVAILABLE

Strangling vines and meat-hungry flora fill this unruly garden of strange stories, selected for their significance as the seeds of the villainous (or perhaps just misunderstood) 'killer plant' in fiction, film and video games.

Step within to marvel at Charlotte Perkins Gilman's giant wisteria and H. G. Wells' hungry orchid; hear the calls of the ethereal women of the wood, and the frightful drone of the moaning lily; and do tread carefully around E. Nesbit's wandering creepers...

Every strain of vegetable threat (and one deadly fungus) can be found within this new collection, representing the very best tales from the undergrowth of Gothic fiction.

British Library Tales of the Weird collects a thrilling array of uncanny storytelling, from the realms of gothic, supernatural and horror fiction. With stories ranging from the nineteenth century to the present day, this series revives long-lost material from the Library's vaults to thrill again alongside beloved classics of the weird fiction genre.

We welcome any suggestions, corrections or feedback you may have, and will aim to respond to all items addressed to the following:

The Editor (Tales of the Weird), British Library Publishing,
The British Library, 96 Euston Road, London NW1 2DB

We also welcome enquiries through our Twitter account, @BL_Publishing.